EDITED WITH AN INTRODUCTION BY

STEPHEN COONTS

COMBAT

Volume 3

HAROLD COYLE

RALPH PETERS

JAMES COBB

R. J. PINEIRO

FORGE®

A TOM DOHERTY ASSOCIATES BOOK
NEW YORK

This is a work of fiction. All the characters and events portrayed in this book are either products of the author's imagination or are used fictitiously.

COMBAT, Volume 3

A Forge Book
Published by Tom Doherty Associates, LLC
175 Fifth Avenue
New York, NY 10010

www.tor.com

Forge® is a registered trademark of Tom Doherty Associates, LLC.

ISBN: 0-812-57617-9
Library of Congress Catalog Card Number: 00-048451

First edition: January 2001
First mass market edition: March 2002

Printed in the United States of America

0 9 8 7 6 5 4 3 2 1

Praise for *Combat*

"American troops go to hell and back to save the free world. Push comes to shove, then Fire-away! And Carrumph!" —*Kirkus Reviews*

"Editor Coonts has gathered an impressive group of technothriller authors for this testosterone laden anthology. These John and Jane Wayne meet *Star Wars* tales offers a chilling glimpse into warfare in the 21st century. The most successful focus is not on weird military technology, but on the men and women who must actually fight . . . best of all is Ing's tightly wrapped tale, "Inside Job." —*Publishers Weekly*

"War is as inevitable in this new century as it was in the past. A thought-provoking, plausible, and exciting look at the "interesting times" the proverbial ancient Chinese curse says that we are condemned to live through." —*Library Journal*

"This anthology reads quickly. It has the kind of pages that keep you turning them long into the night, your sleepless eyes glued like a terrified double-agent on the run from the bad guys . . . can be considered a mission success." —*Readers and Writers Magazine*

"As the Bush administration undertakes a review of the who, what, when and where of military spending, *Combat*—through the eyes of ten well-respected experts—offers a realistic look at what American men and women may face on the battlefields of the not-so-distant future." —*The Ocala Star-Banner*

To the memory of the seventeen sailors who
lost their lives on the USS *Cole*

Contents

INTRODUCTION

The milieu of armed conflict has been a fertile setting for storytellers since the dawn of the written word, and probably before. The *Iliad* by Homer was a thousand years old before someone finally wrote down that oral epic of the Trojan War, freezing its form forever.

Since then war stories have been one of the main themes of fiction in Western cultures: *War and Peace* by Leo Tolstoi was set during the Napoleonic Wars, Stephen Crane's *The Red Badge of Courage* was set during the American Civil War, *All Quiet on the Western Front* by Erich Maria Remarque was perhaps the great classic of World War I. Arguably the premier war novel of the twentieth century, Ernest Hemingway's *For Whom the Bell Tolls*, was set in the Spanish Civil War.

World War II caused an explosion of great war novels. Some of my favorites are *The Naked and the Dead, The Thin Red Line, War and Remembrance, From Here to Eternity, The War Lover,* and *Das Boot.*

The Korean conflict also produced a bunch, including my favorite, *The Bridges at Toko-Ri* by James Michener, but Vietnam changed the literary landscape. According to conventional wisdom in the publishing industry, after that war the reading public lost interest in war stories. Without a doubt the publishers did.

In 1984 the world changed. The U.S. Naval Institute Press, the Naval Academy's academic publisher, broke with its ninety-plus years of tradition and published a novel, *The Hunt for Red October,* by Tom Clancy.

This book by an independent insurance agent who had never served in the armed forces sold slowly at first, then became a huge best-seller when the reading public found it and began selling it to each other by word of mouth. It didn't hurt that President Ronald Reagan was photographed with a copy.

As it happened, in 1985 I was looking for a publisher for a Vietnam flying story I had written. After the novel was rejected by every publisher in New York, I saw *Hunt* in a bookstore, so I sent my novel to the Naval Institute Press. To my delight the house accepted it and published it in 1986 as *Flight of the Intruder.* Like *Hunt,* it too became a big best-seller.

Success ruined the Naval Institute. Wracked by internal politics, the staff refused to publish Clancy's and my subsequent novels. (We had no trouble selling these books in New York, thank you!) The house did not publish another novel for years, and when they did, best-seller sales eluded them.

Literary critics had an explanation for the interest

of the post-Vietnam public in war stories. These novels, they said, were something new. I don't know who coined the term "techno-thriller" (back then newspapers always used quotes and hyphenated it) but the term stuck.

Trying to define the new term, the critics concluded that these war stories used modern technology in ways that no one ever had. How wrong they were.

Clancy's inspiration for *The Hunt for Red October* was an attempted defection of a crew of a Soviet surface warship in the Baltic. The crew mutinied and attempted to sail their ship to Finland. The attempt went awry and the ringleaders were summarily executed by the communists, who always took offense when anyone tried to leave the workers' paradises.

What if, Clancy asked himself, the crew of a nuclear-powered submarine tried to defect? The game would be more interesting then. Clancy's model for the type of story he wanted to write was Edward L. Beach's *Run Silent, Run Deep*, a World War II submarine story salted with authentic technical detail that was critical to the development of the characters and plot of the story.

With that scenario in mind, Clancy set out to write a submarine adventure that would be accurate in every detail. Never mind that he had never set foot on a nuclear submarine or spent a day in uniform— his inquiring mind and thirst for knowledge made him an extraordinary researcher. His fascination with war games and active, fertile imagination made him a first-class storyteller.

Unlike Clancy, I did no research whatsoever when writing *Flight of the Intruder*. I had flown A-6 Intruder bombers in Vietnam from the deck of the USS *Enterprise* and wrote from memory. I had been trying to write a flying novel since 1973 and had worn out two typewriters in the process. By 1984 I had figured out a plot for my flying tale, so after a divorce I got serious about writing and completed a first draft of the novel in five months.

My inspiration for the type of story I wanted to write was two books by Ernest K. Gann. *Fate Is the Hunter* was a true collection of flying stories from the late 1930s and 1940s, and was, I thought, extraordinary in its inclusion of a wealth of detail about the craft of flying an airplane. Gann also used this device for his novels, the best of which is probably *The High and the Mighty*, a story about a piston-engined airliner that has an emergency while flying between Hawaii and San Francisco.

Gann used technical details to create the setting and as plot devices that moved the stories along. By educating the reader about what it is a pilot does, he gave his stories an emotional impact that conventional storytellers could not achieve. In essence, he put you in the cockpit and took you flying. That, I thought, was an extraordinary achievement and one I wanted to emulate.

Fortunately, the technology that Clancy and I were writing about was state-of-the-art—nuclear-powered submarines and precision all-weather attack jets—and this played to the reading public's long-standing love affair with scientific discoveries and new technology. In the nineteenth century Jules Verne, Edgar Allan Poe, Wilkie Collins, and H. G. Wells gave birth to science fiction. The technology at the heart of their stories played on the public's fascination with the man-made wonders of that age—the submarine, the flying machines that were the object of intense research and experimentation, though they had yet to get off the ground, and the myriad of uses that inventors were finding for electricity, to name just a few.

Today's public is still enchanted by the promise of scientific research and technology. Computers, rockets, missiles, precision munitions, lasers, fiber optics, wireless networks, reconnaissance satellites, winged airplanes that take off and land vertically, network-centric warfare—advances in every technical field are constantly re-creating the world in which we live.

The marriage of high tech and war stories is a natural.

The line between the modern military action-adventure and science fiction is blurry, indistinct, and becoming more so with every passing day. Storytellers often set technothrillers in the near future and dress up the technology accordingly, toss in little inventions of their own here and there, and in general, try subtly to wow their readers by use of a little of that science fiction "what might be" magic. When it's properly done, only a technically expert reader will be able to tell when the writer has crossed the line from the real to the unreal; and that's the fun of it. On the other hand, stories set in space or on other planets or thousands of years in the future are clearly science fiction, even though armed conflict is involved.

This third mass-market paperback, containing original novellas by Harold Coyle, James Cobb, R. J. Pineiro and Ralph Peters, completes the *Combat* collection.

Harold Coyle was a professional army officer who began writing as a hobby. After he served in Desert Storm, he left active duty to become a full-time writer. Coyle's novella about cyberwar published here is an interesting look at a highly classified area, and will leave you thinking. Coyle and Ralph Peters are, in my opinion, the best two authors writing today on ground combat.

Essayist, novelist, and consultant Ralph Peters is an acknowledged expert on all facets of the military. His novella, *There Is No War In Melnica*, is an ironic tale based on political reality as tangible as the book you hold in your hand.

If you think that man's conflicts won't spill into space in the years ahead, wait until you read R. J. Pineiro's *Flight of Endeavour*. Like me, you'll find it fascinating. Pineiro is an expert on high tech, a requirement if one plans on writing this type of tale.

James Cobb is a talented young writer we will hear much more about in the years ahead. His novella, *Cav*, which appears here, is set in Africa. One suspects that in the years ahead the conflicts and tensions of that poor, overcrowded continent will again require the commitment of American armed forces. Perhaps the debacle in Somalia taught our politicians something. Then again, maybe it didn't. Read Cobb's tale—it's good.

STEPHEN COONTS

CYBERKNIGHTS

BY HAROLD COYLE

One

---

combat.com

The secluded community just outside of Valparaiso, Chile, slumbered on behind the high walls and steel-reinforced gates that surrounded it. Other than the lazy swaying of branches stirred by a gentle offshore breeze, the only sound or movement disturbing the early-morning darkness was that created by the rhythmic footfalls on the pavement of a pair of security guards patrolling the empty streets of the well-manicured community. The two armed men did not live in any of the homes they were charged with protecting. Even if either one of them had been fortunate enough to possess the small fortune that ownership of property in the tiny village required, neither had the social credentials that would permit him to purchase even the smallest plot of ground within these walls. If they harbored any resentment over this fact, they dared not show it. The pay was too good and the work too easy to jeopard-ize. Their parents had taught them well. Only fools take risks when times were good and circumstances didn't require it.

Still, the guards were only human. On occasion a comment that betrayed their true feelings would slip out during the casual conversation that they engaged in during the long night. Upon turning a corner, one of the security guards took note of a flickering of light in a second-story window of one of the over-size homes. Slowing his pace, the hired guardian studied the window in an effort to determine if some-thing was out of kilter. Belatedly, his partner took note of his concern. With a chuckle, the second guard dismissed the concerns of the first. "There is nothing going on up there that we need to bother ourselves with."

"And how would you know that?" the first asked as he kept one eye on the window.

"My sister, the one who is a cleaning woman, chat-ters incessantly about what she sees in each of these houses. That room, for example, is off-limits to her."

Rather than mollify his suspicions, these com-ments only piqued the first guard's interest. "And why is that? Is it the personal office of the owner?"

Letting out a loud laugh, the second guard shook his head. "Not hardly. It is the bedroom of a teenage boy."

Seeing the joke, the first guard let out a nervous chuckle. "What," he asked, "makes the bedroom of a teenage boy so important?"

"The boy is a computer rat," came the answer. "My sister says he has just about every sort of computer equipment imaginable cluttering the place."

"What does your sister know about computers?" the first asked incredulously.

Offended, his partner glared. "We are poor, not ignorant."

Realizing that he had unintentionally insulted his comrade, the first guard lowered his head. "I am sorry, I didn't mean to . . ."

"But you did," the offended guard snapped. "What goes on in those rooms is not our concern anyway. We are paid to guard against criminals and terrorists, not speculate about what our employers do within the confines of their own homes." With that, he pivoted about and marched off, followed a few seconds later by his partner.

Neither man, of course, realized that the only terrorist within miles was already inside the walls of the quiet little community. In fact, they had been watching him, or more correctly, his shadow as he went about waging an undeclared war against the United States of America.

Alone in his room, Angelo Castalano sat hunched over the keyboard of his computer, staring at the screen. As he did night after night, young Angelo ignored the pile of schoolbooks that lay strewn across the floor of his small room and turned, instead, his full attention to solving a far more interesting problem. It concerned his latest assignment from the commander of the X Legion.

The "foot soldiers" in the X Legion were, for the most part, the sons of well-to-do South American parents, people who could be correctly referred to as the ruling elite. While Angelo's father oversaw the operation of a major shipping business in Valparaiso owned by a Hong Kong firm, his mother struggled incessantly to keep her place in the polite society of Chile that was, for her husband, just as important as his business savvy. Like their North American counterparts, the information age and modern society left them little time to tend to the children that were as much a symbol of a successful union as was a large house in the proper neighborhood. That Angelo's father had little time to enjoy either his son or house was viewed as a problem, nothing more. So, as he did with so many other problems he faced, the Chilean businessmen threw money and state-of-the-art equipment at it.

A computer, in and of itself, is an inert object. Like a projectile, it needs energy to propel it. Young Angelo and the electricity flowing from the overloaded wall socket provided that energy. But engaging in an activity can quickly becomes boring if there is nothing new or thrilling to capture a young, imaginative mind, especially when that activity involves an ultra-modern data-crunching machine. Like the projectile, to have meaning the exercise of power must have a purpose, a target. That is where the X Legion came in.

The X Legion, properly pronounced Tenth as in the roman numeral, was a collection of young South and Central American computer geeks who had found each other as they crawled about the World Wide Web in search of fun, adventure, some sort of achievement. In the beginning they played simple games among themselves, games that involved world conquest, or that required each of the participants to amass great wealth by creating virtual stock portfolios. Slowly, and ever so innocently, the members of the X Legion began to break into the computer systems of international companies, not at all unlike those owned or operated by their own fathers. They did this, they told each other, in order to test their growing computer skills and engage in feats that had real and measurable consequences. "We live in a real world," a legionnaire in Argentina stated one night as they were just beginning to embark upon this new adventure. "So let us see what we can do in that world."

At first, the targets selected for their raids were chosen by the legionnaires themselves, without any controlling or centralized authority. This, quite naturally, led to arguments as fellow members of their group ridiculed the accomplishments of another if they thought the object of a fellow legionnaire's attack had been too easy.

"Manipulating the accounts of a Swiss bank must have more meaning," a Bolivian boy claimed, "than stealing from a local candy store." Though intelligent and articulate, no one had a clear idea of how best to gauge the relative value of their targets.

To resolve this chaotic state of affairs, a new member who used the screen name "longbow" volunteered to take on the task of generating both the targets to be attacked by the members of the legion and the relative value of those targets. Points for the successful completion of the mission would be awarded to the participants by longbow based upon the security measures that had to be overcome, the creativity that the hacker used in rummaging around in the targeted computer, and the overall cost that the company owning the hacked site ultimately had to pay to correct the problem the legionnaire created. How longbow managed to determine all of this was of no concern to the young men like Angelo who belonged to the legion. Longbow offered them real challenges and order in the otherwise chaotic and shapeless world in which they lived, but did not yet understand.

When they were sure he was not listening, which was rare, the rank and file of the legion discussed their self-appointed leader. It didn't matter to An-

gelo and other members of the X Legion that longbow was not from South or Central America. One of
the first clues that brought this issue into question
was the English and Spanish longbow used. Like all
members of the X Legion, longbow switched between the two languages interchangeably. Since so
many of the richest and most advanced businesses
using the World Wide Web communicated in English, this was all but a necessity. When it came to
his use of those languages, it appeared to the well-
educated legionnaires that both Spanish and English
were second languages to their taskmaster. Everything about longbow's verbiage was too exact, too
perfect, much like the grammar a student would use.

That longbow might be using them for reasons
that the young Latin American hackers could not
imagine never concerned Angelo. Like his cyber
compatriots, his world was one of words, symbols,
data, and not people, nationals, and causes. Everything that they saw on their computer screen was
merely images, two-dimensional representations. In
addition to this self-serving disassociated rationale,
there was the fear that longbow, who was an incred-
ible treasure trove of tricks and tools useful to the
legion of novice hackers, might take offense if they
became too inquisitive about longbow's origins. The
loss of their cyber master would result in anarchy,
something these well-off cyber anarchists loathed.

While the security guards went about their rounds,
protecting the young Chilean and his family from
the outside world, Angelo was reaching out into that
world. As he did each time he received a mission
from longbow, Angelo did not concern himself with
the "why" governing his specific tasking for the evening. Rather, he simply concentrated on the "how."

Upon returning from school that afternoon, Angelo had found explicit instructions from longbow on how to break into the computer system of the United States Army Matériel Command in Alexandria, Virginia. This particular system, Angelo found out quickly, handled requests for repair parts and equipment from American military units deployed throughout the world.

The "mission" Angelo had been assigned was to generate a false request, or alter an existing one, so that the requesting unit received repair parts or equipment that was of no earthly use to the unit in the field. Knowing full well that the standards used to judge the success of a mission concerned creativity as well as the cost of the damage inflicted, Angelo took his time in selecting both the target of his attack and the nature of the mischief he would inflict upon it. After several hours of scrolling through hundreds of existing requests, he hit upon one that struck his fancy.

It concerned a requisition that had been forwarded from an Army unit stationed in Kosovo to its parent command located in Germany. The requesting unit, an infantry battalion, had suffered a rash of accidents in recent months because of winter weather and lousy driving by Americans born and raised in states where the only snow anyone ever saw was on TV. Though the human toll had been minimal, the extensive damage to the battalion's equipment had depleted both its own reserve of on-hand spare parts as well as the stock carried by the forward-support maintenance unit in-country. While not every item on the extensive list of replacement parts was mission essential, some demanded immediate replacement. This earned those components deemed critical both a high priority and special handling.

With the commander's approval, the parts clerk in Kosovo submitted a request, via the Army's own Internet system, to the division's main support battalion back in Germany to obtain these mission-essential items.

As was the habit of this particular parts clerk, he had waited until the end of the normal workday before submitting his required list of repair parts. In this way the clerk avoided having to go through the entire routine of entering the system, pulling up the necessary on-screen documents, and filling out all the unit data more than once a day. Though parts that had been designated mission essential and awarded a high priority were supposed to be acted upon as soon as they landed on the desk of the parts clerk, lax supervision at the forward-support unit where the clerk worked permitted personnel in his section to pretty much do things as they saw fit. So it should not have come as a great surprise that the parts clerk in Kosovo chose to pursue the path of least resistance, executing his assigned duties in a manner that was most expedient, for the clerk.

This little quirk left a window of opportunity for someone like Angelo to spoof the United States Army Matériel Command's computer system. Since the request was initiated in Kosovo and relayed to the forward-support battalion's parent unit after normal working hours in Kosovo, the personnel in Germany charged with reviewing that request were not at their desks. Those personnel had the responsibility of reviewing all requests from subordinate units to ensure that they were both valid and correct. They then had to make the decision as to whether the request from Kosovo would be filled using on-hand stocks in Germany or forwarding back to Army Matériel Command to be acted upon using Army-wide sources.

All of this was important, because it permitted Angelo an opportunity to do several things without anyone within the system knowing that something was amiss. The first thing Angelo did, as soon as he decided to strike here, was to change the letter-numeric part number of one of the items requested to that of another part, an item which Angelo was fairly sure would be of no use to the infantry unit in Kosovo.

The item Angelo hit upon to substitute was the front hand guards for M-16 rifles that had been cracked during one of the vehicular accidents. Switching over to another screen that had a complete listing of part numbers for other weapons in the Army's inventory, Angelo scrolled through the listings until he found something that struck his fancy. How wickedly wonderful it will be, the young Chilean thought as he copied the part number for the gun tube of a 155mm howitzer, for an infantry unit to receive six large-caliber artillery barrels measuring twenty feet in length instead of the rifle hand guards that it needed. Just the expense of handling the heavy gun tubes would be monumental. Only the embarrassment of the unit commander involved, Angelo imagined, would be greater.

Selecting the item to be substituted, then cutting and pasting the part number of the artillery gun tube in its place, was only the beginning. The next item on Angelo's agenda was to move the request along the chain, electronically approving it and forwarding it at each of the checkpoints along the information superhighway the request had to travel. Otherwise, one of the gate-keeping organizations along the way, such as the parent support battalion in Germany, the theater staff agency responsible for logistical support, or the Army Matériel Command in Virginia, would see that the item Angelo was using as a substitute was not authorized by that unit.

To accomplish this feat Angelo had to travel along the same virtual path that such a request normally traveled. At each point where an organization or staff agency reviewed the request, the young Chilean hacker had to place that agency's electronic stamp of approval upon the request and then whisk it away before anyone at the agency took note of the unauthorized action. This put pressure on Angelo, for he had but an hour or so before the parts clerks in Germany and the logistics staffers elsewhere in Germany switched on their computers to see what new requests had come in during the night. Once he had cleared those gates, he would have plenty of time to make his way through the stateside portion of the system since Chile was an hour ahead of the Eastern time zone.

It was in this endeavor that the tools and techniques that longbow had provided the legionnaires came into play. By using an account name that he had been given by longbow, Angelo was permitted to "go root." In the virtual world, being a "root" on a system is akin to being God. Root was created by network administrators to access every program and every file on a host computer, or any servers connected to it, to update or fix glitches in the system. Having root access also allows anyone possessing this divine power the ability to run any program or manipulate any file on the network. Once he had access as a root user on the Army computer system that handled the requisitioning and allocation of spare parts, Angelo was able to approve and move his request through the network without any of the gates along the way having an opportunity to stop it. In this way the request for the 155mm artillery howitzer gun tubes for the infantry battalion in Kosovo was pulled through the system from the highest level of the United States Army's logistical system rather than being pushed out of it from a unit at the lowest level.

To ensure that there was no possibility that the request would be caught during a routine daily review, the Chilean hacker needed to get the request as far along the chain as he could, preferably out of the Army system itself. To accomplish this little trick, he used his position as a root operator within the Army Matériel Command's computer to access the computers at the Army's arsenal at Watervaliet, in New York State. It was there that all large-caliber gun tubes used by the United States Army were produced.

Once in the arsenal's system, Angelo rummaged around until he found six 155mm gun tubes that were already on hand there. Using the actual bin number of the on-hand gun tubes, he generated shipping documents for those items. Copies of those documents were then forwarded to the computers of the Air Force Military Airlift Command. The result of these last two actions would all but ensure that the request would go through. Upon arriving at work the following morning, the Department of the Army civilian employees at Watervaliet would be greeted by Angelo's instructions for the disposition of the gun tubes issued through the Army Matériel Command's computer in Alexandria, Virginia. Odds were the DOA civilian would not question this, since all the proper electronic documentation, including a code designating it as a high-priority item, were valid. At the same time the computers at the headquarters of the Military Airlift Command would spew out the warning order that a priority shipment for an Army unit forward-deployed in Kosovo was due in. As was their charter when dealing with such a request, the Air Force staff would immediately allocate precious cargo space on one of its transports headed for Kosovo, assign the mission a tasking number, generate their own mission tasking orders, and issue them to all commands who would be involved in the movement of the gun tubes. When all was set, the Air Force would relay disposition instructions back to Watervaliet, instructing the DOA civilian employee to deliver the gun tubes to the air base from which the designated transport would depart.

All of this took time, for Angelo needed to make sure that he not only hit every point along the long chain, but that each action he took and document he generated was correct. An error anywhere along the way would result in someone going back, up or down the actual chain, to ask for clarification or a retransmission of a corrected request. The chances of someone catching the hack would, as a result, be all but certain.

It was only when he had dotted his last virtual i and crossed his last digital t that Angelo noted the time being displayed on the upper right-hand corner of his screen. It was nearly 3 A.M. Shaking his head, the Chilean hacker raised his arms and glanced at his wristwatch. Why, he found himself wondering, had all this taken so long? While he appreciated that he had eaten up a great deal of time searching for the perfect target, and then finding an appropriately useless item to send them, Angelo found he could not explain the disparity. He had, after all, been involved in spoofs that were far more complex and involved than the one he had just completed.

Easing back in his seat, Angelo considered this incongruity with the same highly developed analytical tools that all the members of the X Legion possessed. Doing so proved to be no easy task, for his eyes were blurry and his mind, exhausted by hours of tedious labor, was not focusing. While there was always the possibility that the fault lay with the American Army's computers, Angelo quickly dismissed this. They had, as best he knew, some of the fastest and most capable systems in the world. Even when the United States had been in the throes of a major crisis, Angelo had never experienced anything resembling a delay on the networks he so enjoyed hacking. This evening had been a relatively slow evening, with network traffic, if anything, being a bit lighter than the norm. So the young Chilean quickly dismissed this possibility.

This made his computer suspect. Perhaps, Angelo thought, it was time to run a diagnostic check of his system and clean up some old files, repair any fragmented sectors on his hard drive, and generally clean house. So, despite the late hour and his yearning for sleep, he leaned forward, pulled up his utility tools, and accessed the program.

Once the disk-repair routine was running, Angelo had little to do but sit back and watch. The images that flashed across his screen were, to Angelo, a bit silly. It showed a little figure, dressed in white with a red cross on his chest, turning a disk. Every now and then, the figure would stop, bend over, and give the appearance of examining a spot on the disk. After a second, the figure would straighten up and continue his search for another "injured" disk sector. Angelo no more enjoyed watching this mundane sequence than he did sitting before a television screen displaying a test pattern. Yet like the late-night viewer too tired to sleep, the Chilean continued to stare at his screen. Even the fact that the little stick figure before his eyes was going about its mindless chores slowly and with jerky motions couldn't shake Angelo from his inattention.

In was in this semiconscious, almost hypnotic state that something utterly unexpected happened. The entire screen before him simply went blank. There was no flickering or shrinking of the image that is characteristic of a loss of power. Angelo did not hear the snapping that usually accompanies the tripping of the monitor's on-off switch. Nor was there a change in the steady hum of the computer itself that would have occurred if hit by a surge. One second the screen had been up and active. Then the next, it was pitch-black.

After blinking in an effort to clear the glaze from his eyes, Angelo stared dumbstruck at the unnatural blackness before him. Already troubled by the previous problem he had been attempting to resolve, this new development further confused the Chilean hacker. He was just beginning to wonder if the diagnostic tools that he had turned to were the cause of this calamity when, on the left-hand side of his screen, he saw a figure appear. The peculiar figure, attired from head to toe in green medieval armor and mounted on a barded horse, sported a long lance and carried a shield. Mesmerized, Angelo watched as the knight, measuring about two and a half centimeters, rode out into the center of his screen. Once there, the horse turned until the small green knight, lance still held at a forty-five-degree angle, was facing Angelo head-on. The figure paused only long enough to lower his lance and tuck his shield up closer to his body. Then, with a quick swing of his feet, the green knight spurred his mount and charged forward.

Fascinated, Angelo watched. While one part of his mind wondered where this image was coming from, another part of the young man's brain found itself captivated by the details of the computer-generated knight and its lifelike motions. As the virtual knight loomed closer and grew larger, more and more details were revealed. Quickly Angelo came to realize that the knight was not all green. Instead, the armor of the growing image before him began to blossom into a motley pattern of light greens, dark greens, browns, tans, and splotches of black, not at all unlike the camouflage pattern worn by modern combat soldiers. Even the bard protecting the knight's steed was adorned with the same pattern. Only the shield clinched by the charging knight failed to conform to this scheme. Rather, the shield's background was as black as the rest of the screen. Upon that field, at a diagonal, was the symbol of a silver lightning bolt, coursing its way from the upper right-hand corner almost down to the lower left. On one side of the bolt there was a yellow zero, on the other a one, numbers that represented the basic building blocks of all computer languages.

Completely engrossed by the video presentation, it took Angelo's mind far too long to realize that the advancing knight, filling more and more of the screen before him as it charged home, was not meant to be entertaining. Rather the symbol of military virtue, power, and untiring quests was the harbinger of disaster. When this horrible fact finally managed to seep its way into his conscious mind, the young Chilean all but leaped out of his chair, as if struck by a lighting bolt not at all unlike the one adorning the knight's grim, black shield. With a jerk he reached for the master power switch in a determined effort to crash his own system before the unheralded knight struck home and did whatever mischief its creator intended.

Had he been thinking straight, Angelo would have saved himself the trouble, accepted his fate calmly, and enjoyed the show. For the knight he saw was not the initiator of electronic doom, but rather a messenger sent forth from an implanted program within Angelo's machine to announce that a sequence of destruction designed to destroy the Chilean's toy had run its course. The South American hacker had been blindsided by an assault launched across the World Wide Web by another cyber combatant, a young boy not at all unlike himself. Like so many other intruders before, Angelo Castalano had been struck down by America's new front-line guardians, the Cyberknights of West Fort Hood.

Two

Virtual Heroes

The tunnels and chambers that honeycomb the hills of West Fort Hood had been built in another era. They had been part of a national effort to fight a foe that no longer existed, using weapons designed to be delivered by aircraft and missiles that had been relegated to museums. In underground chambers encased by reinforced concrete, nuclear weapons had been stored and assembled before being wheeled out onto the tarmac of the adjoining airfield, where the city-killing devices were hosted in the waiting bomb bays of B-47s. For many years the people of the United States had depended on those bombers to stand guard and protect them from foreign intruders. In time new weapons, weapons that were more precise, more advanced, replaced the free-fall bombs that had once been hidden away under the scrub-covered hills of West Fort Hood.

Strangely, the usefulness of the facilities that had been little more than storerooms during the Cold War long outlasted the weapons system they had been created to house. When the bombers had flown off for the last time, and the bombs themselves moved to other underground bunkers, new occupants moved into the spaces left behind.

This subterranean world had much going for it. For one thing, the earth and rock that concealed the underground work spaces created a constant environment and temperature. Other than providing a steady flow of fresh air, little needed to be invested in the heating or cooling of the facility to a round-the-clock temperature of just under seventy degrees. For those who have not had the opportunity to enjoy the month of August in Texas, this was a very big plus. Nor did people need to concern themselves a great deal with physical upkeep. There were, after all, no lawns, walkways, windows, or exterior walls that needed to be tended to. Even the interior was rather robust and carefree. The baby-shit green glazed tiles that covered the walls, while monotonous and difficult to work with, made painting all but unnecessary. There were, of course, issues and difficulties that were well-nigh impossible to overcome. For one thing, the all-male draftee Air Force of the early 1950s had far different ideas about the minimum requirements when it came to the latrines than did the mixed workforce that followed them in later decades. And when it came to updating the electrical web that supplied power to everything from the overhead lights to high-speed computers, architects and engineers first found themselves having to redefine the meaning of creativity.

The attraction of the underground complex, however, went beyond these concerns over simple creature comfort. The very nature of the facility made access difficult. Since there were so few outlets, movement into and out of the underground complex could be readily controlled. The access tunnels which did connect the outside world to the work spaces within were long, straight, unobstructed, and narrow. This permitted security personnel manning the checkpoints at both ends of these tunnels clean fields of fire. The posts themselves, holdovers from the days when top-secret weapons had been stored there, were in fact bunkers. From behind bulletproof glass and using gun ports designed to sweep the entire length of the tunnel as well as the area immediately outside, the military police on duty could employ their automatic weapons to deny entrance into the complex completely.

This tight control extended to more than the coming and going of those who occupied the complex. Electronic equipment operated within the underground chambers was protected by the same dirt and rock that provided the humans who operated it with a comfortable environment. While not impossible, efforts to eavesdrop electronically from the outside were complicated. Nor could electronic emissions from computers escape, except though the cabling that provided power and communications from the outside world. To prevent this, filters and sophisticated countermeasures at selected points along the wiring leaving the complex denied unauthorized monitoring and filtered out emissions. If the powers that be wanted to, the entire complex could be shut down and isolated in every way imaginable.

Isolation, however, was not part of the charter for those who currently occupied the West Fort Hood complex, known by its occupants as the Keep. Quite to the contrary. From clusters of workstations that

numbered anywhere from four to eight, young men
and women sat before state-of-the-art computers, following the day-to-day activities of computer opera-
tors throughout the entire United States Army. With
the twirl of a trackball and the click of a button, the
cybersnoops at West Fort Hood could pull up the
screen of any Army computer that was plugged into
the World Wide Web or one of a dozen closed-loop
systems used by units that handled hypersensitive
material. Everything the unsuspecting computer op-
erators "out there" did and saw on their machines
could be monitored, recorded, and studied from the
complex.

While the on-screen antics of some of the Army
personnel and the civilians who work alongside of
them in cyberspace could be entertaining, the resi-
dents of the subterranean labyrinths were not concerned with them. Rather, they searched the Army's
network of computers in search of those who did not
belong there, young hackers from the outside like
Angelo Castalano who used their computers to generate electronic mischief and mayhem on systems
the Army depended upon to keep itself going. This,
of course, was nothing new and far from being a
secret. The hunting down and tracking of unauthorized intrusions into an organization's computer system by the government and civilian businesses was
practiced universally.

What made the West Fort Hood cybersleuths different than that of other, more mainstream agencies
was what they did once they latched on to someone
fiddling about in an Army computer. The computer
geeks of the FBI, CIA, NSA, Secret Service, banks,
and corporations all relied on laws, both federal and
international, or protective countermeasures to deal
with violators they came across. While this was usually

sufficient to do the job, the use of established courts to punish or end unauthorized intrusions and electronic vandalism took time. In some cases, the lack of laws or a foreign nation's inability to enforce existing laws made retribution impossible. And there were more than a few instances where the nature of the violation demanded an immediate response.

It was to provide the United States Army with the ability to deliver that response that 401st Signal Detachment was created. Sporting a simple black unit crest with nothing but a zero and a one separated by a lightning bolt, personnel assigned to the 401st went about their assigned duties without fanfare. Together this collection of intelligence analysts, computer experts, and hackers stationed at West Fort Hood was rather unspectacular. The didn't sport a beret, worn at a jaunty angle. Nor did they wear a special skills qualifications badge over the upper left pocket of their rumpled BDUs like that given out to paratroopers, expert infantrymen, or combat medics. To those who did not have a security clearance sufficient to read the unit's mission statement, it appeared that the 401st was simply another combat service support unit swelling the ranks of the Army that already had far too much tail and not near enough teeth.

Only a handful of senior officers in the Army knew that this was just not so. The 401st provided neither service nor support. It had teeth, real teeth and a mandate to use them. For the fangs that the 401st sported had not been created to serve as a show of force or deterrent. Unlike their more conventional counterparts, the computer hackers who wore the black "Oh Slash One" crest had but one mode of operation: attack. Collectively known as Cyberknights, their charter was not only to find intruders, but to strike back using every means possible. The motto adopted by this quiet little unit pretty much summed it all up in three words, "Seek, Strike, Destroy."

From their small workstations tucked away in casements where nuclear weapons once sat, the Cyberknights of the 401st went about their task with enthusiasm. For many of the young men and women assigned to the unit, this was the ultimate in jobs, a nonstop video game played against a foe that was always different, and just as articulate as they in the ways of cyberspace. Most of the "foot soldiers" belonging to the 401st were in their early twenties. With few exceptions they had been recruited by the Army on campuses of America's most prestigious universities and colleges. The typical candidates targeted to fill the ranks of the cyberwarfare unit were well-educated students who had more ability than they did drive, ambition, and money. Better than half had been on academic probation when the recruiter from the 401st approached them. Faced with the prospect of being cast out into the real world, where they would not have a degree to help them find a job sufficient to pay off student loans and credit-card debt they had accumulated along the way, the Army's offer was a lifeline.

Without fanfare and often without the knowledge of the administration of the campus on which the recruiting was taking place, the FBI scanned records to detect discrepancies between the potential of students enrolled in computer-engineering courses and their actual performance. When prospective candidates were found, discreet inquiries were made into the habits of the student as well as the reasons for the poor academic showing. When a student matched the profile the 401st had established as be-

ing susceptible to what it had to offer, the action was
passed off to the administrative branch of the 401st
which dispatched one of its recruiters. These officers
tracked down the candidate and made offers few in
their positions could refuse.

Some in the unit's chain of command disapproved
of the procurement practices. Older officers who had
been educated at West Point and had proudly served
their nation for years without compromising the eth-
ical values which that institution took pains to instill
saw the methods used to induce young people at risk
to join the 401st as rather predatory, a tad intrusive,
and a shade too far over the line that separates that
which is legal and that which is not. Few of the former
students, however, complained. Plucked out of college just when things in their tender young lives could
not have gotten any bleaker, they were offered an academic version of a golden parachute. In exchange
for a three-year obligation, debt they had incurred
during their ill-fated academic pursuit of excellence
would disappear in the twinkling of an eye. While that
alone would have been sufficient to bring over a
number of prospective recruits, the Army offered
more, much more. To start with, there was a tax-free,
five-figure cash bonus paid up front. Coupled with
this windfall was a college fund that grew with each
year of honorable service. And for those who had
trepidation about shouldering a rifle or slogging
through the mud, a promise that their nights would
be spent between two sheets and not standing a
watch in a country whose name they could not pro-
nounce was more than enough.

In most cases, however, such inducements were
unnecessary once the new members of the 401st entered the Keep. To young men and women who had

learned to read while cruising the World Wide Web, the Keep was a virtual wonderland, a field of dreams for cyberpunks and hackers. A flexible budget and a policy that permitted the unit's automation officer to ignore normal Army procurement procedures ensured that the Cyberknights were well equipped with state-of-the-art systems. Once they were on the job, the new Cyberknights employed every cutting-edge technology and program available, not to mention a few that were little more than a glimmer on the horizon in the world outside. This last benefit came via a close relationship the 401st maintained with both the NSA and the CIA. This gave the equipment and technologies procurement section of the 401st access to whatever those agencies had, both in terms of equipment and techniques.

While the Keep was, for the Cyberknights, akin to a dream come true, not everyone found their assignment to the 401st to their liking. As he trudged his way down the long tunnel en route to his office located at the heart of the Keep, Colonel Kevin Shrewsbery tried hard not to think about his command.

An infantry officer with an impeccable record and a shot at the stars of a general, his selection to command the 401st had come as a shock. The mere fact that neither he nor any of his peers in NATO headquarters in Belgium had heard of the 401st when his orders had come in assigning him to that post should have been a warning. "What the hell are you people doing?" he yelled over the phone to his career-management officer at Army Personnel Command. "Whose brilliant idea was it to assign me to command a signal detachment? What happened to the brigade at Bragg I was promised?"

Equally ignorant of what, exactly, the 401st was,

the personnel officer could only fumble about in search for an explanation. "You were asked for by name," he replied to the enraged colonel on the other end of the line. "The request for orders assigning you to the 401st was submitted by the Deputy Chief of Staff for Special Operations himself."

Rather than mollify the irate colonel, this response only served to confuse the issue. In the Army, young up-and-coming officers that bear watching are tagged at an early stage in their careers. The field from which a future Chief of Staff of the Army is chosen is pretty much narrowed down to a select few by the time the rank of major is achieved. Those who have a real shot at that coveted position are usually taken under the wings of a more senior officer, an officer who can guide the Chief of Staff of the Army in waiting along the maze of peacetime career assignments that are mandatory checkpoints. This senior officer, known as a rabbi in the Old Army, ensures that all the right buttons are pushed, and all the right tickets are punched by his charge in order to ensure that his candidate wins the four-star lottery.

Major General William Norton, the current Deputy Chief of Staff for Special Operations, was Shrewsbery's rabbi. So it was not surprising that the designated commander of the 401st took the unprecedented step of calling Norton at his home at the earliest opportunity. With as much respect and deference as circumstances would permit, Shrewsbery pleaded his case. "Sir, I have never questioned your wisdom or judgment. But assignment to a signal unit? What is this all about?"

Since the phone line was a private home phone and not secure, Norton could not tell his protégé a great deal. "Kevin," the general stated in a tone that conveyed a firmness that could not be missed, "the

Army is changing. The world of special operations and the manner in which we wage war is changing. In order to advance in the Army today, you must ride the wave of change, or be crushed beneath it." While all of this was sound advice, advice that he had heard time and time again, neither Norton's words or the fact that he, Shrewsbery, would be reporting directly to Norton himself while commanding the 401st did much allay the colonel's concerns. His heart had been set on a parachute infantry brigade. Though considered by many an outdated twentieth-century anachronism, the command of a whole airborne brigade was his dream assignment, a dream that now was beyond his grasp.

That was the first chip on Shrewsbery's square shoulders. As time went on, more would accumulate until it seemed, to Shrewsbery, that he would be unable to walk along the long access tunnels leading into the Keep without bending over.

If there had been a casual observer, one who had the freedom and the security clearance necessary to stand back and look at the 401st from top to bottom and make an objective evaluation of the unit, they would have compared it to a piece of old cloth. In the center, at its core where Shrewsbery sat, the fabric retained its old structure. The pattern of the cloth could be easily recognized and matched to the original bolt from which it was cut. But as you moved away from the center, out toward the edges, the fabric began to unravel, losing its tight weave, some of its strength, and as well as the neatly regimented pattern.

Around the center the observer would see an area populated by the 401st support staff. The recruiters who provided manpower for the unit were assigned here, as were the technocrats who maintained and modified the computers and networks that the Cyberknights used. These staffers liked to think of themselves as the Lords of Gadgets. The Cyberknights called them the stableboys. Also counted as part of the support staff was the intelligence section. While not the equal of the knights in the scheme of things, it was the wizards behind the green door who did much of the seeking.

The intelligence section worked in its own series of tunnels, isolated from the rest of the complex by a series of green doors, a quaint habit the Army's intelligence types had adopted years ago. There they took the first steps in developing a product that could be used by the operations section and, if necessary, the Cyberknights themselves. Rare information concerning computer hacks on military systems was funneled to them from throughout the Army. Once deposited behind the green doors, the intelligence analysts studied each case handed off to them for action. They looked at the incident and compared it to similar events they had come across in the past in an effort to determine if the intruder was a newbie, or someone that the 401st had met before in cyberspace. Next the analysts were expected to make a judgment call, based in part upon the facts they had on hand, and in part on intuition, as to the nature of the hack.

By the time one reached the edges of the material, the original color and pattern could no longer be discerned. All that one could see were individual strands, frayed ends that were barely connected to the cloth. Each strand, upon closer inspection, was different. Each had a distinct character that little resembled the tightly woven and well-regimented strands that made up the center. Yet it was there, among these strands, where the real work of the

401st took place. For these strands were the Cyber-knights, the young men and women who sallied out, into cyberspace, day in and day out to engage their nation's foes. And while the terms these Cyber-knights used were borrowed from computer games, and the skirmishes they fought with their foes were in a virtual world, the consequences of their actions were very, very real.

While Colonel Kevin Shrewsbery settled in for an-other long day, Eric Bergeron was in the process of wrapping up his shift. In many ways Eric was the typ-ical Cyberknight. At age twenty-five he had spent five years at Purdue in an unsuccessful pursuit of a de-gree in computer science. Rail-thin, his issued BDUs hung from him as they would from a hanger, making it all but impossible for him create anything resem-bling what the Army had in mind when they coined the term "ideal soldier." Being a Cyberknight, young Bergeron did nothing to achieve that standard. His hair was always a bit longer than regulations permit-ted. The only time there was a shine on his boots was when he splashed through a puddle and the wet footgear caught a glint of sunlight. Only his baby-fine facial hair saved him from having to fight a daily hassle over the issue of shaving.

Making his way along one of the numerous interior corridors of the Keep, Eric didn't acknowledge any of the people he passed. He neither said hello nor both-ered to nod to anyone he encountered on his way to the small, Spartan break room. It wasn't that he was rude or that he didn't know the names of those he came across. Rather, his thoughts were someplace else. Like most of the Keep's population, Eric's mind was turning a technical problem over and over again. At the moment he was going over his last engagement. Though he had triumphed, it had taken him far too long to ride down the kid in Valparaiso, Chile. This had brought into question his skills, which he took great pride in, as did most of the Cyberknights. This was a far greater motivational factor than all the inducements that had been showered upon them to secure their enlistments or the official rating they all received periodically.

Recognizing the *Lost in Space* stare, Captain Brittany Kutter waited until Eric was almost right on top of her before she called out to him. "Specialist Bergeron?"

Startled, Eric stopped dead in his tracks and looked around. "Yes?"

When she was sure she had his attention, Kutter stepped up to the befuddled Cyberknight. Flashing the same engaging smile she used when she was about to ask someone a favor that was, in reality, an order, Kutter motioned with her right hand toward a rather forlorn figure who stood behind her. "I know you've just finished a long shift, Specialist Bergeron, but would it be possible to show a newly assigned member of the unit around the complex while I find out where he will be assigned?"

Eric made no effort to hide his feelings. He hated it when people like the captain before him assigned his tasks in this manner. Why in the hell, he thought, didn't they just behave the way soldiers are supposed to, like the colonel, God bless his little black heart.

Stepping forward, the young man who had been following the female captain reached out, hesitantly, with his right hand. "My name is Hamud Mdilla. I am sorry to be of bother, but . . ."

Realizing what he had done, Eric managed to muster up a smile. "Oh, please. No bother at all."

Taking advantage of the moment, Kutter broad-

ened her smile as she stepped away. "Well, I'll let
you two go. When you're finished, come by my office."

Eric waited until he was sure that she was out of
earshot before he spoke again. "You'd think," he
mumbled, "they'd drop all their phony pretenses
once they've reeled in their latest catch and start acting like normal human beings."

This comment offended Hamud. "I am sure that
the young captain is more sincere than you give her
credit for."

Looking over at the newly recruited Cyberknight,
Eric smirked. "Yeah, right." Then, with a nod, the
veteran stepped off. "Come on. I'll give you a Q and
D."

New to the Army, Hamud hesitated. "Excuse me?"

"Q and D," Eric explained. "Quick and dirty. I'll
show you around."

Though the tour was an impromptu one, Eric executed his assignment using the same methodical approach he used when dealing with any issue. As he
did so, he engaged the new Cyberknight in conversation. In part, this was to ease the tension that their
awkward introduction had created. But Eric also
took advantage of this opportunity to probe and take
a measure of Hamud's abilities. For even though the
foes the Army wanted them to seek out and destroy
were the ones lurking about in cyberspace, the Cyberknights engaged in an in-house competition that
pitted one against another.

"So," Eric chirped. "Where'd they find you?"

"MIT," Hamud stated glumly. "I was in my third
year there."

"MIT! Wow. I am humbled in your presence."

Glancing over at his rumpled guide, Hamud

wasn't sure if he was being mocked. "Yes, well, it sounds more impressive than it is."

"The best I could do was a few years at Purdue before I reached the end of the line," Eric countered. "The credit line, that is."

Use of experienced Cyberknights to take newly assigned members of the unit was a practice that Colonel Shrewsbery had introduced. He figured that these soldiers, for all their shortcomings, were no different than any others in the Army. The old hand, he reasoned, would do more than show the 'cruit his way around. He would use the opportunity to lord it over the newbie, to demonstrate his superior knowledge as well as brag about his accomplishments. In this way the new man would have an opportunity to gain insights that a nontechno type could not hope to pass on.

"Not every assault on the Army's network poses the same threat," Eric explained as they wandered about the section of the Keep where the wizards of intelligence sorted through incoming material. "And not everyone who breaches security systems does so for the same reason. Most of the intruders are pretty much like us, young cyberpunks with more time and equipment on their hands than smarts."

Nodding, Hamud listened, though he had never considered him-self to be a cyberpunk and very much resented being lumped together with them.

"They utilize their personal high-speed computers and the World Wide Web to wreak havoc on unsuspecting sites for any number of reasons," Bergeron continued. "The sociologists assigned to the unit say most of them are young people harboring feelings of being disenfranchised by whatever society they live in. They use their equipment, given to them by dear old Mom and Dad, to vandalize the very society which their parents so cherish. Of all the intruders that violate Army systems these hackers, known collectively as gremlins, are rated as being the lowest threat to the system as a whole, and generally rate a low priority when it comes to tracking them."

"But they can still cause a great deal of damage, can't they?" Hamud asked.

"Oh, of course," Eric replied as he led Hamud to the next stop. "But nine times out of ten they have neither the expertise, the number-crunching power, or the persistence to crack the really tough security used to protect mission-essential systems."

"The Vikings," Eric stated with a wicked smile as he moved on to the next stop along the tour, "are a different story. They're organized in bands. With their superior organization and, in the main, better equipment they can mount a serious and sustained offensive against the Army's computers. Their ability to network, exchange information, refine techniques, and share insights coupled with an ability to strike along multiple routes using multiple systems simultaneously makes them far more lethal than gremlins. The more vicious bands of Vikings can crash all but the Army's most secure sites." Pausing, Eric turned and looked at Hamud. "But that doesn't keep them from trying."

"Are they all just vandals?" Hamud asked. "Or are some politically motivated?"

"If by political motivation," Eric answered cautiously, "you are referring to terrorist groups, the answer is yes. Though the intel wizards seldom tell us everything, it doesn't take a genius to figure out why the people we are assigned to take down are making the hack."

Pausing, Eric cocked his head as if mulling over a thought. "Of course, there have been instances where a band of relatively harmless Vikings has been hijacked by someone who was, as you say, politically motivated."

Having no qualms about showing his ignorance, Hamud shrugged. "Hijacked?"

"Yes, hijacked," Eric explained as he resumed his tour. "We refer to politically motivated hackers who work for foreign groups or nations as dark knights. Normally, they will operate out of their own facilities, some of which are probably not at all unlike this place. But on occasion a dark knight will search the web for an unattached band of Vikings. By various means of subterfuge or deception, these roaming dark knights, or DKs, work their way into the targeted band. Often, they use bribes such as techniques that he hasn't observed the Viking band he's been tracking use as a means of worming his way into the targeted band's good graces."

When he heard this, Hamud's pace slowed. Turning, Eric saw a pained expression on the new recruit's face. Knowing full well what that meant, the veteran Cyberknight smiled and waved his right hand in the air. "Oh, I wouldn't worry. We've all been duped by some predatory sack of shit. Just make sure you don't get sucked in here."

Forcing a sickly smile, Hamud nodded. "Yes, I can appreciate that."

"Now the DKs," Eric went on as he picked up both his conversation and tour where he had left off, "can be quite vicious. Unlike the gremlins and lesser Viking bands, most DKs and the war bands they belong to have unlimited funds. That means they can not only buy the best that's out there, but even when we fry their little brains, it's only a matter of time before they come back, but only smarter and better prepared for battle."

"So what do you do then?" Hamud asked innocently.

"Then," Eric shouted, thrusting his right arm up,
index finger pointed toward the ceiling as if he were
signaling a charge, "we have ourselves some real
fun."

Three

www.quest

With growing reluctance, Lieutenant Colonel James Mann glanced down at his fuel gauge. In his sixteen years in the United States Air Force, he had never seen that particular indicator dip so low. Drawing in a deep breath, he struggled to control his emotions as he pressed the PUSH TO TALK button. "Quebec Seven Nine, Quebec Seven Nine. This is Tango Eight Four, over." After releasing the PUSH TO TALK button, Mann stared out of the cockpit of his F-16, vainly searching the night sky as he waited for a response from the KC-10 aerial refuelers using the call signs Quebec Seven Nine.

After what seemed to be an eternity, Mann called out without bothering to use call signs. "Does anyone out there see anything that looks like a tanker?"

At first no one answered as five other pilots craned their necks and searched the black sky that made their isolation seem even more oppressive, more ominous. Finally, Mann's own wingman came back with the response no one wanted to hear. "Boss, looks like someone missed the mark."

Rather than respond, Mann flipped through the notes he had taken during their preflight briefing. When he found what he was looking for, he glanced up at his navigational aids. The coordinates, the time, the radio frequency upon which they were to make contact with the tankers all matched. Everything was exactly as it was supposed to be. Everything. Yet, there were no KC-10s out there waiting to greet them with the fuel they would need to complete their nonstop flight to Saudi Arabia.

In the midst of checking and rechecking all his settings on the aircraft's navigational system, another voice came over the air. "Colonel, I'll be sucking fumes in a few. Maybe it's time we start making some noise."

Mann didn't answer. The deployment of his unit was part of a major buildup in southwest Asia in response to threats being directed against the Saudi government. With the exception of conversations between themselves and the aerial tanks, strict radio listening silence was the order of the day. The arrival of the air wing that Mann's flight belonged to was meant to be a surprise to the local despot. "We're going to come swooping down on that little shit," their wing commander told his pilots at their final briefing, "like a flock of eagles on a swarm of field mice." Now, as he peered out into the darkness, Mann accepted the horrible fact that the only thing he and his companions would be swooping down to was the cold, dark Atlantic below. Even if the tankers did show up in the next few minutes, which he doubted, there would be insufficient time to go through the drill and refuel all of the aircraft in the flight. Some, if not all of them, would have to ditch.

Faced with this awful truth, Mann prepared to issue an order that went against his every instinct. "Roger that," he finally responded with a heavy sigh. "Everyone is to switch over to the emergency frequency following this transmission. Though I know some of you will be able to go on for a while, I don't want to make it any harder for search and rescue than it already is. As soon as the first plane goes in, we'll circle around him and maintain as tight an orbit over that spot as we can. Acknowledge, over."

One by one, the other pilots in Mann's flight came back with a low, barely audible "Roger." With that, the Air Force colonel gave the order to flip to the designated emergency frequency and began broadcasting his distress call.

Even before the last aircraft belonging to Lieutenant Colonel James Mann began its final spiral into the dark sea below, frantic efforts to sort out the pending disaster were already under way. When the Kansas National Guard KC-10 tanker failed to rendezvous with Mann's F-16s at the designated time, the commander of that aircraft contacted operations. A commercial pilot by trade, the tanker's commander was less concerned with the operational security than he was with the lives he knew were in the balance.

Back at Dover Air Base, from which the KC-10 had been scrambled for this mission, a staff officer pulled up the tasking orders on his computer screen that had dispatched the KC-10. As the pilot of the tanker continued to orbit at the prescribed altitude, over the exact spot he had been sent to, he waited for the operations officer to confirm that they were in the right spot. Unable to stand the tension, his copilot broke the silence. "That yahoo back in Dover better get a hustle on or there's going to be a lot of unhappy Falcon drivers out here with nowhere to land."

From behind them the navigator glanced down on a sheet of paper he had been making some calculations on. After checking his watch, he cleared his throat. "I'm afraid it's already too late."

Both the pilot and copilot of the KC-10 turned and looked at him. In return, the navigator stared at the pilot. "What now, sir?"

The commander of the tanker had no answer. Without a word he looked away.

When he reached his workstation to begin his shift, Eric Bergeron didn't bother to sit down. Posted in the center of his screen was an international orange sticky note. The reliance of some members of the 401st on such a primitive means of communications caused the young hacker to chuckle. Even in an organization whose whole existence centered on keeping a sophisticated communications network functioning properly, there were many who didn't trust it. Of course, Eric thought to himself as he pulled the note off and read it, after seeing what people like the ones he hunted down could do, he really couldn't blame them.

From his little cubicle next to Bergeron's, Bobby Sung leaned back in his seat until he could see around the divider. "I see you've been zapped by the overlords."

Waving the sticky note about, Eric nodded as he gathered up a notebook he kept next to his computer monitor. "Yes, I have been summoned." In the parlance of the 401st, the overlords were the operations officers, the men and women who assigned the Cyberknights their missions, which the knights themselves referred to as quests. The orange sticky note, reserved for use by the operations section, indicated that this was a priority mission.

"Well then," Sung stated as he made a shooing motion with his hands, "begone with you, oh wretched soul."

Bending over, Eric contorted his expression. Then he did his best to imitate Dr. Frankenstein's deformed assistant as he limped away, grunting as he went, "Yes, master. Coming, master."

In a small briefing room tucked away in one of the numerous casements that sprouted off of the long internal tunnel of the Keep populated by the unit's operations section, Eric met with several members of the staff as well as some outlanders. The conniving officer was no less than the chief of the unit's operations section himself, Major Peter Hines, a name that caused him much grief in an organization with more than its fair share of irreverent cynics. He sat at the head of the long, narrow table in accordance with the military protocol that the regular Army staff stubbornly clung to.

Seated to the major's right, along one length of the table, was the Queen of the Wizards, a title bestowed upon Major Gayle Rhay, chief of the intel section. To her left were the outlanders, outsiders who were not members of the 401st. They wore the typical bureaucratic camouflage that all visitors from Washington, D.C., favored, dark suits and tightly knotted nondescript ties. Farther along that side of the table was an Air Force colonel. That this senior an officer was placed to the left of the pair in civilian attire clued Eric to the fact that the outlanders were pretty well up there on the government's pay scale.

The presence of the outlanders and the officer

from a sister service was not at all unusual. Often-times the 401st handled a high-priority mission that originated within another service or government agency. What was disconcerting to the young hacker was the presence of the Master of the Keep himself, Colonel Shrewsbery. Seated away from the table against the wall, Shrewsbery was situated in such a manner that only Hines could see him without having to turn his head. Eric had noted that Shrews-bery often did this when one of his subordinates was running a meeting or briefing that he wanted to at-tend but not, officially, participate in. During the course of the proceedings the chair of the meeting would glance over to wherever Shrewsbery had placed himself, checking for subtle signals from the colonel. There was, Eric concluded long ago, a sort of mental telepathy used by the careerists within the unit that neither he nor any of the other Cyber-knights were privy to. Not that he wanted to be part of that strange clique.

Without preamble, Major Hines launched into his presentation. "Our records show, Specialist Berge-ron, that you have engaged a DK using the screen name longbow."

Without having to look, Eric knew that the major's use of the term "DK" had caused Shrewsbery to grim-ace. Despite the fact that the colonel had been with the 401st for the better part of a year, the terms his staff resorted to when dealing with Cyberknights still irked him. To him it was unprofessional to indulge in the video game terminology the Cyberknights fa-vored. Still, like every professional officer who en-tered the Keep, he adapted.

"Twice," Eric corrected Hines. "Once just last week during our quest against the X Legion down in South America, and a few months ago when he was working with Der Leibstandart in Germany."

"Yes," the major stated, annoyed that he had been interrupted. "I know." Leaning forward, Hines folded his hands on the table in front of him. "Well, he's back."

Now it was Eric's turn to be surprised. "So soon?" Not that this was unexpected. The Cyberknights themselves had reached a consensus after their second run-in with him that longbow was a DK working for a national-level interest. That he was back already, after only a week, confirmed speculation that had been bantered about between the Cyberknights that this particularly bothersome Dark Knight had access to funds and equipment that only a well-financed organization could provide.

Using a pause to break into the conversation, Gayle Rhay provided some additional information. "He's currently using the screen name 'macnife' and, for the first time, making the hacks himself. Yesterday he hit the Air Force."

Looking over at the rep from that service, Eric noted that the Air Force colonel was avoiding eye-to-eye contact with anyone.

Eric was quick to appreciate that the new screen name was a feeble attempt to cyberize the character's name from the song "Mack the Knife." Nor did he entertain any doubt that macnife and longbow were one and the same person. The one thing that he had learned during his tenure with the 401st was that when the military, the CIA, and the NSA were able to put aside their petty turf battles and pool their combined intelligence assets, no one and nothing could get by them. Even the most sophisticated hacker, exercising the greatest of care, left tracks that were both distinct and traceable.

To start with, a hacker tends to use the same system and computer language. Though he may be familiar with many different types, like an auto mechanic he can't be an expert on every system out there. So he specializes. Nor could he change his ways. As with the mechanic, every hacker has a repertoire of tools that he uses when breaking into a system and while rooting about in it. The sequence in which he employs these tools and the manner in which he operates when confronted by security systems may vary some, but not so much that they cannot be used to assist in pegging who's engaged in making the break-in. It was this particular trait that alerted the 401st that longbow was behind the hacks made by the X Legion, for the novice hackers of that Viking band slavishly mimicked everything longbow taught them. "It's like watching half a dozen junior longbows," an intel Wizard told Eric when they were preparing for that counterhack.

Even more insidious, in the eyes of a hacker, was the ability of intelligence agencies such as the NSA to ID an individual by simply studying the speed and manner in which someone typed. It was far more involved than just counting the number of keystrokes someone makes within a given period of time. Certain irregularities, such as the habit of misspelling the same word, or the use of a certain phrase, tagged an individual as surely as his or her own fingerprints. With the enormous number-crunching ability of the NSA, the American intelligence community had the capability to run the record of a hack through their library of past attacks and look for a match. No doubt, Eric thought as he listened to the briefing, longbow and all his past activities had been puked out as soon as they had done this, just as his own would if he were the target of such close scrutiny.

*   *   *

"He managed," Rhay continued, "to change the mission tasking orders for a deploying flight of aircraft."

"The F-16s," Eric chirped with glee as if he had just guessed the right answer to a pop quiz. Then, when he belatedly remembered that all six pilots were still missing and assumed dead, the Cyberknight's expression changed. "He did that?"

From across the table, one of the outlanders joined in. "The administration considers this attack to be nothing less than an act of war." He made this statement using the sanctimonious tone that many from inside the Beltway seemed to favor when dealing with a flyover person. "As such, the President has directed that the National Security Council come up with an immediate and proportional response."

In an effort to regain control of the meeting, Hines cleared his throat as he looked over at Rhay and the two outlanders, using a spiteful glance as he did so to warn them to back off. When he was ready, the ops major took up the briefing. "That's going to be your mission, Specialist."

Given the events that had brought this about, Eric did his best to hide his excitement. Still, he could see something big was in the offing. "Will this be a duel?"

In Cyberknight speak, a duel was a one-on-one confrontation between one of their own and a dark knight.

Shaking his head, Hines continued. "No, not in the traditional sense."

Leaning back in his seat, Eric eyed Hines and the array of faces across the table from him. "You tagged me because I am familiar with longbow, yet you don't want me to go head-to-head with him. Explain, please."

"It is obvious," the older of the two outlanders

stated, "that not only is this character very, very good, but he has the backing of a very robust and well-financed support system. This makes him a very dangerous threat, since each run-in serves to enhance both his reputation and his experience level."

The second outlander picked up the thought. "Since we can't seem to terminate this particular hacker by direct means, we have been given the mission of finding another way of putting an end to his career."

Like a wrestling tag team, the older outlander took over. "We hit upon the idea of discrediting this hacker, now operating under the name 'macnife.' "

Looking back and forth between the pair of unnamed outlanders, Eric shrugged. "How do *we* plan to do that?"

Used to working with the Cyberknights and the way they could become quite unruly if allowed to, Major Gayle Rhay cut in. "We are fairly confident that another nation is using macnife, formerly known as longbow, and his nation as a surrogate, a platform from which to strike at the United States."

"Other than raising hell and poking the tiger," Eric asked, "what's their motivation?"

"The second party, the one supplying equipment and funding to macnife's nation for his use, may be doing so in an effort to test our computer security and try new techniques on us," the intelligence officer explained. "By going through a surrogate, the second party nation is able to gain valuable experience without having to expose its own nation's cyberwarfare capability to countermeasures or foreign intelligence agencies."

"Huh," Eric grunted. "Sounds like a Tom Clancy plot."

"Were this not actually taking place," Rhay replied,

"it would make a rousing good read. But unlike a technothriller, we can't be sure the good guys are going to win."

Unable to restrain himself, Eric began to grin. "So, you've come to me, the Indiana Jones of cyberwarfare. What, exactly, is it you want me to do this time?"

Without any noticeable objections from Major Hines, the older of the two outlanders gave Eric a quick, thumbnail sketch of what the operation would entail. "You will begin the operation by breaking into the system used by macnife. Once there, you must establish yourself as the root, preferably without anyone noticing."

"Is there any other way?" Eric asked in mock innocence.

In unison, the two outlanders looked at each other, searching each other's expressions in an effort to determine if this was a serious question. Since neither was sure, the older outlander chose to ignore it and continue. "Now comes the hard part. Once in, you're to assume macnife's identity. Using his own system, you're to access several computer systems within the nation that has been supporting macnife's adventures."

"The object here," the second outlander stated in a crisp, monotone voice, "is to create suspicion and distrust."

"I see," Eric replied as he reflected upon the implications. "By making the supplier think that macnife is using their own equipment against them, you're hoping to break this unholy alliance."

"Exactly," the older outlander stated. "Otherwise, the cycle will simply repeat itself, with macnife becoming smarter and the nation supplying the equipment and funding getting away scot-free."

"Do you folks have any specific targets in mind?"

Eric asked as his enthusiasm for this operation continued to mount.

"We have been assigned two targets," Major Hines stated as he finally found an opportunity to elbow his way back into the briefing he was chairing. "The first hack is the supporting nation's cyberwarfare center. We want you to get inside the system there and see what you can find."

Excited, Eric blurted out his questions as he thought of them. "Is this a simple snoop and scoot?"

"If possible," Hines stated, annoyed at the interruption, "we want you to plant a Trojan horse, which the NSA rep will provide you with."

To hackers, a Trojan horse is an implanted code or program that runs an operation or performs functions that the host computer user is unaware of or alters an existing program so that the original functions do not behave as they were intended to. If done well, a Trojan is all but impossible to find and can totally corrupt the original program.

"Okay, so far, this sounds like a piece of cake," Eric quipped.

Again, the two outlanders turned to face each other before continuing. "The second hack is a straight-out attack against a chemical plant located within the supporting nation."

Suddenly, Eric's tone changed. "A denial of service attack?" he asked cautiously.

"No," the older outlander stated without betraying any emotion. "The objective of this hack is destruction. Whether this can be best achieved by altering settings or by incapacitating automated safety protocols will be determined once you're into their system. It's the results that matter."

It was more than the words that caused the hairs on Eric's neck to bristle. It was the cold, unemotional manner in which the outlander mouthed them that bothered the Cyberknight. "If it's a chemical plant," the young hacker stated cautiously, "then we're talking serious roadkill. Aren't we?"

Though they never saw it up close and personal, the loss of human life as a result of their hacks, referred to as roadkill, bothered even the most hardened Cyberknight. So long as there was no blood shed as a direct result of their activities, the young hackers belonging to the 401st could engage in a bit of self-deluding disassociation. But once that line was crossed, once they became aware that their activities, if successful, would produce death, many a Cyberknight hesitated. On more than one occasion, a Cyberknight even declined to execute an assigned task.

Realizing what was going on, Colonel Shrewsbery chose this moment to insert himself into the proceedings. "I am well aware of the fact, Specialist Bergeron," he stated in a gruff voice that commanded everyone's attention, "that you do not think of yourself as a soldier, at least not in the conventional sense."

Eric looked across the room and into the dark, unflinching eyes of the colonel. "I do not believe," the Cyberknight whispered, "in the taking of human life."

"Unfortunately," Shrewsbery countered without hesitation, "those who oppose us do not share that sentiment. While it would be wrong to characterize them all as monsters, let there be no doubt in your mind that they are willing to do whatever they need to in order to achieve their national goals." Pausing, Shrewsbery reached down, without breaking eye contact with Eric, and picked a newspaper off the floor. With an underhanded toss, he flung the paper on the table, faceup, in Eric's direction.

Reaching out, the young Cyberknight stopped it just before it slid off the table and into his lap. In bold print the paper announced that any hope of finding the F-16 pilots alive was waning. Below that banner headline was a photo of one of the pilots' wife, looking up into the empty sky, as she clutched a crying child to her side. As Eric read the caption accompanying the photo, Shrewsbery continued. "How many tears do you think the folks behind that hack shed?"

Looking up at the colonel, Eric's resolve hardened, but only for a moment. "I cannot speak for them, sir."

"I'm not asking you to, son," Shrewsbery replied as he moderated his tone. "All I am asking you to do is to do your best to keep that sort of thing from becoming a daily occurrence. While none of us can bring those pilots back, we damned sure can do something to protect those who are still out there, doing their duty, just like you."

Unable to find a suitable reply, Eric again looked at the photo before him. Then he lifted his eyes and looked over at the people gathered about the table. They were all staring at him, waiting for him to say something.

Glancing back at Shrewsbery, Eric found that he was barely able to contain his anger. How he hated it when someone like the colonel rubbed his nose in what he, and the other Cyberknights, really did. Eric knew that the 401st was not a video arcade. He understood, on an intellectual level, that his actions had very real consequences that affected very real people. He just didn't want to be reminded of this day in, day out. Like the bomber crews in World War II, the young Cyberknight managed, for the most part, to insulate himself from what he was doing.

That's why he and all the other Cyberknights used the colorful terms they did. Such words hid the meaning of their actions. Nor did the Cyberknights allow themselves to think of their foes as real people. And, like the young men who had flown the planes that had smashed Coventry, flattened Dresden, and eradicated Hiroshima, once they had finished an action, they moved on. No need, he often found himself thinking, to bother himself about what lay behind in his wake. He was, after all, simply following orders. Let the people who generated those orders lose sleep over the price.

But every now and then, reality took a bite out of this cherished isolation. As the saying went in the Keep, even Disneyland has a cloudy day.

"Okay," Eric finally whispered as he took the newspaper before him and flipped it over. Mustering up as much enthusiasm as he could, he turned to face Major Hines. "Let's get it on."

Four

The Pit

The days when a high-school kid, parked in front of his computer in the comforts of his bedroom, could rain down death and distraction upon the world were gone. So was the Lone Ranger approach, especially within the 401st. When executing a major operation, known as a hack attack, the exercise had all the intricacies of a Broadway production. The room in which they made their attack was not as nearly as sophisticated as one would have imagined, though it did have more than its fair share of bells and whistles common to most government operations. Yet even these, like everything found in that room, nicknamed the Pit, had a purpose.

The Pit was isolated for reasons of security. The official name of the Pit, posted on the red door that separated it from the rest of the tunnel complex, was Discrete Strike Operations Center, or DSOC, pronounced "dee sock" by the operations staff. Within the DSOC were two chambers, the Pit itself, where the actual cyberattack would take place, and a second, in which observers, straphangers, and miscellaneous personnel not directly involved in the mechanics of the attack could watch via closed-circuit TV and dummy monitors. The Army staff called this the observation suite. The Cyberknights referred to it as the Spook Booth.

Whenever Eric Bergeron had been in the Pit it had always been dark. The only illumination in the room was that which was thrown off by the computer monitors located there and small reading lights at each workstation. Everything else was so dark that if asked by someone, he would be unable to tell them what color the walls were.

The furniture in the Pit was quite sparse, consisting of two long tables, one set upon a platform behind the other. Along one side of each table were armless chairs. These chairs faced a wall that was actually one huge screen that covered that surface from ceiling to floor. Both tables were fitted out with four computer workstations, though there were power trees bolted at either end of the tables and space to accommodate two more if required. Unlike the normal haunts where the Cyberknights went about their day-to-day activities, there were no dividers between the individual workstations. This was done to permit quick access, both verbal and nonverbal, between the members of the 401st at each of the tables. A person working at one position could easily reach in front of anyone to their left or right to pass on a handwritten note or sketch. Even though everyone in the strike center wore a headset with a tiny boom mike that permitted them to speak to other members of the team, it had been found that there were times when these notes worked best, especially when the personnel in the Pit didn't want those in the Spook Booth to know something.

Located at each of the eight permanent workstations was a computer. Each was set up to perform a discrete function during an attack. The primary assault computer, labeled PAC, was the center-right workstation on the front table. It was from this position that Eric Bergeron would make his way into macnife's computer, then on to those that ran the chemical plant located in the supporting nation. To Eric's immediate right sat the primary foreign language expert, or FLE. While much of the traffic on the World Wide Web was in English, many of the programs and protocols, especially those concerning security and safety, were written in the language of the actual user. Hence there was a need for someone to be there, at Eric's side, to translate in real time. These interpreters, recruited in much the same way as the Cyberknights were, had to be as computer savvy as the knights themselves. This was how Bobby Sung, a second-generation Chinese American, had made his way into the ranks of the Cyberknights. Since this hack attack would be going into the systems of two different nations, there was a second FLE located at a computer at the right end of the table, set up at the overflow slot.

The left-center workstation belonged to the systems expert, or SE. While good, the Cyberknights could not possibly know every nuance and quirk of the computers they were working from or hacking. The SE was one of the many on-site civilian tech reps ordinarily charged with maintaining machines supplied by their companies. During an attack, an SE familiar with the targeted systems was brought in to answer any questions Eric might have during the hack or assist if the Cyberknight came across something that he did not quite understand. Oftentimes these SEs were members of the design team who had actually manufactured the computer being attacked. To the SE's left was a language/programs expert, or LPE. Like the hardware specialist, the LPE was on hand in case Eric needed help with the software he encountered.

Immediately behind the primary assault computer, on the rear table, sat the electronic-warfare station. Manned by a second Cyberknight, the operator of this computer had the task of assisting the hacker whenever he ran into a firewall or other security measure during the break-in. Once the hacker was in, the electronic-warfare knight, EWK for short, monitored the systems admin and security programs of the hacked network. It was his responsibility to protect the hacker from countermeasures initiated by automated security programs or systems administrators.

This feat was accomplished in any number of ways. The preferred countermeasure was simply to lie low, or cease the hack, until any detected security sweep was completed. If it appeared as if someone was starting to become wise to the hack, the EWK attempted to spoof the systems administrator by making him think everything was in order. When this failed and the administrator started to track the unusual activity that the hack was causing, the EWK began to feed his foe data that would create the appearance that the security program was malfunctioning. More often than not, this made the system administrator hesitate as he tried to determine if the suspect activity was nothing more than an anomaly in the system or a glitch with the security program of his computer. When this ploy didn't work, the EWK was forced to employ the least desirable trick in his bag, the dreaded red herring.

Every EWK had a totally fictitious hack sequence loaded on the EW computer and ready to initiate with nothing more than the touch of a special function key. Often they used the screen name and tactics of another hacker that the Cyberknights had come across during their day-to-day efforts to protect the Army's computers. This ruse was designed to be both sloppy and obvious, yet not easily countered. When initiated, more often than not, it gave the primary hacker more than enough time to finish his attack and back out before the system administrator caught on. Occasionally, however, the defensive measures taken against the feint were too quick. When the EWK saw that he was losing the fight to keep their foe at bay, he would call out, "eject," signaling the hacker he had to stop the hack, no matter where he was.

To the right of the EWK was an intel wizard. Major Gayle Rhay herself frequently took this seat. Like the systems or the language/programs experts, the intel officer was there to provide the primary hacker with advice and recommendations should he run across something that was unfamiliar or unexpected. The presence of someone from the intelligence section in the Pit also had the benefit of providing the wizards themselves with valuable firsthand knowledge of the capabilities of their foes.

The station to the left of the EWK was occupied by a recently recruited Cyberknight. Since a highly technical hack attack such as the one Eric was about to undertake was both difficult and involved operations against a sovereign power, only the most senior Cyberknights were permitted to make them. To qualify for what was, among the Cyberknights, these most prestigious assignments, a novice had to observe six actual hacks in the Pit and successfully complete twelve consecutive simulations. On this day, the honor of checking off his first observed Pit hack fell to Hamud Mdilla, the bright young newbie Eric had shown around.

Most people who wander onto the World Wide Web from their home computers give little thought about how their input makes it from the keyboard sitting on their laps to the sites they are seeking. Nor do they much care that so much data about who they are, and where they are, is bounced about the web in a rather haphazard manner, from one web server to another, in search of the most direct route to the site desired. Few appreciate how much personal data is left behind, like footprints, during this process.

Things were not that easy for the 401st. They could not simply dial up a local server, plug into the Web, and charge out into cyberspace in search of hackers messing with the Army's computers. This was especially true when going head-to-head with a foreign power who possessed the same ability to tap into servers around the world in search of a foe. Since this was how the Cyberknights themselves found most of their adversaries, it was safe to assume that their counterparts working for other masters would do likewise.

To counter this threat, every major cyberattack, such as the one which Eric was about to embark upon, followed a pathway along the Web plotted out by a network-routing specialist. To the Cyberknights, they were the pathfinders. Working at the computer located on the far left of the rear table, the pathfinder opened the route the hack attack took through the World Wide Web. This normally involved going through a number of servers located around the world. Unlike the home web surfer, there was nothing random about the pathway that data would travel. Yet it had to appear that way. To accomplish this little trick the pathfinder mimicked the route that a hacker the 401st had dealt with in the past had followed. This not only served to confuse the cyberwarfare specialist who might come back at them later, but it also covered the unit's own tracks as the Cyberknights crawled along the Web en route to their target. Any webmaster monitoring a Web server along the way who caught the Cyberknights hack would think that it was the same hacker who had visited them before.

This intricate course through the Web also served to protect the security of the 401st and the Keep. By knowing, in advance, where the outgoing data packets were going, the EWK would be able to go back, when the hack attack was over, and erase any record of the traffic at selected servers. This would make it impossible for anyone tracing the hack to discover the real point of origin. Since the Keep was, at that moment, a one-of-a-kind facility, protecting it was always a major concern. While the attack Eric and the team assembled in the Pit was important, it was not worth compromising the entire unit, a unit that could very well be needed to parry the opening attack of the next war.

The last member of the assault team, the officer in charge, had a seat at the rear table, but no computer. This paradox was the result of a decision made by Colonel Shrewsbery's predecessor when the operational procedures for the 401st were being drafted. Since the officer in charge had the responsibility for the attack, the first commander of the 401st felt it was important that he or she be unencumbered by a computer. "Who'll be keeping an eye on the overall ebb and flow of the attack, the big picture of what's going on," the unit's first commander pointed out, "if the OIC is fiddling about with a computer mouse." Though none of the Cyberknights since then understood how the OIC of a hack could run things without a computer, the issue was never debated or discussed.

A well-orchestrated hack attack did not simply happen. How various Cyberknights thought of their collective efforts was reflected by the terminology they used. Those who followed professional sports spoke of scoring when they accomplished an assigned task, or fumbling the ball when a hack went astray. Other Cyberknights with an ear for the classics liked to think of themselves as members of a well-tuned orchestra. And, of course, there were those who enjoyed spicing up their mundane lives by taking on superhero personas that would make Walter Mitty blush.

None of these alternate realities, however, could disguise the fact that this was, from beginning to end, a military operation. Once the officer in charge of the hack had assembled his team, all pretenses were dropped. With few exceptions these officers were like Shrewsbery, professional soldiers with a muddy-boots background who had been pulled into the 401st because they had a demonstrated ability to lead troops.

Their task was not at all an easy one. Most hackers, by their nature, were loners. They did not readily surrender their cherished individualism since so much of their self-worth was based upon what they, and they alone, could do. To overcome this common personality quirk, every OIC staged a rehearsal once all the preliminaries had been completed and the various players felt they were ready. While standing before his assembled strike team, the OIC walked through the hack attack step by step, from beginning to end.

Since most of the officers in the 401st who served as OICs for attacks could not hope to match the technical expertise of the people they would be in charge of, these professional soldiers relied upon the published execution matrix. This document, set up like a spreadsheet, listed each and every step that would be made during the attack down the left-hand edge of the page. Across the top of the matrix was the title of each member of the team, listed at the head of a column. By following that column down the page, everyone in the Pit could see what action he or she was expected to take as the attack unfolded.

With this execution matrix in hand, the OIC would point to the member on the team whose responsibility it was to initiate the next action. As he and every other person in the Pit listened, the soldier or technician the OIC was pointing to explained in detail what he would do at that point. When finished the OIC would turn to another team member, sometimes chosen at random, sometimes selected because they were required to support the event in progress, to spell out what was expected of them. Every now and then the OIC threw in a "what if?" scenario before moving on to the next item in the sequence. Though he already had an idea who needed to respond to his hypothetical question, the OIC would not point to that person, waiting, instead, for them to respond to the unexpected situation. Only when he was satisfied that everyone knew his or her role in the pending operation would the OIC report to Colonel Shrewsbery that they were ready to execute.

The timing of these attacks varied. The classic window chosen to hack into a system was during off hours, when the traffic on the targeted system was light and the chances of someone noticing something unusual was minimal. There were times, however, when hackers wanted to get lost in the traffic, or when the traffic on a busy system was actually necessary, especially when the hacker was trying to collect authentic screen names and passwords which he could use later. Because the hack attack Eric was about to embark upon required him to assume the persona of macnife, the attack had to be staged at a time when the real macnife would not be at his computer.

The other factor that played into the equation was the desire to keep the number of casualties at the chemical plant low. When the OIC of the attack, an artillery captain by the name of Reitter, mentioned that during the rehearsal, Eric Bergeron could not help but laugh. Normally such outbursts were ignored. In the eyes of the professional officers assigned to the 401st the Cyberknights were not real soldiers and therefore unfamiliar with the proper military etiquette and protocol normally expected from soldiers belonging to "the real Army." Reitter, however, was the sort that could not let such a breach of decorum go unchallenged. "As best I can see," he snapped back, "there's nothing funny about what we're about to do, soldier."

Eric didn't shy away from the captain's rebuke. "It's not the fact that we're going to be taking human life that I find laughable," Bergeron explained. "What I find amusing is the concept that somehow, by killing only fifty people instead of one hundred and fifty, we're being nice, or compassionate to the poor schmucks we're zapping."

Up to that point, Colonel Shrewsbery had been content to stand against the rear wall of the Pit, saying nothing as he listened while Reitter walked the assembled team through the operation. Eric's comments and explanation, however, were both uncalled for and way out of line. "That'll be enough of that, mister," the infantry colonel bellowed. "We are soldiers, soldiers who have been given a mission. Executing that mission, and that alone, is all we are concerned with. Period."

For several seconds, no one said a thing as Eric and the commander of the 401st locked eyes. Only when he was sure that he had made his point did Shrewsbery look over to where Reitter stood, seething in anger. "Carry on, Captain."

When he was sure that their colonel was not looking, and while Reitter was fiddling with the note cards he had been briefing from, Bobby Sung leaned over till he was but a few inches from Eric's ear. "Ve vere only following orders, herr judge," Bobby whispered, using a mock German accent. Though they often joked about such things, the Cyberknights understood that they were playing the deadliest game there was. Only through the acceptance of the party line, as well as adopting the sort of graveyard humor soldiers have always used to preserve their sanity, did the Cyberknights manage to go on.

The one thing that would not be present in the Pit during the attack was something that no one in the 401st ever gave a second thought to, a gun. Once past the two MPs posted on either side of the Discrete Strike Operation Center's red door, no one was armed. Yet the war that was about to be waged there was just as vicious, and deadly, as any war that had gone before. Only the tools, and the type of warrior who wielded them, had changed.

Five:

Hack Attack

From his post in the Spook Booth, the commander of the 401st watched the bank of monitors as the members of his command prepared for combat. Just as the business community had been dragged kicking and screaming into the information age, so, too, had the Army. Professional soldiers such as Shrewsbery knew, in their hearts, that units like the 401st were necessary. While some saw this change as being inevitable, and others freely embraced it as a brave new world, all who had been raised on the heroic traditions of their fathers grieved in silence as Eric Bergeron and his fellow Cyberknights took their place in the front ranks of America's military machine.

Joining Shrewsbery to monitor the attack were a number of advisors. One of the most important members of this second-tier staff was a lawyer from the Army's Staff Judge Advocate Corps. Of all the people involved, her position in the scheme of things was the least enviable, since everything that was about to happen was illegal. Not only were there no federal laws that sanctioned what the 401st did on a day-to-day basis, the United States supported every effort in every international forum it could to counter cyberterrorism. While they understood the necessity to aggressively seek out and destroy those who sought to attack their country under the cover of cyberspace, it didn't make anyone pledged to uphold the law feel good about what they were seeing.

If all went well, the JAG officer would have nothing to do. Her presence there was in case something went astray and the activities of the 401st or members of that unit had to be defended in a court of law. The JAG officers assigned to the 401st likened their plight to criminal defense attorneys retained by the mob.

Though he was also charged with enforcing the laws of the land, the FBI liaison in the Spook Booth viewed the undertaking with envy. As a member of that organization's computer crimes unit, the FBI Special Agent followed everything that the hack attack team did. His presence there was more than a matter of courtesy. Despite the fact that the Bureau could not use the same aggressive techniques employed by the 401st, watching a hack from inception to completion served to improve his abilities to devise ways of catching domestic cybercriminals his agency would have to combat once his tour with the Army unit was over.

Also joining Shrewsbery in the Spook Booth were the CIA and NSA reps who had generated this mission as well as the Air Force colonel who was, himself, connected to the Air Force's own cyberwarfare center in Idaho. Collectively theirs would prove to be the most difficult burden during the hack attack. While they had been the ones who had come up with the plan, none of them could do a thing once the attack had been initiated. Like the dummy monitors they watched, they would be powerless to influence the action.

This was not true of the final man in the room. As a member of the National Security Council, he had direct access to the national command authority. If all went well, he would have no need to use this access. Like the other people in the Spook Booth who were not assigned to the 401st the NSC rep would merely go back to Washington, D.C., once the hack was over and submit a written report to his superiors on what had happened. If, however, things got out of hand, the NSC rep would be the one who would pick up the phone and talk to the President and his advisors. While the NSC rep was friendly enough, Shrewsbery likened being confined in the small observation room with him to being locked in a cage with a tiger.

"Okay, people," Reitter announced over his boom mike after his assembled team signaled they were ready, "Here we go. Comms, open the channel."

The first step in any hack attack was to connect the Pit to an outside commercial network. This was done to keep dark knights from doing to the 401st what Reitter and his team were about to do to the cyberwarfare center macnife was operating from. The communications section of the 401st, located in another part of the Keep, literally had to plug the cable leading from the Pit into an external access port. These ports were arranged in a row on a panel painted bright red. Each of these connections was covered with a spring-loaded cap that snapped shut when the internal cable was removed. While there were written warnings posted all over the room, across the top of the red access port panel, and over each cover, a further audio warning was initiated as soon as a cap was lifted, announcing that the connection now exposed was a commercial line. When the connection was made a banner announcing that fact flashed across the top of the big screen in the Pit. This cued the pathfinder to initiate the attack.

Entry into the World Wide Web from the Pit was rather unspectacular. The procedure used by the pathfinder was not at all unlike that used by millions of his fellow Americans on a daily basis. The pathfinder dialed up the Internet server he desired and waited for the link to be made. Patiently he watched the display on his monitor. The plotted pathway that would take them from the Keep to macnife's system was displayed using a rather simple wiring diagram. Each server along the chosen pathway was listed in the sequence that it would be tagged. Within the hollow wire box each server was identified using its commercial name, the access code the pathfinder would need to use to connect with it, the type of equipment the server used, the nation it was located in, and the language the local webmaster used when tending to it.

The box representing each of these web servers was initially blue, the same color this particular specialist had chosen for the monitor's desktop. When a server was being contacted the box went from blue to yellow. Once the connection was made, it would turn red on both the pathfinder's monitor and the big screen on the wall. Only in the Spook Booth, where the nontechnicals watched, did the screen displaying the servers the hack was being routed through show up as an actual map. "Nontechnicals" was a catchall term applied to visitors to the Keep like the rep from the National Security Council and people who were not as computer savvy as the Cyberknights or their support team. When the Pit was being set up it had been decided that it would be far easier for these people to understand what was going on if they saw a map rather than the simplistic wiring diagram used by the pathfinder.

When a civilian web surfer goes out into cyberspace, he usually has a destination in mind but little concern over how he gets there. He simply instructs the web navigational program on his computer to take him to a Web address. This program does several things. It translates the user's message into a protocol that will allow the user's machine to interact with all the servers on the Web as well as the system at the destination site. This internet protocol, or IP, creates header information which includes both originating and destination addresses as well as the message or any additional information the sender has included. Once sent, this data is broken down into packets of data which then bounce about the World Wide Web looking for a server that is both available and capable of taking the message along to its destination. When the connection is made between the user who initiated the communications and the site he was looking for, the data packets are reformatted into a computer language that the receiver, or the system can understand. If the data is a simple e-mail message, the traffic is deposited in the memory of the computer to which it was sent or the service provider if a connection to the final destination is not open at that moment. If the sender has a desire to communicate in real time with someone on the other end, or access and manipulate information stored there, the connection between the two systems remains open until one party or the other terminates it.

Since he wanted to hit specific servers in a fixed sequence, the pathfinder had to organize the address portion of the packets so that they followed a specific route. If a selected server had no open ports, progress along the Web stopped until access was gained. Once in a server, the address for that server was stripped away, revealing the pathfinder's instructions to send the routing message along to the next server.

The assembled Pit team sat in silence as they watched the pathfinder's display on the big screen. Bobby Sung, a patient soul, could be as dispassionate as the computer that sat before him. Eric Bergeron, on the other hand, was unable to contain the nervous energy that was gnawing away at him. With nothing better to do with his hands, he tapped the table with a pencil. While there might have been some sort of rhythm in the Cyberknight's head driving this subconscious response, his hand did a poor job of translating it into anything resembling melody. Instead of music, the female interpreter seated next to him heard disjointed thumps that only served to heighten her own jitters. Without a word, she reached over and snatched the pencil out of Eric's hand. Offended by her action, Eric turned and stared at her. The interpreter met his indignant glare with an expression that all but said, "Go ahead, make my day."

In the midst of this nonverbal exchange, the pathfinder broke the silence. "Okay, boys and girls, we're in." After giving the interpreter one more spiteful glance, Eric turned his attention back to the big screen.

By the time he had refocused his attention to the progression of the attack, Bobby Sung was already at work. As the electronic-warfare knight for this operation, it was his task to break through the security systems that protected the host computer macnife worked from. Since the system they were breaking into was based on an American design, and both the network-level firewalls and the application-gateway firewalls had not been modified by macnife's sponsors, this task was relatively easy. For the first time that day, Bobby Sung betrayed the excitement he felt by humming "The Ride of the Walküre" while his fingers flew across the keyboard before him.

In the Spook Booth, the CIA agent chuckled when he heard Wagner's oft-played piece. "Sounds like your people have been spending too much time watching old war movies."

Kevin Shrewsbery looked over at the visitor from Langley. "I'd rather that than have them use the training we give them here to empty my bank accounts."

While the CIA man stared at the Army colonel, the FBI liaison chuckled. "You've got that right."

Back in the Pit, Bobby Sung was finishing his tasks. "Righto, mate," he called out to Eric Bergeron, "we be in business."

Taking a deep breath, Eric studied his screen. "Let's see now," he mumbled. Bobby Sung, using an old technique, had managed to enter an open port in the host computer macnife worked from by sending a message using an address that macnife's system was familiar with. Once past the security gateways, the body of the message was not checked by the security programs, since it followed the address of a trusted user. That body consisted of a sequence of commands, written in the computer language used by the system under attack, that established a new root account.

Neither the nation that had provided the computers nor macnife's native country altered the basic programming language, making it easy for Eric to pull up the directory of the host computer and get to work. The first phase of the attack involved the downloading of a Trojan horse. While there are several variations to this sort of attack, the one Eric introduced to macnife's host computer involved that system's Internet protocol instructions.

Rather than destroy a single computer which could easily be replaced, the NSA had convinced the members of the National Security Council that it could nullify the effectiveness of future attacks by keeping track of where the dark knights from that country were going in cyberspace. Their solution was to modify the header portion of the Internet protocol instructions currently on macnife's host computer so that every time macnife and his compatriots connected with the internet, the NSA would be alerted. The Trojan horse in this case did nothing other than send the NSA an info copy of everything that was sent out onto the Web. With that information in hand, the NSA would be able to warn any site that was the target of an attack as well as gather information on who this particular nation was working with.

Methodically Eric made his way into the operating system of macnife's host computer. With root access, this was rather simple. What was not going to be easy was the substitution of codes. To do that Eric would have to operate on the old code. That could create a momentary interruption in service, much in the same way that a surgeon performing open-heart surgery must stop the heart in order to work on it. Everyone using macnife's host computer that was connected to the Internet would experience a momentary delay of service. If this interruption became pronounced, the system administrator would, quite naturally, assume that there was a problem either with his connections or his system. Either way, he would become active and begin an aggressive effort to resolve the problem while ignoring the phone calls from angry users.

To prevent this Bobby Sung would momentarily block all outgoing traffic. To the average user this interruption would appear to be nothing more than a delay in finding an open circuit at his or her Internet service provider. Even the most astute computer geek would have difficulty detecting the hiccup Bobby Sung's break in service would create.

"Hey, Bobby," Eric called out. "You ready?"

The EWK looked up at the big screen, where he could clearly see that Eric had the existing IP header information highlighted and ready for deletion. "On the count of three," Bobby Sung replied. Then he began his count, "Three, two, one, break."

In the Spook Booth, the NSA agent pointed to the screens displaying what Bobby Sung and Eric were doing. "The interruption in service comes first," he explained to the rep from the National Security Council. "Then the Cyberknight making the hack wipes away the old header information and substitutes the one we came up with, the Trojan horse."

Though he really didn't understand everything that was going on in the Pit, the NSC rep grunted and nodded knowingly.

* * *

Back in the Pit, Eric drew his hands away from his keyboard and into the air. "Done!"

Bobby Sung, alerted to this by his compatriot's actions and announcement, removed the block from the targeted system. When the warning banner on his screen was replaced by a "Service resumed" message, the EWK let his hands fall away from the keyboard and to his sides. Dispassionately he watched his monitor, which was now showing him the same thing the systems administrator of the hacked computer was seeing. If anyone had noticed the break in service, they would notify the system administrator, who would, in turn, initiate some sort of action to find out what had happened.

Again the Pit became still as everyone watched for a flurry of activity on the portion or the big screen showing them Bobby Sung's screen display. From his seat the OIC took note of the time. It had been decided that a thirty-minute pause would be sufficient to allay any fears that their insertion of the Trojan horse had gone undetected.

As before, Eric found himself unable to contain his nervous energy. With all his pencils out of reach, Eric began to drum his fingers on the tabletop as he watched the big screen. He was in the middle of rapping out a tune when he felt a sharp slap across the back of his right hand. Stunned, he looked over at the interpreter next to him. Surprised by her action and the scowl she wore, Eric pulled his injured hand up to his chest and began to rub it as he stared at his attacker as if to ask, *"Why did you do that?"*

Having anticipated this, the interpreter shoved a note in front of his face. In angry strokes, the note read, *"Stop with the noise, before I am forced to break your fingers."*

Reaching over and snatching the pencil from her

hand, Eric turned as he took up his notepad and jotted out a response. When it was finished, he flashed his response at her. *"Oh yeah!"* it read. *"You and what army?"*

Seeing an opportunity to pass time by engaging in something more exciting than watching the big screen, Eric and the female interpreter exchanged a flurry of notes.

They were still at it when Captain Reitter broke the silence. "It looks as if the Trojan horse is in place and doing its thing. It's time to move on to phase two."

Before breaking off the silent war of words, Eric scribbled out one more message to his neighborly foe. *"We'll continue this later."* After delivering that, he swiveled about in his seat and took up where he had left off. "Okay, Scottie," Eric announced over the intercom, "beam me up."

Without a word the pathfinder prepared to launch back out into cyberspace from the computer they had hacked into and on to the one at the chemical plant chosen for destruction. Using macnife's screen name, he initiated the new hack from macnife's own computer. Unlike before, he made no effort to cover his tracks or weave his way through the Internet along a predetermined route. For this part of the operation to be successful, the pathfinder had to leave a traceable path from macnife's machine to the chemical plant for the cyberwarfare specialists in the other nation to find.

The point of entry at the new site was the computer system at the chemical plant that handled the shipping and tracking of the plant's products. This point, according to the system expert, would be the easiest port through which they could enter and gain access to the rest of the system. While he watched the pathfinder hand off the attack to Bobby Sung so that he could crack the security codes, the system expert unfolded a diagram of the chemical plant's network.

As before, Bobby Sung wormed his way through the security gateways and worked his way through the system until he had reached the network's root directory. From his seat, Eric looked at up the big screen before him. "Gee," he muttered as he took in the screen before him. "I thought you said this plant had been built by a German firm."

"The plant is German," the SE replied. "But the computer network is based upon an American design."

"I sure hope the American firm got some royalties out of this deal," the interpreter remarked.

Bobby Sung snickered. "Not likely."

From his seat, Reitter called out. "Let's settle down and deal with the issue at hand."

Unlike the previous sessions that had passed in near-total silence, a lively exchange began between the system expert, who guided Eric through the computer network that ran the plant, the interpreter, who translated when they came across something in Chinese, and Eric himself, who asked them both questions. To assist in this effort, each of these three had laser pointers with which they could point to the word or section of the plant's computer screen that was now displayed on the big screen.

"Okay," the SE stated triumphantly. "The second file down contains the program that runs the control panel."

"Well," Eric mused as he highlighted the file and clicked his mouse. "Let's see what we shall see."

After taking a moment or two to study the series of computer commands, the language/program expert heaved a great sigh of relief. "They've not changed a thing. All the pre-programmed defaults are still set."

The system expert nodded. "Agreed. We can proceed as planned."

Leaning forward, Eric locked his fingers and flexed them as a concert pianist would before playing. "Thank you, ladies and gentlemen. Now, for my first number, I shall play, 'Let's fuck with the emergency shutoff.' "

"He's a cocky little bastard," the NSA agent commented to the group assembled in the Spook Booth.

Coming to Eric's defense, Colonel Shrewsbery countered. "He's twenty-five years old, playing the world's most sophisticated computer game." Turning, he looked over at the NSA man. "Like you, we recruit brains, not personality."

Quickly Eric moved from item to item, changing the settings. In some cases he reversed values, so that when the computer screen in the control room showed the operator that a valve was open, it was actually closed and vice versa. Simple mathematical formulas were added to lines that displayed temperatures of the huge vats where chemical reactions and mixing took place. The inserted formulas were written so that the measured temperature at the vat showed up on the control room's computer as being substantially lower than it actually was. Together with the disabling of the automated-shutdown sequence and fire-suppression system, the new settings were designed to initiate an uncontrolled chain reaction. Not only would the personnel in the control room be unaware of what was going on until it was too late, when they did take steps to shut down the plant or activate emergency procedures, the false readings they were seeing and the reversed controls they were manipulating would only serve to increase both the speed of the disaster and its magnitude.

When he was finished, Eric leaned back in his seat, pushed his chair away from his workstation, and looked up at the big screen. Slowly, he checked each line he had altered, character by character. When he had finished, he twisted about in his seat and looked up at Bobby Sung. "What do you think, old boy?"

Sung, who had been watching every move Eric had made, took another long look at the big screen before he nodded in approval. "Bloody good show, old boy. I'd say we have a keeper here."

Though annoyed by their lighthearted manner, Reitter said nothing. The two Cyberknights, like everyone else in the Pit, were under a great deal of pressure.

When the hackers were satisfied, Eric next turned to his left. "Do you see anything that needs a second look?"

Both the systems expert and the language/programs expert took a few extra moments to scan the altered settings and formulas. In turn, each gave Eric a thumbs-up when they were satisfied.

With that, Eric glanced back at the pathfinder. "Okay, Scottie. Take us home." As was his particular habit, the pathfinder clicked his heels three times, repeating the old cliché, "there's no place like home," each time while he backed out of the chemical plant's main computer and prepared to quit the Internet. Finished, he clapped his hands. "We're out."

Without hesitation, Reitter called out over his boom mike. "Comms, break down the link. I say again, break down the link."

In the Pit, the red banner that warned that they

were connected to the World Wide Web suddenly disappeared. Standing up, Reitter looked about the room. "It is now nineteen thirty-five hours. Our initial after-action review will take place commencing twenty hundred in the main conference room." Though this briefing was standard, the assembled team let out a collective groan. Then, without further ado, all of the players began to gather up the material they had brought with them and prepared to leave.

From his seat in the Spook Booth, the representative of the National Security Council blinked before he looked over at Shrewsbery, then at the NSA and CIA reps. "That's it?" he asked incredulously.

As one, everyone connected to the 401st, as well as the special agents from the CIA and NSA, looked about, wondering if they had missed something. Confused, Shrewsbery looked back at the NSC rep. "What were you expecting? Armageddon?"

"Well," the NSC rep asked, still not sure of what had just taken place, "how do you know if you've succeeded?"

Shrewsbery did his best to hide his disgust. It was obvious that this refugee from inside the Beltway had expected to see explosions and death and destruction in real time, just like in the movies. When he had composed himself, Shrewsbery stood up. "Well," he stated as tactfully as he could, "as far as the Trojan horse goes, it will be a few days before the NSA will know just how effective that is."

"What about the chemical plant?"

Shrewsbery shrugged. "My advice is to watch CNN tomorrow morning. If we succeeded, it'll be all over the news."

"And the ploy to foment distrust between the two nations?" the NSC rep continued.

"That, sir," Shrewsbery answered, making no effort to hide his irritation, "we may never know."

Stymied, the civilian advisor stood there, looking about at the men and women gathered about in the Spook Booth. "So, that's it? This is how we will go about fighting our wars in the twenty-first century?"

Bowing his head, Colonel Shrewsbery reflected upon that comment for a moment. He had asked himself the same question time and time again until the truth had finally sunk in. "Yes," he answered, making no effort to hide the regret he felt over this state of affairs. "That's pretty much it." Then, sporting a wicked smile, he looked over at the NSA rep and gave him a wink. "Last person out, please turn off the lights."

Without another word, the infantry colonel pivoted about and made for the exit. In so many ways, his job was finished.

HAROLD W. COYLE graduated from the Virginia Military Institute in 1974 with a B.A. in history and a commission as a second lieutenant in Armor.

His first assignment was in Germany, where he served for five years as a tank platoon leader, a tank company executive officer, a tank battalion assistant operations officer, and as a tank company commander. Following that he attended the Infantry Officers Advanced Course at Fort Benning, Georgia, became a branch chief in the Armor School's Weapons Department at Fort Knox, Kentucky, worked with the National Guard in New England, spent a year in the Republic of Korea as an assistant operations officer, and went to Fort Hood, Texas, for a tour of duty as the G-3 Training officer of the First Cavalry Division and the operations officer of Task Force I-32 Armor, a combined arms maneuver task force.

His last assignment with the Army was at the Command and General Staff College at Fort Leavenworth, Kansas. In January 1991 he reported to the Third Army, with which he served during Desert Storm. Resigning his commission after returning from the Gulf in the spring of 1991, he continues to serve as a lieutenant colonel in the Army's Individual Ready Reserve. He writes full-time and has produced the following novels: *Team Yankee, Sword Point, Bright Star, Trial by Fire, The Ten Thousand, Code of Honor, Look Away, Until the End, Savage Wilderness,* and *God's Children.*

THERE IS NO WAR
IN MELNICA

———

BY RALPH PETERS

A workman tossed him a skull.

Green had played football at West Point and should have made an easy catch. But the gesture was unexpected. He got a couple of fingers on the dirty bone, not enough to grip. The skull dropped on a flat rock and rolled into the dirt. Undamaged. Skulls are hard.

The excavating crew laughed and bantered in their own language. Green was supposed to understand, but the dialect was too thick. He smiled, unsure.

"Assholes," Sergeant Crawley said. He canted his head toward the valley. "More company coming, sir."

Green looked down through the trees. Autumn

had chewed off most of the leaves on the mountain-side, but he still heard the vehicle before he saw it. The putter and choke was a leftover sound of Socialism, from the days when nothing quite worked. Now freedom had come, and some things did not work at all.

A small, light-blue truck with a flat bed bounced up the track that led toward the mass grave. It would have to stop down below, where Green and his NCO had left the embassy's armored Jeep Cherokee. Then the visitors would need five minutes to climb to the massacre site. Unless they were drunk. It was afternoon, and the drinking started early, and the men who drank carried guns. If the visitors were drunk, their climb would take longer.

Green picked up the skull and looked at it. He felt things he could not put into words. Except for the anger and disgust. He could express that. "Fuckers," he said to himself. Then he climbed down into the ravine where the victims had been shot and lightly buried.

His orders were to observe, not to interfere. The embassy had gotten the report the day before. Yet another massacre site, this time in the mountains down south, outside the village of Melnica. The defense attaché, a small, brave man who did not look like a soldier and therefore had not been selected for promotion, had told Green:

"Take Crawley down there for a couple of days and have a look. Get plenty of Kodak moments and GPS the site. Joe Friday them when they give you the song and dance about NATO intervention and American neglect."

Lieutenant Colonel Andretti had been passed over for promotion and was slated to retire, but the Army had asked him to extend his tour as attaché because the system that was forcing him out could find no replacement with his skills. Balkan expertise had long been a career-killer, and now the military was scrambling. Andretti did what was asked of him, with his daughters in high school back in Springfield and their mother remarried. The dark circles under Andretti's eyes reached halfway to his knees. He had been in-country for five years, and none of those years had been good ones.

"And Jeff," the attaché had said as Green was leaving the office, "the cease-fire's holding in that sector. There's no war in Melnica at the moment. Don't you and your cowboy sidekick go starting one, all right?" But Andretti was smiling, kidding. "Take care of yourself."

Green slipped on a clot of leaves, almost dropping the skull again. He resurrected himself and spanked the dirt from his jeans with his free hand. Avoiding the exposed rib cages and hip bones, the femurs and decayed rags of clothing that had emerged from the pit, he made his way toward the foreman of the dig.

The foreman was the only man in uniform, if you called a mismatched collection of military scraps a uniform. He wore an unzipped camouflage-pattern jacket and a gray cap that reminded Green of the German mountain troops he had gotten to know back in his Garmisch days. But the resemblance stopped there. This man was unshaven, despite his captain's insignia, and he carried two automatic pistols on a web belt cinched into his big belly. The calluses on his hands would have stopped a knife. Even his eyes seemed shabby.

The captain saluted Green, despite the American's jeans and Gore-Tex jacket. Green had been open about his rank and purpose. He saluted back, although he would have preferred not to.

He had been trained in Russian, back when the Russians still mattered, and the local language—spoken by all sides in the fighting—was related. He could get through the basics, but could not conduct a geopolitical discussion of any nuance. Two months in-country had not been enough time to gain fluency, but Green understood more than he could form into words of his own.

"Major Green," the captain said in mashed English. "Very bad things *those people* do. You see?" He reached down and picked up a faded rip of fabric. Once, it had been red. "You see?" he repeated, breath steaming in the cold. "Woman's dress. No man's clothes. Dress of woman. Who kills woman, child? Bad, bad."

Green nodded. It was very bad. He offered the captain the skull.

The shorter man seized it and tossed it in his hands. "Maybe woman. Maybe very pretty." He held up the skull. "Not pretty now." Suddenly, his expression blackened. He tossed the skull onto a lattice of bones. "Why America stays away? Those people . . . they kill the little babies. Why America stays away?"

"I'll report what I've seen to the embassy."

"The American Army must come," the captain said in his own language. "With American airplanes. Or there is no justice."

"Listen . . ." Green struggled for words in a language he found as jagged and difficult as the mountains surrounding him, ". . . you need to be careful . . . how you dig up the bodies. You'll destroy . . ." He struggled to remember the word for evidence.

The captain snorted. "Look. You see? Everything is there. How many bodies? I count skulls, I know how many. How many those people have killed of my people. That is all I must know."

Green rearranged what he wanted to say into words he could reach. "All this . . . should be done scientifically."

The shorter man had a lunch of onions on his breath. The workers had sat around the edge of the pit, unbothered, as they ate.

"I fuck science in the ass," the captain said. "Bullets. No science."

Green turned away and took more photographs. The war, in a lull for several months, had left many massacres in its wake. Some sites contained a single family, others an entire village. Some graves held only male bodies, while others had seen equal-opportunity killings. Green had visited two other locations, but the digging had been finished days before he arrived. He had expected freshly uncovered bodies to stink and he had braced himself for it. But the corpses had been in the earth long enough to lose all of their liquid and most of the flesh, and the only smell was of the disturbed earth.

"Call me Frankie," the man from the blue truck said in English. He had introduced himself as Franjo Sostik, late of Milwaukee and now the proprietor of an inn down in the village of Melnica. "No bedbugs or shit like that," he told Green and Crawley.

Frankie had the kind of looks that draw women's eyes, but he was reaching the age when he would no longer be able to convince women he was young. He wore a pullover with the sleeves crushed up above the elbows. His forearms were thick. Black hair grew down onto the back of his hands.

He gestured at the mass grave.

"Can you believe this?" he asked, talking mostly to

Green, the officer, but including Crawley with a glance now and then. "Look at this. Like the fucking Middle Ages or something. Is this nuts, or what? I got to ask myself why I came back here."

"Why did you?" Green asked.

Frankie lifted his shoulders and held out his hands, palms up, weighing the air. Black birds settled on the branches above the dead.

"What the fuck you going to do?" Frankie said. "I got relatives, family. They need me. But I don't have to like it. No way, man, am I going to buy into this shit. When the war started, I said, 'To hell with that shit. Frankie-boy's a lover not a fighter.' " He made a spitting gesture, but his lips were dry. "Back in the States? I had me this woman, you know? Drop-dead gorgeous, man. We're talking serious, high-energy pussy. And clean about herself. Not like the barnyard animals around here." He raised a fist, protesting the fate that had brought him back to this place. "Christ, I *love* America. The States are my real home now. But what are you going to do? A man's got to look out for his family."

"You served, though, right?" Sergeant Crawley asked. "In the war?" The NCO's voice remained casual, as if he hardly cared about the answer.

Frankie shook his head in disgust. "Naw. Not really. Not my style, man. I mean, what is this about, huh? Let those people stay on their side, I'll stay on mine. Live and let live, you know? I mean . . . I carried a gun and all that shit. Kind of like National Guard stuff. Weekend warrior. But I was never in any real fighting. Melnica lucked out."

Green looked down at the tangle of bones, at the workmen with their spades.

"Who are they?"

"Local guys. With nothing better to do."

"I mean the bodies."

Frankie shrugged. "Makes you want to puke, don't it? I mean, who needs to kill women and children?" He nodded toward the top of the mountain. The new border lay on the other side of the ridge, in deep forest. "We might be stupid peasants. But those people are goddamned animals. Fucking sickos."

"But the bodies . . . aren't from Melnica?"

Frankie repeated the shrug. It was a gesture that seemed to refresh him, get him going. "Who knows? Maybe some of them. People disappeared. Drive down the road, never come back. Go up in the fields after the cows, never come back. We lost some. I lost family members myself. But I don't want to make this a personal hate thing. The truth is those people could have been marched up here from anyplace in the valley. They're ours, that's all I know. From our valley. Our people didn't do this shit."

The valley. When the Cherokee came down the pass, with SFC Crawley at the wheel, the panorama had been pure tourist brochure: the river reflecting the sun, and the low fields, the slopes open for pasture below an uneven treeline and the leaves falling up above. Tan houses clustered in the villages, while here and there a farmhouse with a tiled roof stood alone. It reminded Green of Italy, where he had taken a girlfriend when he was stationed in Germany.

Then you reached the valley floor and saw the shell holes in the roofs and the burn scars, the windows shot out and the walls pocked by heavy-caliber rounds. Craters pitted the road and half the fields had gone to bracken. Ranks of stumps told where apple and plum orchards had been cut down, for spite, during a slow retreat. Bitterness seemed to have soaked down into the earth, it pierced the air like rot. In the towns, which had changed hands several times, the Catholic and Orthodox churches had been desecrated in turn. There had been few Muslims in the valley and their small mosques were gone without a trace. The Muslims were the Washington Redskins of the Balkan league.

Green already had a catalog of destruction in his head from other observer missions, but the fighting had been particularly cruel here. The combatants had tried to make the towns of their enemies uninhabitable. When they had been in a hurry, they had only destroyed the clinics, schools, and municipal buildings. When time permitted, they wrecked the houses, too, and blew in the water pipes in the towns.

Green had been a mech infantry company commander in Desert Storm, but no one in his entire brigade fired a round in combat. They just steered their Bradleys across the barren landscape, and the troops joked about the most expensive driver's training exercise in the world. The worst thing about Green's experience of war had been the need to wear MOPP gear in the desert heat. But he was a dutiful soldier, ambitious within the bounds of honor, and he had studied war since his plebe year at the Point. He wanted to understand, and he took what books could give. But nothing he had read had spoken of this kind of hatred.

There was an upside, though: the way the people refused to quit. The towns and villages were struggling back to life, with new glass in many of the windows, shops reopening, and posters for the coming election. No one wanted the war to reignite, though everyone said it would.

The Jeep passed a white UN vehicle, its occupants straining not to see anything.

Then, toward the end of the valley, up a mountain

road with defensible approaches, the village of Melnica sat untouched, a museum display of a destroyed
world. The war had taught the people to pay attention to little details, and they figured out from the
license plate and vehicle make that Americans had
come to visit. Everyone had been anxious to offer
directions to the site of the mass grave, with the men
interrupting one another and the children blooming
from sullenness to giggles and greed. It had been
difficult keeping volunteer guides out of the Jeep.

"Do they listen to you?" Green asked Frankie. The
captain down in the ravine had given the innkeeper
a vague salute, maybe just a wave, when he showed
up.

Frankie spit. "They're dumb shits. Uneducated.
Dumb-dick farmers, you know? They don't listen to
anybody. But they figure I'm smart because I been
to America. I mean, they're *good* people. Just kind of
stupid." He gestured toward the riddle of bones.
"They don't deserve this shit. Nobody deserves this."
He nodded across the mountain again. "Those people . . . they're not Europeans. They're fucking animals."

"You should tell them to be more careful," Green
said as a worker swung a pickax in the pit. "They're
destroying the forensic evidence."

Frankie looked at him as he might have looked at
a child. "They don't want evidence, man. They want
revenge."

"Well, if they expect anybody to come to their aid,
evidence matters."

Frankie smiled. "Oh, come on. It's like I tell them.
When they start all that shit about America riding to
the rescue. I tell them, 'Hey, America doesn't even
know you exist. We might as well be in goddamned
China or on the moon or something. Américans . . .

they live good. They don't need our shit. America got no interest in this.' "

Green had not been prepared for the display at his feet, for the rawness of it, and he was trying to keep his temper with the world. How could you prepare yourself for this? It was important not to show any emotion, he knew that. But every word he said felt phony and hollow and useless to him. He believed in justice, and he believed in the goodness of his country, and he only wanted to know who was right and wrong. But he had never been anyplace where right and wrong were so hard to figure out.

He wanted to *do* something. But he did not know what to do.

"Well, if they want anybody to *get* interested," Green said, gone peevish, "it's going to take evidence. Who killed who. When. Whose troops were in control at the time of the massacre. Ages and sex of victims. Proof that they were noncombatants. They need to wait until people get down here from the capital, people who know what they're doing."

Frankie looked at him with an expression close to wonder. "Major . . . Melnica lucked out, you know? Couple mortar rounds. No big deal. But we lost people. In ones and twos, like I told you. Some old farmer. A girl with no sense. Everybody got a missing brother or cousin or something."

"All the more reason they should be careful. So they can identify—"

Frankie closed a hand over Green's forearm. He had a powerful grip. "You don't under*stand*, man. These are mountain people. They don't want . . . like for their daughter or something to become some kind of medical exhibit. The truth is . . . they don't want to know exactly who's in the grave. Not names and shit like that. They've had enough bad news."

Sergeant Crawley, who had spent his career in Special Forces and had over a year in-country, said softly, "Different world, sir."

Green understood that the NCO was telling him to back off and let it go.

A whistling noise came down the mountainside: wind sweeping along like a tide. The pitch rose and then, suddenly, cold air flooded through the trees and poured over the grave site. The captain down in the trench clutched his hat. The earth smell rose, and leaves tore away from their branches. The workmen paused and looked at the sky.

"Hard winter coming," Frankie said. "Like these poor shits don't have it tough enough already. So, hey, tell you what. You're not going back today, right? I mean, you don't want to drive that road in the dark. There's still mines in the ditches. You got to stay at my place. 'Yankee Frankie's.' I even got American music. Liz Phair, man. Hot little bitch like that. And Mariah Carey. All that shit."

Sergeant Crawley, who wore a plaid wool shirt for this peculiar duty, spoke again. With the endless NCO suspicion in his voice: "How much you charge for rooms, Frankie-boy?"

Frankie smiled. "No charge for the room. If it wasn't for America, I never would've been able to buy the place. You're Frankie's personal guests. You just pay for dinner, cause I got to pay the yokels for the produce and shit, keep the local economy going. But the room's free. I even got running water. But no MasterCard or crap like that. This is hillbilly country, man. Cash only."

Green wanted to be a good officer. He wanted to appear strong, impervious to physical discomforts. But the thought of a warm bed had more appeal than a fall night in the mountains crunched up in the Cherokee, engulfed by the decline of Sergeant Crawley's digestive system. And it was standard practice to stay on the economy when there was no fighting in the area. The small talk with the locals sometimes paid off. Random facts led to revelation.

Green was imagining a warm room and dinner when a worker approached him with a bundle. The man laid the corpse of an infant, reduced to leather, at the American's feet.

"I've been from Bolivia to Bumfuck, Egypt," Sergeant Crawley said, "and nothing's ever simple." He sipped from his can of Coke. *Hergestellt in Deutschland.* The rule was no alcohol during a mission, and Green and Crawley both honored it, though grudgingly. The sign advertising Austrian beer was a wicked tease.

The room held half a dozen tables, a corner bench, and the bar. It was a poor man's copy of a German *Gasthaus*, down to the Balkan kitsch that substituted for Bavarian kitsch on the walls. Business was slow, but the place was warm and surprisingly clean. An old R.E.M. disk whined in the background. America had had its effect on Frankie Sostik, who stood behind the bar, drying glasses and talking to a man with a scar that ran from his ear down across his cheek then back into the collar of his jacket. It was the kind of ragged slash inflicted during a hand-to-hand struggle.

Frankie and his customer were drinking shots. Leaning against the bar, Scarface looked like a made-for-television movie's version of a thug. He showed no interest in the Americans. The only words Green overheard were "girls" and "cigarettes."

"I know it isn't simple," Green said. Crawley was a helpful, closed man, hard to get to know. Shaped by the special ops world, he was a masterful soldier. He made Green, most of whose soldiering had been on training ranges and in schools, feel amateurish. Yet the NCO was never condescending, and he let Green take the lead without resentment. Crawley was a team-player in a world of yes-men who thought they were team players, and Green learned from watching him. In the two months they had been working together, they had spent enough time on the road and in the office late at night to know each other's habits, health, and appetites. They disagreed, almost angrily, on politics and music. But the two men were becoming friends—even though Crawley, with an NCO's reverse snobbery, still refused to call Green by his first name.

"Nothing's simple until the shooting starts," the sergeant said. "Then things have a way of coming clear. Shit, I wish I had a beer." He settled his can on the cardboard coaster.

"Buy you one when we get back. Listen, I know it isn't simple. But you saw the grave. And it's not just one. And there don't seem to be very many of them on the other side of the border."

Crawley made a so-what face. "Most of the fighting was on this side of the border."

"Most of the victims were ethnic—"

"Come on, sir. That's only because these guys didn't have the firepower. If these jokers had had the big muscle on their side, the atrocity ratio would have been reversed. I say to hell with all of them. We don't have a dog in this fight."

Green didn't buy that. "When women and children are butchered, somebody has to be punished. We can't just talk forever. For God's sake, Bob. It has to be clear . . . that atrocities are unacceptable."

The song "It's the End of the World as We Know It," came on the stereo.

"You really want our troops plopped down in the middle of this sewer," Crawley asked, "trying to figure out who's zooming who? These people have to settle their own business. What do you want, major?"

Helpless, Green looked down at the table and pruned his face. "Justice. For a start."

The NCO began to laugh, then stopped himself. "Look, sir. It's ugly. I'm not blind. And I'm not heartless. But I'm not stupid, either," Crawley said. "We can't fix this one, boss. Hell, we can't even tell the players apart."

Scarface dropped a pack of cigarettes on the bar and he and the proprietor lit up. Green sipped his Coke. The German stuff was sweeter than the Coke he was used to. He didn't like it.

"We can't just ignore genocide," Green said. "*I* can't."

But the sergeant was in his stubborn mode. He was a good man, and honest to the nickel, Green knew, but his service and a string of failed marriages had hardened the NCO.

"Why not, major? We always ignored it before and did just fine." His mouth hooked up on one side. "You see genocide, I see the local version of bingo night. Some of these jokers like things this way. I mean, those drive-by diplomats don't understand that there really are evil fuckers in this world. Not everybody wants peace, boss. And people don't execute women and children because they hate the work. Some guys *like* it." Crawley had three years on Green, but he looked a decade older in the lamplight. "Or just look at it this way: we've got our means of conflict resolution, they've got theirs. We sue, they shoot. Every place I've been, people have their own way of settling scores. And, near as I can tell, this crap's been going on forever in Mr. Frankie's neighborhood. We just know about it now. Thank you, Mr. Turner." The sergeant shook his head in naked sorrow. "I've been in seventeen years. And I've seen more damage done by ignorant men with good intentions . . . Christ, I ought to write a book."

Back when the Soviet empire was coming apart, Green had been trained for special duties in the East. One of the bennies had been travel, and one of the trips had taken him to Eastern Europe, just as the locals were slipping their leash. In Poland, he had visited Auschwitz.

There were haunted places on the earth, and the gas chambers of Auschwitz were among them. The ghosts crowded you, and you felt a kind of cold that had nothing to do with thermometers. You felt the weight of death.

Auschwitz had been a benchmark for Green. He was not a particularly sentimental man, and his church attendance was erratic. But he wanted to believe in the goodness of mankind. And he believed that good men had to face down evil.

He believed that someone had to be at fault in the Balkans. Crawley was wrong about that. Genocide was not some kind of local folk tradition that had to be respected by outsiders. When the crime was a massacre of unarmed human beings, someone had to be punished.

Green longed to know who to punish. He knew that Crawley was right about some things, too. It was not simple. So Green went carefully. Waiting for clear evidence, for the muddle to sort itself out, and for more powerful men to decide what must be done.

The sergeant played with his empty soda can. They had eaten spiced sausages, green beans, and peppered rice, with crusty bread and goat cheese on the side. There had even been pudding for dessert. Frankie had pulled out all the stops, to the extent that the war had left him stops to pull. And, to Green's relief, their host had let them enjoy the meal in peace, with no more tales of sexual conquests and the splendors of Milwaukee.

"What the hell," Crawley said abruptly. "Maybe you're right. I *hope* you're right. Because I see us getting into this, God help us, no matter what Sergeant First Class Robert G. Crawley thinks about it. I mean, the president hasn't consulted me personally on this one. And that guy Vollstrom, Mr. Negotiator, he's just set on making his mark on history. We'll be in it, alright. And then I'm going to retire on the spot and set up a concession business selling little touches of home to the GIs. You know, *Hustler, Tattoo World,* action videos." He grimaced. "Maybe get this Frankie-boy to go in with me, take care of the local connections and pay-offs and shit. Start us a real nice whorehouse with the local talent. Because once we're in, we ain't getting out in no hurry. We'll be here till the cows come home. And I figure I might as well make a profit on stupidity of such magnitude."

"You'll never retire."

"Just watch me, major."

"I wish I knew what was right."

Crawley looked at him. "Sometimes, sir, right is just staying alive and keeping your nose clean." He snorted. "Other times, the judge tells you to pay alimony. But it's never like in those books you read."

Green smiled. "And how do you know? If you haven't read the books?"

"Oh, I read them alright. It just wasn't a lasting relationship. Guard the fort, I got to take another piss. Army life's been hell on my kidneys."

When Crawley went past the bar, Scarface held out a glass and gave him a broken-toothed smile.

"Good," Scarface said. "Slivovitz. Very good."

The NCO waved him off. "I gave at the office."

Scarface grumped his mouth for a moment, then knocked back the shot himself. He said something to Frankie in a low voice. Frankie laughed. Then they both stared across the room at Green.

"Hey, major," their host called. "He wants to know what kind of man turns down a free drink."

Green returned the stares.

"There are no free drinks," he said.

Frankie laughed again. Frankie liked to laugh. "I told him Americans get this religious bug up their asses. It makes them crazy."

Yes, Green thought. Except we don't butcher each other over it.

Scarface caught the word "crazy." He tapped a finger against his temple, grinning. His teeth looked like he had been in a thousand fistfights and lost every one.

"Yeah," Green agreed. "We're crazy, alright."

Scarface muttered again, but he did not lose his smile.

"He says you're crazy for not bombing those people over there. With your *Star Wars* airplanes."

"Tell him we don't want to spoil his fun. He looks like he could handle them all himself."

Scarface liked that. But he was disappointed that Green would not accept a shot of plum brandy in the interests of eternal friendship with America.

"He says, how you going to fight if you don't drink?" Frankie translated.

Green was tired of the game. But he had no excuse for turning his back until Crawley returned. So he said, "Tell him I'm like you. Tell him I'm a lover, not a fighter."

Frankie hooted, then translated. Scarface chuckled. It was the sound of a forty-year-old Ford starting up.

"He says that's worse. Lovers need to drink even more than fighters. Women need to be afraid of you."

A woman appeared in the doorway. Early to mid-twenties, she wore jeans and a purple roll-collar sweater. Dark blond hair fell over her shoulders, and her hair and the sweater glistened from the light rain that had drifted over the village. Even at a distance, Green could see that she wore too much makeup, but so did every woman in the Balkans who didn't walk with a cane. By any standard, the woman was attractive. She did not look like village goods.

She considered Green, then walked hastily to the bar. Scarface grunted at her, but she ignored him and spoke to Frankie. He shrugged his shoulders, his favorite gesture, and the woman nodded and smiled uncertainly.

She turned toward Green. But her steps faltered. It seemed as if she were giving herself orders to keep going. As though she were afraid. A few feet away, she stopped, briefly met his eyes, then looked down.

Up close, she was genuinely lovely. Green hoped she was not a hooker. He did not want any part of that, and he did not want her to be that sort. There was something about her that made you want better things for her. She did not look strong. And war sent people down ugly paths.

"May I . . . speak with you?" she asked. Her voice was low, almost masculine in pitch, but it quaked. "I heard that you have come, and wish to practice my English, please."

Good opening for a hooker, Green thought sadly. But the night wasn't going anywhere. If she wanted to sit, he didn't mind the company.

"Please," he said, rising slightly. "Have a seat."

She brushed by him and he smelled the musk of her, and the wet wool of the sweater. After she sat down, Scarface and Frankie lost interest.

"I am Daniela," she said.

"I'm Jeff."

"Cheff?"

"Right. 'Daniela' sounds Italian."

She smiled. Her teeth were straight and fairly white, a blessing by local standards. Odd, how you noticed different things in different situations, Green thought. In the Balkans, you checked out their teeth.

"I think my parents have taken it from a film. Is it a pretty name, do you think?"

"Yes. Very much so."

Sergeant Crawley came back in, wet. Green realized the NCO had been checking the lock-up on the Cherokee and getting the last of the gear into their room, which was in a double cabin out back. With a good lock on the door. Crawley had little ways of shaming him by taking care of duties they should have shared.

The NCO did a fast intel estimate and headed for the bar instead of the table. Green heard him ask for another Coke.

"I do not ask about my name's attractiveness because I seek flattery," Daniela said. "But for practice."

"Practice is very important."

A thick strand of hair fell forward and she flipped it back over her shoulder. The corner of her mouth began to twitch and she quickly set her fingertips over it. Her fingers were rough and scarred, and cuts striped the back of her hand. The sight startled Green. The hand did not match the rest of her.

When she removed her fingers from her lips, the twitch had stopped.

"So . . . are you a teacher?" Green asked. Trying to figure her out.

She shook her head. "There is no school now. Maybe next year. Do you have a cigarette, please?"

From Belfast to Belgrade, the women of Europe still had not gotten the word. They all smoked.

"I'm sorry. I don't smoke."

She looked down, embarrassed at having asked for something, sensing a greater error she did not understand. "I'm sorry. There is no need."

But Green called to his host, "Frankie? Got a pack of cigarettes?"

"German okay?"

Green looked at the woman. She kept looking down.

"It doesn't matter," she said.

"Whatever," Green said to Frankie. Then he asked the woman, "Would you like something to drink?"

She raised her face. There was a little struggle in her eyes, manners at war with appetite. "I think so," she said. "Perhaps there is coffee?"

Frankie dropped off a rose-colored pack of cigarettes and a box of matches with Cyrillic lettering. Leftovers. And yes, there was coffee.

Green opened the pack and held it out for the woman to help herself to a cigarette. Then he laid the pack down on her side of the table and lit a match for her.

Those scarred hands.

She closed her eyes and sucked the smoke deep. As if it fortified her.

"You wish to know what I do?" she asked.

"If you want to tell me."

"But I cannot. You see, there is nothing to do now. I live with my mother. My father is gone. In the war. We do not know any facts about him. But we have hope." She stilled the twitch at the corner of her mouth again. "I have studied at the university until the war's beginning. I studied English literature. But I do not speak so well now. There is no opportunity here."

"You speak English very well."

"Perhaps you know the books of Mr. George Orwell?"

Green remembered reading *1984* and *Animal Farm* in high school. But he was not certain he was prepared for a literary discussion.

"I think they are very true, the books of Mr. Orwell," she went on. "I cannot agree with the people who say *1984* is wrong because the year has come and is gone. The year is not important. I think it is like walking toward the horizon, you see. This *1984* is always ahead of us, no matter how far we go. I think there are always too many people who would like us to behave in such a way."

Green could only remember Big Brother. And the mask with the rats.

"And I think that *Animal Farm* is very important. There are many such pigs."

Green read regularly, but most of the books he chose were histories or biographies. The last novel he could remember reading was a thriller he had picked up in an airport, a story about Washington intrigue and POW/MIAs seized by the Russians during the Korean War. It had not impressed him.

"But I like Mr. Thomas Hardy as my favorite," the woman said, smoke frosting her thick, damp hair. "He is so romantic and sad. But there is an unfortunate lack of books now."

"Maybe you can go back to the university?"

She looked into the smoke. "I would like that very much. But it is difficult. I think the war will come back. And only the people who make black-market business have money." She lifted her head and managed to meet his gaze for several seconds. Her eyes were green, almost gray in their lightness of color. She touched her fingertips to the side of her mouth and looked down again.

"But I think it is not polite to talk so much about my person. We will talk about you now, Mr. Jeff. Where are you from?" She smiled.

"Wheeling, West Virginia, ma'am."

She nodded. "Wheeling is very beautiful."

That was news to Green. "Ever been to the states, Daniela?"

She shook her head. A decided no. "But I know it is beautiful, and the people are very happy. Except for the Negroes, who are in the cities. Are there Negroes in Wheeling?"

"Some."

"Are you afraid of them?"

"Not particularly."

She considered that. "I think they are violent people. I do not like violent people."

"Not all blacks are violent," Green began. "In America—" He caught himself. It was hardly the time or place for Race Relations 101. "Anyway, Wheeling's not the most beautiful city in the United States. But there's pretty country nearby."

"I think it must be beautiful. I would like to see it very much."

The conversation went dead for a moment. Then Frankie brought the coffee, brewed by invisible hands in a back room. It smelled like instant. But even that was a rare treasure in these parts. In the capital city, though, the war had brought wealth to a new class and you could get espresso, which was the new name for the Turkish coffee that had been brewed in the region for centuries. In the capital city, there were late-night cafes and discos, all smoke and loud Euro-pop, where young men with sleek black hair wore suits with padded shoulders, and the women, faces bitter as coffee grounds, wore short dresses and brutal high heels. Everybody had a deal in the works.

Daniela lit another cigarette before she drank. "Thank you. I think you are a gentleman. Perhaps you are married?"

Green smiled at the transparency of the question. These were direct times.

"No. Not married."

"Then, perhaps, you are divorced?" She pronounced the last word with three syllables.

"Nope. Never married."

"That is very strange, I think. And you are an officer?"

"Yes." I am an officer. And, yes, it's very strange. And I would have married Caroline, and she would have married me, and it was all very beautiful when she flew over to visit and we went to Italy, but it was not beautiful enough. Because she would not give up her career for me, and I would not leave the Army for her. And that was love at the end of the century.

"Why have you never been married?"

She leaned toward him, cigarette between the fingers of her closed fist, head leaned against her wrist.

Green wished he could wash the makeup from her face. She was very pretty, maybe beautiful in the way it took a little while to see. It was sad because he sensed she had put on the makeup, which she would have hoarded, especially for him. She made him feel lonelier than he had felt in months.

"Just never found the right woman," he said. "I'm a challenge."

She was not having any of that. "Perhaps this woman will find you," she said firmly. "I think you are a lucky man. You are looking to me like a lucky man."

By local standards, Green figured, he was very lucky, indeed.

"You are living in the capital?" she said. She sipped her coffee with the daintiness of a cat.

"When I'm not on the road."

"You have been there long?"

"Just over two months."

"You will stay for a long time?"

"I'm on a six-month TDY."

She put down the cup, which was chipped around the rim, and looked at him quizzically.

"It means I'm a loaner model. Only temporary. Six months."

She thought about that. "Six months is very long sometimes. I think time is longer in the winter than in the summer. Do you have a girlfriend in the capital?"

Green wanted to be serious, but he could not help smiling.

"No girlfriend."

"You do not think our girls are pretty?" Another cat-sip of coffee.

"Very pretty. But I haven't had much time off."

"I went to university there. If I lived there now, I would show you everything."

He almost said, "Maybe you'll get up there some-time," but stopped himself. He did not want her to read it as an invitation. But he did not want her to leave the table, either.

"It seems like a pleasant city," Green lied. With its obese Habsburg architecture, and its fierce grayness, and the leaden food. The people looked down as they walked, and only the whores and hustlers met your eyes.

"Do you know the cathedral?"

Green nodded. He had gone there, a dutiful tour-ist. The ornamentation had seemed squalid and fussy at the same time.

"I think it is beautiful," she said.

"Are you religious?"

She laughed for the first time. If sound had color, her laugh would have been amber. "Oh, no," she said. "Only the old people are religious now."

"And the people who made the war?"

Her mouth began to twitch again. It was a slight movement, but he could tell that it shamed her. She did not laugh this time.

"They have no religion. For them it is only words. It is an excuse they make."

"Would you like another coffee?"

She shook her head. "I think it is very expensive. One cup is enough, you see."

"Daniela . . . what's your last name? Your family name?"

"Kortach. And yours?"

"Green. Jeff Green. Pleased to meet you, ma'am."

She smiled and stared off to the side of his face. "*Zelen.* That is 'green' in our language. *Zelen.*"

He nodded. Really, he was the one who needed to

practice his language skills. But he was tired. And the
girl was lovely. And she did not seem to be a hooker.
Just another soul washed up and stranded by the war.

You could not let yourself get too close. But it was
difficult sometimes.

"I think I must go now," she said. "It has become
late. And this is not a good place for a woman. The
people in the village . . . they are not open of mind
like the city people. They think bad things."

"You should go then."

The words saddened her. He had only meant to
be polite, but had said the wrong thing.

She touched her fingers to the side of her mouth.
"How long will you stay in Melnica?"

"We go back tomorrow."

She seemed to shrink into her sweater. As if he
had slapped her and she was cowering under the
threat of the next blow. He made her for a lonely
girl desperate for any chance to get out. Suffocating
here. With her memories of books and the greater
world. Willing to risk her reputation for a slim
chance of escape, in a place where reputation still
mattered in a way it had not mattered for a century
in his own country.

"Perhaps you will come again," she said.

"Perhaps."

"Then you will visit with me. To practice English."

"Yes."

"I hope very much that you will come again."

She stood up. He stood, as well. Old manners. And
the miseries of West Point, with its fascist etiquette.

She thrust out her hand to show she was a Western
girl. He took it, and let go too soon. Afraid of himself, of doing something foolish. Even if she was a
fairy-tale princess, he was in no position to play

Prince Charming. A ghost of warmth remained in his grip.

She turned away and he called, "Daniela?"

But he only wanted to give her the rest of the pack of cigarettes to take along.

"I don't smoke," he explained.

Her eyelids fluttered. Too quickly. "I think that is good, not to smoke" she said, turning away again.

She didn't just leave. She fled.

Crawley came over to the table and repossessed his seat. He looked at Green through the veil of smoke the woman had left behind.

"Don't go native on me," the NCO said.

The men at the bar laughed over their own little joke. You could hear the liquor level in their voices. Frankie came over to the table and stood before the two Americans. But he only looked at Green.

"You like her?"

"She's a pretty girl," Green said cautiously.

Frankie grunted. "She's a fucking nutcase. They got her during the war. Gang bang." He punched his fist rhythmically into his palm. "Twelve, fifteen of them." He laughed. "Hell, maybe a hundred. They kept her up in the woods for a couple of days. Now she's the town slut. Would've been better if they'd cut her throat."

Green looked down at the tabletop. The last of the smoke curled and drifted.

"Hey," Frankie said, "you want to fuck her? I'll send her to your room. You can both fuck her. Won't even cost nothing."

"Life sucks, then you die," Crawley said. He sat on his bed checking his 9mm. The oiled-paper blinds were drawn down as far as they would go. A light bulb hung from the ceiling. Commo gear and everything else that could be removed from the Jeep covered the floor between the old iron beds. "Those sausages are doing a number on my stomach. What the hell kind of peppers do they put in them?"

Green was not in a talking mood.

Finally, the NCO laid the pistol on the blanket. "Look, boss man. I've been around the block. I understand the mope you got on, all right? A good-looking woman all cozy at your table, batting her eyes and getting all soulful with you. Then you find out her life's gone off the rails. Way off. And now you don't want to take her home to meet your parents anymore. But you feel bad about feeling that way, 'cause we're all supposed to be sensitive New-Age guys or something, and, yeah, she got dealt a bad hand." He slapped his palms down on his knees. "Well, let me tell you something. Life ain't fair. If it was, you'd feel as sorry for some pot-bellied creepo as you do for the Sweetheart of the Balkans. But you don't, and I don't. And nobody else will, either."

The sergeant clicked his tongue in a parody of shame. "When they packed my ass off to eastern Zaire—that one really got to me. Not for the right reasons, though. Much as I hate to admit it, those people didn't seem real. Not the way your blondie does. Oh, they smelled real enough. Cholera ain't no air freshener. But even the little kids. In my brain I knew they were human just like me, but it didn't move me the way it should have. Not the way American kids would've done. And you know what really flipped me out? This black captain honchoing our A-team? He had the same goddamned reaction. Couldn't relate to people in funny clothes talking mumbo-jumbo and crapping themselves to death. And that's how we get along. There's plenty of suffering out there. We could just about start a

genocide-of-the-month club. So we're kind of programmed to pick and choose. And you've got to do
it that way. Sometimes you just have to turn your
back. Because there's so much suffering it'll just rip
you to shreds if you let it. And if you try to fix everything, you end up fixing nothing. So stay in your
lane. And be prepared to keep on marching past
other people's misery."

Green snapped the clip back into his own pistol.
You didn't make a big thing of it, but you did not
go unarmed into Indian country. "Rack time? Listen
. . . Bob . . . maybe I'm not the right man for this. I
mean, that grave today. The little kid who looked
like a piece of beef jerky. Then the girl, on top of
everything else. My feelings *do* get in the way. It's
sloppy, I know it. Intellectually, I understand. But I
can't help it, goddamn it. And I'm not sure I want
to help it. Maybe I'm not the right guy for this mission."

"There is no 'right guy,' " Crawley said. "You'll get
over it. You get calluses where you need them." He
laughed to himself, a rusty-pipes sound. "Want to
turn off that light?"

"Door locked?"

"Door's locked, I'm locked and loaded, and the
carburetor's under the bed. I would've taken off the
tires, major, sir, but it was raining and I'm delicate."

"Screw off, Crawley."

"Sweet dreams, Romeo."

But Green did not have any dreams at all. He lay
awake for a time, thinking unhappily about the
woman, then disgusted about the way he found himself thinking of her. He decided that Crawley was
probably right, that every emotion was driven by bi-
ology. But he could not make himself accept the
idea. He recognized that there was something cheap

and selfish—too easy—about his sense of sorrow, but
he still believed it would be worse to feel nothing at
all. And he figured Crawley felt more than he was
willing to let on. You couldn't go through this and
feel nothing. Then Green thought of the woman—
Daniela—again. He expected bad dreams. But it had
been a long day and when he fell asleep there was
nothing on his channel.

The first blast shook the walls and woke him. After
a stunned instant, he heard Crawley yell, *"Get down,"*
and he rolled off the bed.

He landed on the commo gear and pack frames,
all knees and elbows and a thin t-shirt. Then he remembered to reach back under the pillow and grab
the pistol. The next explosion hit close, but they got
lucky. The concussion shattered the windows without
blowing them in, and the blinds channeled the falling glass.

"Fuck me to tears," Crawley said. "Mortars. Fuck
me to tears."

"You all right?"

The night was black between the flashes.

Green felt the NCO reaching over him and
smelled the man's familiar smell. Then the mattress
from his bed fell on him.

Crawley was tucking him in.

"Just stay down," the sergeant said. "I've been
through this shit before."

This time, Green heard the whistling before the
impact.

Close.

The floor shook and the remaining glass blew out.
Stings pierced his socks, down where the mattress
did not reach.

"What—"

"They know we're here," Crawley whispered. "This ain't no accidental timing. Let's hope they're just saying hello."

A woman's voice shrieked in the distance. Instantly, Green thought of Daniela. But he made himself focus on business again. He was shaking. But he was ready to go, to move, to act. He just wasn't sure what to do.

"Get your gear on, sir," Crawley told him. "Jeans, boots, jacket. In case we have to run. You hear any more whistling, get back under that mattress."

Green fumbled in the darkness. He had positioned his jeans at the bottom of the bed so he could find them easily. But pulling off the mattress had made a mess of that plan.

Then they heard the shots.

"Oh, shit," Crawley said.

The shouting began.

"You think this is about us?" Green rasped. He had his jeans now, feeling for the leg holes.

"I *know* it's about us. I just don't know what they're out to prove. We need to un-ass this place."

A smaller explosion sounded nearby. Grenade. Then the automatic weapons fire kicked in again. The screaming resumed, and there were male shouts now. Green yanked on his hiking boots. His fingers were unsteady. But they did as they were told.

"Maybe something about that grave," Crawley said. "I don't—"

Something struck the wall inside the room. It was a flat sound, followed by the clang of metal on metal.

"*Shit,*" Crawley yelled. Then he landed on top of Green, covering the major's body with his own, barrel chest grinding Green's head into the floor.

The grenade's blast lifted the sergeant away and stunned Green. He did not even know if he was wounded. He felt as though he had been thumped on every side of his head at once. There was an avalanche in his ears. His body was numb. Then he tasted salt and wet, and sensed the pulsing from his nose.

He could not move, but did not know what that meant. Time warped and would not go forward.

"Bob?"

The sound of his own voice seemed slow to Green. It lingered in the air, surrounded by a bronze roar. In another world, automatic weapons continued to fire. Rounds struck metal. He imagined he was inside a big metal room. There was laughter.

His head hurt. It was so bad his mouth stayed open in a scream without sound. He imagined his skull shrinking, squeezing his brain.

The door swung open. Green wanted to rise, to defend himself. But his body would not move. He could think again. But none of his parts would go. He wondered if that meant he had been paralyzed. The thought stunned him.

Boots. Rampaging through the room. He only realized his eyes were open when a flashlight found them. His neck muscles recoiled.

"On zhiv." The voice seemed pleased and angry at the same time. He heard it over the enormous, constant ringing. *"On zhiv."*

Zhiv. Alive. That was him. A string of obscenities followed.

Suddenly, his arm moved. Without his command. Or maybe he had intended to move it a long time before. Somebody inside him, a ghost from a previous life, reached for the pistol.

A boot came down on his forearm.

Whatever else he had lost, he had not lost his language skills. He understood the words, "American scum."

"Bob?" he called again. It was hard to keep focus. "Sergeant Crawley?"

He had to spit the blood from his mouth. Gagging.

Outside the cabin, a man laughed again. A woman's wail colored the distance.

Rough hands yanked Green to his feet. To his astonishment, he found he could stand. But the darkness would not hold still and he nearly toppled. The sound in his ears rolled and rolled. Instinctively, he raised a hand to wipe the slime from his mouth and chin, but a gunbarrel forced the hand back down.

Someone threw something at him, shouting. He had been unprepared. The object—heavy fabric—hit his chest and fell.

The skull. He remembered the skull.

The voice commanded him to pick up the object and put it on. It was his jacket.

That was when he realized they were not going to kill him right away.

Someone thumped him between the shoulder blades and told him to get outside. Green stumbled toward the different darkness. Dizzy. Nauseated. The air was damp and cold, with the smell of a rifle range. His ears still pushed sounds away, making them small and hard to hear. But he could see clearly.

Where was Crawley?

Dark figures in masks. A fire in a house beyond the inn.

Green bent and hacked up the blood he had swallowed. Then he wiped his face with his hand. No one stopped him this time.

The Jeep rested on flattened tires, shot up. The

vehicle's armor was light, intended to stop assassins with pistols and sloppy shooters during a drive-by, and really all it meant was that you could not roll the windows down. Now the Cherokee looked like a butchered animal.

Green was afraid. And ready to puke from his lack of equilibrium. But training counted for something, however useless. He noted the assortment of weapons the men carried. Belgian FNs, Kalashnikov variants, one jagged little HK. He counted seven raiders, then an eighth man came out of the shadows. There was still screaming and clatter up in the street, so there would be more of them. Their uniforms were as confused as their armaments, ranging from full cammo to jeans and leather jackets. The only thing they had in common was the black commando mask each man had pulled down over his head and neck.

Two of the men tied Green's hands behind his back with rubber-coated wire. They were good at their work. Then a tall, thin man with a young voice barked at him in dialect. When Green didn't respond, the man shoved the butt of his rifle into his gut, driving him back against the Jeep.

The rain had blown over and a few tough stars shone between the clouds. But most of the light came from flashlights, a couple of them big and rectangular like the kind a conscientious driver might keep in the trunk of a car back home.

"Get the other one. Let's get going." Green understood that.

There was a brief, low-voiced argument. Then the thin man and another gunman in a ragged *Bundeswehr* parka slung their weapons behind their backs and went into the cabin.

They lugged Crawley's body outside, belly down, and dropped him on the gravel. His back was shredded, the blood dark as wine under the beams of light. His neck was broken and he had bled from the mouth. The sergeant's pants were stained. As if he had been hung.

A stocky man bent over the corpse. Crawley's hair was cut very short and the man lifted the head by an ear. A big hunting knife extended from his right fist. He took a practiced stance and swung the knife down like an executioner's axe. He knew his business, but it still took four hacks to separate Crawley's head from his body.

The butcher laughed and held up the head, giving some sort of cheer Green did not understand. If he could have killed all of them, slaughtered them, Green would have done it. But he just stood against the wrecked Jeep, hands bound, helpless.

The man bent down again and cleaned his knife on Crawley's shoulder, then sheathed it. He took the head in both hands, stretching out his arms, and shook out as much of the blood as he could. Bits of pulp splattered the earth. When the gore tapered to a few drips, another of the men held out a plastic shopping bag and the butcher dropped the head in it.

Routine business.

Green closed his eyes, but it did not help.

A muzzle prodded his bicep.

"Hajdemo!" Let's go.

He did not understand the rules. His captors carried their weapons at the slack, unworried about a counterattack from the villagers. And there had not been much of a fight, really. There was so much Green could not explain. He wondered if Melnica had survived because it had cut some kind of deal not to resist.

They forced him to walk through the spread of Crawley's blood.

In the street in front of the inn, Green saw the woman, Daniela. On her knees. Begging.

The four men encircling her laughed.

"Hajdemo!"

Two of the raiders lifted Daniela to her feet. One of them kicked her.

Green did not even think to protest. He had trouble walking straight. And his hearing still had an underwater feel.

The column turned up the street that led to the mountain. In a little barn, a cow gave an annoyed moo. The houses remained shuttered and blacked out.

Daniela was four places ahead of him in the line. She was not bound, but she did not try to flee. Instead, she pleaded with the men to let her go back to her mother. She sounded like she was ten years old. Except for the occasional joke, the gunmen ignored her.

It was cold. Green had not had the presence of mind to zip the jacket before they bound his hands. And even the thought that he might die soon did not make the cold any less a bother. His feet stung and itched and hurt.

Much of life was adaptation to your environment. Even the shorter, stockier gunmen were accustomed to climbing. Green kept himself in good shape, but his legs soon strained at the steepness and pace. When he slowed even a little, a muzzle jabbed him in the back.

He had seen them cut off Crawley's head. It had been indescribably real, immeasurably repugnant. Yet now, on the mountainside, the death was already hard to believe. He remembered the NCO saying something about the attack being aimed at them. And Green remembered the man covering him with his body. The things men did. The marvel of courage. He doubted his own bravery, that he would have done such a thing. He had thought of himself as a real hotshot, a first-rate officer. Now he hardly felt like a soldier at all. He felt as though he had been faking it his entire career.

He saw himself as a failure and an ass, and he was afraid. Fighting the tears in his eyes. Glad of the darkness.

They pushed through a grove of evergreens. The wet branches slapped him and soaked through his jeans. But the pine smell was gorgeously alive.

He saw the pulp of Crawley's hacked neck. He saw the head, with the sleepy look of the open eyes.

That was how it looked.

Green fantasized about escaping, trying to imagine how it might be done. But his hands were tied, and the trail was steep, and he did not know the way. They would catch him. In moments. And perhaps kill him for annoying them.

The girl sobbed and kept climbing.

He did not know exactly where the border lay. Somewhere over the crest. But he realized that was where they were going. He was a prisoner of the people from the other side.

Despite the muzzle prodding him, he had to turn from the path and gag up more of the blood he had swallowed. His nosebleed had stopped, though not the dizziness.

Yes. The people from the other side. The butchers. The men who made the mass graves. It was as if they had sensed where his sympathies were headed. And came for him to make him pay.

But what was the angle? What did they hope to

achieve? Their leaders were telling every lie imaginable to fend off the NATO airstrikes that had been
threatened because of the cease-fire violations. What
could they hope to gain by killing Americans? Or
kidnapping them?

He knew that not everything had logic here. Or
perspective. Perhaps they imagined he was much
more important than he was. Or maybe this was just
a renegade band with its own lunatic agenda. The
attaché had warned him, just after Green signed in
at the embassy, that the big warlords could not always
control the little warlords, and the little warlords
could not always control the militias, and the militias
could not control the smugglers, except when they
all worked together. And when they were not collab-
orating with somebody on one of the other sides.

Maybe it was the gravesite. Maybe that was why
they had come after him and Crawley. Maybe there
was more to it. Maybe he had seen something he did
not even realize he had seen. Or maybe they were
afraid he might see something and bring down the
UN and the NGOs and a major investigation.

What had Crawley said? Something about that.
Green could not remember.

He needed to sit down. Just for a minute.

The gunbarrel stabbed his kidneys.

The trees fell away and the trail grew rockier. It
made walking difficult. Green stumbled again and
again. His legs ached. Then it was so rough for a
stretch that he could not think about anything but
his footing. He wondered if they would shoot him if
he turned his ankle and could not go on. The muzzle kept poking his back.

"Fuck you," he said finally. But he sounded pa-
thetic to himself. The metal bore rammed him again,
and he kept marching.

Toward Crawley's head. Floating in the darkness. It was there whether his eyes were open or closed.

He saw the knife descending. Chopping. Hacking. Through flesh so recently alive.

It seemed to Green as though there must be a way to reverse time and undo the damage. How could Crawley be dead? So easily?

That was what the textbooks failed to convey. You read the words. And understood nothing.

Just below the crest, with a high wind blanketing the sound of their voices, the raiders stopped for a powwow.

Witch's sabbath landscape. Rocks pale, the scrub and lichen dark. Blacker clouds in a black sky. And the shrieking wind.

The dark men clustered, masked heads bobbing. Green found himself standing hardly a body length from the woman.

She was looking at him.

This time he was the one who was ashamed, the one who looked away.

He wondered why she didn't run for it. Perhaps she knew they would kill her if she did. She would know the local rules. And dying was the worst thing for most human beings, no matter what the books said.

He hated his helplessness more than he hated his captors now. When he looked up, the woman was still watching him. He could not make out any of the details of her features. Except for her eyes. They gleamed.

The tall, thin gunman broke from the huddle and strode over to Green. Roughly, he undid the cords binding Green's wrists. Then he said something.

Green didn't get it. The dialect.

The man chuckled and tried another word.

He was telling Green to take a piss, if he needed to.

"Stay on the trail," he said. "Landmines."

Green tried to guess how long they had been marching, how far they had come. Still no hint of light in the sky. He felt as tired as at the end of a marathon field exercise, as though he had not slept for days. Only his brain was alive, fueled on fear. Eyes wide, body dead.

No. Not dead. Crawley was dead. That was what dead meant.

The man bound Green's wrists again.

Daniela was squatting with her face in her hands.

"Don't fly away, little bird," the gunman told her.

Then the discussion ended. Three of the men headed back down the trail. Rear guard? Green wondered.

The nine who remained shoved and cursed, far more than necessary, to get their prisoners moving again.

They crossed over a saddle between two outcroppings of rock. The footing was even more treacherous going down the eastern side of the ridge. Green fell once, landing on his backside and bound hands. Rock bit his knuckles.

The man behind him kicked him to his feet. Then they entered the treeline again, going deep into more dark, wet pines, and the trail leveled, traversing the side of the mountain. The party followed it into a draw that was shielded from the wind, a natural refuge. It was so overgrown and deep-set that Green missed the outline of the huts at first. It was a partisan camp. Maybe, Green thought, it had been one for centuries. And a smuggler's lair between wars.

Except for the footfalls and grumbling of the raiders, the world had gone silent.

They gave him another chance to empty himself, an odd courtesy, then tied him, sitting down, to the trunk of a dead tree. The wood was as hard as stone.

"We stay now," a new voice told him, in English.

"What do you want with me?"

"We stay now," the man repeated. "One day." He hitched up his trousers and shadowed off.

The gunmen must have been tired, too. But they were not too tired for the girl. They pulled her toward one of the huts. She fought them now. But only until they beat her to the ground. Then she gave up and let them drag her.

"American," she called. She had forgotten his name. *"Help me."*

Green closed his eyes.

But his hearing had returned unmercifully. The sounds were worse with his eyes shut, and soon he opened them again. The men felt secure enough to light a small stove in the open and they sat around it, sharing a bottle and waiting their turn. The night was so quiet in the glen that Green could hear the bounce of an old-fashioned bed. Sometimes the girl cried out, begging them to stop, not to do any more. Then she would cry for her mother again. One of the men cursed her, and Green heard the sound of fists. The girl screamed, then whimpered, and finally went quiet. The bed started up again.

Green wept. He did not understand this world.

He remembered her scarred hands.

She had told him she was not religious. But when one of the masked men led her out in the morning light, barely able to walk, bleeding and naked from the waist down, she prayed. First she prayed standing. Then, when they nudged her over to the edge of the rocks, she prayed on her knees. Green made himself watch, in penance for his helplessness. He could not see her face now, only the torn purple sweater not quite covering her rump and the bare, dirty soles of her feet. But he heard her, the mumbled familiar rhythms. She was still praying when one of the men put a pistol to the back of her head and fired.

The raiders untied Green's hands and offered him a share of their breakfast. Sliced salami, bread, and gruel. He shook his head.

The man with the tin dish in his hand laughed and told his comrades:

"He's angry. He wanted to fuck her, too."

"He can still fuck her," another man answered.

They had not buried her. They only kicked her body off the rocks.

A squat man rose from the cluster around the little stove. He had a businesslike stride. He undid the rest of the cords binding Green. When Green stretched out his legs, it felt so good it made him close his eyes. When he opened them again, he saw the man standing before him, holding out the tin plate. There were stains around the mouth of the man's commando mask.

"Pojesti."

Green shook his head again. It was only a slight movement.

"Pojesti."

"No. Fuck you."

With the speed of a professional fighter, the man dropped the plate and punched Green just below the eye. It knocked his head back against the tree.

He had never been hit so hard. He slumped over. It felt as though his neck had snapped.

The man kicked the plate with its remnants toward him.

"Pojesti."

The instant the man turned, Green launched himself. He hit him behind the knees in a perfect beat-Navy tackle and scrambled on top of him as soon as the man's torso thumped the ground.

Green landed one fist. Then they were all on him. When he woke up, he was tied to the tree again. He had to twist his body as hard as he could not to puke on himself.

His eye was swollen and it left Green with a narrowed view of the world. And his feet itched and burned. It seemed ridiculous to him that, waiting to be executed, he should be so bothered by his feet.

Except for a pair of sentinels, the men drifted into the huts to sleep out the day. Eventually, Green slept, too, head drooped above the lashings that bound him to the tree. He half-woke a few times—once he felt crazed by the unreachable itching and cramping of his feet—but every part of him had worn down and the need to sleep finally slammed him down like a whisky drunk.

He dreamed he was back in Wheeling, buying a new car. Except that the car lot was one he recognized from Copperas Cove, in Texas, and he could not square that because he knew he was in Wheeling. A woman he had dated at Fort Hood appeared, excited him, and vanished. There was a problem with the paperwork at the dealership. He needed to prove something and could not. Buying the car was a major commitment, and he needed to get it done before he thought too much about it. He recognized his weakness, knew he was watching himself in a dream.

He woke to twilight and the smell of grilling meat. The sky was deep and cloudless. The fragrance of mutton, a vivid living smell of death, made his stomach ache.

In the shadow of the trees, the gunmen sat and ate, pulling the meat from the skewers with their fingers and gnawing bread torn ragged from a loaf. They shared an oval brandy bottle. Only five of them left now. The tall, thin boy who had marched him up the mountain was gone, Green could tell that much even though the men still wore their stocking masks.

Three of the remaining men stood up and slung their weapons over their shoulders. Green could not make out what was said, but he sensed it was a parting. And he was right. The brandy went around one more time, then the men marched off in a file. Ten minutes later, Green saw their shrunken figures emerge from the treeline, climbing toward the pass. The man at the rear turned around, as if he sensed that he was being watched. In the dying light, Green saw the white dot of an unmasked face.

The masks had only been for him.

He wondered, for a moment, if he had gotten it all wrong. If these men were not ethnic warriors at all, but only bandits imagining a fat Yankee ransom.

Again, he thought of Crawley's severed head.

Not ransom.

One of the pair who had stayed behind to mind him stood up and swaggered toward Green. He was stocky, with a submachine gun slung across his back. Not one of Green's earlier abusers. He untied Green and pointed toward the little grill and his companion, who sat cradling an airborne-variant AK. Watching.

Green stumbled at first, almost fell. His legs were numb. And he still had difficulty with his balance.

The man who had untied him grabbed Green

from behind, taking a fistful of his jacket collar.
Abruptly, he steered Green toward the huts. A bolt
of panic shot through Green's chest and stomach,
piercing right down to his bowels.

Was this it?

No. It couldn't be. They had killed the girl over
by the rocks. That was the killing place.

Something else.

What?

Green felt himself shaking. He hated it, did not
want to seem a coward, but could not control his
body. He felt supernaturally alert, but not in a way
that engaged reality. His dream had been more real
than this.

He understood it now. Why the people had walked
to the ovens at Auschwitz. Because you did not know
what else to do, afraid that any action you took would
only make things worse. And because you were
drugged on hope, even as you faced the executioner.

The gunman shoved him between the huts, prodding him toward a trough that caught the water from
a mountain spring. He told Green to wash his face.

The water was beautiful, and delicious.

Afterward, the gunman herded Green to the little
stove then pushed down on his shoulder. Green sat.
The second raider fingered his rifle, watching everything through the slits in his mask. The stocky one
bent down behind Green. A strong-handed man, he
jerked Green's left ankle back and tied it to his left
wrist, hobbling him but leaving his right hand free.

The stocky man lifted a last skewer of mutton from
the grill and pushed the meat off with dirty fingers.
The chunks fell on the flattened grass in front of
Green.

This time Green ate. The men gave him bread,
and offered him their plum brandy. He almost ac-

cepted it. But finally shook his head. When the last of the meat was gone, Green licked his fingers. Wanting more.

In the gloaming of the little draw, the stocky man reached toward his comrade, straining to grasp the brandy bottle. And Green saw a flash of pale skin below the mask.

A scar traced down the gunman's neck, from below his ear into his collar.

It was not the smartest thing Green ever did or said. But he was far beyond cool judgment. He spoke to the man on the other side of the stove, the one with the collapsible-stock AK.

"Why'd you kill the girl, Frankie?"

The jerk of the head confirmed it. Even Scarface understood English well enough to understand what had happened.

After a moment, Frankie reached up and peeled off his mask. He ran his hand back over his liberated hair.

"Fucking shit things anyway," Frankie said.

Scarface spoke rapidly. In a tone of alarm. But Frankie made a dismissive gesture.

He looked at Green. "It doesn't matter now. We're going to kill you. You know that."

But Green refused to think about his own death. He kept his eyes on Frankie. "You sonofabitch. Why kill the girl?"

Scarface pulled off his mask and shook his head hard. But he let Frankie do the talking.

"What the fuck do you care? You have plans to marry her or something?" He laughed and said something in dialect to Scarface. Scarface laughed with the old Ford rumble Green remembered.

"Look," Frankie said, "this isn't America. People

here have values. You can't just go slutting around in a village like that. That bitch was damaged goods."

"You said she was raped."

Frankie rolled his eyes in the glow of the stove. "And that's supposed to make it all right?" He breathed out heavily, a killer's sigh. "You'll never understand. We have to purify our race. A woman who's been raped . . . by those people . . . she doesn't belong here anymore. Anyway, Daniela was nothing but a slut."

"She was one of *your* people, for God's sake. She was educated. She could have helped you rebuild . . ."

Frankie leaned on his gun. "She was a whore, man. Nobody around here's going to marry a whore. And no whore's going to teach our kids. Shit, she was even ready to go away with you last night. All you would've had to do was ask." His eyes burned. "Do you know it's a scientifically proven fact that every man who screws a woman leaves his trace in her, his mark? Then, when she has a baby, the baby's got traces of all of them, of every one who's been in her. That's why those people rape. To infect our genes."

"That's nuts."

"It's science," Frankie said. "*Sci*ence."

Green closed his eyes. He wished he had not eaten the mutton. "You're sick," he said. "You gang-rape one of your own people . . . put a bullet in her head . . . and that's okay? That's some kind of good deed? To keep the race pure? What fucking race? You're all fucking the same, for Christ's sake."

Frankie's tone turned to disgust. "Don't make some big drama out of it, man. She was a disgrace to our people. *Our* country's going to be built on racial purity. Outsiders don't understand. We can't allow genetic pollution. None of *their* filth. And no

Turk filth, either." Frankie glanced at Scarface. "Look at Ivo here. He was her goddamned cousin, man. And he was all for blowing 'her fucking head off. He under*stands*."

"You're sick," Green repeated.

"Yeah? And you're going to be dead."

In despair, Green spoke aloud to himself. "What . . . in the name of God . . . is this all about?"

Frankie grinned. "Which God? Ours, or theirs?"

"Nothing personal," Frankie told him as they went down the trail in the darkness. Scarface walked point, weapon at the ready. Green followed. Frankie brought up the rear. A three-quarter moon lit the path where it broke out of the trees. The fields shone silver. Frankie spoke in a softened voice, as though listening for danger all the while. "You're a sacrifice for a greater cause. You should be proud."

"Fuck you."

Frankie gave a snorting laugh. "Yeah, well. We owe you. I got to admit. Maybe we'll put up a little monument to you somewhere when all this is over. 'Major Jeff Green, who brought America into the war and rescued our people with his sacrifice.' Kind of nice, when you think about it. I mean, what the fuck, man. *Your* death's going to have meaning. Not like most of the poor suckers who get wasted around here."

"America won't intervene because of one major."

"Oh, yeah?" They passed through another belt of low pines and a branch caught Green across the mouth. "Anyway," Frankie went on, "it's not just you. You're just going to be the straw that broke the camel's back. All the atrocities and that shit. Those people have it coming. And your people know it. They just need a little push."

They marched down the mountainside. Green

thought hard. His mind went too fast or too slow, but never just right. Ideas trotted by, then galloped off before he could harness them. And Sergeant Crawley was always with him. Crawley and the girl.

"All this . . . even the mortars on your own village," Green said. "It was all staged. To look like the other guys killed us, or kidnapped us, or whatever."

"Hey, first prize, Mr. Fucking Wizard."

"And you're taking me across the border . . ." Green had trouble getting the next words out, ". . . so . . . you can kill me on their side. So I'll be found where the guilt will seem indisputable."

"Man, you should be on *Jeopardy!* or something. You know I miss American TV? *Baywatch* and shit. And, by the way, I appreciate your consideration. In not biting it back at the inn. We would have had to lug your dead ass over the mountain, which would have been a significant hassle. And the corpse wouldn't have been nice and fresh for those UN fucks to find."

They passed along the high end of a meadow. The autumn night had a scent of rotting apples. Again, the smell of death made Green feel vividly alive.

"And the head? Sergeant Crawley's—"

"It'll turn up. We'll be sure to let your people know."

Scarface dropped to one knee and readied his rifle. Frankie put a hand on Green's shoulder and shoved him down. His voice was only a whisper now.

"Fuck around, and you die right here."

But there was nothing. Only the mountain ghosts.

They came down into a dead world and there was no more talking. The moon had passed its apogee, and the air was colder in the foothills than it had been on the mountainside. Fields of weeds paled with frost. Green put his pride on hold and asked if he could zip up his jacket. His hands were raw with the cold, but he knew he could do nothing about that. Frankie slapped him hard on the back of the head for opening his mouth, but whispered to Scarface to hold up for a minute. Instead of releasing Green's hands from behind his back, Frankie closed up the jacket himself.

"All comfy?" he asked. "Now shut the fuck up."

They came to the head of a cart track and Scarface consulted Frankie. Then they both nudged Green into the underbrush.

He wondered how deep into the country they planned to take him before they killed him.

"Got to stay off the roads," Frankie said. "Lazy fuckers are all sleeping. They aren't worth shit unless they got artillery behind them. But they drop mines all over the place."

They skirted a farmhouse, and saw the sky through its burned-out windows. It truly was a dead place, with not even a stray dog. The weather had put down the insects. And if there were forest animals, they had learned to lie low. Black, burned-over patches scarred the fields in the moonlight.

They crossed a stream by stepping on rocks. Ivo got a wet foot and started cursing. Frankie told him to shut up in the same tone he had used on Green.

"I guess you're some big deal?" Green said. "Local warlord, the big stud back from America."

"You shut the fuck up, too, smart guy. I told you."

"What have I got to lose?"

Frankie's head shook, silhouetted by the fading moonlight. "Man," he whispered, "you really don't understand shit, do you? I mean, really? You'll be *begging* me. For just one more minute. Just five more seconds of life, man. Everybody does. Except the crazy ones. Like Daniela. The crazy ones know better." He laughed, pleased at his vision. "But you. You remind me of this old guy. This doctor fuck. Thought that made him safe. He stayed behind in a clinic to take care of their wounded. Then he makes this big scene when we start waxing the fucks. All this big-shot, big-shit dignity of human life crap. I took that shitbird outside myself. And when he finally got it through his skull that all that education and what the fuck wasn't going to save him, he starts begging. Like some little kid. 'Please, don't kill me yet. Oh, please, not yet. Just one more minute, just one more minute.' " Frankie gave Green a punch on the shoulder to get him moving again. "I bet that's how you'll be. You still think your fucking passport or the cavalry's going to rescue you. But you're already dead, pal."

Green got the sense that his captors knew the way, but not precisely. Darkness took its toll, and they seemed to wander for a while. He remembered his own confusion at Ranger camp, exhausted in the darkness, trying to follow an azimuth in the mountains of northern Georgia. And he recalled his pride in meaningless achievements. It really was nothing but vanity.

There was no training in the world for this.

The march led past a field of staggered crosses, slapped together from wood scraps. Each cross had two horizontals, the lower one wider.

"We didn't kill enough of them," Frankie said.

They came to a hamlet before dawn. The moon was down and the darkness had the texture of flannel. But you could still see that every structure had been destroyed. On both sides of the lane, broken walls rose and rubble narrowed the passage. The earth crunched underfoot.

Frankie and Scarface had a discussion that turned into a spat. Green got the words "patrols" and "stay." Abruptly, Scarface threw up his hands, giving in. Frankie turned to Green.

"We're going to hang here and check out some property. Find some little fixer-upper. See if we can get a good deal."

They went carefully behind the ruins, nervous of booby traps. They sent Green in front now, telling him where to go.

The only structure that offered a decent hiding place was a barn. It stank, although the village must have been destroyed months, if not years, before. But the sky had begun to gray and it was time to go to ground.

In order to avoid leaving traces outside, they took care of their needs at the back of a stall. Then Scarface tied Green to a post where the barn door opened, making no attempt to hide him from anyone who might come nosing inside. Scarface was in a surprisingly good mood, considering that he had spent all night walking through Indian country and had just lost an argument. He tried his bits of English on his captive.

"Door open," he said. "See American." He cocked his fingers into a play pistol and put the index finger to Green's temple. "Bang, bang."

"What's he's trying to say," Frankie explained, "is that anybody comes around here, they bust in the door and they're going to shoot anything they see alive. So they shoot your ass. And give us time to unload on them. That's how this shit goes down."

"Then what?"

"What?"

"Then what happens? All the killing. Daniela. Me. All the others. What's the point anymore? There's a cease-fire down here. You've got your shitty little country. What more do you want?"

"I want those people dead, man. All of them. They still have our land. It was ours for centuries. I want it back." He made a whistling sound. "And you saw what they did to our people. That grave. Those people are savages. You can't live with them."

It was Green's turn to smile, to share what he had figured out. Maybe Frankie would kill him. But he would not die fooled.

"Yesterday, you mean?"

"Yeah. Like that. Women. Little babies. Those people are fucking animals."

"Except the bodies in that grave weren't your people. Were they, Frankie? That's why you were going at them with pick-axes, wrecking the evidence. You wanted to show us another mass grave, to pile it on. But you didn't want us to look too hard. Because the corpses weren't your people at all. And you knew where the grave was because you did the killing."

Scarface looked at Frankie. Frankie's face had gone mean in the gray light.

"Americans can't understand," he said at last, "what's it's like here. It's kill or be killed. Them or you. There's no choice."

"Women and children? That's real hero's work, Frankie."

"Women have babies. Babies grow up to kill you. Children don't forget."

"So everything's okay. Anything for the cause. Butcher people. Massacre your neighbors." Green glanced back and forth in the murky light that filtered through the walls and the little window. "Destroy villages like this."

Frankie laughed. Green still did not get it.

"*This* village? We didn't do *this*, man. Those people did it for us."

Green looked at him. With a question on his face.

Frankie put on an expression that pitied Green's naivete. "This was a *Muslim* village, man. Nobody gives a shit about those scum. Me, I almost like them, in a way. 'Cause those people spend so much time and energy killing them. A bullet in a Turk's head means one bullet less for mine."

Green leaned back against his post. Scarface said something to Frankie. Frankie nodded. Scarface stood up and drew a dirty rag from his back pocket.

"Too much talk," Frankie explained. "Got to be quiet now."

As Scarface approached him with the gag, Green said, "You're wrong. This wasn't a Muslim village. You can smell the pig shit."

Frankie laughed. Green's was the funniest act of the season.

"I didn't say they were *good* Muslims," Frankie told him.

They did not wait for the twilight this time. The afternoon was falling golden through the window when Scarface kicked Green awake, tore off the gag, and untied his hands. Then Scarface pulled a heel of bread from his jacket pocket and dropped it in Green's lap. Green was so dry he could hardly chew or swallow. But he tried not to waste a crumb. This time, he took a swig of the brandy when it was offered.

"They're lazy fuckers, those people," Frankie explained. "They wrap up their patrols by the middle of the afternoon. Then they get fucking drunk. They have no culture. Just appetites, you know? They're not Europeans. But at least it makes things easier for us."

They let Green go to the back of the stall alone.

"Take a good one," Frankie called. " 'Cause it's going to be your last. We just got time to get to the highway and take care of business before the UN trucks come back." After a moment, he added, "They're stupid, too. I hope those dickheads don't just drive over your body and turn all this into a waste."

Scarface muttered and walked off. He opened the door and brilliant light poured into the barn.

"He's just checking if the coast is clear," Frankie said. "Then it's time for our walk."

The explosion shook the birdshit from the rafters of the barn. Frankie grabbed his rifle and took off, abandoning Green. After a delay of a few seconds, the screams began.

Green had never heard such an intensity of shock and pain in a human voice. Even the girl's cries had not been as piercing.

The window was set high, at the back of the barn. It was small. But Green thought he could fit through it. He was just pulling himself up to the sill, when he heard the voice behind him.

Frankie had come back. *Get the fuck down. Get out here. Now.*

The sunlight was hard as metal. Scarface lay on a pile of rubble. Thrown there. He had no legs.

He was screaming and rocking, trying to tourniquet himself with a belt. The only words Green could decipher were "Help me, help me."

Scarface looked up from the shreds of meat and bone and rags where his legs had been. Looking at Frankie.

Frankie stood there. Fingering his rifle.

Scarface pleaded. He was nothing but a little pile of bloody meat. Sprawled on blown cinderblocks, broken beams, and masonry. The ultimate bed of nails.

"You." Frankie said, turning to Green. "Get down. Lie down."

Green stared at him.

Quick as a boxer, Frankie slammed him on the shoulder with his weapon, then beat him across the back. The barrel cracked against a rib and the sight tore through Green's jacket.

"Get down, motherfucker. Lie down on your god-damned belly."

Green lay down. A couple of body-lengths away, Scarface shrieked and begged.

"Spread out your arms and legs," Frankie told Green. "*Do* it."

Green did it.

"Now don't move. Or you're history."

Green understood more of what Scarface was saying now. The man was pleading with Frankie to make Green carry him back over the mountain, to help him stop the bleeding, to do something, anything . . .

Frankie picked up a chunk of cinderblock.

Green could just see Scarface's eyes. The terror. The legless man scuttled and twisted, trying to bring his weapon around. But Frankie threw the cinder-block.

It struck Scarface in the chest, stunning him for a moment.

Frankie shoved his AK behind him, grabbing a rock with one hand and another piece of cinder-block with the other. He was quick.

"*Ne,*" Scarface screamed. "*Ne, ne . . .*"

Frankie stood over him and hurled the rock at his comrade's head.

Scarface dropped back onto the rubble. After the pile of rocks and masonry settled again, there were no more sounds.

Frankie switched the piece of cinderblock to his right hand. This time he bent low and brought it down on the side of Scarface's head, with all of his weight behind it. He swung with so much force he fell onto the body.

Green could not quite see the effect of the blow. But he heard the sound of a dropped pumpkin.

Frankie knelt over the man for a moment. Gasping. Then he smashed the chunk of cinderblock down again. Making sure. The shard trailed a spray of blood as it descended. Then more blood splashed upward, catching Frankie's face.

When he stood back up, Frankie had blood on his face and hands, on his jacket and on the legs of his pants. His face had the blankness of an icon in an old church, with a saint's huge eyes.

He let go of the cinderblock and glanced at Green.

"Martyr to the cause," Frankie said.

Green was racing on adrenaline now. It brought his brain back to life. He understood why Frankie had done it. Killed the comrade he could not save and could not leave to be captured. With a shard of cinderblock instead of one clean shot. Because a stray animal can set off a mine, but only human beings fired rifles. At the sound of a shot, the other side would have shaken off their torpor and come at a rush to find out what happened.

Their world had begun to make sense to him. He felt as though he had realized something huge that could not be put into words. Something he needed to tell his own people.

Frankie had gone savage. He beat Green up to his knees with the stump of metal where the rifle's stock collapsed forward. For a bewildered moment, Green imagined Frankie was going to beat him to death, too. But Frankie only wanted to get going. Before a patrol showed up. He made Green bend forward and touch his forehead to the earth, then he hurriedly tied Green's hands behind his back again. Green's wrists were already raw and Frankie pulled the cords so tight it made him wince.

Frankie knew the way now, in the daylight. He steered Green down rows of knee-high stumps that had been orchards and on into the forest. Cursing, yet keeping his voice low. He raged against the Muslims, the "Turks," until the complaints were almost hypnotic.

"Fucking Turks," he said, over and over. "Fucking goddamned animals. Fucking Turks."

Finally, Green said, "How do you know it was the Muslims? How do you know it wasn't the other side? Or even your own people?"

"You shut the fuck up. Just shut up. Only the Turks set booby traps like that. It's the way they think. They don't fight like men. They sneak. Fucking cowards. All they want to do is get Christian women doped up and fuck them. They need to be exterminated. Wiped from the face of the earth. Every one of them."

Madness, Green thought as he listened. And I was wrong. We were all wrong. It's not a little madness, not something you can reason away or treat. Not even with airstrikes. It's a big madness. Devouring. Reason doesn't exist here. It truly is another world.

"That bitch Daniela," Frankie said. "Her goddamned father was half Turk. She was born a worthless slut. You see what happens?"

Madness, Green thought. It struck him with the force of revelation. That one word. *Madness.*

They were crossing a field of stubble when they heard the dogs. Yaps echoing up the valley. They were miles away. But they frightened Frankie.

He still has to get away, Green realized. After he kills me.

"Get going," Frankie said. "Move it."

Green watched for a place where he could make his break. Desperate now. With his hands tied behind his back, he could not outrun his captor. And he certainly could not outrun a bullet. He needed a change in the terrain. A bank he could roll down. Or another village. Some way to put some initial distance between them, or obstacles to make it hard to aim.

The land had flattened. In the forests, the trees were well-spaced, with very little underbrush. The fields had been harvested. Green never found his opportunity.

He sensed death coming. Thinking: This is how an animal must feel. He longed to just run. To take his last chance. But he marched along and went where he was told.

He could not tell if the dogs were gaining on them or not. There was so much distance between them. And, if they closed in, Frankie would certainly kill him first. Even if he didn't, those people would do it and blame it on Frankie.

Green understood them now. He got the logic that was not the logic of his kind. It seemed a terrible waste that the knowledge would die with him. When it could be so useful to those who did not understand. To those who imagined sanity waiting to be awakened like some political Sleeping Beauty.

He did not really believe he would die. Not at every moment. Part of him could not conceive of such a thing. Something would happen. He would be saved. It made no sense for him to die like this.

No, he realized. It made all the sense in the world. In *this* world.

He heard vehicles. The grunt of military diesels. But these, too, were far away.

Frankie marched him faster.

The late afternoon light glazing the land was as beautiful as anything Green had ever witnessed. Indian summer weather back home. The best time of the year. Football games, in high school then at West Point. The scent and feel of the girls as they tested themselves against life. The safe, privileged world from which he came. Where you caught footballs, not bullets, and danger meant getting caught by your father with beer on your breath, then, later, missing your ride and overstaying your weekend pass. Or just an upperclassman in a bad mood.

He recalled the crisp mornings when the hills smoked above Wheeling, then the brilliant days when the wind swept down the Hudson. Young women who never gave a thought to gang rape in their lives, who had left the village a hundred years behind them. Who would never be killed because their father was half-something. His land of wonder.

Vehicles groaned on the other side of the trees. Maybe a pair of football fields away. Abruptly, the motion sounds stopped and the engines went into idle.

Frankie shoved his gunbarrel into Green's back and said, "Get down. Flat."

Green got down. And heard voices. No dogs, except for those in the distance. But voices asked each other questions. He could not make out any words, but the intonation was universal. They were looking for something.

Green wanted to shout. To take his chances with those people. To take any chance left to him at all.

Frankie held the muzzle to his head.

The searchers remounted and drove away. Maybe it had just been a piss stop, after all.

"Get going," Frankie said. "It isn't far now."

They passed through a glade where the earth was suddenly soft underfoot and the colors of summer held out. Dark greens hard as lacquer. And pale woodland ferns.

"Tell me one thing," Green said.

"Shut up. Move."

"Why'd you come back? From the States? For this?"

Frankie did not answer immediately. The ground rose slightly and hardened underfoot. The earth sounded cold under their boots again.

The yapping of the dogs had grown fainter, almost inaudible.

As they detoured around a clearing, Frankie answered him:

"Americans got no pride. No dignity. A man isn't respected."

"Lost your job? Girlfriend dump you?"

"Fuck you. You don't know what it's like. Big-shit officer." They marched a dozen paces. "Here . . . things make sense. People respect you. For the right reasons. Not just because you're some rich Wall Street fuck. Because of your family. Because of who you are. Because of who your old man was."

From a treeline, Green glimpsed a paved two-lane road half a mile away.

That would be it.

Frankie paused for a moment, judging the land-scape, the safest approach. Before he got them moving again, he looked at Green. Measuring him.

"You think I'm some kind of nutcase. Right? You probably got your skull crammed full of that equal opportunity shit. All that equality crap just means niggers get to fuck your women and you can't say nothing about it." He pointed to the east with his rifle. "It doesn't make sense to you that those people nailed my grandfather to a tree and skinned him alive and now I want to take a piece of their skins. Does it?"

Green wondered at the man. His teachers had been wrong. They did not even belong to the same species any more. All men were not created equal.

"My uncle . . . my father's older brother . . ." Green said, ". . . was killed by the Japanese. And I drive a Honda back home. We put the past behind us. That's our strength."

Frankie looked at him with raw disdain.

"That's not strength," he said. "That's weakness."

They followed a gulley between two fields. The beeches lining the depression had lost most of their leaves and Green ploughed through drifts of yellow and brown that rasped and splashed around his knees.

Apple cider. Sweaters. Parties. Kids goofy in their Halloween costumes. Vampires and ghosts. Ninjas. They had no idea what was frightening. The really terrifying creatures did not wear costumes or have horns or fangs or claws.

He worried that Frankie was right. That he would beg at the last minute. If he had to die . . . if he was going to die . . . he didn't want the end to shame him.

What was he doing here anyway?

What on earth was he doing here?

He wished he had never become a soldier. Or that he had resigned his commission and married Caroline.

He had been so proud. Of his service, his rank. Of the achievements he had imagined held genuine importance.

This is what it came down to.

The leaves made a heart-wrenching sound as he crushed through them. Brutal with memories.

It was going to break his mother's heart. And his father's. His father had always been so proud of him. It was his mother who worried. About football injuries, or the wrong girl for him. About wars.

Did this even count as a war?

He decided he would fight at the end. No matter what. Even if he could only kick.

Unless he saw a chance to run.

He did not know what he would do.

Behind his back, Frankie was humming. Maybe the beauty of the afternoon had reached him, too.

The road had been built at an elevation above the fields, which lay in a floodplain. Its embankment rose before Green like a wall. The gulley narrowed to a culvert, with a half-blocked drainpipe showing daylight under the roadbed.

"Stop."

Not here. Frankie would want to do it right up on the road. There was still time.

"The UN dicks are always on time, at least," Frankie told him. "French colonel's got himself one of their sluts over in the town. Noon to five, then he's on the road again."

Green waited. He sensed Frankie sniffing, sensing the world, listening.

Silence. No dogs, no motors. Not even a bird. Green shifted his weight and the leaves rustled. He tried one last time to work his hands free. Trying to do it discreetly. But the cords were ungiving.

"Okay," Frankie said. "Get up there. Get going."

The time to run would be just when he reached the flat of the road, while Frankie was still climbing the embankment. That would be his best chance. Run and jump down the other side. Then keep on running like hell. He couldn't see yet, but he hoped the ground might drop even lower on the other side of the road. Maybe there would be some undergrowth. Anything that would give him a scrap of advantage.

He walked across a strip of ploughed-under field. With the air cold and thin in his lungs.

"God, please," he prayed. "Please, help me now."

He started up the embankment, struggling to keep his balance with his hands bound behind him.

As he approached the top, he saw that it was hopeless. There was only another field on the other side, wide open for at least two hundred meters before it ended against the next treeline.

He got ready to run anyway.

But Frankie's hands were not bound. He beat Green to the top and covered him with the rifle, moving just in front of him, stepping backward.

Without prompting, they both stopped in the middle of the road.

"This is it, motherfucker."

Green stared at the man who would kill him.

Frankie wasn't smiling now. "Turn around," he told Green. "You've got one minute. Pray, or do whatever you want. One minute."

The last blue sky.

Green took off. He ran harder than he had ever

run on any football field. He ran and waited for the shot.

He heard the crack of a rifle.

But he was still alive, still running.

And the sound had not been right. It had not been close enough.

He ran a little farther. When there was no second shot, he stopped. And turned around.

Frankie lay crumpled in the roadway. With his brains strewn over the asphalt. His eyes were open and stunned.

Green saw them then. Emerging from the far tree-line. Someone shouted to him to stay where he was. Men in grayish fatigues. Bearded men. Wearing those little caps that always made him think of the old Howard Johnson's hot-dog rolls. Silly caps. *Those people.*

Green sat down hard in the middle of the road and waited.

The hand-over took place on the border that night, with no time wasted and the usual suspects in attendance: the rag-tag killers who had saved his life, a French colonel, and a Dutch major. The U.S. attaché, Lieutenant Colonel Andretti, was on the receiving end.

Driving back to the embassy, Andretti listened to Green's story. Green did not sugarcoat it.

"I was sure they were going to kill me," Green concluded, rubbing his foot. His feet stank, but Andretti understood. "First that sonofabitch Frankie, then me. And pin it on him. I guess my cynicism's showing."

The attaché snorted and offered him another Diet Coke from the cooler. Real gringo Coke. "You got lucky. One man's misfortune . . . you want another sandwich?" Andretti's rough skin gleamed as a flash of headlights lit the back of the sedan. "Couple of reporters just found the biggest mass grave of the war. Seven, eight-hundred bodies, minimum. UN, Red Cross, NGOs, the press—everybody's all over those people. Even the Russians look like they're ready to back airstrikes against their little bearded brothers." He snorted again. The bad air in the capital city had given Andretti asthma at the back end of his career. "You were their good deed for the day. After a decade of atrocious ones. They had everybody they could muster out looking for you. One-legged distance runners and one-armed paper-hangers. We had to jump up and down to keep them on their side of the border. They figured out what was happening quicker than we did. And they were not going to take that rap, if they could help it. They've got enough on their plate already."

Green considered the universe, then condensed it. "I keep thinking about Bob Crawley."

The little attaché settled back into his seat. "You'll think about him for the rest of your life, Jeff."

The President's special envoy, a former ambassador playing hooky from Wall Street, had flown into the capital city that morning. His visit had nothing to do with Green, whose disappearance had been a sideshow in the circus of international relations. Nicholas Vollstrom was in the middle of another round of shuttle diplomacy, with airstrikes in the offing if the villains of the moment did not back down and do his bidding.

The diplomats assigned to the region had been trying to communicate the complexity of the situation to the President's envoy for months, but had failed. Now, with Vollstrom anxious to go wheels-up for Brussels, where he had a come-to-Jesus session with the SACEUR the next morning, the ambassador had the attaché usher Major Green into the embassy's secure bubble. In a last attempt to inject some reality into the envoy's view of the world.

Green had not even showered. There had barely been time to wash the last crusts of blood from his face in the men's room and change into the suit he kept in the office for meetings with the local bureaucrats. He had seen Vollstrom getting into a limo once. And he had read plenty about him. In person, the president's man was beefy, running to fat. He wore glasses and spoke in a loud, high-pitched voice.

Green tried to tell his tale soberly and efficiently. But less than a third of the way into the story, Vollstrom cut him off, thumping his fist down on the table.

"I've just spent the afternoon and most of the evening with the president of this republic. With whom I have built a relationship of trust. He briefed me personally on what you were doing down there, major. Clowning around, stirring up trouble. And it backfired on you. Got one of you killed. And now you want to shift the blame." He grimaced in disgust. "You'll be lucky if you aren't court-martialed. Goddamned lucky."

"Sir . . ."

The envoy leaned across the table toward Green. His neck swelled out of his collar and his face turned the color of raw meat.

"Get this straight, son," he said. "There *is* no war in Melnica."

RALPH PETERS is a novelist, essayist, and former soldier. His fiction includes *Traitor, The Devil's Garden, Twilight of Heroes, The War in 2020,* and other novels. He is also the author of the acclaimed book on strategy and conflict, *Fighting for the Future: Will America Triumph?* His commentaries on strategic themes appear regularly in the national and international media. He entered the U.S. Army as a private in 1976 and retired in 1998, shortly after his promotion to lieutenant colonel, so he could write and speak freely. His military service and research travels have taken him to fifty countries, and his duties led him from an infantry battalion to the Executive Office of the President. His novella in this collection, "There Is No War in Melnica," is based on his personal observation of the Balkans from 1972 to the present.

CAV

——————

BY JAMES COBB

Excerpts from The New Ways of War: Politico-Military Evolution in the Opening Decades of the Twenty-first Century.
Professor Christine Arkady,
University of Southern California Press, 2035

Much to the consternation of the international community, the African race wars raged on into the new millennium, but not in the format of the old black and white South African conflict. African and *Afrikaner* came to accommodations with comparative rapidity following the end of apartheid in the 1990s. Replacing it was a new, ominous, and growing confrontation between black and brown.

In a great arc across the African *Sahel* from the Atlantic to the Sudan, an almost continuous series of border clashes and minor insurgencies sputtered and flared between the Arabic-Moorish nations of North Africa and the Black African states of the Sub-Sahara. Fueled by racism, newborn nationalistic pride and old tribal enmities, and fanned by self-seeking political leaders and Islamic radicals, the potential for an open conflagration loomed large within the region.

The flash point came in the fall of 2021. The Islamic Republic of Algeria, the new primary trouble-maker among the northern tier Arabic states, began beating the drum of *Jihad* against Mali, its immediate neighbor to the south. Taking up the cause of a small Mali-based group of Tuareg separatists with a sudden and suspicious vociferousness, the Algerians launched a major military buildup along the Mali border, all the while calling for a "liberation of our Muslim brothers from the black animists."

This in the face of the fact that the vast majority of Mali's population was also Islamic, albeit of a decidedly more moderate cast than the Revolutionary Council in Algiers.

Mali, in and of itself, was no great prize for any would-be conqueror. Wracked by drought and desertification, it was a strong contender for the title of the poorest nation on Earth. In a strategic military sense, though, it represented a pearl beyond price for any potential empire builder coveting North-western Africa. The largest of the West African states, Mali is set in the literal heart of the region. Every other nation around the West African periphery is vulnerable to an invasion staging out of Malian territory.

Reacting to that threat, and to the pleas for assistance from the Malian government, the West African Economic Federation deployed counterforces into Mali in the first major regional security operation ever launched by that fledgling organization. However, although willing, the WAEF combat units were woefully outnumbered and underequipped to face the armored juggernaut being assembled by the Algerians. Chairman Belewa of the Federation Board of Unity, an intensely realistic statesman, dispatched an urgent request for military assistance to both the United States and France.

France replied with a *Force d'Intervencion* task group built around the First *Regiment Etranger d'Cavalerie.* The United States deployed the Second Army Expeditionary Force with two attached elements: the Thirteenth Aviation Brigade (Support) and the Seventh Cavalry Regiment (Armored Strike).

It was hoped that the presence of the Legionnaires and the Garryowens on the ground in Mali would serve as a trip-wire deterrent to Algerian military adventurism.

The hope proved to be false.

The Western Sahara
300 Km North-Northwest of Timbuktu
1454 Hours, Zone Time; October 28, 2021

Lieutenant Jeremy Bolde rode in *ABLE*'s open commander's hatch with the balanced ease born of long practice. His wiry, well-muscled form flowed with each jolt and lurch of the big Shinseki armored fighting vehicle in much the same way as a skilled rider moved with the trail pacing of his horse. In that portion of his mind not involved with his focused and deliberate scanning of the surrounding terrain, the words of a song from the old army circled past, his sun-cracked lips pursed in an unheard whistle.

"In her hair she wore a yellow ribbon.
And she wore it proudly so that every man could see.
And when we asked her why a yellow ribbon.
She said it's for my lover in the U.S. Cavalry . . ."

Abruptly, the shrill alarm tone of the threat board squalled in the earphones of his helmet. At the same instant, Bolde felt *ABLE* swerve sharply beneath him as his driver, Specialist Third (Vehicle Operations) Rick Santiago locked the wheel over in an instinctive turn-and-accelerate evasion.

Bolde hit the seat control selector with the palm of his hand, dropping himself down through the commander's cupola and into the cab beside Santiago, the hatch lid thudding closed over his head.

"What do we have?" he demanded.

"Our point drone was just painted by a ground scan radar," Warrant Officer First (Velectronics Operations) Bridget Shelleen reported crisply from behind Bolde's shoulder.

"Any indication of a targeting acquisition?"

"I don't think so." The intense little redhead leaned into the drone operations station on the starboard cab bulkhead, her fingers dancing across the keypads as she pumped a series of commands into the datalinks. "*CHARLIE* was just cresting a dune line when he was blipped. I've reversed him back into the radar shadow. Contact broken. With the luck of the Lord and Lady, they'll think he was a dust transitory."

"How about us, Brid? Are we still clean?"

"No painting indicated. *CHARLIE* is running about ten klicks out ahead of us. We're still below the scan horizon of whatever is out there."

"Right. Recall *CHARLIE*. Low speed. Minimize dust plume. Rick, find us a hide. We're going to ground."

"Doin' it, LT," *ABLE*'s wheelman yelled back over the whir and rumble of the wheels. "We got a *qued* off to the left. I just gotta find us a go-down."

At eighty kilometers an hour, the armored cavalry vehicle roared along parallel to a dry wash. Such *queds* were one of the few, rare terrain variances to be found amid the broad expanses of sand-and-gravel *fesh fesh* plain that predominate in northern Mali.

Driving right-handed, Santiago used his left to manipulate the settings of the ride control panel, backing off the air pressure in *ABLE*'s eight massive Kevlar-belted tires from HARD SURFACE to ALL TERRAIN and dialing a few extra inches of ground clearance into the suspension.

Ahead he saw a point where the *qued* bank had collapsed, giving him a steep but usable access ramp to the ravine floor. "Okay going down. Hey, back in the scout bay! Hang on! Rough ride!"

He braked hard, swung the wheel over, and avalanched his vehicle down the crumbling slope. The suspension sprawled and angled, autoconforming to the terrain and keeping *ABLE*'s twenty-two tons centered over her wheelbase. Tire cleats dug in, then slipped, and the big war machine slither-crashed to the floor of the twenty-meter-wide dry streambed in an explosion of dust and sprayed earth, the pneumatic seats of her crew bouncing hard against their stops. Santiago leaned on his accelerator and *ABLE* lunged forward again, the eight-by-eight drives scrabbling for traction in the sand.

Another avalanche could be seen in the sideview

mirrors. *BAKER*, Saber section's second gun drone, waddled down the slope after the command vehicle, its onboard artificial intelligences obediently station-keeping in their tactical default mode.

"How far you want me to work up the wash, LT?"

"Get us clear of our entry point." Bolde computed artillery spread patterns in his mind, judging clearances. When they'd put two bends in the streambed between themselves and the spot where they had disappeared from surface view, he nodded to his driver. "Okay, Rick, shut down and power down!"

ABLE shuddered to a halt, her turbines fading out with a whispering moan. A metallic hiss followed as the cavalry vehicle hunkered closer to the ground, her suspension lowering into a vehicular crouch.

In the forward compartment, an instinctive stream of orders flowed from Bolde.

"Brid, raise the sensor mast and go to full passive scan. I want a threat review! Rick, prep the Cypher for launch. Mary May! Deploy your ground pickets!"

"Yes sir," Spec 5 (Ground Combat) Mary May Jorgenson yelled from the scout team bay back aft. "Ramp going down. Scouts, set overwatch! Go!"

The tail ramp thudded open, and boots rang on aluminum decking.

Even as he issued his commands, Bolde personally involved himself in the security of the laager point. Accessing onboard fire control through the commander's station, he assumed direction of *ABLE*'s primary weapons pack.

In road mode, the boom mount of the weapons pack normally rode angled back over the stern of the cavalry vehicle like the cocked stinger tail of a scorpion. Now it straightened and extended, lifting the twin box launchers of the Common Modular Missile system above the lip of the wash. The telescopic

lenses of a target-acquisition sensor cluster peered
from between the launchers, as did the stumpy barrel of a 25mm OCSW (Objective Crew Served
Weapon). Much like the attack periscope of a submarine, the weapons mount began a slow and deliberate rotation, scanning the horizon.

Scowling, Bolde watched the camera image pan
past on his master display. Nothing moved out across
the desert except for the perpetual heat shimmer.
To the north, toward the rippling dune line, a single
thin streak of dust played along the ground. A blue
computer graphics arrowhead hovered over it, however, designating a friendly. *CHARLIE* drone returning from his point probe.

As the camera turned to the south, more friendly
activity was revealed. A figure clad in desert camouflage snaked over the edge of the *qued.* Carrying his
SABR (Selectable Assault Battle Rifle) over his forearms, Specialist Third Nathan Grey Bird snaked
across a narrow stretch of gravel in a fluid infantry
crawl, vanishing into a low clump of rocks with a deft
alacrity that would have brought pride to the heart
of his Shoshone-Bannock warrior ancestors.

Specialist Second Johnny Roman had his outpost
established on the opposite bank of the *qued* and
Specialist Second Lee Trebain could be seen
through *ABLE*'s Armorglas windshield, establishing a
sentry point farther ahead along the wash floor. Sensor systems were all well and good, but the "mark
one eyeball" was still the hardest sensor in the world
to fool. Saber section would not trust its security to
electronics alone, not while one Lieutenant Jeremy
Bolde commanded.

Bolde disarmed the weapons pack and allowed the
boom to retract back into travel mode. Arming off
his bulky HMD helmet, he replaced it with the dust-

and sweat-stained cavalry terai that had been riding atop the dashboard, settling the hat over his short-trimmed, sandy hair at the precisely proper "Jack Duce" angle. The black slouch-brimmed Stetsons had been revived by the new cavalry as their answer to the berets of the Ranger and Special Forces regiments, a distinctive badge of branch individuality. The difference was that the Airborne units looked upon their signature headgear as being, for the most part, ceremonial. The Cav looked upon theirs as essential field equipment.

"Pickets are out, Lieutenant. Ground security set." Mary May Jorgenson came forward from the scout compartment through the narrow passage between the two mid-vehicle powerbays.

Man-tall and broad-shouldered for a woman, Mary May was one of the elite few female personnel to match the rigorous physical parameters required by the Army for a Ground Combat Specialist's rating. Yet for all of her inherent and repeatedly proven toughness, there was still a large degree of the mellow Nebraska farm girl in her blue-eyed and lightly freckled countenance.

Wearing BDU trousers and a flak vest over a khaki tee shirt, she carried an M9 service pistol on her right hip. However the 9mm Beretta automatic was carried in a left-handed holster, butt forward in the old dragoon's draw. She, too, wore a battered terai cocked low over her brows.

"What's up, Lieutenant?" she inquired, leaning back against the rear bulkhead. "Are we in contact?"

"With something," Bolde replied, rotated his seat so it faced the systems operator's station. "How about it, Brid. What do we have out there?"

"A single battlefield-surveillance radar," the systems operator replied, her attention still focused on the telepanels of her console. "With our mast up, I'm receiving an identifiable side lobe from it. Emission ID file indicates a Ukrainian made Teal/Specter system. . . . Multi-mode . . . About five years old . . . And it matches a unit type known to be in Algerian service."

She sat back in her seat and looked across at Bolde. "We are indeed in contact with the enemy, sir. And given the emission strength and beam angle, the unit must be operating from an elevation."

"Hell!" Bolde permitted himself the single short curse. "They beat us to the pass."

Terrain defines the battlefield. Unfortunately, for all intents and purposes, northern Mali doesn't have any. No rivers, no mountains, no forests, no swamps. Just extensive, arid plains of baked earth and *fesh fesh* intermittently blanketed by the migrating sand dunes of the Sahara.

The one exception was the El Khnachich range. A line of low, rugged hills arcing from east to west, midway between Algerian border and Timbuktu, it was the sole high ground in an ocean of flatness.

The Taoudenni caravan track, the closest thing to a road that existed in this part of the world, ran southward through a pass in the range. For centuries, the Taoudenni track had been a link joining Algeria with the Niger River valley. Thirty-six hours before, when the Algerian army had stormed across the undefended and indefensible Mali border, one entire mechanized division had been vectored down this beaten sand pathway, its mission to seize that route southward into Mali's fertile heartland.

In a countermove, Troop B, First of the Seventh had been ordered north from its patrol base in Timbuktu to meet the thrust, a fanged and venomous mouse charging an elephant. For the first time in modern human history, the hills of El Khnachich were important.

The systems operator called up a tactical map on her main display. The hill range and the pass lay perhaps twenty-five kilometers ahead on the section's line of advance. Blue IDed unit hacks glowed near the bottom of the map, indicating the position of Saber section's dispersed elements. A single hostile target box pulsed in the southern mouth of the pass.

"Darn!" Mary May yanked off her hat and slid down the bulkhead to sit on the pebbled rubber antiskid of the vehicle deck. "I thought the noon sitrep said that the Algies were still watering up at Taoudenni oasis."

"The bulk of the division was," Bolde grunted, his angularly handsome features impassive. "But they were already starting to push their lead elements south. I suspect they rammed some fast movers forward to play King of the Hill. Any sign they've got anything over on our side yet, Brid?"

The SO shook her head, her firefall of hair brushing the back of her neck. "Nothing's indicated. *CHARLIE* didn't spot anything, and I'm not picking up any tactical communications on the standard Algerian bands. If they have any units fanning out on this side of the slope, they're running an extremely tight EMCON, and that's not like them. We'll have to go eyes up to be certain, though."

"Then let's do it. Get off a contact report to Bravo six then put up the Cipher. I want to see what we have crawling around out there."

The Cipher reconnaissance drone was literally a flying saucer. Or perhaps to be even more precise, a flying doughnut, a flattened discoid aeroform four feet in diameter with two contrarotating lift fans in its center. A puff of compressed air launched it out of its docking bay on *ABLE*'s broad back. Bobbling in a hover for a moment over the dry wash, it autostabilized then darted away to the north, skimming an effortless ten feet above the desert's surface.

The drone rotated slowly as it flew. The television camera built into the rim of its sturdy stealth composite fuselage intently scanned the surrounding environment, the imaging being fed back via a jitter frequency datalink to its mother station in *ABLE*'s cab. There, in turn, a slender hand on a computer joystick clicked a series of waypoints onto a computer-graphics map, guiding the little Remotely Piloted Vehicle on its way.

On the main screen, the rusty red wall of the Khnachich range rose above the dune lines.

"I'm not seeing anything moving out there," Mary May commented from her position, seated cross-legged on the deck.

"Nothing as big as an armored column at any rate." Bolde glanced at the ECM threat boards. "And nobody is emitting except for that one radar on the high ground. Brid, take the drone out to the west a ways and then take it up to the ridgeline. We'll move it back east along the crest and have a look down into that pass."

Shelleen nodded her reply, her expression fixed and intent on the drone-control readouts.

Even at the Cipher's best speed, it took over a quarter of an hour to maneuver the drone into its designated observation position. At one point, as the RPV climbed the jagged stone face of the hill range, the video image on the display flickered and the datalink inputs faded as line of sight was broken between the drone and its controller. Instantly, Shelleen's hands flashed across the keypads, rerouting the links through one of the flight of Long-Duration Army

Communications drones orbiting over the Mali theater at a hundred thousand feet.

The imaging smoothed out and Bolde rewarded his SO with a slight, appreciative nod of his head.

In due course, the drone's position hack on the tactical display and the image on the television monitor indicated that the drone was approaching the gut of the pass. Shelleen eased the RPV to a hover just below the crest of the last saddleback. "No closer," she advised, "or they'll hear the fans."

"Okay. Blip her up. 'Then we shall see' as the blind man said."

The systems operator tapped a key. Twenty miles away, the drone's motor raced for an instant, popping the little machine an additional hundred feet into the air. For a few seconds before dropping back out of sight below the lateral ridge, the RPV's sensors could look down into the mouth of the pass.

"Oh yeah," Mary May commented. "They beat us here all right."

Bolde reached forward for the monitor playback controls and froze the image.

It was the usual multinational hodgepodge of military equipment that had become commonplace in the post–Cold War Armies of the Third World.

The previously detected Teal/Specter radar track and its generator trailer sat parked in the center of the road. Mounted on the hull of a BMP 3 Armored Personnel Carrier, the radar unit's slablike phased-array antenna swung deliberately in a slice-of-pie scan of the desert below.

Backed deeper into the cut behind it, deftly positioned to blast any radar-hunting fighter-bomber or gunship making a pass on the Teal/Specter unit, was a massive, tracked antiair vehicle, its rectangular turret bristling with multiple autocannon barrels and missile tubes. A Russian 2S6M *Tunguska* or, more than likely, an Indian-produced copy of the same.

Then there were Scylla and Charybdis, a pair of eight-wheeled *Otobreda Centauros* parked out on either flank of the pass entry. The long-tubed 105mm cannon mounted in the turrets of the big Italian-built tank destroyers angled downward, covering the narrow road that switchbacked up from the flats.

In the face of the day's heat, the Algerian crews swarmed around their vehicles, concealing them not only with visual-sight camouflage netting, but also with RAM antiradar tarpaulins and anti-infrared insulation. Stone defensive revetments were being stacked up as well, indicating that this was more than a brief stretch-and-cigarette stop.

"Okay, Brid. Walk us over the pass. Let's see what else they have down there."

"What else" proved to be half a dozen more armored fighting vehicles dispersed along the winding floor of the pass. Tracked and low-riding, with the Slavic design school's distinctive flattened "frying pan" turret shape mounted aft of center, their crews were hard at work digging them in as well.

"Six Bulgarian BRM-30 scout tracks and a pair of *Centauros*," Mary May commented. "That's a full Algerian Recon company. The radar rig and the *Tunguska* would be mission attachments."

"The question being just what that mission is." Bolde slid out of his seat and hunkered down on the deck beside the system operator's chair to get a clearer view of the station displays. "Brid, take us north a little more. I want to get a view of what's happening on the other side of this ridge."

"Not a problem," she replied, setting the new waypoint.

It wasn't. In another minute or two the drone went

into hover again, offering its masters a panoramic vista of the plains to the north of the El Khnachich. The caravan road was a pale trace across the desert floor. Clustered about it, perhaps fifteen kilometers beyond the hill range, a number of massive dust plumes rose into the air.

"There's the rest of your division," Shelleen commented, "or a goodly chunk thereof."

"Agreed," Bolde replied slowly, "but not in road column. It looks like they're dispersing."

"They are, LT," Santiago added. The driver had swiveled his seat around, joining the ad hoc command conference. "From the look of that dust kickup, you got a series of company-sized detachments peeling off the main road and fanning out."

"Yeah." Mary May nodded up from the floor. "If I didn't know better, I'd say those guys were dispersing to go into a night laager."

Bolde glanced down at his head scout. "Why do we know better, Mary May?"

The young woman shrugged. "Because they've no reason to stop and lots to keep going, Lieutenant. You never halt on the near side of a low river ford or a clear mountain pass. It might not be low or clear the next day when you want to move again."

"Yeah. That's how we'd do it. But then the gentleman who's running that outfit may not necessarily play by the same rules that we do." Bolde let his voice trail off as he contemplated possibilities.

"Probably," he said after a half minute's pause, "that Algi division is strung out along a good seventy–eighty kilometers of the Taoudenni road about now. They're stuck with staying on it because their logistics groups are still using trucks instead of high-mobility all-terrain vehicles. They can't move too fast for that same reason. That caravan route is literally just a camel trail.

"Now, a lot of Third World commanders still aren't too comfortable with large-unit operations after nightfall. Let's also say that the Algi general running this outfit is a conservative and cautious kind of guy, again like a lot of Third World commanders.

"He's got night coming on, a replenishment coming up, and he knows that there's likely U.S. and Legion Armored Cav out here hunting for him. The idea of being draped across this range of hills with some of his maneuver elements on one side and some on the other come oh dark hundred might not appeal to him too much."

"It wouldn't to me either," Shelleen noted thoughtfully. "There are things a raider could do with a situation like that."

"Indeed there are, Miss Shelleen," Bolde agreed, lifting an eyebrow. "And I was hoping to try some of them out tonight. Unfortunately, our Algerian friend appears to be playing it safe. He's run a fast recon element out ahead to secure this pass. That will do a couple of things for him. For one, it'll plug up the obvious route another mechanized unit would have to take to get at his main. For another it will give him an observation post on the high ground.

"That battlefield radar will give him early warning of any major force moving in from the south. If one shows up, he can engage at long range with artillery, spotting from the pass mouth. He knows he's got way more tubes and rails on this side of Mali than we do, so he'll have the edge in any potential gun duel.

"So covered, he figures he can safely fort up overnight north of the pass to regroup and resupply. Come first light, when he doesn't have to worry so much about being bushwhacked, he can push his entire division rapidly through the choke point of the pass. Once he's got his maneuver battalions out into open country again, he can trust in his massed firepower to bust him through any light-force screen we can throw in front of him."

Bolde's planning staff exchanged glances, wordlessly discussing their leader's analysis. Bridget Shelleen voiced their findings. "That very well could be what we're seeing here, sir. The question is, what are we going to do about it?"

"What indeed. What indeed." Bolde accessed a secondary screen on the workstation, filling it with a graphics-map tactical display of the immediate region. He added an overlay showing Saber section's position as well as that of the known hostile units. Using the console touch pad, he drew in the potential laager sites of the remainder of the Algerian division. Then he considered once more.

Minutes passed and Mary May Jorgenson stirred restlessly from her seat on the deck plates. "It wouldn't be too much trouble to mess up that recon outfit in the pass. My guys and I could get up on the ridges overlooking their positions and laser designate for our CMMs. We could take 'em out, no problem."

"Yeah, we could do that," Bolde replied slowly. "But how much would that gain us or cost the bad guys? We could kill that recon company, all right. But is that our best potential shot? If we are serious about slowing the Algis down, we'll have to maximize our strike effect. We'll have to nurse as much bang out of our buck as is conceivable, even if it means stretching the sensibility envelope to a degree."

"*L'audace, l'audace, toujours, l'audace,*" Shelleen murmured.

"Precisely. The problem is that we are down here—"

Bolde's fingertip touched the blue position hack at the bottom of the map display—"and all the really good stuff is up there." His finger climbed up the map to the Algerian laager zone. "Tonight, the Algis are going to be in static positions, refueling and re-arming. Their logistics groups are going to be up forward and intermixed with their maneuver battalions. That's when they will be at their most vulnerable and when we could do the most damage.

"Thing is, the Algis are playing it smart. They've read their copy of *Jane's All the World's Weapons Systems* and they're going to ground far enough back from this hill range so that we can't toss anything over the rocks at them. If we want to hurt them, really hurt them, we'll have to get over on that north side with them, and they can't know we're there until it's too late."

Bolde looked back over his shoulder at his driver. "How about it, Rick? Can you get us over these hills without using the pass?"

The lean and moustached Latino gave a slight shrug. "It's gonna depend on the surfaces and gradients, LT. Miss Shelleen, could you show me the slope profile on that stretch of range ahead of us?"

"Coming up." Pad keys rattled.

A new overlay appeared on the tactical display, a mottled red, yellow, and blue transparency draped across the contour lines of the map. This was a gauging of the slopes and angles of the El Khnachich range as laser and radar surveyed by a Defense Mapping Agency topographical satellite cross-referenced with the cross-country performance capacity of the Shinseki Multi-Mission Combat Vehicle family.

"Yeah, we got somethin' here." Santiago levered himself out of the driver's seat and crowded in with the others around the workstation. "See," he indicated in interlocking sequence of yellow and blue areas on the map. "It looks like I can get us over that next saddleback to the west of the pass. The grades look good anyway."

"How about surfacing?" Bolde inquired.

"I kept an eye on the visuals we were getting from the drone. It looks like we got some shale-and-gravel slopes and some boulder fields, but nothing we can't beat."

"And how about the Algis? Do you think they might suspect somebody could crawl through that hole?"

A faintly condescending smile tugged at the driver's lips. "Treadheads always have a problem believing what a Shinseki can do, LT. The Algerians don't have a vehicle that could get over that saddleback. I'm willing to bet that they'll figure we don't either."

Santiago straightened and took a step back, collapsing into the driver's seat again. "The problem is, sir, while I think I can get us over that sucker, I'm not going to be able to do it fast. Especially if I have to be sneaky while I'm doing it."

"How about if you don't have to be sneaky? We'll be tiptoeing going in, but we'll be pretty much running flat out when we extract. Can you get us back out over this route before the Algis can zero us?"

Santiago held out his hand, palm down, and rocked it in an ominously so-so manner. "The main force isn't what's sweating me, LT. My beast and I can outrun pretty much anything that moves on treads if we get half a chance. What I'm worried about is that recon company up in the pass. They can't cut us off moving laterally along the ridge. Like I said, their vehicles can't hack the climbing. But if they move fast enough, they could either drop down

out of the pass and intercept us short of the hills as
we fall back, or they could be waiting for us over on
the other side. It wouldn't take much. They'd only
have to hold us in place for a couple of minutes, just
long enough for their pursuit forces to close up and
engage and . . . *fiit!*"

Santiago drew his thumbnail across his throat,
matching graphic action to graphic sound.

"A valid point, Rick," Bolde replied, rocking back
on his heels. "To secure our line of retreat, we're
going to need to give that recon company in the pass
something else to think about. Mary May, you were
talking about taking those guys out. Do you think
you and your team could do the job without the direct support of the vehicles?"

The young woman tilted her head down so that
the brim of her hat concealed her eyes and her expression as she thought. When she lifted her head
again, she looked composed and confident. Only a
faint reddening of her lower lip indicated how she
had bitten it. "No problem, Lieutenant. We'll have
the terrain and the surprise factor. We can keep 'em
busy."

"Okay then. Brid, recall the Cipher." Bolde
glanced around the cab of the command vehicle,
meeting his troopers' eyes as he spoke. "Here's how
we're going to do it. We've got some pretty good
cover here, so we'll lie doggo for the rest of the afternoon. We'll keep the pass under observation, run
some mission prep and get a little rest. If the Algis
do go to ground and if we have the same tactical
situation come nightfall, we'll develop an Ops plan.
We all good with this? All right, then let us proceed."

The remaining hours of the afternoon passed in a
breathless shimmer of heat, the smears of shade pro-

duced by the walls of the *qued* a priceless commodity beneath the torchblast of the sun. The expanse of desert around the vehicle hide remained empty, barring the passage of a herd of rare Saharan gazelles. As they materialized out of the mirage fields, their delicacy and grace stood in stark contrast to the harshness of the land.

The only hint of war came when two pairs of frost-colored contrails climbed above the horizons, one pair coming from the north, the other from the south.

They met and tangled lazily in the desert zenith, sparks of sunflame glinting from cockpit canopies and banking wingtips. One by one, over a period of a single minute, the snowy streamers of yarn terminated, turning dark and arcing toward the earth below, or ending abruptly in a smoke blotch against the milky azure sky.

The lone survivor turned away to the south. Bolde and his troopers watched for any sign of a descending parachute but all that was seen was the tumbling flicker of falling metal fragments.

Tired of its day's brutality, the sun drifted below the horizon.

[SABER 6-BRAVO 6***WHAT SUPPORT ELEMENTS WILL BE AVAILABLE WITHIN MY OPSFRAME?]

Jeremy Bolde typed the words onto the flatscreen of the communications workstation, located on the left-side bulkhead behind the driver's seat. Reaching forward, he tapped the transmit key. Instantly, his sentence was encrypted and compressed down into a microburst transmission too brief to be fixed on by a radio direction finder. Tight-beamed up from the dish antenna atop *ABLE*'s cab, the blip transmission was received by a station-keeping relay drone and then fired downward again to the Bravo Troop command vehicle some two hundred miles away to the southeast.

Awaiting the response, Bolde tilted the console seat back, the creak of the chair mount loud against the only other two sounds in the cab, the low purr of the air-conditioning and the quiet snoring of Rick Santiago. *ABLE*'s driver had his own seat tilted back to its farthest stop and his terai tipped down over his eyes, raking in a few precious minutes of sack drill. Even when *ABLE* was in laager, Rick could generally be found lounging behind the cavalry vehicle's wheel, an aspect of the almost symbiotic relationship he had developed with his massive armor-sheathed mount.

Bolde was pleased his driver could get some rest. He wished he could do as well. Maybe later.

Then the answer to his query flashed back on his screen, erasing any thought of sleep.

[BRAVO 6-SABER 6***EFFECTIVELY NONE.]

The datalink transmission continued hastily.

[BRAVO 6-SABER 6***I'M DAMN SORRY, JER, BUT WE ARE AT SATURATION. ALL AVAILABLE IN-THEATER AND LONG-RANGE AIR ASSETS ARE COMMITTED TO SUPPRESSION OPS AGAINST ALGERIAN AIR FORCE. HONCHO 2ND HAS EFFECTIVELY ASSUMED COMMAND OF ALL IN THEATER GROUND FORCES. 1ST LEGION CAV, 2 & 3 OF 7TH, AND WAEF MOBILE FORCE ARE MASSING IN EASTERN SECTOR FOR COUNTERSTRIKE

AGAINST ALGERIAN ARMORED CORPS
ADVANCING SOUTH ALONG TESSALIT-GAO
HIGHWAY. HEAVY INITIAL CONTACT
PROJECTED FOR TONIGHT. ALL AIRCAV, ALL
L-R ARTILLERY ELEMENTS ARE ENGAGING
ENEMY MAINFORCE AT THIS TIME. YOU CAN
CHECK THE STRIKEBOARDS BUT I THINK THE
CUPBOARD IS BARE UNTIL AT LEAST FIRST
LIGHT TOMORROW.

There wasn't anything else to do except to type

[SABER 6-BRAVO 6***ACKNOWLEDGED. ANY
FURTHER INSTRUCTIONS.]
[BRAVO 6-SABER 6***JUST SCREEN AND
DELAY, JER. 2ND RANGER, 6TH AIRCAV AND
9TH RIFLE HAVE ALL BEEN COMMITTED AND
ARE DEPLOYING BUT WE CAN'T EXPECT TO
SEE THEM ON THE GROUND FOR 36–92
HOURS.
SCREEN AND DELAY AND BUY US SOME TIME.
CARBINE AND PISTOL SECTIONS BRAVO HAVE
FOUND ANOTHER TRANSIT POINT OF THE EL
KHNACHICH RANGE TO THE EAST OF YOU
AND ARE GOING DEEP, HUNTING FOR
ALGERIAN LOG UNITS. ALPHA AND
CHECKMATE TROOPS 1ST ARE
REPOSITIONING TO TIMBUKTU PATROL BASE
BUT WILL NOT BE A FACTOR UNTIL 06–07
HUNDRED TIME FRAME TOMORROW. . . .

A secondary screen on the console lit off, indicating that a data dump was under way from the troop
command vehicle carrying intelligence updates, re-
freshed battlemaps, and weather projections, the
sole aid their CO could dispatch.

... DO THE BEST YOU CAN WITH WHAT YOU
HAVE, JER.]
[SABER 6-BRAVO 6***IF IT WASN'T A
CHALLENGE, SIR, IT WOULDN'T BE THE
CAVALRY. SABER-6 DOWN]

Bolde secured the transmitter and retracted the
roof antenna. For a long moment, he studied the last
glowing lines on the communications screen. After a
moment, he chuckled with soft self-derisiveness.
What was that line George C. Scott had said in *Patton*? The one just before El Guettar, "All of my life I
have dreamed of leading a large number of men in
a desperate battle."

Well, while he had no large number of men, the
desperation level was certainly adequate. Brid Shelleen, with her somewhat "different" worldview would
say that he had created this moment and this situation for himself. He had asked and the universe had
given.

For he, Lieutenant Jeremy Randolph Bolde, had
dreamed of being a warfighter, not merely a soldier,
or a career army officer, but a combatant. For as long
as he could recall, Bolde had hungered for what Patton had called the "sting of battle," for the chance
to test himself in the ultimate crucible.

Such concepts and attitudes were decisively not
"PC" these days, not even within the Officers' Corps,
or within his own old Army family. But they had
smoldered on deep down in his belly where he lived,
and they flared hot and bright now.

*Hail, Universe! If this night is your gift to me, I thank
you for it.*

Bolde called up a large-scale tactical map on the
big screen. Tilting the seat back, he studied the dis-

play, absorbing each terrain feature and deployment point.

They would be overwhelmingly outnumbered, but that was almost an irrelevancy. Classically, cavalry almost always fights outnumbered. But then again, the cavalry trooper almost always had three good allies ready to ride at his side: speed, shock, and surprise. Utilize them properly, and they could go a long way toward leveling the odds. He must use them in precisely the right way tonight.

Also, while the modern armored cavalry section was, pound for pound and trooper for trooper, the most tactically powerful small military unit in history, he must dole that power out one critically metered spoonful at a time to maximize its effect against the enemy. Definitely a most interesting exercise.

Without Bolde realizing it, his lips pursed and a whispering whistle drifted around the command cab.

> *"For seven years I courted, Sally,*
> *Away, you rollin' river.*
> *For seven years she would not have me.*
> *Away, I'm bound away, crossed that wide*
>   *Missouri . . ."*

Mary May Jorgenson stood beside *CHARLIE* in the twilight, putting the gun drone through a systems check cycle. As with the section command vehicle, *CHARLIE* was an MM15 Shinseki Multi-Mission Combat Vehicle configured for armored cavalry operations, a sleekly angular boat-shaped hull the size of a large RV, riding on eight man-tall tires. Unlike *ABLE*, it carried a decisively different payload of systems and weapons. *CHARLIE*, and his brother *BAKER*, were the dedicated stone killers of the team.

Configured for robotic operation, *CHARLIE*'s cab

windshield and crew gunports had been plated over.
Squat sensor turrets were mounted in the driver's
and commander's hatches, giving the drone a
slightly froglike appearance. A low casemate had
been fitted atop the aft third of the hull, the mount
for a Lockheed/IMI 35mm booster gun. The slender, jacketed tube of the hypervelocity weapon extended the full length of the drone's spine to a point
five feet beyond its nose.

Using the trackball on the remote testing pad,
Mary May tested the fifteen-degree traverse and elevation of the booster gun, then cycled the chain
drive of the action, carefully keeping the magazines
and propellant tanks on safety. Her head tilted in
the dimming light, she critically listened to the clatter of the rotary breech mechanism, trusting her own
judgment as well as the pad displays.

The blip of another key tested the twelve CMM
artillery rounds slumbering in their vertical-launch
array in the drone's forward compartment. The
touch of a third verified the readiness of the Claymore reactive panels scabbed onto *CHARLIE*'s composite armor skin. Checks done. Boards green. Mary
May unjacked the remote pad from the drone's exterior systems access. They were ready to rock.

Boots crunched on the gravel of the *qued* as Nathan Grey Bird trudged up from *BAKER*'s parking
point. Her assistant scout leader had been running
an identical testing cycle of the second drone.
"How's Mr. B looking, Nate?" Mary May inquired.

"Pretty much good," the stocky, bronze-skinned
trooper replied. "One of the secondary link aerials
was acting sort of shorty, so I replaced it. And that
first wheel motor on the right side's leaking oil
again. I topped it up and we'll be okay for tonight,
but for sure we got a busted seal on that unit."

Mary May nodded. "I'll write it up. The next time we see the shop column, we'll get it pulled."

"Whenever that might be." Grey Bird grinned, white teeth flashing. "We pulling out soon?"

"The LT says as soon as we hit full dark. I'd say that'll be inside the hour." Mary May passed Grey Bird her testing pad. "Secure that for me, will you, Nate. Then go on up to *ABLE* and kill some rations. We'll eat, then switch off on picket with Johnny and Lee so they can get a not-on-the-move meal, too."

"You got it, Five. You comin' along now?"

"In a minute. Save me the pizza MRE if Rick hasn't already snagged it out of the box."

Mary May caught up her carbine from where it leaned against one of *CHARLIE*'s wheels and started back down the wash. Warrant Officer Shelleen had walked down the draw a few minutes before, and the scout wanted to verify that everything was all right with her. Or at least that was the excuse Mary May gave herself.

In actuality, she was motivated by a continuing and nagging curiosity about Saber's systems operator. When Mary May had elected to join the Army, one of her reasons had been to see new things and meet new people. Never in her wildest imaginings however had she ever visualized herself serving beside a genuine, spell-casting, card-carrying witch.

A smile tugged at the corner of her mouth. She never mentioned Warrant Officer Shelleen's religious preferences in any of her letters home. Mary May's family were all hard-shell Lutheran, and she didn't need Uncle Joseph and Aunt Gertrude writing their congressmen.

Mary May lightened her footsteps as she approached the shallow bay in the wall of the wash that she had seen Warrant Officer Shelleen enter, not de-

siring to disturb, yet aware that she might. In the
growing shadows she noted a slender figure kneeling
on the sand of the *qued* floor, facing away to the
south. A palm-sized splash of diesel oil burned bluely
on the ground before her, and the silver-hafted dagger the SO carried lay on the sand at her knees, its
blade aimed at the heart of the flame. Bridget Shelleen's arms were uplifted shoulder high, and her
head was lowered, a soft whispered pattern of words
escaping from her lips.

Mary May hesitated, a ripple of unease touching
her, the discomfort sometimes felt by the average
person when in the presence of a truly and genuinely
devout individual.

Shelleen's whisper faded away and the whicker of
the wind in the wash was the only lingering sound.
For a long minute, the systems operator continued
to kneel, statue-still. Then, gracefully, she leaned forward and scooped up a double handful of sand and
poured it over the patch of flame. Lifting the dagger
from the ground, she made a decisive gesture with
it as if she were slashing through some invisible line
or thread that surrounded her. The blade disappeared into her boot sheath and the redhead rose
and turned to face Mary May, her movements an effortless catlike flow.

Unnerved at so suddenly finding herself regarded
by those large and level green eyes, Mary May asked
with a forced lightness, "Casting a spell on the Algis,
Miss Shelleen?"

A wisecrack wasn't at all what she had wanted to
say but she'd had to do something to recover her
equilibrium.

"Oh no," Shelleen replied with a calm seriousness.
"The Law of Return would make that a very bad
idea."

"The Law of Return?"

"Yes. One of the root laws of all magic," the systems officer replied, picking up her flak vest and pistol belt from where she had set them aside. " 'So as you conjure, so shall you receive back fourfold.' Invoking a negative conjuration, a black magic if you will, against the Algerians could come back and hit us far harder than it would the enemy. I was only addressing the Lord and the Lady, asking them for strength, protection, and wisdom for us all this night."

Mary May tilted her head questioningly. "You mean like you were only praying?"

"Essentially." Shelleen smiled back.

The two women started back up the ravine to the vehicle hide through the deepening shadows. Overhead, the first star seeped through the darkening blue of the sky.

"War," Mary May asked eventually. "Can I ask you something?"

"Why not?"

"Well, the word is that you were once a model in New York or something. How did you ever become . . . a soldier?"

Again, "soldier" wasn't what she'd meant to say, but that's how it had come out. The warrant officer shot her a knowing glance and smiled again.

"Yes, I did have the start of a modeling career once," she replied, slinging her flak vest over her shoulder. "I also had the start of a very unhappy, meaningless, and self-destructive life. So I started to look around for something to hold on to. Eventually, I found the beliefs of my Celtic ancestors, Wicca or Paganism as it is known to some. It was something that worked for me, giving me a degree of peace although not of contentment.

"I continued my studies and, upon my becoming a priestess, I elected to confront my destiny once and for all. I undertook a time of fasting and spiritual seclusion, a spirit quest as it is called by the American Indian. During it, I asked for the Lady to show me the path I should be following during this stage of my life."

"Did she?" Mary May asked, intrigued in spite of herself.

Shelleen nodded. "She did. She came to me as the Lady of the South Wind, armor-clad, the guardian and the woman warrior. I had my answer. So, I went back to New York, fired my agent, tore up my contracts, and joined the Army."

She smiled a sudden impish grin. "And yes, there are any number of people who think that I have gone totally and completely insane."

Mary May chuckled. "A lot of my family think the same thing about me. What do you think now? Was it the right call?"

Bridget Shelleen paused just short of *ABLE*'s tail ramp and swept her arm around the vehicle hide. "Here, I find I am centered," she replied, looking into the scout's face. "Here, for the first time in my life, I can say that I am exactly where I'm supposed to be. If you can do that, I suppose you aren't doing so badly."

Mary May Jorgenson could not disagree.

The South Face of the El Khnachich Range
Three-quarters of a Mile West of the Taoudenni Caravan Road
2335 Hours, Zone Time; October 28, 2021

The only illumination within the cab came from the glow of the instrument displays, that odd gray-green unlight that is compatible with night-vision systems. The only light beyond the sloped windshield issued from the cold and distant stars.

At the walking pace of a healthy man, the three vehicles of Saber section ground upward toward the saddleback, the two gun drones trailing *ABLE* nose to tail, like obedient circus elephants. Normal operating doctrine called for an unmanned vehicle always to be out on point, cybernetically scouting and taking the initial risk. However, the rugged irregularity of this night's drive mandated that a human intelligence break the trail.

As *ABLE* hunched and clawed her way upslope, Rick Santiago relished the feel of handling the big war machine. As a kid back in Arizona, there wasn't a tractor pull, off-road race, or monster truck bash within a hundred miles of Wickenburg that he hadn't attended. By the time he'd graduated from high school, he'd built up both a perilously hot Ford F150 pickup and a terror-of-the-desert reputation.

Unfortunately, few job prospectuses listed driving crazy in the dirt as a prime desired attribute.

Then came the day when an enterprising Army recruiter brought a transport variant of the Shinseki Multi-Mission Combat Vehicle to a hill climb outside of Yuma. Rick and a lot of other young people stood by in awe as that magnificent eight-wheeled monster shamed some of the best ATVs and 4X4s in the Southwest, Rick had filled out his enlistment papers that day, sitting in the Shinseki's cab.

"Okay, people," Lieutenant Bolde murmured over the helmet intercom. "We're getting in close. Column stealth up and go to batteries."

Miss Shelleen replied with a soft verbal acknowledgment as she dialed the command into the drone datalinks. Rick answered by clicking a switch se-

quence. The breathy whine of *ABLE*'s twin turboge-
nerator sets faded away, leaving only the purr of the
multiple drive motors and the crunch of the mountain rubble beneath the mushy all-terrain tires.

The key to the Shinseki's amazing flexibility and
performance was its composite electric-drive system.
Two lightweight UMTec 1000 ceramic gas turbines
spun a pair of electrical generators. The generators
pumped power into the banks of rechargeable iron-
carbide batteries under *ABLE*'s deck plates, and
these batteries, in turn, fed the 150-horsepower radial electric-drive motors built into the hubs of each
ground wheel. No gears, no clutch, no driveshaft,
just instant power on demand.

There were other advantages as well. Spinning
constant speed at their most efficient RPM setting,
the turbines drew the maximum power potential
from each liter of fuel consumed. And for those
times, such as now, when stealth was at a premium,
the turbines could be shut down. Operating on battery power alone, the armored cavalry vehicle's thermal and audile signatures were greatly reduced.

Through his night-vision visor, Santiago noted a
change in ground texture ahead. A shale patch on
the hillside angled down to the left. He eased the
all-wheel steering over, hunting uphill for better traction.

But not quite far enough.

Rick felt the hill shift beneath *ABLE*, the deck
slewing and tilting as loose shale slid away beneath
the left-rear tires. The cavalry vehicle lurched, threatening to twist crosswise and slide in the beginning
of its own avalanche. Santiago's foot rocked forward
on the accelerator, slamming 1200 horsepower into
the ground. *ABLE* responded like a hard-spurred
cow pony. Lunging upgrade, she scrabbled to solid

ground, tire cleats paddlewheeling in the stone fragments.

Rick Santiago grinned into the night. ¡Hijole! *And
they're paying me for this!* "You're gonna want to edge
the drones over to the right a few yards, Miss Shelleen," he called back to the systems station. "We got
a little patch of soft stuff here."

And then they were at the crest of the saddleback
with only the downslope and a great darkness before
them. Bolde cycled through the vision modes of his
helmet visor and surveyed that darkness. By standard
light, there was only the starblaze of the sky and the
black horizon line of the not-sky. By switching to
the night brite option, he could use the starlight to
make out another great expanse of gravel pan and
sand dune stretching out from the northern face of
the range.

Here and there, well out into the desert, were also
occasional flickers and flares of transitory illumination. Bolde recognized them as light leaks caught by
his photomultipliers: dashboard glow, lantern gleam
escaping through a gap in a tent door, a sloppily
used flashlight. Hints of the presence of a bivouack-
ing army.

It was not until he switched from the gray world
of the night brite vision to the glowing green one of
the thermographic imager that all was made clear.
Glowing cyan geometries like the patterns on a
snake's back stretched across the horizon. Other individual dots of light and stumpy luminous caterpil-
lars crept and crawled between them.

This was the infrared portrait of an army at rest.
Each geometric was a company-sized laager point,
each dot of light the signature of a parked armored
fighting vehicle. The steel hulls stood out as they ra-

diated the heat absorbed during the day back into the chilling night. No doubt the Algerians had anti-IR tarps deployed, but insulation could only do so much against the vivid thermal contrasts of the Sahara environment.

The moving green points of light would be liaison and supply vehicles bringing up the food, the fuel, and the thousand and one other things an army on the march required. They were like the red corpuscles of a bloodstream, carrying oxygen to the muscles of a limb, giving it strength. And as with a bloodstream, if that flow was cut off, gangrene and death would rapidly follow.

"Column . . . halt," Bolde said lowly.

ABLE crunched to a stop, *BAKER* and *CHARLIE* following suit in robotic obedience.

"Okay, Mary May. We're at drop point. Your people set to take a walk?"

The scout leader moved forward to crouch beside Bolde's seat, her tall and rangy frame bulked out by full field gear.

Curved ballistic plates of bulletproof ceramic had been slipped into the plate pouches in her BDU shirtsleeves and trouser legs and snugged tight with Velcro strap-tabs. An interceptor flak vest shielded her torso as a combat helmet protected her head. In addition to its integral squad radio and night-vision system, spring-wire leads connected the helmet's HUD (Heads-Up Display) with the SINCGARS Leprechaun B communications and navigation system clipped to Mary May's load-bearing harness and to the BattleMAC tactical computer strapped to her left forearm.

This night she would be carrying thirty-five pounds of body armor and personal electronics alone, without the consideration of weapons, ammunition, incidentals, and the gallon of water in her MOLLE harness reservoir. Such was the reason females were still rare within the Ground Combat Specialists' rating. Even in the twenty-first century, the foot soldier still required a healthy dose of pack mule in their genetic makeup.

"Set, LT," she replied. "Ready to go down the ramp."

"Acknowledged, Five. You've got the drill. Get into position. We'll coordinate the strike and recovery as the situation develops. You've got the satellite beacons with you?"

"Two of them, yes, sir."

"Good enough. Take one of the water cans as well and cache it somewhere, just in case. Bravo six knows you're up here. If something Murphys on us, and we don't make it back for pickup, trigger a beacon and lie low. The regiment will get you out."

Mary May grinned through the black-and-brown camouflage paint that covered her face. "I'm not worried, sir. I always leave the dance with the guy who brought me."

Bolde grinned back. "We'll make that our beautiful thought for the day, Five. Take off."

"Yes sir. See you later guys."

"*Adios*, Five. Watch your ass out there."

"Blessed be, Mary May."

Jorgenson moved aft to the scout bay. A brief rattle of equipment followed a whispered command and the tail ramp whirred down. Boots scuffed on anti-skid decking, then crunched on gravel and a cool puff of outside air traveled up the passageway from the rear of the vehicle. The tail ramp closed again and a single whispered word issued from the radio link.

"Clear."

In the starlight beyond the windshield, four
patches of shadow trickled up the right-hand slope
of the saddleback. The three remaining in *ABLE* cab
found themselves acutely aware of their intensified
aloneness.

Bolde spoke in the darkness. "You journeyed this
night, Brid. What do the spirits of this place have to
say about us?"

"The old ones who dwell here wish us neither
good nor evil," the Wiccan warrior replied levelly,
her face underlit by the glow of her console screens.
"They do not know us. They will judge us by our
actions and then make their decision."

"Then let the judgment begin. Okay, Rick. Column forward!"

The only sound over the scout team's tactical circuit
was the rasp of heavy breathing caught by the helmet
lip mikes. It was a half mile climb to the top of the
saddleback ridge that overlooked the pass, mostly
a thirty-to-forty-degree assault up loose shale and
crumbling sandstone. Sometimes the hill was man-
ageable by leaning into the slope, at others a clawing
scramble on hands and knees was required.

Boots sank in and slid back ten inches for every
twelve gained. Clutching fingers gashed on jagged
stone and the dust quenched the flowing blood.
Lungs burned and legs ached beyond all condition-
ing.

Johnny Roman and Nathan Grey Bird bore the primary burden of the Javelin launcher and Johnny
considered himself the luckier half of the team. He
only bore two reload round canisters and their car-
bines. Nat had taken the burden of the launcher itself.

The Jav was a good old piece that could still do a

thorough job on most anything that might be encountered on the battlefield. But the price paid for that kind of firepower was weight. A Javelin launcher with a missile preloaded in the tube weighed fifty pounds. Johnny wryly acknowledged that you couldn't kill an armored fighting vehicle with something you could carry in your hip pocket.

The other fire team didn't have it all that much better either. He could see Mary May and Lee Trebain laboring farther ahead upslope. They were tricked out for grenadier work with SABRs slung across their backs and half a dozen spare magazines each of 20mm grenade and 5.56mm NATO to feed the over-and-under barrels of the twin gun systems. All that plus another Javelin reload each.

All in all, each member of the scout team was humping the near equivalent of his or her own weight up that night black ridge.

Beside Johnny, Nate Grey Bird's feet slithered out from under him and he went facefirst into the slope with a muffled curse. He started to slide backward and Johnny grabbed out for him, snagging his harness.

"You okay, Nate?"

"Yeah, I'm okay," the fiercely whispered reply came back. "It's just that this goddam piece of sewer pipe won't pack worth shit. It keeps throwing me off!"

"You want me to take it for a while?"

"No, I'm okay. It's only a little way to the crest now. I'm gonna take a breather for a second."

"Good idea."

The two troopers collapsed against the slope, striving to catch their breath long enough to take a swig from their water packs.

"When I get back to Purdue to finish my degree,

you know what I'm going to do?" Johnny said after a minute.

"I dunno. What you gonna do, white man?"

"I'm going to write a paper. A combined science and philosophy paper about how environment and situation can affect the theoretically immutable laws of physics."

"I don't get you."

"It's like this. Climbing this damn hill, it feels like we're lugging every damn weapon in the world on our backs. But over on the other side, when the shooting starts, I suspect it's going to feel like we're hardly carrying anything at all."

A dozen yards below the eastern crest of the saddleback, Mary May angled her team into a jagged rock formation that jutted from the scree slope like a miniature castle. "Okay, guys," she said, unslinging the Javelin reload she carried. "Go to ground and set overwatch. I'm going up to take a look around."

"You want me to come too, Five?" Lee Trebain asked from the pocket of shadows he'd claimed.

"Nah, just cover me," she replied, thumbing the takedown stud for her SABR. Disassembling the big weapon into its three primary components, she set aside the grenade launcher and locked the sighting module directly onto the grab rail atop the receiver of the carbine. The repeatedly drilled act took only seconds.

"You sure you don't want me up there?"

"For Pete's sake, Lee, I'm only going to be about forty darned feet up the hill," Mary May snapped back in an aggravated whisper, locking out the carbine's folding stock. "I don't need anyone breathing down my neck. Just watch my back."

Mary May removed an anti-IR cape from a harness

pouch. Drawing the foil-lined camouflage cloth around her, she secured it with a silent, "stealth" Velcro neckband and drew the hood over her helmet. Crawling out of the rock outcropping, she snaked her way upslope on knees and elbows. In a few moments she was at the crest.

Still prone, she eased herself ahead the last few feet, then froze in place. The gut of the pass lay below her.

For the next several minutes she lay unmoving, slowly and deliberately scanning the terrain below and across from her. The barren, steep-sided ridges and precipitous ravines reminded her strongly of the Dakota badlands back home. Deliberately she toggled in the night vision visor of her helmet between thermographics and photomultiplier, seeing what each sensor view had to offer.

Her helmet visor had more to offer than just enhanced vision. It also served as a Heads-Up Display for her other systems. A graphics compass rose scrolled across the bottom of her vision field, giving her an instantaneous bearing on anything she observed. Time and radio-frequency hacks glowed in the corners of her eyes and, as she turned her head, threat arrows pulsed redly, aiming down at every known and plotted hostile position in the area, graphics prompts giving her the range to target.

A look back over her shoulder revealed a trio of blue arrows hovering over the rock formation downslope. Her own team, their location microburst transmitted to her Leprechaun B navigation system from the GPS receivers of their own Leprechaun units.

And in the distance, and drawing steadily farther away, another trio of blue arrows, the troop vehicles and their crew en route to this night's destiny. The only other "blues" within a two-hundred-mile radius.

Mary May shivered in spite of the growing pocket of body heat trapped beneath the IR cape and returned her attention to the pass below.

One of the Algerian scout tracks was parked within her field of vision, the residual heat signature of its armor beginning to fade with the chill of the desert night. A dazzling point of thermal radiation burned close abreast of it, however, possibly a small fuel pellet stove. Given the steam plume rising above it, someone must be heating water for tea or coffee. Spectral green shadows huddled close about it, Algerian soldiers warming their hands in the stove glow and maybe thinking of the night's watch or about home.

Other luminescent forms hovered away from the stove, one in the track's turret, two more on station above and below the vehicle hide. *Sentries*, she thought, staring out into the dark.

Mary May started to ease back below the ridge crest when suddenly she caught more movement in her visor. She froze in place like a startled lizard.

On the barren ridge across from her, a line of four small cyan dots bobbed slowly along.

Lifting her hand up to her helmet, Mary May flipped up her night-vision visor, blinking for a moment in the onrush of true darkness. Then she lifted and aimed her carbine, not to fire but to utilize the magnification and imaging of its more powerful sighting module. The pressure of her thumb on a handgrip stud zoomed her in on target.

An Algi patrol. Each of those Algerian BRM-30s carried a four-person scout team, just like her own, and one such team was conducting a security sweep along the high ground beyond the pass. And if there was a patrol over on that side, likely there was one somewhere over on this side as well.

The other scouts looked up as Mary May slid back into the shelter of the rock pile. She flicked aside her helmet's lip mike, deactivating her squad radio, then spoke in a whisper. "Here's how we're going to work it, guys. The Algis are deployed below us along about a kilometer of the pass floor. Nate, you and Johnny work your way to the south end of the pass, staying out of sight below the crest of this saddle-back. You have the Javelin and you take out the heavies at the pass mouth. Kill the *Tunguska* first! Got that? From down in the bottom of this canyon, the *Centauros* and the BRMs will have trouble elevating their main armament high enough to engage us up here. The quad 30s on that antiair vehicle could saw the top of this ridge right off though. It goes first!"

"He's first blood, Five," Grey Bird's soft reply came back.

"Okay, Lee and I will work our way north. We'll take out the two northernmost BRMs with the grenade launchers, each of us engaging one of the tracks. All initial attacks will be coordinated with Lieutenant Bolde's move on the main body of the Algerian division. We get into position and we wait for the LT to give us the word to open fire. Until we get that word, we are strictly hide and evade. Nobody, and I mean nobody, fires a shot for any reason!

"Once the music starts, the two teams will work in toward each other, picking off the remaining Algi elements as the shots present themselves. These rocks will be our rendezvous point for fallback and extraction. Lock it in."

Fingers touched keypads, calling up and storing GPU fixes in personal navigation systems.

"Set, Five."

"Got it."

"Same."

"Right. Watch your backs. Make your kills. Get back here. That's the show. That and one other thing. We may have some company up here tonight."

Like an infantryman hunkering under cover, *ABLE* retracted its suspension and sank behind the shelter of the low dune, *BAKER* and *CHARLIE* going to ground a quarter of a kilometer off on either flank. Electronic Countermeasures masts unfolded and suspiciously sampled the ether.

The interior of the cab was silent except for the tick and creak of contracting metal and the purr of the systems fans. "Any sign of a ground-scan radar on this side?" Bolde inquired over his shoulder.

"Negative. Just two big air-search systems well off to the east and west," Shelleen replied. "Mobile SAM batteries covering the laager sites. I'm getting tastes of a constant-wave datalink though. They might have a scout drone up."

"We'll watch for it. Rick, you take tactical security while we plot the strike."

"Doin' it, LT," Santiago acknowledged. Accessing the sensors in the commander's cupola via one of the driver's station telescreens, he began a deliberate scan of the surrounding environment.

Bolde assumed control of *ABLE* weapons pack, elevating the boom to its maximum fifty-foot extension for a high-ground overview of their selected objective.

The lead Algerian mechanized battalion had deployed on an open gravel pan, straddling the Taoudenni caravan trail roughly four kilometers beyond Saber section's position. The three maneuver companies were in laager at the points of a two kilometer triangle, the base oriented to the south with the Headquarters Company in the center. Each company position was a weapon-studded island in the desert, creating a mutually supporting archipelago of firepower.

Bolde zoomed in on the nearest laager. The Algerians had learned a few things about desert fighting over the years. They had abandoned the old heavily structured Soviet doctrine in favor of the more flexible and efficient Western-style mixed combat team. One three-tank platoon mated with two four-track infantry platoons. All of the AFVs were parked nose outward in a hundred-meter-wide radial pattern that faced their heaviest protection and armament toward any potential threat.

There would be a sentry posted in every one of those vehicle turrets and a shell or ammunition magazine fed into every gun action. As Bolde looked on, one of the tanks panned its main tube warily across the horizon.

Once upon a time, it had been a Russian-made T-72. However, as Bolde recalled from his technical briefings, little remained that was actually "Russian" barring the bare hull and suspension.

A lightweight Japanese turbocharged diesel had replaced the original power plant, and a Korean-produced copy of a German-designed 120mm smoothbore had been fitted in the turret, replacing the cranky 125mm main gun. A revised velectronics suite had been manufactured in Taiwan, the reactive armor jacketing had come from a factory in Brazil, and the redesign and rebuild had taken place in an Egyptian armaments works.

The end result was an international battlefield "hot rod" considerably more efficient and deadly than the machine that had first rolled out of a Soviet foundry thirty-plus years before. Similar performance upgrades had been applied to the ex-Soviet

BMP Infantry Fighting Vehicles of the infantry elements as well.

Again, located in the center of the position, were the unit headquarters tracks and a covering antiaircraft vehicle. Also present were a pair of massive semitankers and a number of smaller deuce-and-a-half utility trucks. The logistics group was up, bearing with it the fuel, food, water, and ammunition that would be needed for the next day's march. Figures worked around the parked vehicles, unrolling fueling hoses and unloading stores, no doubt thankful for the night's cool.

A swift scan of the other company sites indicated that similar replenishment operations were going on there as well. The timing was right, and the Gods of Battle were smiling.

"Brid, we've got sixteen rounds of antivehicle and eight of antipersonnel in the drone silos. You program the AVs. I want one dropped in on each of the fuel tankers and the command vehicles. I'll take the APs."

Overlooking the pass, Nathan Grey Bird and Johnny Roman struggled on against the burden of both the rugged terrain and their augmented munitions load. They were still several hundred meters short of their firing position. Time was growing tight, and the ridgeline looked even more broken ahead of them.

"Hey Nate," Johnny wheezed. "Hold up. I got an idea."

"Such as?"

"Such as, why don't we cache a couple of these spare Jav rounds here so we can move faster. We'll be working back this way again. We can just pick 'em up when we're ready to use 'em."

"Damn, white man! I'm proud of you! You're starting to think like an Indian. Let's do it."

Farther to the north along the saddleback, Lee Trebain peered cautiously through his firing slit between two boulders. The youthful Texan could see his designated target on the floor of the pass below him. His position was good, the BRM-30 had been backed into the slope between a couple of crude stacked-stone fighting positions. Its tail ramp was down, and Trebain could intermittently make out movement both inside the track and in the gun pits.

Moving with silent care, he verified that a clip of smart rounds was in the grenade launcher of his SABR and that the magazine of 5.56 NATO was well seated in the carbine section. Then he slipped a second clip of 20mm antiarmor projectiles out of a harness pouch, setting them where they could be grabbed in an instant. He'd worked out just exactly how he was going to do this thing. All he had to do was to stay ready for the word.

Trebain tried to keep focused, but he couldn't keep from glancing away toward the north. Toward that next blue friendly arrow glowing in his visor display.

She wasn't moving anymore. She must be set, too. And she had to be all right, right? She was on the squad circuit and she could have yelled for help if something had blown. And there hadn't been any gunfire, and, besides, Mary May could take care of herself.

But then, damn it all entirely, wasn't the guy supposed to look after a girl? That's the way it always been where he'd grown up and the instinct was hard to shake, even when the girl was two inches taller than you were and had three grades of seniority. Lee

closed his eyes and shook his head, trying to clear it
of a confused jumble of emotions and images. He
snapped them open them again when the audile
prompt of the tactical datalink sounded in his helmet earphones. The glowing line of a communication was scrolling across the bottom of his vision
field.

***SABER 6 TO ALL SABER
ELEMENTS***STAND BY TO
ENGAGE***ACKNOWLEDGE READINESS
STATE***

Lifting his hand to his helmet, Lee tapped the
transmit key at the base of his lip-mike boom, giving
his go signal. Flipping his visor up, he settled the
SABR against his shoulder and peered through
the sighting module. Safeties off. Weapons selector
to GRENADE. Mode selector to POINT DETONATION.
Finger on trigger.

Lee Trebain's mind was suddenly as cold and clear
as a mountain spring.

The same message flashed before the eyes of Nathan
Grey Bird and Johnny Roman just as they threw
themselves flat on the overlook above the mouth of
the pass. Below them, at the foot of a steep scree
slope, was a quarter-mile-wide plateau notched into
the range side and the fighting positions of the Algerian blocking force. They'd made it, but just
barely.

"Johnny, let the LT know we're in position! Then
get those reloads ready!"

"Doing it, Nate." Roman blipped the acknowledgment, then popped the end caps off the first of the
two spare Javelin canisters.

Grey Bird plugged the connector lead from the missile launcher's firing unit into his helmet's remote jack and a targeting reticle snapped into existence in the center of his field of vision. Choosing the Javelin's "ballistic engagement" option, he eased up onto his knees. The boxlike firing unit with its handgrip nestled against the side of his head, the connected launcher tube swiveled to angle down his back, its muzzle pointing to the sky. Turning his head slightly, he set the death pip of the sight on the top of the turret of the Algerian antiair track.

Nathan felt his lips peel back in a feral grin. Back in Idaho, his sister had never been happy with his decision to go career Army. Intensely into American Indian activism, she had felt he was selling out his heritage by joining the service that had defeated his people. And she had been extremely unhappy when he had chosen the cavalry as his preferred branch.

Nathan had pointed out in reply that their ancestors had been some of the best mounted warriors the world had ever seen. What greater heritage did he have except as a cavalryman?

She had retired grumbling before he'd had the chance to mention that the regimental assignment he'd been given was to the Seventh. *Hoya,* she was going to go through the roof on that one.

Grey Bird eased down the first trigger, giving the missile its initial look at its target.

"All CMMs designated and the scout teams are in position," Bridget said quietly. "No detected changes in tactical environment. Ready to engage on your command, Lieutenant."

Bolde swallowed with deliberation before replying. All of the preparations, all twenty-five years of them, were over.

So you think you're good, Jeremy Bolde, good enough to take your life into your hands this night. But how about these six other lives you'll be carrying? Does your surety stretch that far? It had better, for when this battle is over, whatever remains will be your responsibility.

"Right. Stand by for conversion to direct linkage control. I'll take *BAKER*. You've got *CHARLIE*. Stand by for turbine start. All units!"

"Turbine start armed on drones."

"*ABLE* ready to light off, LT."

Bolde typed the ***ALL SABER ELE-MENTS***COMMENCE ENGAGEMENT NOW*** command into the scout team datalink and poised a finger on the transmit key. "Good luck to us all, ladies and gentlemen," addressing those who were present and those who were not. "May we all be discussing this over a cup of coffee come morning. Open fire!"

Flame geysered from the backs of the gun drones. Twelve rounds per vehicle, launching at half-second intervals, a spreading fountain of destruction. The Common Modular Missile rounds, configured for an artillery-fire mission profile, climbed almost vertically until booster burnout. Then guidance fins snapped out of the main stages and dug into the air. Arcing over the Algerian armored formation, the missiles pitched nose down, hunting for targets.

The infrared sensors in the noses of the anti-vehicle rounds scanned for a specific geometric size and shape on the ground. One that matched that of the prey assigned to them. The antipersonnel rounds steered in via Global Positioning System fix, the proximity fuses in their warheads concentrating on their altitude above ground. As each missile locked in, its main engine ignited, blasting it through the sound barrier and down out of the sky.

The antipersonnels detonated while still a thousand feet in the air. Each "beehive" warhead burst to release a spreading conical swarm of needle-nosed and razor-finned flechette darts, thousands of them, in a supersonic steel rain, a titanic shotgun blast sweeping the open ground clean of life.

The antivehicle rounds arrived a split second later, before the standing dead even had a chance to fall to the earth. Flaming pile-driver strokes that crushed and destroyed.

The targeted fuel tankers popped like bursting balloons, sprayed diesel flaming as the warheads exploded deep in their guts. Likewise the headquarters tracks lurched, belching fire and shredded flesh out through their doors and hatches. The command personnel whose task it was to coordinate a defense, perished before they even knew an attack was under way.

And amid the chaos and confusion, no surviving sentry immediately noted the three small thermal plumes that hazed into existence out in the desert night, the one turning away and the two closing the range.

The charge had been sounded.

From his firing position between the two boulders, Lee Trebain dropped his grenades in around the Algerian scout track, being exceedingly careful *not* to place them too close to the parked vehicle. From personal experience, Trebain knew what the first instinct of a fighting vehicle crewman was when suddenly placed under attack. *Saddle up and get under armor!*

Trebain had no desire to interfere with that instinctive reaction. Not yet.

The turret of the scout track swiveled around and

up-angled, ripping off a 30mm reply to his volley of grenades. The autocannon shells tore a gash across the slope twenty meters below his position, kicking up dust and stinging stone fragments. Hot damn! Mary May had called it right! They couldn't fire up out of the gorge!

The turret gun raved off another long futile burst, covering the figures scrambling aboard through the vehicle's lowered tailgate. Through the thermographic sights of the SABR, Trebain saw a luminous green mist belch from the track's exhaust as the engine kicked over, the ramp beginning to close.

Now! Now was the time to take them!

Trebain ejected the empty clip from the grenade launcher and slammed the fresh magazine of anti-vehicle shells into its place. Holding the death dot of his sights on the turret of the Algerian scout track, he again pulled the trigger.

Like many armored fighting vehicles, the Algerian BRM had reactive armor panels scabbed to its hull and turret. Made up of sheets of low-grade plastic explosive sandwiched between two thin metal plates, reactive armor defeated shaped-charge antitank warheads by exploding upon the impact of the warhead, the counterblast "defocusing" the warhead's detonation, leaving the protected vehicle undamaged.

Unfortunately for the Algerians, each reactive panel only worked once.

Lee Trebain rapid-fired the six rounds in his launcher magazine, the SABR's recoil thumping his shoulder. The first two grenades kicked reactive panel flares off the BRM's turret. The next four drilled cleanly through steel.

The holes punched by the grenades were only the diameter of a pencil. Each puncture, however, spewed a supersonic jet of flaming gas and molten metal into the confined space of the track's interior. One such jet, as hot and destructive as the fire blade of an acetylene torch, slashed across the ammunition tray of the turret gun.

The BRM shuddered to a halt. Its deck hatches blew open and a protracted series of detonations flickered and reverberated within the vehicle, like a string of firecrackers dropped into a trash can. Afterward nothing emerged from the vehicle except for a growing plume of smoke.

Trebain became aware of more explosions around him. Some were nearby and echoing sharply through the canyon. Other heavier blasts rolled in from the northern horizon, a skyline that now glowed an angry flickering orange.

Trebain backed crablike out from between the two boulders and slid a few meters down the reverse slope of the saddleback. Hugging the ground, he flipped his night-vision visor back down. Warily he scanned his environment as he dug a fresh 20mm clip out of a harness pouch.

Running footsteps sounded behind him and he whipped around, freezing his trigger pull as he caught the blue flash in his Heads-Up Display. Mary May dropped beside him a moment later. "How'd you make out?" she demanded.

"Clean house. Track and crew. How 'bout you?"

"Same. That's two down. Let's go see how the other guys are doing."

"Right behind you, Five."

A half klick to the south, Nathan Grey Bird's finger closed around the Javelin launcher's second trigger.

The hollow thump of the launching charge followed, kicking the missile out of the tube. The missile itself did not ignite until it was well clear of the

launcher and the operator both. Flaming away in a
high-curving trajectory, it dived on its target from
above, the one angle of attack unshielded by either
reactive armor or heavy steel.

The *Tunguska* exploded spectacularly, bursting
30mm shells intermixing with flaming rocket fuel.
"Ayeee!" Grey Bird screamed. "I count coup! Feed
me, white man, I'm on a roll!"

"Loading!" Johnny Roman slammed the next missile into the smoking breech of the launcher, then
rolled aside. "Round loaded! Clear!"

The launcher barked again and the second round
burned across the sky, wobbling slightly as it hunted
for the heat signature of its target, stabilizing again
as it found what it sought. The more distant of the
pair of *Centauro* tank destroyers lifted off the ground
on a pad of flame, its turret blowing off and flipping
away.

"That's two! Keep 'em coming!"

Above the crackle of ammunition heat firing in
the burning wrecks, screams and shouts echoed up
from the pass mouth along with the sound of crank-
ing diesels. The Algerians were reacting to the attack.
Wildly and without coordination, but that would
come swiftly as the shock effect wore off. Grey Bird
and Roman had only seconds of clear time remaining.

The second *Centauro* was the closest of their three
targets, immediately below them at the foot of the
steep slope that led down into the pass mouth.
They'd saved it for last because it would be the easiest snap shot. Nate locked the launcher into direct-
fire mode as Johnny slammed the last Javelin into
the tube. Springing to his feet and aiming downward, Grey Bird acquired the target in his helmet
sight and squeezed the trigger.

At that instant, the *Centauro*'s driver, reacting to the sure and certain knowledge that a moving target is harder to hit, slammed his eight-wheeled mount into gear and floored his accelerator. The tank destroyer lurched forward, not swiftly enough to escape the homing missile fired at it, but enough to divert its impact point. The Javelin clipped the flank of the *Centauro*'s turret and a reactive armor panel detonated, swatting the missile aside. Undamaged, the tank destroyer roared out of its field revetment, its turret gun traversing and elevating.

Roman and Grey Bird could only stare at each other and at the empty launcher.

"Uh-oh."

"To which I can only add 'Oh shit'! Let's get out of here!"

Below, the *Centauro*'s driver rammed the front wheels of his vehicle up the slope, giving his gunner the extra angle he needed to engage the ridgeline. An instant after the two scouts had thrown themselves back down the opposite slope, a 105mm round gouged a notch in the hill crest, the concussion and battering spray of stone fragments sending both men sprawling into the jumble of broken rock that covered this section of the saddleback.

They would become grateful for that momentarily.

Dazed, and with his ears ringing, Grey Bird lifted his head. "Johnny, you okay?" he yelled.

"Yeah. Nate." A familiar but equally groggy voice replied over the squad circuit. "What do we do now?"

"We crawl back and get those other two Javelin rounds, that's what we do. Then we kill that damn tank destroyer before the Five and the LT find out how bad we screwed up."

Grey Bird started to pull himself upright. He spotted Johnny's "friendly" prompt in his helmet visor,

pointing down into a boulder field a short distance
to his left. However he also spotted an ominous, un-
marked green glow downhill at perhaps a hundred
meters.

"Algis! Down!"

Assault-rifle fire spattered his rocks a split second
after he dived back behind them. With his own carbine still slung over Johnny's shoulder, Grey Bird
yanked his Beretta out of his belt holster. A handgun
was a poor second in any kind of a serious firefight
but at the moment it was far better than nothing.

A short chopping burst of 5.56 NATO sounded
from off on his left. "I got four of them spotted,
Nate," Roman reported. "They're trying to work a
skirmish line up toward us. They must be one of
those Algi scout teams the Five warned us about."

Behind their position, another shell ripped into
the ridgeline, showering the two pinned troopers
with a fresh barrage of stone fragments. Grey Bird
burrowed closer to the jagged rock he lay upon.

"You know something, white man?" he said, spitting a mouthful of grit aside.

"What?"

"All of a sudden I'm developing this great feeling
of empathy for General Custer."

Jeremy Bolde's hand closed around his console joystick, and suddenly he was looking through *BAKER*'s
cybernetic eyes, the imaging from the onboard cameras feeding into the Heads-Up Display of his helmet.

You could maneuver and deploy gun drones via
microburst transmissions over a datalink, in effect is-
suing suggestions to the onboard artificial intelligences. Actual combat, however, required a human
telepresence. It was as if he rode the back of the

charging steel beast in the ultimate video game gone real.

The system was configured to trackfire mode; the cart-wheel sights of the booster gun hovered in front of his eyes. Wherever he aimed those sights, so would the drone steer itself. Data hacks glowed around the perimeter of his vision: speed, ammunition, vehicle systems status, and ahead glowed a small forest of hostile target arrows stabbing downward accusingly at the enemy. His forefinger tightened on the throttle trigger and a flick of his thumb lifted the safety cover off the firing switch, triggering the hot gun warning tone.

"Right through the middle, Brid," he murmured. "I'll work left to right. You have right to left. Engage."

"Engaging," the quiet one-word reply returned over the inter-phone.

Bolde laid his sights on the first silhouetted armored fighting vehicle as he might have aimed a target pistol and pressed the thumb button.

Two kilometers away, the first round cycled into *BAKER*'s booster gun. It wasn't a shell in a conventional sense, rather it was a slender "kinetic kill" dart encased in a sabot sheath, a simple finned crow-bar of superdense inert uranium encased in a superhard tungsten steel alloy.

The dart itself carried no propulsive powder charge. Instead, injectors spewed a metered dose of a liquid explosive propellant into the breech chamber behind the round. Ignited by an electric arc, the incandescent gas of this initial detonation hurled the dart on its way as with a conventional cannon. However as the projectile accelerated down the barrel, secondary injectors spaced down the length of the smoothbore cannon tube fired in sequence, building the breech pressure and pushing the dart to a velocity far higher than could be obtained from a conventional weapon.

Three rounds were fired in as many seconds, an X of blue-white flame spewing from the cannon's muzzle brake.

Downrange, an Algerian T-72 died. Neither its reactive armor nor the heavier steel beneath were enough to save it. The tungsten-and-uranium darts passed through the tank's hull like heated needles through butter. The passage converted kinetic energy into heat and instead of solid projectiles, jets of metallic plasma exploded into the tank's interior, burning at the temperature of a star's surface.

Bolde swung his sights onto the next target in the laager. Shock and surprise had done their parts. Now they must rely on speed, wreaking as much havoc as they could before the Algerians recovered.

The vehicles around the laager perimeter flared like the candles on a birthday cake as the fire streams of the two gun drones converged. Over the intercom link Jeremy could hear Bridget Shelleen's whispered supplication with each press of her trigger key.

"Lord and Lady . . . Hold your hands above us this night . . . Grant pardon for these lives we must take . . . Grant peace to those we must slay . . ."

"Scout lead! We got trouble here!"

Mary May paused in her jogging run and dropped to a crouch beside a stone slab. Lee Trebain following her lead an instant later. "Go, Nate. What's happening?"

"We're blown," the Indian trooper rasped back over the squad circuit. "We been nailed by an Algi patrol."

"Tac situation? Are either of you hit?"

"We're under good cover, but pinned. Four hostiles on our front. Johnny and me are both okay, but we can't maneuver. We bitched the strike and one of the *Centauros* is still operational. It has the ridgeline covered behind us. We can't fall back."

"Oh, jeez! We're hearing small-arms fire from the south. That must be you guys. Can you hold?"

"For a while, Five."

"Understood," Mary May acknowledged. "We'll be up with you as soon as we can. Hang in."

"We don't have all that much choice," Grey Bird replied with wry grimness.

Trebain had been monitoring the same series of transmissions, and now he scrambled. "The guys are in trouble. Let's go!"

"Like I said, we'll get to them as soon as we can." Mary May started back up to the ridge crest. "We still have four Algi scout tracks down in that canyon we have to take care of."

"Hey, Mary May. Nate and Johnny are in trouble!"

"Darn it, Lee. I know it!" she snapped over her shoulder. "But the lieutenant and Miss Shelleen and everybody will be in trouble if we let those tracks bust out! Now load antiarmor and come on!"

Trebain swore under his breath and followed.

The growl of engines and the squeak and chatter of tracks echoed up from the pass floor. The Algerian BRMs were on the move. Rolling north at a fast walking pace, they had their scout teams deployed as flank guards. Warily, the Algerian mobile troopers advanced, scanning the walls of the pass on either side. There would be no surprising this bunch.

Lying side by side, Mary May and Trebain watched them advance. "How we working this?" Trebain growled.

"You kill that lead track. I'll peel the infantry."

Mary May flipped her visor up and settled her eye to the sighting module of her SABR. "One magazine, then pull back fast. On my mark. Three . . . two . . . one . . . shoot!"

The two grenade launchers barked out their vest-pocket artillery barrage. The lead BRM flared and exploded under Trebain's fire stream while Mary May walked a string of laser-ranged airbursts down the left-hand column of dismounted flankers.

The surviving Algerian infantry scattered and went to ground. Their earlier-gen night-vision goggles picked up the muzzle flashes on the ridge crest and assault rifles began to crackle an angry response. The surviving BRMs reversed gear and backed up the roadway like a trio of startled crayfish. In the turret hatches, the track commanders swiveled their deck machine guns in line with the threat and opened fire, hosing streams of greenish tracers into the night.

"Lee, fall back!" Mary May rose to a half crouch, intent on dropping the last shell in her clip in on the second track in line.

"Mary, get down." Trebain lunged to his feet, grabbing for her harness. Then the bullet hail was chopping up the stone around them. Mary May flipped backward off the crest in a credible parachute landing roll. Trebain tried to follow but a 7.65 NATO round took his right leg out from under him. The ballistic plate covering his shin deflected the slug but the limb went numb from ankle to hip.

Lee fell forward in a sprawl. He felt himself start to slide. Good God Almighty, he was falling down the front face of the ridge! He clawed at the crumbling slope, trying for a hold, but he only succeeded in making himself tumble. Caught in the midst of a miniature landslide, Lee lost his grip on his weapon.

Stars burst behind his eyes as he found himself battered away from consciousness.

"Brid, cut across the laager and then engage the command company! We'll use the fires for thermal masking."

"I'm with you." The contralto reply remained cool and focused.

"Rick. Drop Jabberwockys and commence disengagement! Head for the extraction route."

"Doin' it, LT!"

ABLE swerved and accelerated, jinking across the pans like a broken-field runner, her belly racks thumping as the first Jabberwocky beacon kicked clear. Inside the cybernetic world of his battle helmet Bolde's eyes flicked over to the time display, counting seconds. The three S's had done as much as could be hoped for and soon the Algerians would be reacting, violently, to this assault.

The danger now lay in the fact that Saber section had revealed itself by radiating. The continuous-wave datalinks that now connected the command vehicle with its fighting drones could be detected and locked in on by radio direction finders. Because of the jitter frequency technology used, it wouldn't be easy, but given enough time, a minute or two, the Algerian Electronic Warfare battalion would have a fix on them. Once that happened, the word would be flashed to the division's artillery regiment and hellfire and damnation would rain from the sky.

The Jabberwocky decoys, small, high-discharge radio transponders that produced a false signal similar to *ABLE*'s emissions signature, could buy them a little more combat time. So would staying on the move and not presenting a fixed target for the direction finders.

The question was, just how much.

BAKER and *CHARLIE* raced through the perimeter of the shattered Algerian mechanized company. Not a single vehicle remained intact, and flames leaped from the torn hulks. There were still men alive, though, a few stunned survivors, and mostly they fled or cowered in the presence of the angular, multiwheeled demons that had come howling in from the desert. A few, though, still strove to resist.

Bolde caught the backflash of a rocket launch out of the corner of his eye. Some thirty meters to the left, an Algerian infantryman crouched in the shelter of a wrecked BMP, the tube of a light antitank weapon at his shoulder and leveled at *BAKER*. Caught by surprise there was nothing that Bolde could do. However, with light-swift electronic reflexes, the gun drone defended itself.

Thermal sensors recognized the exhaust flare of the rocket and the onboard AIs triggered the Claymore reactive panel in line with the threat. A more sophisticated cousin of conventional reactive armor, the Claymore panel exploded, its front face fragmenting into thousands of small tungsten cubes. Sprayed into the path of the incoming rocket, they chewed the projectile apart in midair. And not the rocket alone, the expanding wave of shrapnel reached out and engulfed the missile man as well.

Moments later the drone tore out through the far side of the laager perimeter and Bolde executed the turn in toward the Algerian Headquarters Company. There was a logic to Bolde's charge directly through the enemy encampment. Any infrared sight aimed at the gun drones from the central enemy position would be blinded by the heat aura thrown off by the blazing hulks of their first kills. Any enemy gunner seeking to engage them would also be presented with the quandary of having his own troops in his line of fire.

The drone's 35s raved on. The last of the communications and command vans died. The mortar carriers and ammo hogs of the Algerian heavy-weapons section exploded, the glare momentarily overloading the videolinks. Wild missiles tore loose from the disintegrating antiair vehicle, jittering madly across the sky. Bolde became aware of a squealing warning tone and a pulsing red flag in his vision field. Barrel overheat! The drones had expended almost half of their two-hundred-round base load, and their titanium-lined gun tubes were going incandescent.

Damnation! Just when they were getting some real work done!

"Brid, deploy smoke! Execute breakaway! Come right to one two zero!"

Multispectral smoke canisters thumped out of secondary projectors, burying the drones in a synthetic fogbank, and the two vehicles turned away from the havoc they had produced, racing back into the undamaged darkness of the night.

Bolde called up a command on *BAKER*'s ordnance menu, releasing a blast of chill carbon dioxide gas down the barrel of the drone's main gun. "Brid, execute a thermal purge. We're going in again."

There was a warning edge to Shelleen's reply. "Lieutenant, may I remind you that we've been radiating continuously for almost five minutes."

"You may, Miss Shelleen, but I want one more Algi company torn up. We'll hit the one to the southeast. Come left to zero eight zero and engage as you bear!"

The drones described a dusty curve across the desert toward their next objective, bucketing over the sand ripples in the plain.

This time it was different. This time the Algerians had been given the opportunity to recover from the initial CMM strike. Tank guns spewed fire and tracer streams snaked along the ground. Bolde weaved and swerved his robotic command, snapping off counter-shots as his sights aligned. One Algerian vehicle burst into flames. A second, a third . . .

Suddenly the image from *BAKER*'s cameras blurred under a concussive impact. A pattern of red-and-yellow system warning flags blazed in front of Bolde's eyes and he caught the impression of the world rolling over onto its side, then the datalink broke and his HMD fuzzed into static.

"Hell!" Bolde tore up his useless visor. "We just lost *BAKER*!"

"I saw him go out," Brid reported. "Direct hit with a tank round. Dead one. Orders?"

Bolde dialed up the self-destruct code on *BAKER*'s crisis menu and beamed it off, hoping there was a functional receiver to catch it. "Disengage! Show's over! Get *CHARLIE* out of there. Put him under autonomous control and head him for the extraction point, then kill our transmitters. Rick, balls to the wall and clear the area! We've pushed it about as much . . ."

Beyond *ABLE*'s windscreen, the desert exploded.

Mary May skidded down the unstable slope to the sprawled form amid the slide rubble. Lee shouldn't be moved after a fall such as he had sustained, but he was also three-quarters of the way down to the pass floor and lying on an open hillside. Algerians had pulled back around the next bend in the gorge, but they would be probing again soon.

Grabbing on to his harness, she dragged Trebain a few yards cross-slope to a clump of thorny brush. It wasn't much, but it was all the cover immediately available. Dividing her attention between the canyon floor and her wounded trooper, she made a fast assessment of Trebain's condition.

He was unconscious but breathing. The ballistic plate shielding his right shin had shattered from a direct hit, but the bullet itself had been turned. The leg was rapidly darkening with a massive bruise, and Mary May suspected the limb wasn't going to be much good for a while. Trebain's body armor had also shielded him from the worst effects of his fall. Beyond a concussion and a sizable collection of bangs and abrasions he appeared intact. A good thing as there wasn't much she could do at the moment beyond applying a few jets of aerosol disinfectant.

As she completed her inspection, she heard him moan softly.

"Hush, Lee. You're okay," she said quietly.

"Mar . . . Five . . . what happened?"

"You took one on the armor and fell down the wrong side of the hill. How's your leg feel?"

"My leg . . . Christ! I can't even feel if it's still attached!"

"It is," she replied, stretching out beside him. Peering out beyond the brush clump, she established her firing position. "It's just numb from the shock. Enjoy it while it lasts. I'll bet you've got one heck of a bone bruise there."

"I can't even get it to move." Trebain shook his head, becoming more aware of his environment. "Shit! How in the hell are we going to get back up to the extraction point!"

He started to sit up but Mary caught him by the

shoulder. "Stay down. We could have Algis moving in on us again. I'm not sure how we're going to get out of here yet, but we are. You're going to be okay, Lee. Nobody's leaving you behind. You got my word on it."

The thermal lobe and glare from the burning Algerian track kept overloading her night brite visor. Mary May flipped it up for a few moments and rested her grainy eyes with a look up at the cool star-speckled blackness of the desert sky. Beside her, she heard a soft, dazed chuckle. "Shit! And all this friggin' time I've been worrying about taking care of you."

Distractedly she reached back and patted Trebain on the shoulder. "We take care of each other, guy."

Flipping her visor down again, she keyed her Leprechaun transceiver onto the voice-channel link with the command vehicle. "I'd better let the lieutenant know we've got problems . . . Scout Lead calling Saber Six. Flash Red. Do you copy?"

She repeated the call three times. There was no answer.

ABLE's hull rang like a beaten oil drum, and shrapnel sparked and howled off of her armor plating. For an instant her crew stared down at the ground through her windshield as the concussion of the multiple shell bursts lifted her tail into the air. Then the cavalry vehicle crashed back onto her eight wheels.

"Incoming!" Santiago bellowed, fighting with the wheel to stave off a rollover.

"Oh really? You think?" Shelleen commented through gritted teeth, clinging to the grab bar above her workstation.

Bolde reached across to the driver's console and

slapped the belly rack release, kicking out another set of Jabberwocky decoys. "Brid. Verify that the transmitters are down! Rick. Hard left! Get us out from under the next pattern!"

The driver replied by skidding *ABLE* through a minimum-radius turn that locked the frame levelers to their stops, shooting the cavalry vehicle off at right angles to their prior course. Instants later, chain lightning played across the desert and man-made thunder roared as eight heavy howitzer rounds tore up the ground where they would have been. The Algerian table of organization was artillery heavy, the divisional commander having over eighty tubes and launchers at his disposal. He was employing this awesome sledgehammer now to eliminate the gadfly that had dared to sting his command. The gadfly's only recourse was flight.

"Rick, hard right!"

ABLE swerved again, sprayed gravel roaring in the wheel wells. Flooring his accelerator, Santiago resumed the dash south for the hill range. But again there came the wail and slam of an incoming salvo, the cavalry vehicle barely scurried clear of the shells dropping in its tracks.

A rapid rhythmic thumping came from back aft as the shrapnel-torn rubber sheathing stripped from one of the tires. The wheel held together; its multiple layers of steel and Kevlar cording could withstand more damage then even a conventional metal tank tread, but a limit would be reached . . . soon.

"Dammit! They're tracking us! Brid, are you sure we've got cold boards!"

"Positive," she called back. "We are not emitting, and the threat board is clear. No laser or radar paints or locks!"

"Then there's got to be a drone eyeballing us!

Find it! Rick, shuck and jive! Buy us some time!"

Bolde called up the weapons pack on his controller, heating up the pair of CMM surface-to-air rounds that were always carried ready for use in the box launchers. Elevating and indexing the mount, he began searching for the Algerian's airborne spy.

"I verify a drone," Brid yelled. "I'm getting a datalink trace."

"Can you jam it?"

"I'll need a minute to analyze and match the jitter pattern."

"We don't have a minute."

Another salvo dropped in on *ABLE*. Again they didn't hit behind but around the fleeing cavalry vehicle and only the luck of the draw prevented a direct hit. With the range established the Algerian gunners would switch to anti-tank scatter packs for their next volley.

Wildly, Bolde swept the IR sights of the sensor group across the sky. There! Off to the west, the sight crosshairs acquired a smear of ruddy heat against the cold stars. The Algerian recon drone was running roughly three klicks out and paralleling their course, targeting for the enemy Artillery regiment.

A flick of his thumb set the tracking lock and a rock forward on a coolie-hat switch zoomed the camera in. Bolde got a momentary impression of the skeletal frame of a miniature helicopter, internally lit by the glow of its rotary engine.

There was only the momentary impression because he was already squeezing the trigger that sent both of the antiair CMMs on their way. The last imaging sent to the Algerians by their drone was two wobbling fire trails converging on it from out of the night.

Bolde observed the flash of the missile kill. "Brake hard! Now!" he bellowed.

ABLE's wheels locked up and her tail came around as she broke loose and slithered to a halt, broadside on. And then submunitions shells burst overhead and the desert hissed and sparkled as hundreds of deadly little antiarmor bomblets rained out of the sky just beyond the stalled Shinseki.

"Might as well just let her sit, Rick," Bolde continued calmly. "If they still have us acquired, we'll never get out from under the next one."

The only sound the soft steady-state whine of the turbines. Bolde, Shelleen, and Santiago sat unspeaking in the darkness, thinking their own thoughts and counting the seconds. When fifteen had passed, the next salvo fell . . . half a mile away along the course they had been following. The next dropped at twice that range as the thwarted Algerians stabbed blindly into the dark. Bridget Shelleen chuckled softly at the wonder of being alive.

Bolde released a breath that he had been holding for what seemed to be an amazing length of time. "Rick, get us out of here. Brid, advise Mary May that we're disengaging and tell her to head for the extraction point. Fun's over, people, let's go home."

At a solid 60 K an hour, *ABLE* and the *CHARLIE* drone roared south toward the looming refuge of the El Khnachich range. Bolde kept *ABLE*'s weapons pack trained aft as they fled, scanning their back trail for signs of enemy pursuit or activity.

Beyond the burning wrecks of the battalion they had decimated, the Algerian division was reacting like a kicked ant's nest. Thermal blossoms dotted the night as hundreds of vehicle engines kicked over, the neat pattern of laager sits dissolving as unit commanders strove to regroup into combat formation.

Flares and flashes of gunfire danced around the perimeter as gunners blazed at ghosts in the darkness or even engaged in "blue on blue" duels with their own side.

Bolde grinned. This kind of battlefield hysteria could do more damage to the enemy in the long run than his own direct assault. The smile rapidly dissipated as Brid spoke up from her station. "We've got major problems with the scout team. They've got the Algerian recon company immobilized with about half of the elements destroyed, but they're pinned down as well. They can't get back to the extraction point."

"Get me a direct link with Mary May."

"Not possible. She's too far down in the pass and we're radio blocked. All we have is a relay through Nate and Johnny on the squad circuit."

Bolde twisted around in the command chair. "What in the hell is she doing down in the pass?"

"Lee Trebain apparently took a bad fall down into the cut. Mary May is with him but he's been injured too badly for them to get back up to the ridgeline."

"What about Nate and Johnny? Can they get to them?"

"Again not possible. Nate and Johnny are pinned down by an Algerian patrol at the southern end of the pass about a kilometer away. They haven't taken hits yet, but they can't move. Both fire teams are requesting instructions."

Requesting instructions. The polite military term for begging the CO for a fast miracle. Bolde lifted his wrist to his mouth and wiped away the salty dust caked on his lips. This was his run. He'd set this plan up, and his people had every right in the world to expect that he would get them out the other side of it. Simple statements like, "I misjudged" or "I over-

looked something" were not an option. Her face out-
lined by the screen glow, Brid Shelleen looked at
him, calmly, expectantly.

"Brid, tell the scouts to hang on and stand by.
We're coming to get them. Then pull *CHARLIE* back
in with us. Rick, new game plan. Forget the route
over the saddleback. We're going out through the
pass."

Through the SABR's infrared sights, Mary May
picked out a ghostly pale sphere hovering a few
inches off the ground, the face of an Algerian
trooper. Gingerly he was crawling forward to peer
around the turn of the pass, hugging close to the
rubble along the edge of the roadway. The face was
there for a moment and then gone as the trooper
ducked back.

Flicking the selector setting to AIRBURST Mary May
rested the sight crosshairs just above the point where
the Algerian had disappeared and squeezed the
SABR's trigger.

At the trigger crossed its first detent in its pull, the
SABR's ranging laser produced an invisible pulse of
coherent light that touched its targeting point and
reflected back. The microprocessor in the SABR's
stock computed a range from that laser reflection
and as the grenade launcher itself fired, an induc-
tance coil wrapped around the launcher's barrel
transmitted that range to a microchip buried within
the shell as it screamed down the tube.

The shell itself dispassionately counted out the distance in flight and, over the target, it detonated,
spraying the environment with a handful of shrapnel.

The Algerian trooper did not return.

"What's happening, Five?" Trebain asked.

"Nothin' much. Just a snooper. How are you doing?"

The breath rasped in the Texan's throat. "You were right about the leg. I liked it a lot better when it was numb. I'm trying to tell myself I'm just imagining it, but I think I got a couple of busted ribs, too."

"That's no fun. That happened to me once when I fell off a hayrack. As long as you're breathing all right you'll be okay. You want a hit of feel good?"

"No. I want to stay clear. Maybe I can do something . . . Mary May, maybe you'd better start thinking about getting out of here. Like you said. I'll be okay."

She rolled onto her side and looked back at Trebain. "What's with you, Lee? Do you honestly think I'm going to run out on one of my guys? Get real!"

"Aw hell, Five. It's just that . . . I don't like the idea of the Algis getting their hands on you is all."

Mary May nestled back behind her weapon stock. "Well, thanks, but I don't like the idea of the Algis getting their hands on any of us. And that's not going to happen. The lieutenant'll get us out of this. One way or another."

Almost as if by one of Brid Shelleen's conjurations, a familiar and most welcome voice sounded in their helmet. "Saber Six to Scout Lead. Do you receive?"

Mary May almost broke the transmit key on her lip mike. "Roger that! We copy, Lieutenant!"

"Okay, Mary May. We've got the Cipher drone up and we're relaying through that," Bolde replied over the circuit. "We also have you and Lee spotted, not to mention our friends the Algerians. We see three BRMs around the bend in the pass about two hundred meters south of your position. Do you verify?"

"I verify, Lieutenant. I can hear their engines

idling. We've hurt them pretty bad. I don't think they're exactly sure of what they're up against yet."

"Better and better. We'll be up with you presently, but we're going to need a little bit of assistance. What's your ammunition state in regard to 20mm grenade?"

"Uh, six clips between Lee and me, counting the one in my weapon. Mixed antiarmor and smart round."

"Excellent," Bolde's filtered voice replied with satisfaction. "When I give you the word, I want you to rapid fire it all down the pass in the direction of the Algis. Don't worry about hitting anything in particular. Just make a lot of noise and keep their heads down. Then you and Trebain stand by to mount up fast. Understood?"

"Understood, sir."

"Very well. Then let's proceed. Stand by to commence firing . . . now!"

Mary May's finger closed convulsively on the trigger. As rapidly as she could she hosed the bend in the canyon with high explosives, the sharp popping of the grenade bursts reverberating up and down the pass, the echoes building upon themselves. Ejected shell cases tinkled around her and the frame of the SABR grew warm and then hot as she poured fire through it. Lee, ignoring the pain of his fractured ribs, fumbled clips out of his own harness pouches, feeding her.

She was down to her last three rounds when two massive, dark shapes roared past on the floor of the pass. *ABLE* and *CHARLIE* running side by side and charging headlong for the bend in the canyon. Mary May realized that her barrage had been performing multiple functions. Not only distracting and suppressing any Algerian forward observers but blanket-

ing the sound of Bolde's charge through the pass.
In a moment someone was going to be most unpleas-
antly surprised.

The cavalry vehicles vanished around the curve
and the silvery glare of muzzle flashes reflected off
the walls of the gorge, strobing with the orange of
explosion flame. The hills trembled with the piercing crack of booster-gun fire, the thudding cough of
grenade streams and the slam of Claymore panels.

And then silence and darkness and a single satisfied voice over the radio link.

"And some damn fools say cavalry is no good in
the mountains."

ABLE reappeared around the bend in the canyon.
Rolling to a halt below Mary May and Trebain's position, its tail ramp swung open. Before the vehicle
had even come to a halt, however, Mary May had
Trebain to his feet. Supporting him they slid-hopped
down the slope toward home.

"See, Lee, I told you we'd get out."

The only answer was a tightening of the arm
around her shoulders.

Mary May lugged the injured trooper into the
scout bay and dumped him into one of the air seats
spaced around the bulkheads. As she secured his
safety harness, the tail ramp lifted, and *ABLE* rum-
bled ahead.

"Hey, Lieutenant," she yelled forward. "There's
still one tank destroyer left at the mouth of the pass."

"Understood, Five," Bolde called back. "Miss Shelleen is sorting that gentleman out right now."

Wired into *CHARLIE* drone's remote cyber senses
through her Helmet-Mounted Display, Brid Shelleen
snaked the big robot through narrowing confines of
the pass, keeping the throttle trigger pressed to its

limits. The enemy knew of their presence and intent. There was no room left for subtlety, no more than there would be in a high-noon shoot out between two old Western gunfighters. Speed and precision would decide this last engagement.

For a split second Brid toggled across to the overhead tactical of the area around the pass mouth. The Algerian *Centauro* was off to the right of the roadway by about fifty meters, covering the exit and waiting.

She built the engagement sequence in her mind. Fire smoke grenades . . . Clear the pass entrance and pivot to the right . . . Switch to thermographics . . . Acquire the target . . . Take the shot . . . *Do it now!*

CHARLIE's grenade throwers hurled a cluster of smoke bombs out into the open ground beyond the pass mouth, the drone plunging into the dense swirling haze produced by the bursting charges. Brid started to brake for the turn when, abruptly, a shadowy outline loomed in her visor.

The problem with any military plan of action rests with the fact that the enemy rarely consults with you concerning his own intents. The Algerian tank destroyer crew had apparently elected at that moment to cut across the entry to the pass. Their intent, no doubt, was to take a snap shot at their oncoming foe. Instead, they had found themselves engulfed in an unexpected smoke screen and had come to a halt directly in the path of the charging US vehicle.

Brid locked up *CHARLIE*'s brakes, but before she could halt the drone it had plowed headlong into the *Centauro,* centerpunching it between its second and third set of drive wheels.

She hit the firing button of the booster gun, but the three-round burst blazed futilely over her opponent's deck. The casemate mount could neither depress nor traverse enough to engage this closer-than-point-blank target. She saw the tube of the *Centauro*'s 105 swing across her video field of vision, then caught the vibration as the gun barrel jammed out of line against *CHARLIE*'s hull. The Algerian gunners were caught in the same conundrum as she, unable to bring an effective weapon to bear.

Unable to reverse away from the deadlock, Brid opted for her only other alternative, she rocked her joystick hard forward and crushed the power trigger to maximum output.

CHARLIE shuddered, its massive tires clawing at the unyielding stone. Red and yellow systems overload warnings flared all around the periphery of Shelleen's Helmet Mounted Display and a grinding vibration blurred the camera imaging. But *CHARLIE* began to gain ground.

As the deck tilted beneath him, the Algerian driver frantically and futilely attempted to break away but the five hundred horsepower of the *Centauro* could not match the twelve hundred of the Shinseki. Remorselessly the gun drone bulldozed the tank destroyer sideways and over, the *Centauro*'s wheels spinning helplessly, until the point of overbalance was reached.

With a final crash the Algerian vehicle went over onto its side. With the deadlock broken, Bridget backed *CHARLIE* off twenty meters and waited. The Algerian crew scrambled out of the hatches of their doomed vehicle, fleeing into the night, and she let them go with a prayer.

I thank you, My Lady, for granting me this option of mercy.

Then she tore open the belly of the tank destroyer with another booster-gun burst.

"The pass mouth is clear, Lieutenant," she said,

lifting her voice to the world outside of her helmet display.

Nate Grey Bird fed his last clip of 9mm into the butt of his Beretta. A lot of extremely odd noise had just come from over the ridge crest, and he sincerely hoped it was indicative of a relief-and-rescue operation.

"Nate, what's your sitrep?" Lieutenant Bolde's voice was coming in over the squad channel now.

"Pretty much the same, sir, except the Algerians are getting closer. They're going to be in hand-grenade range pretty quick, and they have four throwing arms to our two."

"That will be an irrelevancy here in a moment, Specialist Grey Bird. Roman, you still with us?"

"Yes sir!" Johnny's enthusiastic response came back. "Right here."

"All right, here's the package. I have fixes on you and Nate as well as on the bad guys. In a second here I'm going to toss some CMMs over the ridgeline and onto the Algi positions. Crawl under your helmets because they are going to be close. After the rounds hit, the two of you fall back to the ridgeline and drop down to where we're waiting. We're parked almost underneath you."

"Uh, begging your pardon, sir." Johnny's voice had lost a great deal of its enthusiasm. "But that descent is almost vertical. How do we get down?"

"The operative word here, Mr. Roman, is 'almost.' As for how you get down, I suggest you step off the edge and let gravity take its course. You can grow some new skin on your next leave. Dedigitate, gentlemen, we do not have a great deal of time here! Rounds on the way!"

*　　*　　*

Aimed almost vertically, the box launchers belched out their four preprogrammed missiles, the flame spraying over *ABLE*'s armored back.

"Rounds look good," Brid reported from her workstation. "We have hits . . . Johnny and Nate are moving . . ."

"Right. Get *CHARLIE* moving, too, down and out onto the flats. Expedite!" Bolde swiveled the weapons pack around, intent on doing a little housecleaning. The Teal/Specter radar unit still sat at the edge of the plateau. Its crew had bailed out of the unarmed vehicle as the fighting had gotten close, and it was far too valuable an asset to leave intact.

Laying his sights on the generator trailer, Bolde demolished it with burst of 25mm from the OCSW. Elevating fire, he chewed away the antenna array and finally focused on the rear hull doors of the transporter track, caving them in and gutting the systems bay.

"Here they come!" Mary May yelled from the aft compartment. Turning his sights to the rear again, Bolde caught the last of Nate and Johnny's wild slide down the slope face. They still had the Javelin launcher. Good men!

A sharp *tack tack tack* sounded against the windshield and bullet stars danced across the Armorglas. There were still Algerians out there trying to make a fight of it. Bringing the grenade launcher around, Bolde raked the stone outcropping across from their position, covering his last people home.

The ramp dropped and the deck rang as Johnny and Nate threw themselves and their equipment aboard. "In!" Mary May screamed.

Rick Santiago didn't need a "go" order. All hands were thrown back in their seats as *ABLE* lunged forward at maximum acceleration.

*   *   *

Rick fought with the cavalry vehicle's wheel as they tore down the first switchback below the pass. Dios! *This thing is just a goat path! This grade will be hairy enough in daylight and at a sane rate of speed!*

Beside him Lieutenant Bolde chanted a mantra. "Faster . . . Faster . . . Artillery . . . Faster!"

Artillery? Shit! Somebody up there in the pass must still have a working radio. They'd left a whole lot of really pissed off Algerians just on the other side of this hill range, and now they no longer had to worry about the presence of friendly troops!

ABLE tore into the next corner, broadsiding through it like a sports car, her outer set of tires more over the edge than on the road. Rick tore back his night-vision visor and slapped his palm down on the auxiliary panel, kicking on the headlights and running lights full beam. Screw stealth! He had to see!

One . . . two . . . three . . . four . . . five . . . six . . . interminable switchbacks, then a short down grade and then the gravel pans.

"Off the road!" Bolde's yelled command rang in the confines of the cab.

Killing the headlights, Rick swung *ABLE* into the open desert. A dune loomed ahead, and the Shinseki didn't as much drive over it as through it, blasting a bow wave of sand to either side. All eight wheels momentarily left the ground. She hit hard once and then concussion bounced her into the air again as the night cracked open and bloody orange light flooded in. There were no definable single explosions as much as a continuous ear-crushing thunder as the massed time-on-target barrage rained down on the Taoudenni caravan road.

Rick's heart stalled in his chest. But after a moment he realized that they were steadily pulling away from the fire zone. The bombardment wasn't swinging onto them but was only marching down the roadway. The Algerians were firing blind, raking the caravan route, a frustrated tantrum of high explosives hurled after a brazen and escaping enemy.

They were out. They were all out. Backlit by the shell bursts, Rick could even make out the battered silhouette of *CHARLIE* drone lumbering faithfully behind them. Then and there, Santiago made a pledge that the next time he got home, he would remember this night and he would go to church and light some candles. He would also go out and get really, really, drunk, but first, he would light the candles.

Over at the commander's station, Lieutenant Bolde unsnapped the chinstrap of his helmet. Lifting its weight off with a sigh of relief, he ran a hand through his sweat-sodden hair. "Well, that wasn't such a chore now, was it?"

45 Miles Southeast of the El Khnachich Range
0421 Hours, Zone Time; October 29, 2021

"You want me to push her for a while, Rick?"

"Nah, LT. I poured a little coffee down my throat, and I'm good to the replenishment point."

"Just checking."

Steel-splinter stars still gleamed overhead and the cracked cab hatches admitted a stream of pure, chill predawn air that blew away the stenches of powder and sweat and fear. Bolde and Santiago had the driving watch. The others caught what fragmentary rest they could.

Brid Shelleen drowsed intermittently in her workstation seat. Mary May lay on the deck beside her, her head pillowed on her flak vest. Aft, things were silent in the scout bay as well. Even Lee Trebain slept with the aid of a morphine ampoule.

Somewhere over the horizon, an Army heavy-lift quad-rotor was outbound to meet them. Aboard it would be fuel blivets and ammunition reloads and a flying squad from squadron maintenance to help repair their battle damage.

His injured man would be airlifted out to a field hospital for care. And maybe there would be hot A rations and a clean uniform and an extra liter of water for a bath. And maybe a chance to sleep. Maybe really sleep for several hours straight through.

Bolde grinned to himself. Luxury in the eyes of the field soldier. But not yet. Not yet. There were still things to be considered.

What had he done this night? What had he accomplished that had been worth the gamble of the lives of his people?

Destroying the Recon company had poked a sharp stick into the eye of the enemy. Worthwhile. The Algerian army was weak on logistics. There would be no replacements for those destroyed tankers. Another gain. And the attack on that Algerian mechanized battalion would have a cascade effect. Knock out one of a brigade's three maneuver battalions and you cripple that brigade. Cripple one of its three maneuver brigades and you weaken the entire balanced structure of the division. A plus.

More importantly, though, was the time. It would take hours for the Algerians to re-form and resume replenishment. More hours for casualties to be dealt with and replacement supplies to be brought forward. More hours cautiously to probe forward and

learn if any new and nastier surprises were set to be
sprung.

Half a day bought? Maybe a day? It was enough.
What was that rueful joke making the rounds within
Third World military circles? *If you are planning a war,
best also plan to win it before the Americans can get there.*
The Algerian *fait accompli* had been blocked. Their
aggression had been stalled. When they finally ventured south of the El Khnachich range, they'd find
more than just a scattering of cavalry patrols waiting
for them. They'd find an army.

Bolde slouched deeper into his seat. The risk and
return had balance. It had been worth it.

Half-asleep at her workstation, Bridget Shelleen
lifted her head as she heard a soft trilling whistle
grow in the darkness. It had the lilt of the old country to it, and it took her a moment to place the melody over the rumble of the tires. When she did, she
smiled.

> *"Instead of spa, we'll drink down ale.*
> *Pay the reck'ning on the nail.*
> *No man for debt shall go to jail,*
> *For Garryowen and Glory."*

GLOSSARY

Common Modular Missile System—The replacement-to-be for
the US Army's current TOW and Dragon antitank missile systems. An interchangeable family of warheads,
guidance packages, and booster engines, CMM rounds
can be assembled in the field to produce a number of
differently mission-formatted antiarmor and antipersonnel missiles. Capable of being launched from both Army
land and air vehicles.

HMD (Helmet-Mounted Display)—An integral multimode imaging system built into the visor of a combat helmet. It
can be used to present readouts of personal or Velectronics systems, as a video display for operating remote-
controlled vehicles and equipment via telepresence, or
as an access to a virtual-reality environment.

Javelin—A shoulder-fired, infrared-guided, "fire and forget" antitank missile. The replacement for the Dragon
ATM, the Javelin is just entering the US inventory at
this time, making it a veteran weapons system by 2021.

Laager (modern usage)—A temporary camp for a unit of
armored fighting vehicles in the field.

SABR (Selectable Assault Battle Rifle)—The projected next-
generation weapons system for the US Army's ground
fighter. An assumed given in any twenty-first century
conflict situation is that the American foot soldier is
going to be massively outnumbered wherever he (or
she) is going to be committed to battle. The concept
behind the SABR is to give the individual US infantry-
person the same enhanced firepower and survival advantages that precision-guided standoff munitions give
his (or her) Air Force counterpart.

The SABR is a composite weapon, combining a
5.56mm Heckler & Koch G36 assault carbine with a six-
round, clip-fed grenade launcher, the launcher firing a
family of 20mm antivehicle and antipersonnel rounds,
many of which will be cybernetically fused "smart" munitions.

Also mated to the weapon will be a multimode sighting system incorporating thermographic, night brite,
and laser targeting technologies, giving the user the
ability effectively to engage the enemy at all ranges and
in all combat environments.

OCSW (Objective Crew Served Weapon)—The 25mm big
brother to the SABR. Replacing the "Ma Deuce" 50 cal-
iber machine gun and Mark 19 40mm "Chunker," this
vehicle- and tripod-mounted high-velocity grenade
launcher will also be capable of delivering a wide variety
of "smart" and "dumb" munitions.

RPV (Remotely Piloted Vehicle)—A remotely operated, robotic
surface or aircraft.

MM-15 Shinseki Multi-Mission Combat Vehicle—An end result

of Army Chief of Staff Eric K. Shinseki's "Medium-Weight Force" concept. The replacement for the U.S. Army's current force of heavyweight tracked tanks and Armored Personnel Carriers. The concept behind this family of wheeled Armored Fighting and Support Vehicles is that they are light enough to be airlifted rapidly to any global trouble spot. Yet, at the same time, they mount enough advanced technological firepower to deal with any potential crisis.

Track—Military slang. The term "track" might be used for any caterpillar-treaded armored fighting vehicle other then a true tank or a self-propelled howitzer, e.g., "scout track", "antiair track", "command track," etc.

Velectronics (Vehicle electronics)—A ground-combat vehicle's battlefield sensors and onboard electronic-warfare systems. An increasingly critical factor in future conflict situations.

Author's Note—Following the American Civil War, the Seventh U.S. Cavalry Regiment began using the old Irish ballad *Garryowen* as its distinctive signature march, an acknowledgment to the many Irish immigrants who served with both the regiment and with the frontier army as a whole.

So strongly did the regiment become linked with the song that they became known as the Garryowens, a designation the unit still wears proudly today.

JAMES COBB has lived his entire life within a thirty-mile radius of a major Army post, an Air Force base, and a Navy shipyard. He comments, "Accordingly, it's seemed a natural to become a kind of cut-rate Rudyard Kipling, trying to tell the stories of America's service people." Currently, he's writing the Amanda Garrett technothriller series, with three books, *Choosers of the Slain*, *Seastrike*, and *Seafighter*, published. He's also doing the Kevin Pulaski suspense thrillers for St. Martin's Press. He lives in the Pacific Northwest and, when he's not writing, he indulges in travel, the classic American hot rod, and collecting historic firearms.

FLIGHT OF
ENDEAVOUR

———

BY R. J. PINEIRO

One

The soft whirl of the Environmental Control and Life Support System broke the silence of space, the dead calm that Russian Mission Specialist Sergei Dudayev had grown to detest since his arrival at the International Space Station three months before. He knew he didn't belong there, in the pressurized cylindrical modules that had been his entire world for what now seemed like an eternity. A place where "up" and "down" had no meaning, no significance. A state-of-the-art rat cage where humans worked, ate, and slept protected from outer space by layers of metal alloys and insulating compounds.

Outer space. Sergei frowned as he gazed out through the Habitation Module's panoramic windowpanes at the light cloud coverage over southern Africa. The Earth looked peaceful, quiet, majestic.

At five-foot-four, the thirty-year-old Russian cosmonaut was a short man, particularly when standing next to his American or European colleagues. With a neatly trimmed beard, hollow cheeks, and charming smile, Sergei gave the impression of someone who found no pleasure in food. In his long, bony face, Sergei's alert, rather feminine eyes had an Italian softness that made people feel at ease with him. Today, he was banking on his natural ability to make everyone inside the International Space Station feel comfortable in his presence.

Closing his eyes, he listened to the sound of his own breathing as he prepared himself mentally for what he had to do. He felt his heartbeat increasing, the adrenaline rush, the perspiration forming on his creased forehead.

He opened his eyes and stared at a perfectly round bead of sweat floating inches from his face. He placed his index finger and thumb around it and toyed with it for a few seconds before squashing it. The silent explosion projected hundreds of tiny liquid particles in an isotropic that slowly trended upward as they got sucked in by the air-revitalization-system extractors overhead.

The time had come. With *Atlantis* heading back down to Earth and the launch of the shuttle *Endeavour* at the cape being delayed by a week, the ISS's regular crew of eight had been temporarily reduced to five, including himself.

The opportunity to take over the U.S. military's GPATS module would never be so easy. The Global Protection Against Terrorist Strikes module was one of several modules that made up the current core of the station. But unlike its sister modules, which served either as living quarters or to run experiments and collect data, GPATS, the highly classified military payload of a shuttle flight a year ago, housed a prototype hydrogen fluoride chemical laser gun powered by an array of solar cells. Initially plagued with bugs, the laser had already proven itself useful six months ago, when a malfunctioning satellite had come dangerously close to colliding with the space station. The laser had managed to transfer enough energy to the satellite to deflect its trajectory, missing the station by a thousand feet. Since then, the Pentagon, in order to protect the station from space junk, had used two shuttle flights to haul a billion dollars' worth of upgrades to increase its power and accuracy, making it capable of disabling enemy satellites as well as incoming nuclear warheads—its design objective during the Strategic Defense Initiative project over a decade ago. But GPATS also housed another weapon, deployed at the request of the United Nations Security Council: thirty BLU-85 warheads, each fitted with individual Earth reentry boosters. The BLU-85 was the largest nonnuclear warhead made by the United States, big brother of the venerable BLU-82 used during the Vietnam era to clear out large areas of forest for helicopter landing pads. The purpose of the BLU-85 aboard the ISS: a tactical, nonnuclear, first-strike antiterrorist-capability weapon that could be delivered with surgical precision anywhere on Earth within minutes. Each warhead provided the equivalent yield of fifteen thousand tons of TNT, or fifteen kilotons—small when compared to the two-hundred-kiloton warheads atop ICBMs, but large enough for its intended application. A single BLU-85 could level a military compound in a hostile nation, vaporize a terrorist training camp, discourage an advancing army, or destroy a cocaine plantation—all with the push of a button, and guided to its target by its own radar in shoot-and-forget mode. In procedures similar to the ones followed for decades by missile-silo crewmen, the weapons were kept in a state of readiness, their launching controlled by two crew members from the United States, the country that footed the entire GPATS bill. GPATS was the United Nations' ultimate hammer against a rebellious nation or terrorist group, capable of delivering a quick and devastating blow without the large overhead of troop deployments or air strikes, or the political and moral problems associated with a nuclear strike.

And now I will use this weapon against the Russian butchers, thought Sergei, who had become aware of this secret payload during the last month of his training.

Sergei Viktor Dudayev was Russian by birth, but his heart belonged to the struggling people of Chechnya, the land where he'd spent most of his youth as the son of a military officer during the final decade of the Soviet Union. Growing up in Grozny, Chechnya's capital, had allowed the young Dudayev to develop strong bonds with the locals, some of whom were killed during the turbulent civil war period following the fall of the Soviet Union. This secret loyalty had remained very much alive inside Sergei Dudayev after he'd left that war-scarred land, abandoning his friends in their fight for independence. The fire continued to burn in his heart even after he had settled in Moscow and tried to start a new life; even as he himself climbed the military ladder of the Russian military, following in his father's footsteps; even as his distinguished career eventually led him to the Russian space program.

Sergei reached into a Velcro-secured side pocket and extracted a small electric stun gun, capable of discharging a single twenty-thousand-volt shock, powerful enough to incapacitate an average man for thirty minutes. His people in Chechnya had managed to smuggle the tiny gun inside a Progress Russian cargo spaceship, which had arrived at the station just last week. Along with the gun came coded instructions from his Chechen contact in Moscow on the critical timing to take control of the station.

"Hey, Serg. You look pretty depressed today." One of the American astronauts floated past him, patted Sergei on the back, and stopped in front of the food galley. The American was the current resident aboard the ISS from the United Nations Security Council. In addition to standard mission-specialist responsibilities, he was also chartered with the protection of the GPATS module. Ever since the UNSC deployed GPATS, a minimum of one crew member aboard the ISS possessed the training and the weapons to defend the military module.

Sergei didn't respond, his eyes shifting from the American's holstered stun gun to the back of his light blue flight overalls, identical to the ones Sergei wore, except that the muscular UNSC soldier filled his, while Sergei's looked a size too big for his lanky frame.

The tall astronaut turned around, his hands fumbling with a brown pack of dehydrated peaches. His round face, pink and white, went well with his short hair. Curious brown eyes blinked at Sergei. "You okay, pal? You look sick. Have you been getting enough sleep?"

His heartbeat rocketing as he tried to hide the stun gun behind his back without looking suspicious. Sergei forced a smile, slightly closing his eyes as he nodded. "Yes, I am fine. Thank you."

The bulky American shrugged, turning his attention back to his dried peaches.

Sergei Viktor Dudayev tightened the grip on the

stun gun and gently pushed himself toward the food galley, arming the weapon and pressing its bare-wire ends against the soldier's neck.

A light buzzing sound filled the Habitation Module as the pouch flew off, spilling its contents in a brownish cloud. The American jerked for a moment and went limp, his arms floating in front of his body.

First incapacitate, then kill.

Blocking out all emotions, Sergei choked his victim until breathing ceased. Then he felt for a pulse, finding none. Satisfied, he grabbed the dead man's stun gun before pushing his body aside.

Adrenaline rocketing his heartbeat, Sergei stared toward the other end of the Habitation Module, where sleep compartments occupied both sides of the padded walls and the ceiling. A crewman slept in one of them. Another American, the station commander.

The Russian cosmonaut drifted toward him, coming to a rest in front of the compartment. The commander's arms floated loosely to the sides as his head leaned slightly forward. The Velcro straps securing him against the padded board applied just enough pressure on his body to create the illusion of sleeping in a comfortable bed.

Sergei curled the hairy fingers of his right hand around the plastic case of the UNSC soldier's stun gun, and without further thought, drove the hot end of the weapon into the side of the commander's neck. The astronaut opened his eyes and stared at Sergei in surprise, before his eyes rolled to the back of his head and his arms jerked forward, almost as if trying to reach for his attacker. The motor reflex ended a moment later, and, again, Sergei strangled his incapacitated victim.

The Russian unzipped the front of the American's

suit and removed a key attached to a chain around his neck. The American also wore a small badge around his neck. Briefly eyeing the credit-card-size object, Sergei decided to come back to it later. Right then he needed both ISS master keys.

Sergei Dudayev floated to his first victim and retrieved a second key, before approaching the center of the module and eyeing the closed-circuit TV monitors of the operations workstation. There he verified that the remaining crew members, one British and one Japanese, were still inside the U.S. Laboratory Module, the forty-four-foot-long pressurized cylinder similar in shape and size to the Habitation Module. Satisfied, he inserted both keys on the top of the keyboard of the Multipurpose Application Console, linked to the electronic core of the ISS's network. From here, Sergei had control of all onboard subsystems such as electrical power, thermal control, data management, communications, interface with ground control, and even full space station attitude control and orbit altitude.

Sergei Dudayev bypassed all manual overrides of the air-revitalization system and emergency hatch releases of the U.S. Laboratory Module. A few more strokes of the keys and he heard the alarms going off across the station as the computer system automatically isolated the laboratory from the rest of the station by closing and locking the hatches at both ends of the module.

His eyes drifted back to the flat-panel monitor, which now showed two astronauts frantically waving at the camera and reaching for the radio. Sergei turned the intercom system off. He didn't care to hear their pleas, just as the world had refused to listen to the cry of his people as Russian forces raped his beloved Chechnya.

Visions of his explosive youth, of his slaughtered friends, of his hasty departure filled his mind as Sergei typed again. This time he overrode the air pressurization and revitalization control system of the station and began to bleed the air still trapped inside the Laboratory Module into space. The astronauts continued to wave and scream in front of the camera, but their struggle didn't last long. Soon they began to breathe through their mouths. Their movements grew clumsier, erratic, until they went limp.

The Russian quietly followed the bodies floating in the monitor. His soul could hear their screams now, their shouts and pleas for mercy. All four astronauts had died without really knowing Sergei's motive, without an explanation as to why their lives had to end so abruptly inside this man-made pocket of life traveling at thousands of miles per hour over a fragile Earth.

The two keys giving him access to all modules of the station, including GPATS, Sergei quickly typed the appropriate commands on the MPAC workstation, unlocking the latching mechanism that isolated GPATS from the rest of the station. Locking the MPAC system by removing both keys, Sergei used a single arm motion to propel his weightless body across the length of the Habitation Module, where a hatch connected that end of the module to Node One, also known as Unity, a pressurized cylinder fifteen feet in diameter and eighteen feet long sporting six hatches that served as docking ports for the other modules. A hatch connected to the U.S. Laboratory Module, another to the GPATS Module, and a third to the airlock, where the crew could suit up prior to EVAs, extravehicular activities, or space walks. The hatch immediately above Sergei led to a Russian-made Soyuz capsule to be used by the crew of the station to return to Earth in an emergency. Sergei planned to use the Soyuz Escape System (SES) to return to Earth after he had completed his mission.

A fifth hatch attached a cupola to Unity. Composed of eight large windows arranged in a circle over the node, the cupola provided the crew of the ISS with a 360-degree field of view in azimuth and complete hemispheric field of view in elevation of Earth. Part of the instrumentation aboard the cupola was the control system for the ISS robot arm, a larger and more versatile version of the venerable robot arm of the space-shuttle program. Unity's sixth hatch was used to dock with visiting shuttles or Russian Progress supply ships. The other end of the U.S. Laboratory Module connected to Node Two, which led to additional modules on that side of the station, including the Columbus research module from Europe, and the Japanese experimental module.

Using the handholds built in along the padded walls lining Unity, Sergei directed himself into the GPATS Module. Placing his feet into the secure straps in front of the latched hatch, he applied nine pounds of pressure on the hatch actuator lock lever, turning it 180 degrees. The hatch opened to the contour of Unity's inner wall. Sergei pulled it toward him about six inches, before pivoting it up and to the right side, exposing the crowded interior of the GPATS module.

Unlike the other modules, illuminated with soft white overheads, the interior of GPATS had a green glow designed to minimize eye fatigue during prolonged combat situations. Viewed from the inside, the module looked like a half cylinder. The side facing Earth was completely taken up by the BLU-85s, each stored in its own individual compartment and stacked ceiling high for the entire length of the module, leaving a three-foot-wide "walkway" between the wall of shelled warheads and the left side of the compartment. The forward section of the side of GPATS opposite the warheads consisted of two large computer consoles, each capable of launching warheads if the order ever came from the United Nations Security Council. The workstation closest to the hatch had a red light above it, meaning it was the system currently designated as active. The other system, set in standby mode, served as backup.

Farther down the left side Sergei saw the single computer system controlling the powerful GPATS laser, gimbal-mounted above the module. Gliding past gleaming instrumentation and displays, the Russian cosmonaut reached the laser system, whose operation he had had to learn before being qualified as mission specialist. ISS regulations dictated that every crew member aboard the ISS knew the operation of the laser in case of an emergency. The operation of the warheads, however, was limited to UNSC personnel, mostly American. In the event that a mission specialist like Sergei figured out how to operate the warhead-launching system, he would be incapable of doing so without the authorization codes, which were kept in a safe next to the workstation. Sergei had picked up bits and pieces of the launching procedure during a recent drill by eavesdropping on an intercom channel. If the order to launch ever came, the authorized crew would use their keys simultaneously to open the safe and extract the sealed envelopes containing the launch codes, which would then be compared with those received from Earth. If the codes matched, the order to launch one or more warheads would be executed. Such precautions were required given the fact that albeit nonnuclear, each warhead was capable of leveling downtown Washington, D.C. However, no authorization from the Pentagon or the United Nations was required to use the laser, particularly if there was a need to deflect or vaporize space junk in a collision course with the station. Its use in an emergency was at the sole discretion of the station commander.

Sitting behind the controls of the GPATS laser, Sergei activated the search-and-tracking radar, which, in conjunction with the tracking systems of three reflectors positioned in geosynchronous orbit 23,000 miles above the Earth, had the capability of detecting and tracking anything in orbit.

Sergei went to work, commanding the laser's search-and-tracking system to scan the space along an east-to-west elliptical orbit of 274 kilometers in perigee and 150 kilometers in apogee with an inclination of 63.4 degrees—the orbit of Russia's latest Cosmos surveillance satellite, currently Russia's eyes over the border between Chechnya and Dagestan to the north. Sergei adjusted the system's sensitivity to filter out objects smaller than ten feet in length. It took an additional minute before the search-and-tracking system came back with an object roughly the size of a school bus.

Sergei Viktor Dudayev smiled.

I see you.

His fingers moved almost automatically, selecting an energy setting, width of beam, and duration of event. Giving the controls one last inspection, he commanded the laser to fire.

The hydrogen-fluoride chemical laser gun, receiving its power from massive solar-rechargeable batteries, created a high-energy beam of light, which streaked across space to one of three reflective mirrors in geosynchronous orbit. The fifty-foot-diameter segmented mirror, actively cooled by a steady flow of liquid hydrogen running below its reflective surface, and whose angle had already been determined by its radio link with GPATS, deflected the beam with only a four percent loss in energy. The beam continued on its new trajectory, which abruptly ended when it came in contact with the laminated twenty-four-karat gold skin of the Cosmos orbital reconnaissance satellite.

Although the beam only remained in contact with the satellite for a few seconds, the laser's energy changed into intense heat, slicing through the skin, evaporating the metal, and instantly frying the sophisticated electronics housed in its core.

Before manning the workstation controlling the warheads, Sergei used the keys to extract the launching codes from the safe next to the system. He activated the system and spent a few minutes typing the thirty-characters-long codes, working through several menus and levels of security. Another set of codes allowed him to move down the encrypted system until he reached the directory where the launching software resided. A few more keystrokes and the twenty-one-inch Sony color monitor displayed a list of warheads, labeled UNSC15KTSN001 through UNSC15KTSN030 in cyan on a black background.

He placed an index finger, trembling from excitement, over a spring-tensioned trackball—a mouse didn't work well in zero gravity—bringing the cursor to the BLU-85 warhead SN#001. Sergei's plan, which he had secretly worked out two weeks prior to his launch with Nikolai Naskalhov, an aide to the president of Chechnya, was simple: gain control of the warheads as a hammer against the Russian troops threatening to invade Chechnya. The destruction of the Russian satellite had been Sergei's message to

Moscow that the people of Chechnya now had an ally high above the clouds. As he gained control of GPATS, another message was being delivered to the Kremlin: unless the Russian 157th armored division retreated from the border with Chechnya, he would release a warhead over an undisclosed location. More demands would follow.

The adrenaline rush making it difficult to swallow, Sergei clicked the button beneath the trackball. He wanted to activate the warheads and have them ready for launch at a moment's notice.

The UNSC15KTSN001 warhead turned magenta, and a message appeared:

> UNSC15KTSN001 HAS BEEN SELECTED
> INSERT VALID UNSC ACCESS CARD TO
> ACTIVATE
> ******00:59******

A slot opened beneath the monitor and a red LED began to blink next to it.

Sergei froze.

Insert Valid United Nations Security Council access card?

Why would he need one when he had already logged into the system and entered all the authorization codes successfully?

Confused, Sergei glanced at the screen again. It now read:

> UNSC15KTSN001 HAS BEEN SELECTED
> INSERT VALID UNSC ACCESS CARD TO
> ACTIVATE
> ******00:55******

And a second later,

UNSC15KTSN001 HAS BEEN SELECTED
INSERT VALID UNSC ACCESS CARD TO
ACTIVATE
******00:54******

The Russian's soft eyes widened in fear when he realized the system would not let him start the launch sequence unless he inserted a UNSC access card in the slot within the next fifty-four seconds. The UNSC had added a safety feature that he didn't know existed, and if the system was as secured as he expected it to be, he would probably only get one chance at inserting the card before the computers would lock him out.

But where do I—

You idiot! The station commander! The card! He glanced at the screen once more.

UNSC15KTSN001 HAS BEEN SELECTED
INSERT VALID UNSC ACCESS CARD TO
ACTIVATE
******00:47******

Sergei jumped off the chair and propelled himself to the entrance of the GPATS module, floated across Unity, and into the Habitation Module. Shoving aside the American floating next to the galley, he reached the end of the long, cylindrical compartment, halting his momentum by holding on to the edge of the sleeping compartment.

He tugged at the chain around the neck of the dead station commander, but it didn't give. Beads of sweat lifting off his forehead, the Russian raised the chain over his victim's head. Holding the electronic card in his left hand, he kicked his legs against the side of the sleeping compartment, propelling himself back toward Unity. He miscalculated his zero-G flight, crashing his right shoulder against the edge of the passageway. The impact deflected his forward momentum, sending him floating out of control inside Unity.

Wasting precious seconds, ignoring the pain, Sergei clawed at anything within reach to regain control, grabbing on to a built-in handle next to the hatch connecting Unity to the cupola. In the process, he let go of the card, which floated toward his feet.

In one swift motion, Sergei snagged the chain, pulling the card to his chest. Kicking his legs against the cupola's control panel, he shot himself through the D-shaped entry of the GPATS module, reaching the workstation a moment later.

******PROCEDURE VIOLATION******
TIME LIMIT EXCEEDED. SYSTEM RESET IN
PROGRESS
******167:59:54******

Procedure violation! He had missed the window by six seconds!

Sergei tried to insert the badge, but the slot was already closed. He tried to type a command to reset the system manually, but the system would not respond. The keyboard was locked. He tried the power switch on the side of the machine, but it did not have any effect. The system was obviously designed to bypass all exterior input after such violation, and it would remain like that for 168 hours—one week—before it would let him try again.

Sergei was familiar with procedure violations, and the only way to reset the system before the stated time was by entering a special access code known only by four people in the world: The U.S. President, the Russian President, the British Prime Minister, and the Secretary General of the United Nations. The procedure was implemented as a safety measure against exactly this type of intrusion. One week was usually enough time to get either a shuttle or a Russian Soyuz packed with armed United Nations forces up here. During his last six months of training at Johnson Space Center, in Houston, Sergei had seen a platoon of UN Security Forces in similar zero-G training exercises. While Sergei trained to use a screwdriver in space, the soldiers practice zero-G warfare tactics. But fortunately for Sergei, he still had a chance of pulling this off. It just would take a little more time and a hell of a lot more nerve.

Moving up the module to the laser station, Sergei quickly verified his access to the laser. Unlike the warheads, the laser system could never be locked—as long as the user had the right authorization codes. Otherwise, the station ran the risk of getting damaged by space junk. He moved over to the backup warhead-deployment workstation, next to the one he had locked.

Sergei tried his luck at gaining access to the warheads' directory. He got the message:

**SYSTEM LOCKED BY OTHER USERS
PLEASE TRY AGAIN IN 167:58:42**

Frowning at his own stupidity, but grateful that at least he could defend himself and prevent anyone from getting near the station, Sergei deactivated the system and floated back to the Habitation Module, where he prepared a coded message that he sent to a mobile tracking station in Chechnya ten minutes later, when the International Space Station flew over the Caucasus Mountains.

The reply from his controller was very clear: hold your ground. Regain control of the warheads and advise when Sergei was in a position to launch. He would be provided with a priority list of targets at a later time. Right then control of the ISS played a significant role in the ongoing discussions with Russia, providing Chechnya with bargaining leverage against the Russian armored divisions gathered at its border. He was also told that the hearts of the Chechen people were with him at this time.

Afterward, Sergei dragged the bodies of the four astronauts across Unity and into the hyperbaric airlock, which provided an effective and safe mean for the transfer of crew and equipment between pressurized and unpressurized zones.

He gave the interior of the compartment a visual check to verify that all airlock equipment—including the two AMEX AX-5 EVA hard suits and all power tools—were safely secured, before floating back up into Unity. Closing the hatch, he used the small control panel next to the hatch to depressurize the airlock from the normal atmosphere inside the station of 14.7 pounds per square inch (PSI) to 0.5 PSI. As Sergei remotely opened the airlock's exterior hatch, the pressure differential between the vacuum of space and the low pressure of the airlock sucked the four astronauts out of the airlock and into free space.

Sergei closed the exterior hatch, repressurized the airlock, and headed back to the Habitation Module. Although he felt partially victorious for coming so close to accomplishing his lifelong goal of seeking revenge against the enemies of Chechnya, the cosmonaut couldn't help a wave of guilt. After all, this had been the very first time that he had taken another human life. As much as his mind tried to justify his actions, the plain fact remained unchanged. He had killed four innocent astronauts—people that he knew well after training together for over two years.

Sergei stared at his brown eyes in the small mirror by the module's personal hygiene station. *There is no turning back now.*

Closing his eyes, Sergei saw Nikolai Naskalhov's round face. He remembered Nikolai as he told Sergei of the pain inflicted on the Chechen people by the Russians. The rapes, the killings, the abuses, the humiliation, the agony his people had endured for so long while the Americans stood by, while the rest of the world stood by. But Sergei also remembered the feeling of retribution that radiated from Nikolai's burning stare. The presidential aide had suffered as much as many Chechens but was willing to sacrifice everything to strike back, to stand up for his people.

Filling his lungs with the purified air of the Habitation Module, Sergei Viktor Dudayev watched his reflection in silence.

TWO

Wearing one-piece blue coveralls, Mission Commander Diane Williams sat in the rear of one of three firing rooms on the third floor of the Kennedy Space Center's Launch Control Center (LCC), a four-story building located south of the Vehicle Assembly Building, where shuttles were mated to External Tanks and to Solid Rocket Boosters prior to their rollout to Launch Complex 39.

Running a hand though her short, brown hair, the forty-five-year-old astronaut of three previous shuttle flights watched the start of her flight's countdown, initiated with a Call to Stations at T minus twenty-four hours. The retired Marine aviator crossed her arms, which looked as thin as they had been when she was in the military, but without the firmness of daily exercise.

She watched LCC technicians run orbiter checkouts from their workstations by using complex algorithms that monitored and recorded the prelaunch performance of all electrical and mechanical systems and subsystems aboard *Endeavour*. The workstations, linked to the large-scale Honeywell computers one floor below, sent an array of commands to thousands of sensors inside the orbiter. The sensors measured specific parameters and relayed the information back to the workstations for comparison against safety limits stored in the Honeywell's memory banks. The cycle of information and checks would continue nonstop until seconds after liftoff, when control of the mission would be handed off to Mission Control in Houston, Texas.

"What do you think of our new passengers, Diane?" asked Gary McGregor, the thirty-seven-year-old astronaut of one previous shuttle flight scheduled to be Diane's Mission Pilot. McGregor, a former Air Force captain and F-16 pilot, was a short man, almost four inches shorter than Diane's five-ten, with black hair, a carefully clipped mustache, and brown eyes that widened as he grimaced, something McGregor had been doing a lot since the change in mission plans two days before.

Diane glanced at the four "Space Marines," the term adopted by astronauts when referring to the selected team of UN Security Council forces trained to operate in zero gravity.

"Look like your average tough *hombres*," Diane replied with a shrug, her slim brows rising a trifle. "I hope they can handle it up there."

McGregor nodded.

The four soldiers, wearing all-black uniforms, stood roughly thirty feet to Diane's left. Their eyes were trained on a sixty-inch projection screen on the left wall of the firing room, displaying a Titan-IV rocket slowly lifting off Pad 40. The Titan carried a large segmented mirror left over from the Strategic Defense Initiative days. Diane's first priority after reaching orbit would be to chase and rendezvous with the Titan's payload and connect the large mirror to the end of two Remote Manipulator System arms—the fifty-foot-long shuttle robotic arm used to deploy satellites—to protect *Endeavour* from a potential laser discharge by the Russian terrorist aboard the ISS.

Timing was of the essence to complete the mission successfully, before the Russian regained control of the warheads. Diane had to deploy the mirror before the terrorist realized that *Endeavour* had been launched, and he used the laser to destroy the shuttle just as he had the Russian Cosmos satellite. There was a risk of detection, but NASA had minimized it by programming the mission software aboard *Endeavour* to achieve an orbit 180 degrees out of phase with the space station, meaning that the orbiter and the station would be on the same circular orbit, but at opposite ends, with the Earth in between, until *Endeavour* was properly shielded. In addition, to prevent the terrorist from destroying any other satellites, NASA, in conjunction with the Department of Defense, had disabled the mirrors in geosynchronous orbit, and also the Brilliant Eyes search-and-tracking satellites used by the laser's tracking system to zero in on a target. The laser's range of operations had been reduced to detecting and engaging objects within the station's visual horizon.

The UNSC had also considered firing Anti-Satellite (ANSAT) missiles at the ISS to distract the terrorist while *Endeavour* dropped off the Space Marines. That approach, however, carried the risk of a missile slipping through and destroying the station.

The ANSAT option then became a last resort if the shuttle mission failed to prevent the terrorist from gaining access to the warheads.

But by the time we get that close, the mirror will protect the shuttle, she thought, as the Titan broke through the sound barrier and continued its ascent undisturbed.

Diane glanced back at McGregor, who for the past day had began to show signs of stress. "You okay?" she asked.

The native of Tulsa, Oklahoma, brushed a finger over his mustache as his eyes stared in the distance. "I'll be fine."

Diane tilted her head toward the UNSC soldiers. "We just have to get those guys close enough to the station. The rest is up to them. Pretty straightforward."

McGregor didn't respond right away. The current mission plan, after attaching the mirror to the robot arms, called for Diane and McGregor to pilot the shuttle to a concentric orbit six miles above the ISS during the night portion of the orbit, when the station's large solar panels were idle and the laser system drew its power from its backup batteries. The terrorist would probably detect the incoming shuttle and most likely blast away with the laser against the shielded orbiter until it ran out of power. Afterward the UNSC soldiers would use a prototype Lockheed boarding vehicle, currently being loaded into *Endeavour*'s payload bay, to reach the hyperbaric airlock of the ISS, neutralize the terrorist, and regain control of the station. It was a simple plan, but the Marine in Diane knew that military missions didn't always go as planned. And McGregor knew it too.

Fortunately for everyone, the Lockheed boarding vehicle, a top-secret Air Force project that was being

readied for space at the processing facilities of Cape
Canaveral Air Force Station (CCAFS), was scheduled
for launch in six weeks aboard *Atlantis*. Now CCAFS
personnel were working in conjunction with the
Launch Complex 39A team to swap payloads. *Endeavour*'s original payload, two commercial satellites
and one Department of Defense (DOD) satellite,
had already been loaded back into its payload canister and returned to the Vertical Processing Facility.
CCAFS personnel now transferred their secret cargo
from the payload canister to *Endeavour*'s payload bay.
The operation was scheduled for completion in another two hours.

McGregor shook his head. "I'm Air Force, Diane.
I know how these last-minute missions usually go . . ."
He lowered his voice a few decibels. "I mean, we had
no dry runs here. No simulation time on this type of
approach. We're banking *everything* on being able to
connect that damned mirror to the RMS arms, and
also on being able to control the arms and the shuttle attitude verniers to keep that mirror shielding us.
What if something goes wrong? Do you know what
that laser can do to the orbiter? And how about that
classified Lockheed vehicle we're carrying? Do you
know how to use it? And what's that special cargo
labeled UNSC CLASSIFIED in the lockers of the crew
compartment? Do you know?"

Diane shook her head slightly while giving McGregor a slanted glance, pushing out her lower lip
in a resigning pout.

"Neither do I."

"That's not our concern, Gary. We've been given
a mission. Those guys have theirs. Period. You served
in the military, didn't you? What we're doing's called
following orders."

McGregor frowned. "How do you manage to keep it all straight in your head?"

Diane shrugged and looked away. Her mind had already formulated the answer: California. Many years ago. During a training exercise outside the Marines' El Toro Air Station, her F/A-18D Hornet had flamed out, sending her jet into an uncontrollable spin. She had managed to eject in time but injured her back when a gust of wind swung her parachute into the side of a hill.

Diane closed her eyes. She remembered the base's doctor, a petite woman with a heart-shaped face, a pointy nose, and enormous round black eyes wearing a white lab coat and a stethoscope hanging from her neck. She introduced herself as Dr. Lisa Hottle, a physician assigned by the base's commander to look after her. Dr. Hottle explained to Diane the crippling consequences of her spinal-cord injury and the possibility of walking again but only after undergoing extended physical therapy. The Marine aviator immediately withdrew into the tears. Life had dealt her a cruel hand. For the weeks that followed Diane fell into a state of depression. The Marine Corps sent a battalion of psychiatrists to help her cope with the drastic changes in her life, but nothing helped.

Late one evening, Dr. Hottle came into Diane's room to check on her condition. Diane, barely acknowledging the doctor, gazed at the stars through the window next to the dresser. Instead of taking Diane's pulse, Dr. Hottle simply stood at the foot of her bed staring at Diane. *So, you're feeling sorry for yourself?* Dr. Hottle asked. Before Diane could reply, the petite doctor unbuttoned her blouse and reached behind her back, lowering her padded brassiere. The sobering revelation struck Diane with the force of a jet on afterburners as she stared at her breastless chest, a pink scar traversing Dr. Hottle's upper chest from armpit to armpit from a double mastectomy. *You simply go on, my dear Diane. You simply just . . . just fight with all you've got and go on with your life.*

Diane had not only learned to walk again, but within six months of the accident she was back on a Hornet. A year later she had joined NASA and became a shuttle astronaut.

As the Titan rocket shot high above the clouds, Diane Williams let the memories fade. Although she considered this mission the most important of her life, that experience long ago had given her a new perspective in life.

Diane checked her watch. "Looks like the Titan is going to make orbit, and that means we're going up, too. See you in a few."

Diane headed toward the entrance of the firing room, walking by the Space Marines.

"All set, Commander?" asked the senior UNSC officer, a black ex–Army colonel by the name of Frank Ward, his booming voice matching his six-foot-three height and 240 pounds of solid muscle. Ward had been in a bad mood ever since NASA got news of the killings aboard the station. His man aboard the ISS had apparently failed to prevent the terrorist from gaining control of the station. The UNSC had come down hard on Ward, drilling him on every aspect of his operation, questioning his team's capabilities to carry out the assignment for which the UNSC spent over twenty million dollars per year in equipment and training. Now Ward and his team were under extreme pressure to recover the station and save whatever was left of their reputation.

She grinned at the bald colonel with the powerful chest and equally strong arms and legs. A pair of piercing brown eyes stared back at Diane. "We're ready, Colonel."

"Are you certain? This mission is far too important."

"We're *always* ready, Colonel. Are you?"

Ward raised a brow and said, "We'll be there."

"Good. See you at the launchpad."

Three

Fifteen minutes later, Diane peeked inside one of many windowless offices at the KSC's headquarters. A medium-built man in his late forties sitting behind a desk typed on a computer. He wore a pair of dark slacks, a perfectly starched cotton white shirt, and a maroon tie. The keyboard clicking stopped, and he looked up above the edge of the brown monitor, studying Diane for a few seconds through rimless glasses. Narrow streaks of gray on his otherwise brown hair gave him a touch of elegance.

"May I help you?" he asked, returning his eyes to the screen. The clicking resumed.

Diane walked inside the ten-by-twelve office, closing and locking the door behind her. "As a matter of fact I need lots of help."

He looked at her again, smiling. "Exactly what kind of help do you seek?"

Diane reached his desk and sat against the edge, her back now toward him. "Well, you see. I'm about to go on this long and dangerous journey, and I feel I need something else besides my training to help me make it through."

He stood, walked around the desk, and stood in front of her. Standing almost six-foot and weighing 190 pounds, he removed his glasses and, tossing them over the desk, told Diane, "I'm sorry, miss, but I still don't understand exactly what I can do to assist you on this journey."

Diane pulled him toward her before throwing her arms around his neck and kissing him on the lips. A moment later she pulled away, staring into the eyes of Jake Cohen, and saying, "That'll get me from lift-off to Solid Rocket Booster separation. After that I'm afraid I'm gonna run out of motivation."

Jake smiled, taking her in with a greedy stare. He had always loved to play these little games. The businesslike, forty-eight-year-old veteran astronaut and now Capsule Communicator (CapCom) for the past dozen shuttle flights had a private side that never ceased to amaze Diane Williams. Not only was Jake Cohen a refreshing change in Diane's otherwise very organized life, but Jake was also one of the very few men Diane had met who was never threatened by her profession. As a matter of fact, Jake once confessed to her that her brilliant mind and different past had attracted him to her just as much as her stunning looks.

"I heard the Titan launch went clean," Jake said.

Diane nodded while brushing her lipstick off Jake's face. He intercepted her index finger and sucked it gently. She pulled it away. "Pervert."

"Can't seem to control myself around you . . .

speaking of which, most everyone's out to lunch, and you did lock the door, didn't you?"

She quickly pushed him away. "You're nuts, Jake."

"Hey," he said, pulling her close. "You only live once."

"Stop it, Jake. Besides, we got a briefing in twenty minutes."

"That's plenty of—"

"No."

"It's gonna be a long and lonely week."

She smiled. "Are you really going to miss me?"

"Yep."

"Liar. But thanks anyway," she said with an odd little glance at Jake, who had always enjoyed spending time by himself. Diane sensed that Jake probably looked forward to just a little space for the next few days. Since their relationship had gone into high gear six months before, neither of them had done much outside of work besides rolling under the sheets at his or her place. As it turned out, both Diane and Jake had not had a sexual partner for some time. So when Jake's hands had ventured inside Diane's cotton skirt after going through a bottle of Chardonnay late one evening at his apartment during their seventh date in three weeks, Diane had not resisted, figuring Jake not only was the most understanding, decent, and honest man she had ever known, but he also had a similar technical background, which gave them a lot more in common.

Jake suddenly turned businesslike. "Are you okay about this flight? You don't have to go if you don't want to. I mean, there is a lot of risk on this one."

Diane put a hand to his face and smiled. "And I love you too, darling."

Jake grimaced. The issue of her going on this mission had come up in every conversation they'd had in the past two days, since NASA settled on a recovery strategy. Jake had volunteered to go in her place, and that comment had resulted in their first fight ending with Jake's quick withdrawal of his suggestion plus a dozen roses. But as charming and intelligent as Jake Cohen was, he was also a hardheaded bastard who would not give up until *Endeavour* left the launchpad. Trouble was, Diane's head was as thick as his.

"Jake, I don't question your professional decisions, so, please, don't question mine. Besides, you'll be with me on the radio every step of the way."

Jake regarded her with a peculiar grin, at once agreeable and frustrated. "You're some strange piece of work, Diane Williams. But at least you're my kind of strange."

"I warned you about getting involved with me. I'm not an airhead in a bikini walking down Cocoa Beach."

Jake laughed, "But you sure look great in one . . . or out of one."

Diane slapped his shoulder.

"Say, speaking of strange, what do you think of your passengers?"

She shrugged. "We both have a mission, but up there I'm *Mission Commander*, meaning it is *my* pond and up to the point that he leaves the orbiter he *will* follow my orders. I think we understand each other. I am annoyed, however, that NASA won't allow me to inspect the gear they're bringing aboard my ship."

"Look, you and I know that this mission is a bit different from what we're used to flying. In the past at least we were told we were carrying classified cargo, and we were even given some level of detail about it, but absolute secrecy on this one is top priority directly from the top. I know it makes you and

Gary mad as hell not knowing much about this new boarding vehicle or the stuff that they are hauling inside the crew module, but the reality of things is that you two don't have a need to know. That's Colonel Ward's job. Think of him as a mission specialist. Your job is just to get him and his team close enough to the station and then get the hell out of the range of that laser as fast as possible, and stay out of sight until Ward and his men get the situation under control."

"I'll do my part, Jake. I was in the Marines. I know how to follow orders. When is your plane leaving for Houston?" she asked.

"In three hours. Do you want to grab a bite at the cafeteria?"

Diane Williams nodded and leaned forward, kissing him on the cheek before they walked side by side toward the door.

Four

_____

The waiting never got any easier, decided Diane Williams as the digital display of _Endeavour_'s mission timer showed T minus three minutes. No matter how many times she'd done it before, sitting on top of enough chemicals to create a blast as powerful as the BLU-85 warheads aboard the GPATS module in the ISS made her question whether she had chosen the right career after leaving the Marine Corps.

But the reason why she felt even more concerned at that moment than on any of her previous flights was not the fact that _Endeavour_ could become the target in an orbital shooting alley for the terrorist manning the GPATS laser. After all, Diane had been a Marine aviator. She had dodged more than her fair share of antiaircraft fire during the Gulf War. The woman in the astronaut knew there was another reason for her abnormally high heartbeat, for her dried mouth, for her sweaty palms. She had never before felt this nervous about a launch, not even during her first time, shortly after completing her astronaut training.

There was another reason, but it was one the astronaut in her refused to admit, for it made her feel weak in the eyes of her professional mind. For the first time since joining NASA Diane was truly afraid of dying. She had not realized her fear until she'd reached the Operations and Checkout building before dawn that morning to eat the classic steak and eggs breakfast, prior to suiting up and heading for the launchpad. The realization of the danger involved, not only in a routine orbiter flight, but in this particular mission had slowly begun to sink in with every bite she had taken of that medium-well sirloin steak and scrambled eggs. And the reason for the uncharacteristic fear was Jake Cohen. For the first time in her life Diane had fallen in love, and that gave her something that she feared losing.

Jake Cohen filled Diane's life more than anyone or anything else, even flying. She never thought it could happen, but somewhere during the past six months her priorities in life had changed, and the possibility of a life with Jake had superseded all her other ambitions. Perhaps it was the fact that she was forty-five. Or maybe that the pilot in her had seen enough action to last forty-five lifetimes. Or the fact that Jake loved her the way she was. She wasn't sure why it had happened, only that it had. And it had been a revelation she had kept all to herself, refusing to share it even with the man she loved. The fear of lowering her wall of pride and exposing her innermost feelings to Jake Cohen was just as intense as the fear that ran through her body at that moment, while her pale green eyes gazed at a dawning sky through the 1.3-inch-thick windowpane directly in front of her.

Breathing in the oxygen and nitrogen air mixture inside the flight deck while forcing her mind to put her fears aside, Diane checked the timer and gave Gary McGregor a thumbs-up. The Mission Pilot winked and returned the gesture.

The NASA Launch Room controller's voice crackled through the orbiter's speakers.

"T minus two minutes fifty-two seconds. Endeavour: *the liquid oxygen valve on the External Tank has been closed and pressurization has begun."*

The colossal rust-colored External Tank, carrying over 1.3 million pounds of liquid oxygen and 227,641 pounds of liquid hydrogen, and measuring nearly 158 feet in length, began to pressurize the liquid oxygen housed inside its aluminum-monocoque-structured tank to a pressure of twenty-one pounds per square inch—the pressure necessary to force the oxidizer to the three Space Shuttle Main Engines and achieve combustion with the volatile liquid-hydrogen propellant.

"T minus two minutes fifteen seconds: the main engines have been gimbaled to their start position and the pressure on the liquid oxygen tank is at flight pressure. T minus two minutes and counting: the liquid oxygen vent valve has been closed and flight pressurization is under way."

She glanced at CRT#1, one of three CRTs on the control panel between McGregor and her, displaying the status of the main engines. She also glanced at an array of warning lights between CRTs #2 and #3. Nothing seemed abnormal.

"Coming up on the one-minute point on the countdown, everything is going smoothly. The firing system for the ground suppression water is armed."

Diane battled her rocketing heartbeat. *Just like in*

the Marines, Diane. she told herself. *Relax and do what you do best!*

"T minus thirty-seven seconds and counting; switching control of the launch to the computer sequence."

Launch countdown control switched from KSC's Launch Processing System to *Endeavour*'s five General Purpose Computers, four working in parallel, the fifth checking the output from the other four.

"T minus twenty seconds: SRB hydraulic power unit started, the SRB nozzles have been moved to the start position. Coming up on fifteen. Switching to redundant start sequence. T minus twelve . . . eleven . . . ten . . . nine."

Diane closed her eyes and visualized the sound-suppression water system nozzles popping up from the Mobile Launch Platform base, like lawn sprinklers, and beginning to spray water onto the base of the MLP at the rate of 900,000 gallons per minute in anticipation of main engine start.

"Seven . . . six . . . we're going for main engine start!"

The GPCs ordered the opening of the liquid-hydrogen and liquid-oxygen feed valves of the huge External Tank, channeling both propellant and oxidizer to the Space Shuttle Main Engines through seventeen-inch-diameter feed lines, at the rate of 47,365 and 17,592 gallons per minute respectively. The highly cooled chemicals reached each of the SSMEs, where two sets of turbopumps boosted the chemicals to pressures of 6,500 PSI for the propellant and 7,400 PSI for the oxidizer. The chemicals reached the combustion chambers at fulminating speeds before exploding in a hypergolic reaction that created a colossal outburst of highly pressurized steam.

The soul-numbing rumble that followed reverberated through the entire orbiter as each of the three SSMEs, capable of unleashing 375,000 pounds of thrust, kicked into life at 120-millisecond intervals, and automatically throttled up to the ninety percent level.

"We've got main engine start . . . three . . . two!"

The GPCs verified that all three engines had maintained the required thrust level before firing the pyrotechnic device in each of the two Solid Rocket Boosters, and the resulting blast echoed through Diane's soul as the astounding uproar of 7.5 million pounds· of thrust thundered against the cushion of water above the Mobile Launch Platform. The acoustic shock wave pounded the ground on this warm and humid dawn as the brightness from *Endeavour*'s engines illuminated the indigo sky, casting a yellowish glow for miles around.

The GPCs verified proper SRB ignition and, a fraction of a second later, initiated the eight explosive hold-down bolts—twenty-eight inches long and 3.5 inches thick—anchoring the shuttle to the Mobile Launch Platform. All three SSMEs throttled up to 104 percent, and the computers started the mission timer. Diane sensed upward motion.

"Liftoff! We have achieved liftoff!"

The 4.5-million-pound shuttle rose vertically in attitude hold until the SRBs' nozzles cleared the tower by forty feet.

"Houston, *Endeavour*. Starting roll maneuver," commented Diane in a monotone and controlled voice, shoving away all of her fears.

Endeavour began a combined roll, pitch, and yaw maneuver to position it head down, with the wings leveled and aligned with the launchpad.

"Roll maneuver completed."

"Endeavour, *Houston. Got a visual from the ground. You're looking good. Mark twenty seconds,"* Jake Cohen said from JSC.

"Roger, Houston," responded Diane.

Diane glanced at CRT#1, where an ascent-trajectory graph showed the desired ascent route and *Endeavour*'s current position as the GPCs issued millions of commands every second to the gimbal-mounted SSMEs and the SRBs to keep the orbiter on track. With this part of the mission totally automated, Diane and McGregor limited themselves to monitoring equipment and instruments as the shuttle rose higher and higher, leaving behind a billowing trail of steam and smoke.

"Houston, *Endeavour*. Mark thirty seconds. Throttling down for Max Q."

"Roger, Endeavour. Throttling down."

Endeavour's main engines throttled down to reduce the aerodynamic stress on the 21,000 thermal protection tiles glued to the orbiter's all-aluminum skin as the vehicle approached the speed of sound.

"Passed Max Q. Engines back up to 104 percent," reported Diane, as ice broke off from the External Tank and crashed against the front windowpanes. Diane saw their minute explosions before they disintegrated and washed away in the slipstream. One point three Mach. They had gone supersonic.

"Houston, *Endeavour*. Mark one minute ten seconds," reported McGregor. "Five nautical miles high, three nautical miles downrange, velocity reads at 2,300 feet per second."

Diane's eyes drifted to CRT#1. *Right on track*, she thought. The GPCs and their complex ascent phase algorithms performed beautifully. Right next to CRT#1 were the master alarm warning lights. All looked normal. Below it she saw the mission timer.

"Mark one minute twenty seconds, Houston," Diane read out. "Nine nautical miles high, six nautical miles downrange. Three thousand feet per second. Mark one minute thirty-five seconds."

"Roger, Endeavour. We copy you at one minute forty-five seconds. You are now negative seats. Repeat. Negative seats."

"Roger, negative seats," responded Diane as *Endeavour* soared above the maximum altitude for safe use of ejection seats.

Diane checked the chamber pressure of both Solid Rocket Boosters. It had dropped to 55 PSI down from 400 PSI at liftoff. At 50 PSI both SRBs automatically shut off and the GPCs' SRB separation sequence software automatically fired the bolts holding the SRBs to the External Tank.

Diane watched the pyrotechnic display as *Endeavour*, still mated to the ET, rocketed at nearly five thousand feet per second while both SRBs arced down toward the Atlantic almost ten miles below.

"Endeavour, Houston. Confirm SRB sep."

"Smooth, Houston. Very smooth," responded Diane. "Mark two minutes twenty-five seconds."

"Roger, Endeavour."

Diane and McGregor monitored the readings from the CRTs for the next five minutes as *Endeavour* gathered speed and altitude while depleting the propellant and heavy oxidizer in the External Tank. This made the shuttle progressively lighter without a change in upward thrust, allowing *Endeavour* to accelerate to 24,000 feet per second—the speed necessary to break away from the Earth's gravitational pull and achieve an orbital flight.

"Houston, *Endeavour*. Mark eight minutes twenty seconds, altitude sixty-three nautical miles, 645 nautical miles downrange. Standing by for MECO."

"Roger. Endeavour."

Diane watched the GPCs initiating the Main En-

gine Cut Off sequence. All three SSMEs shut off the
moment the feed-line valves connected to the um-
bilical cords coming out of the External Tank were
closed. Eighteen seconds later, the computers jettisoned the ET by firing the explosive bolts anchoring
it to the orbiter. Suddenly engulfed by the silence of
space, Diane watched the ET separating with a velocity of four feet per second. The tank would continue on a suborbital trajectory, which would take
whatever survived the reentry breakup to an impact
location in the Indian Ocean.

"Houston, *Endeavour*. We have ET sep," said
McGregor.

"Roger, Endeavour. *Eight minutes fifty-eight seconds,
confirmed External Tank separation."*

"Roger, Houston. Stand by for first OMS burn,"
said Diane as she armed both Orbital Maneuvering
System engines, vital to perform orbital insertion.
With its current altitude of eighty nautical miles and
inertial velocity of 24,300 feet per second, *Endeavour*
flew a very unstable suborbital trajectory, which
would bring the orbiter directly within the range of
the ISS's laser. In order to boost the orbiter to a safe
orbit fast, one long OMS thrusting burn would be
made instead of the usual two. The OMS engines
consisted of two pods, one on each side of the upper
aft fuselage on either side of *Endeavour*'s vertical sta-
bilizer.

"OMS burn in five ... four ... three ... two ...
one ... now!"

In each OMS engine, highly pressurized helium
forced both hydrazine propellant and liquid oxygen
down to the reaction chamber at great speed. The
chemicals clashed in a hyperbolic reaction, creating
the necessary outburst of thrust. The temporary silence gave way to yet another roaring blast. Diane

felt a mild pressure forcing her against her flight seat as the OMS engines, providing a combined thrust of twelve thousand pounds, began to accelerate *Endeavour.*

"Mark fifteen seconds, Houston. All systems nominal. Helium pressure's 3700 PSI on both tanks. Propellant and oxidizer pressure looks good," reported McGregor.

"We copy, Endeavour.*"*

Three minutes and twenty seconds later the OMS engines shut off, and Diane nodded approvingly. Orbital insertion had been as accurate as anyone could have hoped. *Endeavour* flew a stable orbit 180 degrees out of phase with the ISS, and on an intercept course with the Titan payload, which *Endeavour* would reach in another five hours.

"Good job, Endeavour.*"*

"Thanks."

In reality, besides initiating the single OMS burn, her contribution to the mission had been next to none.

But that changes now, she reflected as she unstrapped her safety harness and watched McGregor do the same.

"What do you think so far?" she asked.

"Well," he responded as they floated side by side behind the seats, "I just hope we can attach that mirror to the RMS arms."

"One thing at a time."

She removed her helmet, and her shoulder-length hair floated above her head. She wore a pair of small diamond earrings.

Diane used a single arm motion to push herself gently to the aft flight-deck station to open the payload bay doors and expose the vi-tal heat radiators to space. The radiators, used by *Endeavour*'s environmental-control system, dissipated the heat generated by the orbiter's equipment and also the heat accumulated on *Endeavour*'s skin during the ascent phase.

That accomplished, Diane dived through one of two interdeck hatches on the flight deck's floor down to the crew compartment, where Colonel Frank Ward and his three warriors, dressed in matching all-black uniforms, had already unstrapped themselves from their seats and were going over a diagram of the space station.

Three of the lockers on the forward section of the crew module, opposite the airlock, were already open, exposing a number of black boxes marked with bright yellow codes.

Colonel Ward raised his head and briefly made eye contact with Diane Williams before motioning one of his men to close the lockers.

Since their brief chat at the firing room a couple of days before, the colonel had kept conversation with the former Marine colonel to a minimum, and that suited Diane just fine. The less interaction she had with him or his men, the happier she felt. Jake was right. All she had to do was get Ward and his team close to the ISS, and then move out until it was safe to return. The rest was up to them.

"Everything okay, Commander?" asked Ward.

"No problems, Colonel. You and your men made it fine?"

"Yes. Smooth ascent."

"Good. I know you and your men are taking all the necessary precautions with your special payload, including whatever it is you have stored in those lockers. I'm sure you realize the danger involved if the air inside the crew module is contaminated. You do remember *Apollo 7,* right? The fire inside the capsule that incinerated three astronauts?"

Ward gave her a long stern look before saying, "All of my equipment was approved by NASA, Commander. Why don't you stick to your job and I'll stick to mine?"

"Fair enough," she responded, as Ward lowered his gaze back to the large blueprint floating in between the four Space Marines. Diane checked her watch and looked over to McGregor making his way through a hatch from the flight deck. "Start prebreathing in two hours, Gary."

McGregor also checked his watch before nodding. Prebreathing 100 percent oxygen was required prior to a space walk to remove nitrogen from his bloodstream. Inside the airlock, they breathed a mixture of oxygen and nitrogen at a pressure of 14.7 pounds per square inch, the same as sea level. But once inside a space suit, McGregor would breathe pure oxygen at a reduced pressure of only four PSI—the pressure required by the Extravehicular Mobility Unit suit for ease of limb movement during EVA without excessive physical effort. The rapid drop in pressure around his body would cause bubbles of nitrogen to form and expand in his bloodstream, causing severe nausea, cramps, paralysis, and even death—the same problem faced by scuba divers when surfacing too quickly following a deep underwater session.

Diane headed for the changeout station to the right of the airlock, and, extending the privacy curtain, she changed out of her crash suit and into the blue coveralls standard for shuttle missions.

She floated back up to the flight deck. She wanted to run some tests on the RMS arms. Its proper functionality was paramount to the mission.

Five

_____

The Flight Control Room was located on the third floor of the Mission Control Center at Johnson Space Center in Houston, Texas. Capsule Communicator (CapCom) Jake Cohen sat back on his swivel chair in the rear of the large room, where almost thirty flight controllers for this mission worked behind console computer displays arranged in rows of six or seven across the entire length of the room. A few projection screens on the front wall displayed different mission-related information, including a world chart that plotted _Endeavour_'s location in orbit and actual television pictures of activities inside and outside the shuttle, like the view of Earth on the screen to the right of the world chart, and a view of the payload bay on the screen to the left. Other displays showed critical data such as elapsed time after launch, or the time remaining before the next maneuver, which in *Endeavour*'s case was the time to rendezvous with the Titan target.

Jake removed his glasses, rubbed his eyes, and loosened his tie. So far, so good. Being CapCom was an important but quite stressful responsibility, particularly since he had to pretty much live inside Mission Control for the duration of the flight. But like his predecessors, going all the way back to the Mercury Program of the early sixties, Jake understood the significance of him being here. He was the primary voice that the crew aboard *Endeavour* heard after launch. He was their primary contact while the astronauts traveled in space at over twenty-four times the speed of sound. In his hands, and in the hands of the Flight Director (called Flight) sitting to Jake's immediate right, rested the responsibility of making sound split-second decisions and passing them on to the crew in space in an emergency. CapComs and Flights have been doing basically the same thing for over forty years: assisting countless crews on countless spacecraft accomplish their missions and return home safely.

Since it opened for business on a 1,620-acre site twenty-five miles southeast of Houston in February of 1964, the responsibilities of the Johnson Space Center have included the design, development, and testing of spacecraft, the selection and training of astronauts, the planning and conducting of manned missions, and many other activities related to help man understand life in outer space. And it all started with the Mercury Program.

The Mercury Program. Jake couldn't help a tiny smile. The term Capsule Communicator was a holdover from those early manned flights, when Mercury was called a capsule rather than a spacecraft. Those had been simpler times, when compared to current events, yet . . . *look at what we have done with our accomplishments.*

Jake felt disappointed that despite all the technical advancements and all the scientific breakthroughs, man was still man. And at that moment one madman was at the controls of the world's most advanced—and most expensive—technological wonder, and the U.S. had sent an equally technological wonder to stop him before he wiped out the downtown area of every major capital in the world—according to a communiqué broadcast just hours ago from Grozny, Chechnya. Unless the United Nations—Russia in particular—agreed to a twenty-point list of demands from the Chechen president, including the acquisition of nuclear missiles to protect itself again future Russian threats, the terrorist would start releasing the GPATS deadly cargo one at a time according to a priority list of targets.

Jake could only pray that Colonel Ward's team was indeed as good as he claimed, and that nothing went wrong with the orbiter. Clearly, there was no other way to regain control of the ISS than by force.

Six

_____

From the aft mission station of the flight deck, Diane Williams guided one of two Remote Manipulator System arms from its stowed position on the main longeron of the starboard payload-bay upper wall to the large segmented mirror hovering thirty feet above the orbiter.

She looked through one of the two rear-facing windows at the fifty-foot-long mechanical arm, which had six joints designed to mimic the human arm. The RMS had shoulder yaw and pitch joints, an elbow pitch joint, and wrist pitch, yaw, and roll joints—all controlled by a joystick-type hand controller.

Slaved to Diane's hand motions, the RMS slowly extended toward one side of the rectangular mirror, nearly as long as _Endeavour_ and just as wide as the orbiter's wingspan. Anchored to the end of the robot arm was Gary McGregor in his Extravehicular Mobility Unit (EMU), an untethered pressurized suit that provided McGregor with a one hundred percent oxygen environment pressurized to three pounds per square inch (PSI), the equivalent atmospheric pressure of 14,000 feet in altitude.

They already almost had to scrub the mission because of the difficulties in retrieving the large segmented mirror from a malfunctioning Titan shroud. The procedure, which NASA had scheduled to take only four hours, had actually taken three times as long, requiring two separate space walks because the oxygen supply inside the EMU backpack only lasted eight hours. Using a battery-operated circular saw, McGregor had cut the faulty latching mechanism halfway through his second EVA, allowing the spring-loaded shroud to separate along its longitudinal axes, exposing the mirror, which then had to be unfolded before attempting to secure it to the ends of the two RMS arms.

This flight was the first time that NASA had loaded two RMS arms aboard a shuttle. Normally, only one robot arm was needed to accomplish most operations involving satellite deployment and retrievals, but this situation was quite different. Two arms were required in order to achieve a strong grip on the mirror, particularly during orbit transfer maneuvers, when *Endeavour* would use the Orbital Maneuvering System engines to change orbits and chase the space station. But loading a second RMS arm aboard the shuttle had come at the price of sacrificing the Ku-band antenna, normally used for communication and data transmissions at a much faster rate than the orbiter's S-band antennas. This was a reasonable compromise to increasing the odds of keeping that mirror snuggled tight against the shuttle.

McGregor disengaged himself from the end of the

RMS arm and grabbed a handle at the edge of the mirror.

"Tether yourself to the RMS, Gary," she said when noticing that McGregor had not secured his EMU suit to the manipulator arm after disengaging from the RMS. If something went wrong at that moment, McGregor could be sent floating out of control away from the orbiter with nothing to hold him back.

"Okay," he responded as he attached one end of a woven cable to the RMS while clipping the other to a metal ring on the side of his pressure suit. *"All right, now bring the end up . . . nice and gently."*

The arm's standard end was only about three feet from the edge of the mirror. Using the two-position slide switch on top of the rotational hand controller, Diane changed the sensitivity of the arm from coarse to vernier. The RMS motors moved now at a fraction of the speed they did before. Operating in this fine-adjusting mode, Diane positioned the end of the RMS within inches of a special fitting welded onto the aluminum-and-graphite frame supporting the segmented mirror.

"All right. How's that?"

"Almost there. Bring it up just a dash."

Slowly, following McGregor's hand signals, Diane brought the end of the arm in direct contact with the latching pin on the mirror, until the latch snapped in place.

Locking the arm, Diane Williams switched control of the Rotational Hand Controller to the second RMS, set the vernier/coarse switch back to coarse, and mimicked the position of the first RMS. This time she did it without the help of McGregor, who was still strapped to the first RMS and was currently engaged in clamping a high-resolution TV camera to the edge of the mirror to be able to see objects on the other side of the mirror.

One of the complications of having two manipulator arms on board was that Diane could only control one arm at a time. Although the wiring for a second hand controller existed, NASA had never installed it because it had never been needed, until now. But such installation would had taken weeks to complete—time the world did not have.

"All right, Gary. I think you can come in now."

"On my way."

McGregor returned to the payload bay by crawling back along the first RMS. When he reached the airlock he said, *"I'm inside."*

"All right. Good job," Diane responded as she commanded the second RMS to pull the mirror closer to *Endeavour*, leaving just a foot between the orbiter's upper fuselage and the honeycomb frame supporting the mirror.

"How much clearance does that gives us?" said Colonel Frank Ward, who had been standing behind Diane for the past minute. The Lockheed boarding vehicle stored in the payload bay needed at least ten feet of clearance between the edge of the cargo bay wall and the mirror.

Without looking at the large black soldier, Diane said, "Not enough for your boarding vehicle. You tell me when you're ready, and I will lift one side to let you out. Otherwise, I'm keeping that mirror as close as possible to the orbiter."

"That's fine," Ward responded.

Diane felt bad enough that the vertical fin, the OMS pods, and a portion of the nose were not covered by the mirror. She didn't want sections of the wings also exposed by moving the mirror around. The OMS pods and the nose had to be exposed since that was where *Endeavour*'s attitude vernier rockets were located. Those rockets were critical for orbital maneuvering, and their exhaust paths could not be obstructed. But anything else was safely hidden behind the segmented mirror.

NASA had estimated the chances of the laser hitting the unprotected sections of the orbiter at less than three percent. And given the fact that she would just be dropping her load and then quickly getting out of the laser's range, she would be exposed to that three percent for just over twenty minutes. To make matters even safer for the crew of *Endeavour*, the mission plan called for approaching the station during nighttime, when the gigantic solar panels of the station would be essentially off, and the only power available for the laser would have to come from the GPATS module's vast array of storage batteries. According to the laser manufacturer, the batteries would only support somewhere around fifteen laser shots, depending on the energy level used and the duration of each event. After that, the Russian terrorist would be unable to fire the weapon until the station came back around into the daylight portion of the ninety-minute orbit. That gave Diane roughly forty-five minutes to make her approach, take the laser hits, drop the UNSCF soldiers and their gear, and get out of Dodge.

"How much time will we have to clear *Endeavour* once we're in position?" asked Ward.

"About ten minutes."

Ward nodded before turning around and propelling himself down one of the interdeck hatches.

Diane thought of Ward's secret cargo stored in the lockers below, hoping it wasn't anything flammable. An explosion inside the crew module would be bad news for everyone aboard. But she didn't realistically

expect NASA to approve the storage of any dangerous substance inside the crew's living quarters.

Diane reached for the intercom. "Colonel?"

"Yes, Commander?"

"Please secure your gear in the crew compartment.
We have a twenty-five-minute window to start our approach to the ISS. OMS burn in fifteen minutes."

"No problem."

"Gary? You're through?" Diane asked.

"I'm getting rid of the EMU." McGregor responded
from inside the airlock.

"Get up here now."

McGregor floated into the flight deck a few
minutes later.

"Diane . . . I think we have a little problem down
there," he whispered, pointing to one of the hatches
leading to the crew compartment below.

"Yes?"

Swallowing hard, McGregor said, "I got a chance
to take a good look at what Ward's been guarding
so carefully."

"And?"

"While I was changing inside the airlock, I saw
them through the hatch's window."

"What is it, Gary?"

"HEP."

"Wh—what?"

"And from the looks of it, those guys down there
were inserting fuses into the plastic. I guess they were
waiting until after we reached orbit to arm the explosives to avoid the strong vibrations during ascent."

Putting a hand to her forehead, Diane Williams
struggled to calm down. She couldn't believe that
someone would be insane enough to bring high-
explosive plastic on-board a shuttle. *And armed?*

She rushed past McGregor and dived through one of the interdeck openings.

"Colonel!" she screamed, reaching the crew compartment and startling the four UNSC soldiers, who were setting up the seats in preparation for the orbital maneuvers to chase the station. Each soldier had an oxygen mask over his face. A plastic tube ran from each clear mask to a pint-size tank strapped to the belt of each uniform. The soldiers were prebreathing pure oxygen in preparation for their space walk.

Ward pulled down the mask. "I'm right here, Commander. There's no reason to scream."

"Who gave you permission to bring explosives aboard this orbiter?"

Ward gave her an odd little glance. "I thought we had an understanding here about our respective roles."

"Not when it involves bringing HEP inside my shuttle."

Ward exhaled slowly, obviously not happy that she had found out about the HEP, but still trying to see if he could reason with her. He put his arms in front of him, palms facing Diane while the other soldiers looked on with curiosity. "Look, nothing's going to happen. We are profession—"

"I want to jettison the explosives immediately," she said.

The UNSC colonel simply crossed his arms. "Can't do that, Commander. The HEP's a critical element of our mission. If we can't regain control of the station before the terrorist regains access to the launching software, then my orders are to blow up the module. Besides, HEP doesn't just blow on accident because of vibrations or anything else. It need to be detonated."

"It wasn't a request, Colonel. It was an order."

"Sorry, Commander. That's an unreasonable request. Besides, I only take orders from the Secretary General of the United Nations. This is the way the UNSC has approved to carry out the mission, and the White House has bought into it."

"Do you realize what can happen if any of those charges go off inside the crew module?"

"*Won't* happen." Ward was beginning to show an edge. "The only time we were at risk was during ascent, and during that time I had the detonators removed from the charges. Now I need to get the charges ready for my mission. You've just told me I would only have ten minutes to get ready after reaching the ISS. That's barely enough time to—"

"We're not going anywhere until you lose those," Diane said, pointing a thumb toward the lockers. "And that's final."

"You're compromising my mission, Commander. I have permission from the UNSC to neutralize anyone who jeopardizes my team's ability to achieve our objective." Ward placed a hand on the stun gun strapped to his belt.

Diane tightened her fists and said, "And who's going to fly this shuttle?"

"Your Mission Pilot."

"He's not going to do it."

"Let's ask him."

Diane didn't like the way this was headed. She was losing control. "I'm calling Houston."

"Be my guest. But do it quickly, or we're going to miss our window."

Fuming, Diane headed back up to the flight deck, where a stone-faced McGregor stood by one of the interdeck openings.

"Jesus Christ, Diane. Let's just do it. Let's drop

them off by the ISS and get the hell away from there until it's safe to return."

Reaching her seat, Diane put on her headgear and contacted Houston using the S-band frequency.

"Houston, *Endeavour*."

"*Endeavour, Houston. Go ahead,*" came the voice of Jake Cohen.

"Houston, I'm afraid we have a problem. Colonel Ward has stored HEP inside the crew compartment. I want to jettison it. We can't afford to have an explosion in here."

"*Ah . . . that's a negative, Endeavour. The explosives are secured, and are a vital component of this mission. HEP is very safe unless purposefully detonated.*"

"Houston, we're talking about high-explosive plastic that could kill us all and destroy the orbiter. This goes totally against NASA policy. Remember *Apollo 7*? We can't allow anything that volatile on board."

"*Sorry, Endeavour. The soldiers must keep the HEP. We don't have a choice on this one. Their orders are to blast the GPATS module if they can't get inside the station. Besides, the Apollo 7 incident happened because the capsule had a 100 oxygen environment. You don't.*"

"But they already have the fuses in and connected to the detonators. All it takes is one electric charge, and they'll blow!"

"*This one comes straight from the top. The HEP stays. And you better get everything secured or you'll miss the window to reach the ISS in time.*"

Diane inhaled deeply. This was a mistake. A terrible mistake. Closing her eyes, she briefly prayed that nothing went wrong with the approach. Although HEP had a long safety record and was very unlikely to go off accidentally, Diane didn't want to add more risk to their mission. A subsystem could explode if the laser hit the wrong spot on the orbiter. Having explosives on board could create secondary explosions if the initial blast happened to be close to the charges.

"*Endeavour, Houston, Confirm orders.*"

Diane shook her head as she said, "I want it on the record that I disagree with the orders, but I will execute them. I will secure all objects in preparation for the OMS burn."

"*Roger, Houston out.*"

Slowly, Diane turned around, only to be welcomed by Colonel Frank Ward wearing a headset. The plastic oxygen mask floated under his square chin. The UNSC colonel had been listening to the conversation. McGregor stood in the back, flanked by two of Ward's men. The short F-16 pilot looked quite helpless next to the large and muscular soldiers in allblack uniforms.

"All set?" Ward asked.

Diane Williams nodded and turned back to her instruments. "We're about to start an orbital-change maneuver. Everyone take your seats."

Ward floated toward the back of the flight deck and disappeared through one of the interdeck hatches. The two soldiers followed him.

McGregor approached Diane as she strapped herself to her seat and put the headgear back on.

"Diane, are you—"

"Is the airlock secured, Gary?"

"Ye—yes. It's secured."

"Good. Strap in. We've got work to do."

Diane refused to let her emotions surface more than they already had. She was a professional. She was *Endeavour*'s commander. She would behave as such for as long as the mission lasted.

Before starting the final approach to the ISS, Diane had to realign the Inertial Measurement Units—

three all-attitude, four-gimbal, inertially stabilized platforms that provided critical inertial attitude and velocity data to *Endeavour*'s General Purpose Computers—to maintain an accurate estimate of orbiter position and velocity during the orbital flight.

She did a quick radio check inside the orbiter to make sure all was secured. Satisfied, she reached for an overhead panel and enabled the Star Tracker system. Talk-back lights on the same panel told her both Star Tracker doors just forward and to the left of the front windowpanes had fully opened, exposing the two sophisticated bright object sensors to the cosmos. In addition to the nose attitude-control rockets, the Star Tracker system was another reason why the segmented mirror could not cover the orbiter's nose section.

The Star Tracker system measured the line-of-sight vectors to the two brightest stars within the system's field of view. The data was fed to the GPCs, which calculated the orientation between the selected stars and *Endeavour* to define the orbiter's attitude and relative velocity. A comparison between the calculated attitude and the attitude measured by the Inertial Measuring Unit provided Diane with the correction factor necessary to null the IMU error.

The newly adjusted position and velocity vectors, or "state" vectors, were then compared to the International Space Station's state vectors fed to *Endeavour*'s GPCs via S-band telemetry communications relayed from Houston. Both sets of state vectors, updated once every millisecond as both *Endeavour* and the ISS orbited the Earth, were fed to the Guidance, Navigation, and Control software running in the GPCs, which in turn fired the Orbital Maneuvering System thrusters.

Diane's eyes drifted to the OMS helium pressure

and hydrazine propellant indicators as the engines came to life, unleashing twenty-six thousand pounds of thrust for fifteen seconds, directing a tail-first *Endeavour* toward its planned delivery orbit, nicknamed Delta. The mild deceleration force pressed her against the back of her flight seat as the southern portion of South America flashed across the top of the front windowpanes before disappearing behind the edge of the segmented mirror frame. In her mind, however, flashed the armed charges shifting inside their containers.

Focus!

A scan of control panel F7, where three five-inch-by-seven-inch green-on-green CRTs displayed the status of *Endeavour*'s vital systems, showed nominal. The array of talk-back indicator lights between CRT#1 and CRT#2, and directly above CRT#3 also showed no warnings. The OMS helium pressure indicator to the left of CRT#3 marked 3,700 pounds per square inch, matching the digital readouts on CRT#1 directly above.

"ETA to Delta Orbit, fifteen minutes," said McGregor, typing a few commands on the right keypad of the center console beneath control panel F7, while checking the readouts of the rendezvous radar measurement, which provided range and range rate to the station. Unlike the late nineties rendezvous radar systems, which could not be used until the orbiter got within fifteen miles of the target, the new system gave them ranging information from as far away as nine hundred miles.

Diane barely acknowledged it, her eyes switching back and forth between the mission event timer and CRT#1. At Delta Orbit, *Endeavour* would have achieved the necessary translational velocity to maintain an orbit six miles behind the ISS.

The GPCs stopped the OMS engines. "Burn complete," she said as the software programmed the aft and forward Reaction Control System verniers to turn the orbiter without disturbing its translational velocity, positioning the mirror toward the ISS. The moment the inertial system detected that the orbiter achieved the desired attitude, the GPCs fired the RCS thrusters in the opposite direction to counter the rotation.

She briefly glanced at McGregor before using a secured S-band radio frequency and speaking into her voice-activated headset. "Houston, *Endeavour.*"

"*Go ahead,* Endeavour." She heard Jake's voice coming through very clear. Audio and video communications, as well as telemetry-data transfer, were established through the S-band frequency. Information from *Endeavour* traveled to one of three Tracking and Data Relay Satellites (TDRS) in geosynchronous orbit, where the signal was amplified and relayed to White Sands Tracking Station in New Mexico, before arriving in Houston. Although the link had been established nearly thirty years before, it still remained the best and most reliable way to establish clean, secured, and uninterrupted communications during a mission.

"Houston, OMS burn complete. ETA to Delta thirteen minutes, twenty seconds, over."

"*Endeavour, you're confirmed.*"

"Will be within firing range in one minute," Diane said while checking the leftover pressure on the OMS helium and propellant tanks, which told her that *Endeavour* now had enough fuel left for two more orbital maneuvers besides the deorbit burn at the end of the mission.

Diane glanced at McGregor, who brushed his mustache with a finger while frowning slightly, obviously feeling as nervous about this whole ordeal as she did.

"We're in range," McGregor said, while releasing his restraining harness and heading to the aft station, where he could make adjustments to the RMS arms if necessary.

Diane turned around and gave McGregor a glance. The Mission Pilot already had planted himself in front of the aft station, his right hand on the RMS hand controller, which was currently set to control the starboard mechanical arm.

As the orbiter quickly reached its orbital position behind the ISS, Diane prayed that the mirror would hold in place and that the soldiers kept the HEP safe.

Seven

His feet secured to Velcro attachments in front of the crew support station of the Habitation Module, Sergei Viktor Dudayev heard the proximity alarms disturb the peaceful whir of the air-revitalization system inside the International Space Station.

He checked the timer on the support station before pulling free of his Velcro anchor and propelling himself across the twenty feet that separated him from the Unity module, which connected to the aft section of the cylindrical module.

His Chechen contacts had been right in assessing the Americans. They were sending a shuttle his way in an attempt to regain control of the station before Sergei could release any of the warheads.

But they do not know what kind of enemy they are facing.

Floating cleanly through the hatch connecting the Hab Module to Unity, Sergei kicked his legs against the padded wall to his right and cut left to snug his short frame through the opening leading to the GPATS module. The screen of the proximity radar, which filled the space three hundred miles around the station with energy, showed an approaching space vehicle. The computers had already identified it as the Space Shuttle *Endeavour*.

Eight

At Houston Space Center, Jake Cohen watched the image displayed on the huge projection screen in the front center of the Flight Control Room on the third floor of the Mission Control Center. The telescopic lens of the camera McGregor had attached to the starboard edge of the segmented mirror captured the image of the ISS in the distance. It looked like a white dot with multiple white lines extending like tentacles. The dot was the core of the station, where all the modules interconnected. The lines were the sections of the scaffoldlike booms supporting the gigantic solar panels. At this moment those panels were not powering the station because the Earth was now positioned between the ISS and the Sun.

Jake clenched his jaw and simply waited for the laser attack that he feared would follow soon.

Nine

"We're here, Colonel. Stay in your seats until we're safe," Diane said over the intercom while still strapped to her seat. Her left hand was glued to the Rotational Hand Controller (RHC), the center stick located in between her legs, which controlled the attitude verniers on the nose and the OMS engine pods. By simply moving the RHC as she would an airplane control stick, vernier rockets in the nose and rear of the orbiter would fire to move *Endeavour* in the desired direction.

A backward glance and she saw McGregor still in front of the aft crew station, right hand on the RMS controller.

"We're gathering our equipment," Ward said over the intercom from below.

"No, no. Stay in your seats. Keep your equipment secured."

"We can't. There isn't enough time."

"But there is no telling how the orbiter is going to take the lase—"

A blinding flash, followed by a powerful jolt. The orbiter suddenly went into uncontrollable gyrations.

Dear God!

"Keep that mirror taut against us, Gary!" Diane screamed, realizing a moment later that the laser had either partially struck the nose of the orbiter, or its energy level was far greater than Los Alamos had predicted. *Endeavour*'s nose was not only blackened, but a number of heat-protection tiles were missing while the rest appeared charred. The laser had damaged the nose's rotational verniers. Two of them were firing sporadic bursts of—

A second laser flash engulfed the orbiter, this time without the direct protection of the mirror as *Endeavour* tumbled across space.

An explosion rocked the orbiter, followed by an even larger blast that sent powerful stress waves across the entire fuselage. Warning lights came alive on the control panel as a second explosion rocked the shuttle. The laser must have sliced through the exposed skin of the orbiter, damaging subsystems.

"Smoke! We've got smoke down there!" screamed McGregor from the aft crew station.

Diane turned around and watched black smoke coiling up from the crew module. The smell of cordite assaulted her nostrils.

"The HEP!" she screamed as her fears became reality. "A charge must have gone off!"

"Jesus, what are we going to—"said McGregor.

"Remain at your post!" she commanded, while her right hand applied forward and right pressure to the RHC to get *Endeavour*'s upper side facing the station again. The orbiter, however, would not respond, as the nose verniers continued to fire at random, making it impossible for her to offset their thrusts with the aft verniers.

"Colonel Ward? Colonel Ward? Do you copy?" she said over the intercom.

Nothing.

"Colonel? Colonel?"

No response.

"Let me go down there and check it out," McGregor said.

"Remain at your post!"

The smoke was now beginning to fill the flight deck, but it was not as thick as it first looked. Most of it was already being sucked out by the air-revitalization subsystem, which was still operational after the explosions.

But smoke was the least of Diane's problems. *Endeavour* was still dangerously exposed to the ISS, and she could not bring it back under control.

"Houston, we have a problem."

"We've heard, Endeavour," came Jake's voice. *"You're showing multiple failures of the payload-bay door system, rotational verniers, and—"*

"Houston, I'm having a hard time correcting the orbiter's attitude," Diane said, as she began to move her hand toward an overhead panel, where she planned to switch from General Purpose Computer control, to manual control of the Orbital Maneuvering System engines. But her hand never made it. Instead both arms got thrown forward from the fierce explosion that followed the intense light of a laser beam that caught *Endeavour* broadside.

In a blur, Diane saw a cloud of thermal-protection white tiles bursting off the orbiter's starboard wing. Several crashed against the front and side window-panes.

"The mirror is loose!" screamed McGregor.

Diane looked up, through the upper windowpanes, and instead of seeing the black supporting frame of the mirror, she saw stars.

"Where is it?" she asked.

"The starboard RMS has broken loose from the payload bay. The mirror's off to the side! I still got ahold of it with the port RMS, but it's no longer shielding us!"

"Jesus Christ," she mumbled as the nose verniers ran out of fuel.

Black-and-white tiles, the Earth, and the stars flashing across her field of view, Diane glanced at the array of warning lights between CRT#1 and #2, and noticed the PAYLOAD CAUTION and the HYDROGEN PRESSURE warning lights on the red. *At least the OMS engines and the aft RCS thrusters are still healthy*, Diane thought as her left hand reached down for the Rotational Hand Controller. Now that she did not have to fight the damaged nose verniers, she had a chance to stabilize the orbiter before using the OMS engines. She could not attempt an orbital burn until the shuttle had achieved the proper attitude; otherwise, the burn would simply send *Endeavour* into even more uncontrollable gyrations.

"Get that mirror under control, Gary!"

"Working on it!"

Her hand applied forward right pressure to the RHC. This time the orbiter responded, but sluggishly because it was operating on only a partial set of rotational vernier engines.

"Houston, Houston, this is *Endeavour*. I'm bringing the orbiter under control. OMS burn in ten seconds. Eight . . . seven . . . five . . . three . . . now." She threw the switch, expecting to feel the slight acceleration from the OMS engines.

Instead, a powerful explosion thrust Diane into her restraining harness. A side view of McGregor's body flying past her and crashing against the front windowpanes brought images of dummies inside automobiles during crash tests. The explosion shook the entire vessel as the CRTs on the center control panel burst in a radial cloud of glass that reached Diane's face before her own hands.

She screamed as razor-sharp glass rushed past her and crashed against the aft crew station of the flight deck.

Bouncing back on her flight seat as the orbiter went into another set of uncontrolled rotations, Diane forced herself to breathe between her teeth to avoid inhaling any glass particles or the floating beads of blood lifting off the multiple cuts on her face and neck. McGregor was out of sight, probably floating somewhere behind her.

Alarms blaring, Diane turned her head, only to see Gary McGregor choking on his own blood from a shard of glass embedded in his throat.

"No, no!" she screamed as their eyes met while she unstrapped her safety harness.

Diane reached him near the center of the flight deck, feeling utterly helpless as McGregor made guttural noises while small clouds of foam and blood left his slashed neck and were inhaled by his opened nostrils. He was drowning in front of her.

Slowly, she reached for the piece of glass and pulled it out, but the stream of spherical blood globules that spewed out of the wound nearly drowned her, forcing her to pull away with her hands on her face.

Holding her breath while waving away the floating blood, Diane refocused on McGregor's eyes, but saw no life in them. She reached with her right hand to close them, but another flash, followed by a horrifying explosion, shoved her against the front windowpanes.

"Oh, God!" she mumbled as her head and right shoulder burned from the impact. Bouncing against the panes, Diane floated right past McGregor and toward the aft crew station, where she hit legs first before bouncing back to the front of the flight deck.

Disoriented from the multiple blows, Diane wildly tried to reach for anything to slow down her momentum and prevent another collision, which came a second later, against the back of her own flight seat.

The disciplined Marine inside her taking command, Diane wrapped both arms around the back of the flight seat and tried to take a peek at the control panel.

Warning lights filled control panel F7, where three rectangular holes showed the place where the CRTs had been a minute before. A look outside the windowpanes revealed nothing but a cloud of broken tiles and other debris she couldn't make out. All she could figure was that the OMS engines had been damaged by the laser and blew up when she had tried to use them.

Finding it hard to breathe, Diane quickly reached for the lightweight headset floating over McGregor's head. She disconnected it from McGregor's portable leg unit, and plugged it in her own unit. Once more she hugged the back of the flight seat.

"Houston, Houston. *Endeavour*, here. Do you copy?"

Nothing.

"Houston, this is *Endeavour*. Do you—"

Another flash, followed by three explosions as the laser cut deeper into the orbiter, destroying its core.

The blasts pressed her against the seat with a force so great that for a moment Diane felt she was pulling Gs in an F-18. She felt the sudden urge to vomit, and bending over, she did, coughing a large cloud of blood from a number of burst capillaries in her mouth and throat. Her eyes filled as she turned her face away from the floating blood moving toward the rear of the flight deck, where it mixed with the smoke still rising from the crew compartment below.

Another glance at the control panel told her of the lost cause she faced. All main systems were gone, including the air-revitalization system, which explained why she was having a hard time breathing. Then she saw the front windowpanes, saw the growing cracks streaking across the 1.3-inch-thick panes.

Diane knew what that meant, and without another thought, she kicked her legs against the back of the seat and pushed her bruised body toward the left interdeck hatch, just aft of her flight seat, where she curled her fingers on the side rails and pulled herself into the mid deck compartment. The smoke there was thicker than in the flight deck, but she could still see her way through the—

The sight almost made her vomit, but the Marine in her took over, forcing control as she stared at the mangled and charred body parts floating in—

Hurry.

She had no time to waste. The moment those panes gave, the vacuum pressure would be unbearable as everything loose got sucked through the openings. The sudden loss of pressure would mean instant death.

Her hands reached the airlock hatch actuator lock lever at the rear of the crew compartment, and she turned it 180 degrees to unlatch it, pulling the D-shaped hatch toward her. The massive door pivoted up and to the side, exposing the roomy interior of the airlock. Diane floated inside and closed and locked the hatch behind her just as another explosion shook the vessel, giving Diane the impression that the orbiter would come apart any minute. The blast shoved her against the opposite side of the airlock, where the back of her head struck one of the aluminum alloy handholds on the sides of the locked hatch that led to the payload bay.

In an instant, the madness around her ceased and Diane Williams lost consciousness.

Ten

_____

Sergei Dudayev watched the wingless orbiter tumble away after he blasted it one last time before the battery level dropped below the fifty percent mark. He decided to stop firing to conserve power in case he needed it before the ISS could reach the daylight portion of its orbit and replenish the battery charge.

Sergei adjusted the resolution of the spotting telescope of the GPATS module. At such short distance it gave him a clear view of the broken front windowpanes, which meant that the flight deck and the crew compartment had lost pressurization. He also noticed a missing payload bay door, most of the wings and vertical fin, and nearly half of the thermal protection tiles. The shield, which Sergei assumed was made out of segmented mirrors since it had deflected the initial laser shot, now floated away from the orbiter with one of the RMS arms still attached to it. Farther away, he saw the missing payload door, now a rotating hunk of twisted, blackened aluminum.

Sergei glanced at *Endeavour* one last time and shook his head. *Fools. Maybe now they will concede to my people's demands.*

He shifted his gaze to the locked workstation.

******PROCEDURE VIOLATION******
TIME LIMIT EXCEEDED. SYSTEM RESET IN
PROGRESS
******32:28:14******

Soon, he thought. *Soon the warheads will be mine.*

Eleven

"Come in *Endeavour*, over. *Endeavour* come in, over."

In the midst of a chaos inside the Flight Control Room, Jake Cohen waited for an answer, but all he got was the low hissing static noise coming from the overhead speakers.

"Sir," said the Electrical, Environmental, and Consumables Systems Engineer (EECOM) to Jake's far left, a blond-headed man of about thirty with fair skin and a wide nose, wearing black-framed glasses. EECOM was responsible for monitoring *Endeavour*'s fuel cells, avion-ics, cabin-cooling systems, electrical-distribution systems, and cabin-pressure-control systems. "We're still getting S-band telemetry from the orbiter through the TDRS-White Sands link, and it shows zero pressurization inside the crew compartment and flight deck. I'm afraid that—"

"Yes, I know," Jake said, more to himself than to

anyone. "*Endeavour* just got hit multiple times by that damned laser!"

Silence in the control room.

"GUIDO," Jake said a moment later. "Status."

The Guidance Officer, call sign GUIDO, sitting a row in front of Jake, was responsible for monitoring onboard navigation and guidance computer software.

While looking at the telemetry data browsing across his twenty-inch color screen, GUIDO said, "Orbiter tumbling along all three axes while maintaining a concentric orbit with the station roughly six miles away. Guidance computer software showing a major malfunction. I'm afraid we can't control the orbiter via remote."

Jake glanced to his right at the Propulsion Systems Engineer. "Talk to me, PROP."

The fifty-year-old PROP, a veteran astronaut himself, was responsible for monitoring and evaluating the Reaction Control and the Orbital Maneuvering System engines. He also managed propellants. PROP kept his eyes on the data displayed in his console. "Doesn't look good. Major malfunctions on the OMS engines. Looks like the laser cracked the propellant tanks and they blew the moment Commander Williams fired them."

Damn. I can't believe this has actually happened. And Diane, the crew . . . God Almighty.

And that Russian bastard is still at large.

Closing his eyes, Jake Cohen removed his glasses, rubbed his eyes, and breathed deeply. He looked to his left. The Flight Director had already left the room to brief the NASA Administrator, who in turn would pass the information to the President and his staff.

"Wait . . . wait," said the blond-headed EECOM.

"The computers are showing nominal pressure inside the airlock. Oxygen content is at thirty-two percent. Pressure is 14.7 PSI." Slowly, he turned to Jake. "Do you think that—"

Jake snapped forward. "Damned right I do! I say we got us some astronauts marooned inside that airlock! What's the status of the pressure-control system and oxygen supply?"

The EECOM's fingers worked on the keyboard as data flashed off and on the screen. After several seconds, he said, "We're in luck. Pressure system is active and still trying to repressurize the crew compartment. My guess is that we got a serious opening to space inside that compartment and the system can't pressurize it. I'm showing two fuel cells down and one still operational."

Jake nodded. "Redirect the pressure-control system to support only the airlock, nothing else. Disconnect all other systems that might be draining the fuel cell. Let's focus everything we have on keeping the atmosphere inside that airlock within the normal range. That will buy us some time."

"Yes, sir."

Since the pressure-control system didn't have to operate at full power because all it was pressurizing was the volume of air inside the airlock, the single fuel cell could last much longer. This was a significant advantage because the oxygen used by *Endeavour*'s life-support system was the same liquid oxygen used by the fuel cell, along with liquid hydrogen, in an electrochemical reaction to produce electricity. The longer the fuel cell lasted, the longer that airlock would be not only fully pressurized, but also filled with air.

"It's done. At the current load, that fuel cell should last us about twenty-four hours, give or take a few, depending on how many astronauts are alive," commented the EECOM.

Jake stared at the blank screen, where only a few minutes before he had seen the images captured by *Endeavour*'s video cameras. Now he was blind, trying to help a dying orbiter while operating in the dark. *Well, almost in the dark*, he admitted. At least partial telemetry data continued to pour in, giving his support crew the information they might need in order to figure a way out of this mess.

Interlacing the fingers of his hands in front of his face, Jake closed his eyes, praying that at least somebody had made it to the airlock. Based on the conversation aboard *Endeavour* before the attack, Jake felt that Diane and McGregor were the two with the best chance of being inside that airlock because they should have been up in the flight deck controlling the orbiter and the RMS arm at the time of the HEP blast inside the crew compartment below.

I should have listened to you, Diane.

Jake Cohen forced the guilt out of his mind. He needed his logical side operating at full capacity in order to guide his staff through this one. Every piece of telemetry data arriving into the Flight Control Room would have to be scrutinized by itself and in combination with other information to try to piece together a possible salvage operation of an orbiter that already appeared beyond salvage.

Twelve

Diane Williams pulled up so fast after releasing her Hornet's ordnance that she thought the Gs would crush her. Her vision tunneled to the information projected on the F-18's heads-up display. Diane kept the control column pulled back. The Hornet shot up into the overcast sky, its wings biting the air as it rolled above the clouds and the sun filled her cockpit, making her feel so detached from the world below. Flying gave her a sense of omnipotence she could get nowhere else. She belonged to a privileged class, an aviator of the United States Marines, pilot of one of the most coveted and feared war machines in the world: the Hornet. Her Hornet. And Diane pushed it, forced it to the outer limits of its design envelope, rammed it into the tightest turns that its titanium-layered honeycomb structure could take, shoved it across the sky in any imaginable way to accomplish the job. To fulfill her promise to America that she would put *every single ounce of her life into doing what she had been trained to do.*

But her engines suddenly flamed out. Lights filled her cockpit as her jet tumbled out of control, alarms blaring. But then the noise went away as fast as it had appeared, and Diane suddenly found herself lying in that hospital bed at El Toro Air Station. The room was dark, humid, quiet. The lamp on her nightstand filled the room with yellow light, but it was enough to illuminate the faces of the others present in that room. Diane saw Dr. Lisa Hottle's face giving her a stern, yet compassionate look. Next to the doctor stood Gary McGregor in blue coveralls gazing at the floor, a large piece of glass embedded in his throat. Then Diane turned to the last person in the room, a large black man wearing a dark uniform. It was Colonel Frank Ward, his left hand holding an HEP charge. Then a blinding light filled the room, followed by a loud explosion and alarms, many alarms . . .

Another siren went off, but it didn't belong inside the hospital room. Diane didn't know where it had come from. The siren wasn't part of the nightmare. The siren was here, inside the sealed airlock of the wounded orbiter. It was the alarm that NASA had installed in all shuttles to give crews a five minute warning before the oxygen supply would run out.

Dizzy and in severe pain, Diane kept her eyes closed. The throbbing on the back of her head challenged the piercing pain from her throat, where blood vessels had burst from the G-like pressure induced by the multiple explosions. The coppery taste of blood filled her senses with the same intensity as the general body soreness from bouncing around the flight deck like a rag doll.

Floating upside down, Diane opened her eyes, feeling what had to be the worst headache of her life. The relentless pounding of veins against her temples seemed amplified by the siren telling her she had less than five minutes' worth of air inside that compartment, and from what she remembered she doubted *Endeavour* had any other pressurized compartment that could support life after the laser attack.

And McGregor, the UNSC soldiers . . .

Concentrate.

Turning off the alarm, she glanced through the four-inch-diameter observation window on the hatch leading to the payload bay, and visually checked the main cargo in *Endeavour*'s payload bay: the new and still untested Astronaut Maneuvering Vehicle—a four-person unpressurized prototype module designed by Lockheed to provide teams of UNSC personnel the flexibility of moving in space quickly and efficiently. The first production AMV was not supposed to be ready for another year, but the problems aboard the ISS called for Lockheed to release its only prototype.

"Shit," Diane whispered when spotting the vehicle upside down and jammed against the rear of the bay. Actually, most everything else that she could see through the narrow opening appeared out of place or missing.

Before she could attempt an Extravehicular Activity to check the damage done to the AMV and the other equipment in the payload bay, Diane had to start the hourlong 100 percent pure-oxygen prebreathing.

After a brief check that the integral oxygen tank for prebreathing was not operational, Diane grabbed the emergency portable oxygen unit off a built-in inner wall to her left. She actually needed the portable unit even if she wasn't planning an EVA because the oxygen level inside the airlock was falling below the safety level.

She placed the clear plastic mask over her nose and mouth and turned a red knob on the pint-size canister connected to the mask through a thin plastic tube. Letting the canister float overhead, Diane stripped naked. Next she opened a compartment containing most of the "underwear" garments she would have to put on prior to donning the actual EMU—the space suit designed to provided pressure, thermal and micrometeoroid protection, communications, and full environmental control support for one astronaut. The EMU's thick skin consisted of a number of layers, starting with an inner layer of urethane-coated nylon, followed by a restraining layer of Dacron, a thermal layer of neoprene-coated nylon, five layers of aluminized Mylar laminated with Dacron scrim, and an outermost layer made of Goretex, Kevlar, and Nomex for micrometeoroid protection.

Diane put on the Urine Collection Device—a pouch capable of holding one quart of liquid, derived from a device used by people with malfunctioning kidneys. She followed that with the Liquid Cooling and Ventilation Garment (LCVG) which, similar to long underwear, consisted of a one-piece front-zippered suit made of a stretch-nylon fabric but laced with over three hundred feet of plastic tubing, through which chilled water would flow to control her body temperature.

The undergarments out of the way, and while still breathing directly from the oxygen canister, Diane connected the LCVG's electrical harness to the upper torso section of the multilayered EMU she retrieved from another airlock compartment. She removed the EVA checklist attached to the upper torso's left sleeve and, having done her share of space walks, she gave it a quick scan before flinging it aside.

She attached the electrical harness to the EMU. Because the orbiter's communications system was dead, the electrical harness—designed to provide her with a biomedical and communications link to Mission Control—would not work until she reached the space station.

Next, she grabbed the connecting waist ring of the lower torso section—or suit pants—of the EMU, and, while floating in the middle of the airlock, she guided both legs into it. The lower torso came with boots, and joints in the hip, knee, and ankle to give the astronaut maximum mobility. Briefly removing the oxygen mask while extending both arms straight up, Diane "dived" into the upper torso section floating overhead, reattached the oxygen mask, and connected the tubing from the EMU to the Liquid Cooling and Ventilation Garment before joining and securing the upper and lower torso sections with the waist-entry closures of the connecting rings.

She checked her watch. According to NASA regulations, she had another forty minutes of prebreathing before she could go outside, but because the crippled orbiter could not provide her suit with cooling water, oxygen, and electrical power during the long prebreathing period to conserve the oxygen and battery power inside the EMU's backpack for actual EVA time, Diane decided to risk a prebreathing shortcut to maximize the eight hours' worth of oxygen of the Primary Life Support System (PLSS) backpack unit. Besides, her emergency oxygen canister would be exhausted in another five minutes and the air quality inside the airlock was already below the safe level.

Diane backed herself against one of two PLSS units and secured it in place. She made the appropriate connections for feedwater and oxygen, and secured the display and control module on the front, which showed alpha and numeric readouts of oxygen level, fuel, and power remaining in the PLSS.

She grabbed one of the helmets, a clear polycarbonate pressure bubble with a neck connecting ring, and rubbed an antifog compound on the inside of the helmet. Next she placed a communications cap on her head and connected it to the EMU electrical harness. Grabbing a pair of gloves and putting them on, she fastened the ends to the locking rings at the end of each EMU sleeve.

Taking a final breath of 100 percent oxygen from the portable unit, Diane removed the clear mask and let it float over head. Next, she lowered the helmet and locked it in place. Powering up the PLSS, she breathed again while pressurizing the suit to 16.7 PSI at 100 percent oxygen, two PSI above the airlock pressure, to create a pressure differential. Diane's body responded with a slight discomfort in her ears and sinus cavities. She tried to compensate by yawning and swallowing, but the pressure in her ears remained. Pressing her nose against a small sponge mounted to her right, inside the helmet ring, Diane blew with her mouth closed, forcing air inside her ear cavities and equalizing the pressure.

Her eyes on the display module attached to her chest, she turned off the PLSS and waited one minute to check for suit leaks. The pressure dropped to 16.6 PSI, well within the maximum allowable rate of leakage of the shuttle EMU of 0.2 PSI per minute.

Satisfied, she dropped the pressure to 14.7 PSI and waited ten more minutes while slowly starting the airlock pressure bleed-down. The moment the pressure outside equaled the pressure inside the airlock, Diane checked the chest-mounted timer.

Forty-five minutes of prebreathing. It'll have to do.

She took two additional minutes to bring the EMU pressure down gradually to six PSI instead of the recommended four PSI for maximum EMU flexibility without excessive muscle fatigue. At pressures higher than four PSI, the flight suit became more rigid, but Diane had no choice when presented with the option between risking nitrogen-induced bends and exerting a little more effort to move. In another fifteen minutes she planned to lower it to four psi to extend the life her PLSS.

She lowered a sun visor over the helmet before reaching for the hatch actuator lock lever and turning it 180 degrees. She pulled the D-shaped door toward her a few inches and then rotated it up until it rested with the low-pressure side facing the airlock ceiling.

Thirteen

"What did you say?" asked Jake Cohen, slowly turning toward the blond-headed EECOM, the Electrical, Environmental, and Consumables Systems Engineer.

"S-band telemetry shows zero pressurization inside the airlock, sir."

"Dammit!"

"No, sir. You don't understand. The pressure didn't leak out. It was intentionally bled out by someone inside the airlock. My data is also showing an opened hatch to the payload bay. Someone up there just started an EVA."

"And we can't talk to the astronaut?"

"I'm afraid not, sir. All we can do is read the telemetry data on S-band."

"Damn. I wish that K-band antenna was there," said Cohen. In reality, *Endeavour* had given up the K-band antenna to accommodate a second RMS manipulator arm. The K-band antenna could have allowed an alternate communications channel between the orbiter and Houston Control after the S-band antenna was damaged during the laser shootout.

Jake Cohen grabbed the phone to update his superiors. Just thirty minutes ago he had gotten word from Andrews Air Force base that a squadron of F-22s armed with ANSAT—antisatellite—missiles was standing by waiting for the order to shoot down the station before the terrorist regained control of the warheads. Now maybe there was a chance that the station could still be salvaged if the surviving astronauts could reach the ISS in time.

Fourteen

———

Diane Williams held on to the handrails to push herself through the opening and into the payload bay, where she closed her eyes to avoid getting disoriented from the multiaxial rotation of the orbiter with respect to the Earth. She had not noticed it before because of her enclosure inside the airlock, but now that she was in the bay, her eyes instantly sent an alarm to her brain. *Vertigo. Nausea.*

Fighting what she knew would be deadly spatial disorientation, Diane opened her eyes, but kept them focused inside the payload bay, forcing herself to ignore anything outside her small world. Breathing slow and deep to get her body under control, she decided that her initial observation from inside the airlock had been correct. Everything seemed out of place, with most of the standard equipment missing, including one of the two Manned Maneuvering Units (MMU) or self-propelled backpacks, one payload bay door, both RMS arms, the segmented mirror, video cameras, one Payload Assistance Module, floodlights. All gone.

Diane pushed herself to the rear of the cargo area, where she reached the open-canopy AMV, realizing that it would take a miracle to get any use out of it. The missing MMU had crashed against the delicate control panel of the AMV, smashing the stealth vehicle electronics, which, on closer inspection, she decided were vital for proper operation of the AMV's jet thrusters.

Appalled at her bad luck, Diane exhaled heavily, pounding a gloved hand against the black composite skin of the crippled vehicle, her only way of reaching the station . . . or was it?

Her eyes darted across the payload bay toward the undamaged MMU, the backpack system used by astronauts since the 1980s for untethered EVA. Although NASA prohibited astronauts from using the MMU at distances farther than three hundred feet from the orbiter, Diane knew that as long as there was compressed nitrogen in the MMU tanks, the jets could propel her for miles. The only problem she faced was that she didn't know which way to go. But Diane noticed that the Lockheed AMV carried a small homing unit, which she unstrapped from the side of the vehicle. She also grabbed one of four HandHeld Maneuvering Units from the back of the AMV. The small HHMUs were most likely intended to be used by the UNSC soldiers to maneuver themselves away from the AMV after arriving at the station. Now Diane would use it as a backup in case something went wrong with her MMU.

Armed with the homing device and the HHMU, Diane pushed herself back toward the MMU parked next to the airlock. She stopped in front of the maneuvering unit, attached to the payload bay wall with a framework that had a stirruplike foot restraint. Diane placed both EMU boots inside the stirrups and visually inspected the unit, checking the battery and nitrogen-propellant readings, both of which showed fully charged.

Turning around, Diane backed herself against the MMU, until the PLSS backpack locked in place. She extended both control arms of the MMU and placed her hands on the hand controllers. The right controller would give her acceleration for roll, pitch, and yaw, while the left one gave her the power to produce translational acceleration along three different planes: forward-back, up-down, and left-right.

Diane used her left hand to reach for the main power switch located above her right shoulder, and a second later the MMU locator lights came on. She reached with her right hand for the manual locator light switch over her left shoulder and turned it off. It was bad enough that the Russian aboard the ISS might be able to pick her up on radar. She definitely didn't feel like flashing her location like a beacon in the darkness of space.

Strapping the small HandHeld Maneuvering Unit to one of the MMU arms, and the homing radar to the other, Diane prepared herself to execute a maneuver she had never done before.

She currently moved with the same translational and rotational speed as *Endeavour*. She had to jettison away from the rotating wreckage without changing her rotational velocity with respect to the orbiter so that a section of the orbiter would not come crashing against her.

Since the orbiter seemed to be rotating around an

axis close to the center of the payload bay, Diane decided to slowly jet herself toward it, reaching a position nearest to *Endeavour*'s zero-rotation point.

She applied full pressure to the aft-facing jets, which spewed nitrogen in one direction and gently pushed her in the other, along a line near perpendicular to the axis of rotation. Twenty seconds later she had moved close to 150 feet from the orbiter, which continued to rotate just as fast as she did.

The Earth, orbiter, and the cosmos flashing on her viewplate, Diane applied two lateral thrusts to counter her clockwise rotation, making a few fine adjustments until she floated upside down, with a large portion of the South American continent hanging overhead.

At that distance she finally saw the damage done to the orbiter, realizing the power of the GPATS laser. Actually, *Endeavour* didn't look like an orbiter anymore, but more like a black-and-white cylindrical hunk of space junk.

Diane also slowly came to terms with the fact that she was alone, forgotten, probably given up for dead by Mission Control. All she had was the gear she had taken with her. The compressed nitrogen inside her MMU tanks. The eight hours' worth of oxygen and pressurization that the PLSS could provide her EMU suit, plus the thirty-minute emergency oxygen reserve unit below the PLSS's main oxygen tanks. She wished she could use her radio, somehow tell Mission Control—tell Jake—that she had survived. But her only link to ground was through an orbiter that no longer existed. Diane was her own spaceship, her own world. The steady flow of oxygen from the PLSS system—carried through a maze of tubes into the back of her helmet—was her life. She depended on it as much as she depended on the system's heater exchange and sublimator to warm the oxygen before it reached the inside of her helmet to avoid fogging the faceplate. Diane depended on the chilled water running through hundreds of feet of plastic tubing lacing her suit liner to maintain her body temperature. She relied on the multiple layers of insulation of the EMU suit to keep her body from direct exposure to temperatures that would boil her blood in seconds.

Diane Williams drew from a distinguished space career and from her decade of military training to shove those thoughts aside and concentrate on the job. She was Mission Commander. She was in control of her space vehicle, regardless of whether that vehicle measured as large as an orbiter or as minute as her EMU enclosure. Being in charge meant keeping her emotions and fears aside, letting her logical side take over. It meant activating the homing unit and steering her MMU propulsion system toward a space station out of her visual range, but a station she knew floated out there, somewhere in the vast emptiness of space.

Diane Williams glanced at *Endeavour* one last time, thought about McGregor and the UNSCF soldiers for one final moment before using the jets to turn around and align herself with the information shown on the liquid crystal display of the homing device. Diane fired the thrusters until she'd put herself in a collision course with the space station. She hoped her orbital trajectory would get her to the station in less than eight hours.

Fifteen

******PROCEDURE VIOLATION******
TIME LIMIT EXCEEDED.
SYSTEM RESET IN PROGRESS
******07:15:14******

Sergei Dudayev stared at the screen while eating from a pouch of dried peaches. The moment was near. During his last orbital pass over the Caucasus Mountains, he had gotten confirmation of the deployment orders. Russia refused to yield to Chechnya's request to take possession of nuclear warheads for self-defense. It had also refused to pull back the tank divisions deployed to the border.

Soon I will show them that we mean our threats.

Sixteen

Seven and a half hours into her journey to reach the station, Diane Williams began to feel the effects of the carbon dioxide her nearly discharged Primary Life Support System backpack could not fully extract from her EMU suit. The centrifugal fan of the PLSS, running at nearly twenty thousand RPM, slowly failed to draw the contaminated oxygen from the normal rate of 0.17 cubic meter per minute down to 0.14 and dropping—according to her chest-mounted display. In addition, the slow warming trend inside the suit also told her that the PLSS feedwater pump and heat exchanger and sublimator, designed to maintain a steady flow of chilled water through the hundreds of feet of plastic tubing lacing the LCVG underwear Diane wore, were also fading.

The situation would only get worse, with the suit slowly turning into a greenhouse as humidity and temperature got out of control, fogging the faceplate and eventually suffocating her.

She had to act, and fast, while she could still see through the pressurized polycarbonate plastic sphere underneath the gold-coated visor protecting her eyes from the blinding ultraviolet rays of a sun that had loomed over the horizon a half hour ago. Diane activated the EMU's purge valve to bleed the carbon dioxide into space before switching to the secondary oxygen pack NASA added to the bottom of the unit to ensure the safety of astronauts in case of main PLSS failure.

Operating in open-loop mode, where the oxygen she breathed did not get circulated back to the PLSS but went through the purge valve, Diane checked the timer on the chest-mounted display. She had around fifty minutes' worth of oxygen left.

That should be enough.

Squeezing the last of the nitrogen pressure inside the Manned Maneuvering Unit's tanks, Diane used the station's long frame, only five hundred feet away, to block the blinding sun. So far, the station showed no sign of alarm.

Soon that'll change, she decided, aware of the station's proximity sensors. Although they had not been sensitive enough to detect her yet, they were designed to detect any object with a radar cross section larger than a half foot getting within five hundred feet of the station.

Her viewplate beginning to fog and her EMU suit temperature climbing out of the comfort zone, Diane opened the purge valve a bit more, which also meant her oxygen supply would decrease at a faster rate. She didn't have a choice. She had to keep the helmet from fogging at all costs while commanding the MMU to thrust her toward the hyperbaric airlock attached to the Unity Module.

Seventeen

UNSC15KTSN001 HAS BEEN SELECTED
INSERT VALID UNSCF BADGE TO ACTIVATE
******00:59******

Sergei Dudayev was ready when the slot under the keyboard opened. Upon inserting the badge, the screen changed to a blinking:

UNCS15KTSN001 IS READY TO LAUNCH

The Russian cosmonaut smiled. Then the station's proximity alarm went off.

Eighteen

Diane Williams noticed a number of red lights flashing on some modules. The proximity alarm motion sensors had detected her. She needed a decoy.

Unstrapping the HandHeld Maneuvering Unit from the side of the PLSS, Diane disengaged herself from the backpack propulsion system that had carried her all the way there. A hard kick against the MMU to push herself toward the station, and Diane watched the MMU tumble out of control away from her.

Now came the tricky part. All she had to propel herself toward the station was the HHMU, very similar to the ones used for EVAs during the Gemini Program of the 1960s, and seldom used by modern-day space voyagers because of the readily available and highly sophisticated MMUs.

Diane held the three-jet maneuvering gun with

both hands. There were two jets located at the ends of the rod and aimed back. A third jet, located at the center of the rod, faced forward. Remembering the technique used by those early space explorers, Diane Williams centered the gun close to her lower chest—the place she estimated to be closest to her center of mass. Visually lining up the rear-facing jets with the airlock hatch roughly three hundred feet away, Diane fired the gun, releasing a symmetrical burst of compressed oxygen from both jets, propelling herself more or less in the desired direction.

Finally learning the limitations of the HHMU— and also the frustration of those Gemini astronauts— Diane found herself making slight correction on the firing angle of the jets while lowering the gun to her waist, below the chest-mounted display to avoid a slight rotational motion induced by firing the thrusters out of line with her true center of mass. Slowly, using a combination of forward thrusts and also firing the reverse thruster to break her momentum, Diane reached the airlock hatch.

Nineteen

The proximity alarms blaring, Sergei Dudayev checked the radar and verified the existence of an object at less than five hundred feet from the station.

Puzzled, he floated back into Unity and up to the cupola. Using a restraint system that enabled him to rotate easily for viewing through any of the windows, the Russian spotted an empty Manned Maneuvering Unit drifting away from the station.

An MMU?

Realizing that the ISS didn't carry any MMUs, Sergei concluded that unless for some very strange law of physics one of *Endeavour*'s MMUs had been dislodged from its flight station and floated in this direction, the presence of the backpack system could only mean one thing.

Twenty

———

After performing an emergency bleed of the air inside the airlock by using the small control panel built in on the D-shaped EVA hatch door, Diane Williams pressed her left hand against the manual unlocking lever while holding on to the adjacent handle with her right. Three full clockwise turns, and she pulled the hatch door back several inches before a spring-loaded mechanism rotated it upward. Floating inside the airlock, Diane closed the hatch behind her and repressurized the compartment.

Twenty-one

Sergei noticed the red lights blinking on the control panel of the crew support station, which told him that an emergency airlock bleed had been done. The EVA hatch had been opened, then closed, and now the airlock was being repressurized.

Cursing his stupidity for assuming that the crew of *Endeavour* had perished in the attack, Sergei kicked his legs against the side of the cupola and reached Unity, sighing in relief when noticing that the hatch connecting the airlock to the bottom of the node was still closed. Without further thought, he locked it from the inside.

Twenty-two

Diane finished pressurizing the airlock and noticed the green light above the hatch connecting her compartment to Unity turning red. Realizing that the Russian had most likely found her, she decided not to depressurize her EMU suit just yet. Instead, she reached for the communications panel on the side of the airlock wall and set it to the standard EVA mode UHF frequency 121 Mhz. Next, she remotely switched on the station's K-band antenna to close the ISS-Houston link via a TRDS and White Sands Tracking Station.

"Houston, this is *Endeavour*'s Mission Commander Diane Williams, over."

"Wh—what? Come in . . . come in, Commander! Jesus Christ! We thought . . . great to hear from you!" Diane heard an unfamiliar voice coming through.

"I have little time before Dudayev catches on and

cuts us off. I've reached the station. I'm trapped inside the airlock and have less than twenty minutes left of oxygen in my PLSS."

"Diane, this is Jake."

Diane smiled thinly. "Jake, the orbiter's gone. McGregor and the UNSCF soldiers didn't make it. The bastard now has me locked out of the station."

"Calm down and listen carefully there might be a way to—"

Diane frowned. "Houston? Houston? Come in, Houston."

Twenty-three

A few keystrokes on the computer keyboard of the Multipurpose Applications Console, and Sergei disconnected the communications link between the airlock and the rest of the station. An American astronaut—Diane Williams—had managed to exchange a few words with Houston Control, and although Sergei had not been pleased with that fact, he had at least gotten a good idea of Diane's desperate oxygen situation. The American was running out of air, and in another twenty minutes she would no longer present any danger to his mission.

He commanded the computer system to purge the airlock.

Twenty-four

"Houston, can you read? Hous—"

The emergency purge alarm went off inside the airlock, conveying the Russian's intentions. Glad that she had maintained EMU pressurization, Diane searched for the maintenance tools stowed inside compartments on all four walls of the airlock, finding what she sought: a heavy-duty, battery-operated drill, to which she attached a four-inch-diameter stainless-steel serrated disk at the end of the drive shaft. She had seen what the tool could do when McGregor had cut open the jammed Titan shroud to release the segmented mirror.

Pressing the tool's on-off switch twice to verify proper operation, Diane unlocked the exterior hatch. Having secured the power tool to a six-foot-long woven line that she clipped to her EMU suit, Diane used the HHMU to move away from the

D-shaped opening, past the modules, and toward the long, thin structural framework that ended in one set of solar panels.

Rapidly exhausting the compressed oxygen inside the handheld propulsion unit, Diane grabbed a tubular member of the truss assembly. Painted black, the tube—made of aluminum-clad graphite epoxy— was both lighter and relatively stronger than metal. Diane hugged it with her left arm while strapping the HHMU to the side of the EMU suit.

Crawling inside the tubular framework, Diane reached a black tube running all the way from a set of solar panels, still a hundred feet away, to the center of the station. The contents of the tube—thick electrical cables—fed the massive array of nickel-hydrogen batteries and the power converter that provided the GPATS module weapons system with the necessary energy to generate the destructive chemical reaction. The battery also fed the computer system that controlled the warheads and their launching units.

Pulling on the woven line, Diane clasped the power saw in her gloves and turned it on. The serrated wheel began its silent, high-velocity spin. Diane anchored herself between adjacent beams before pressing the round blade against the side of the tube, immediately slicing through the soft composite material and into the thick wires, which bathed her in a cloud of sizzling debris. On Earth, such action would have resulted in a cloud of sparks, but in the vacuum of space, the intensely hot particles had no oxygen to burn.

Her EMU gloves insulating her from the 208 volts of electricity generated by the solar panels, Diane made several cuts to achieve a clean separation. Satisfied, she crawled back out of the framework and moved toward where the large laser gun stood atop the GPATs module.

Twenty-five

Sergei Dudayev heard another alarm coming from the GPATS module and instinctively pushed himself out of the Hab Module, through Unity, and into GPATS, where one of the computer screens at the front of the module told him of an EPS recharge system failure. The Electrical Power System no longer received a charge from the solar panels, and had automatically switched to the battery packs, which had a charge life of thirty hours—much less if he had to use the laser system.

Cursing, Sergei floated back into Unity and through the connecting hatch to the cupola, where he watched the American astronaut floating by the base of the laser gun.

No! Not the laser!

Returning to the GPATS module, Sergei made up his mind and pressed the launch button for the selected warhead. Its destination: the Russian troops on the border with Chechnya.

Sergei wished he could release the remaining warheads, but he had to take care of the American first. Without the laser the station would be defenseless against another attack.

Floating back into Unity, Sergei used the remote actuators to close the outer hatch before repressurizing the hyperbaric airlock. He opened the inner hatch and floated toward one of two one-piece AMEX AX-5 Advanced Hard Suits, made of aluminum and containing no fabric or soft parts, except for the joints, enhancing mobility and comfort for the wearer. The suit had integrated helmet, gloves, and boots.

Entering the suit from a hatch in the rear, Sergei slipped in both legs first, followed by the upper part of his body. Once inside, he backed himself against a Self-Propelled Life Support System backpack, which perfectly covered the square hatch opening, creating a seal after the magnetic latches all around the joint snapped in place. Pressing two buttons on his chest-mounted display and control panel pressurized the AX-5 to twelve PSI—one of the advantages of the new suit since it eliminated the need to prebreathe pure oxygen prior to an EVA.

The sound of his own breathing ringing in his ears, Sergei depressurized the compartment and opened the hatch. He could waste no time. The American had already disabled the GPATS battery-charging system and was now about to sabotage the laser.

The AX-5 integrated thruster system—a simplified version of the MMU—consisted of sixteen compressed nitrogen jets instead of the MMU's twenty-four. Operating two joystick-type controls on his chest-mounted panel, Sergei fired the aft-facing thrusters to propel himself away from the station and get a bird's eye view of his enemy.

Rotating himself in the direction of Diane, Sergei once more fired the thrusters. This time, however, he did it for nearly ten seconds, giving himself a forward velocity of around five feet per second.

Twenty-six

Diane Williams had just finished cutting the array of cables that controlled the sophisticated servomotors of the gimbal-mounted laser gun when she noticed an external door opening on the side of the GPATS module.

She cringed when a single sleek cylinder, roughly fifteen feet in length by three in diameter, slowly left the station after being pushed away by its spring-loaded release mechanism, designed to get the warhead away from the station before firing its reentry booster.

With less than ten minutes of oxygen left, and with the warhead floating farther away from the station, Diane decided to go after the warhead while it was still floating near the GPATS module.

Switching off the power saw and letting it float at the end of the woven line, Diane reached for the HHMU, but her hands never got there.

Twenty-seven

Sergei rammed the American female astronaut at a relative velocity of nearly five feet per second. The blow, cushioned by the thick aluminum suit and also by the high-pressure environment around Sergei's body, barely bothered him or his heavy high-technology garment, but it sent the American tumbling out of control toward the framework to the right of the U.S. Laboratory Module.

Twenty-eight

The powerful blow took Diane Williams entirely by surprise. Her forehead crashed against the polycarbonate plastic helmet before the Earth and the station flashed around her. In one of the flashes, she caught a glimpse of what had crashed against her. The Russian terrorist had suited up and come after her in one of the rugged AX-5 suits.

She finished that thought when another blow, this one to the back of her head, nearly knocked her out as she smashed into the tubular framework near the *. . . where in the hell am I?* She pulled free of the stiff latticework just to be welcomed by a foot shoved against her chest-mounted display.

"Bastard!" she muttered in between breaths as her legs got caught in the crossbeams and batons of the framework. Blinking rapidly to prevent her tears from separating from her eyes and floating inside her helmet, Diane saw the Russian thrusting himself upward for several feet before an expulsion of compressed nitrogen gas from the upward-facing thrusters drove him back down at great speed. This time both feet stabbed her midriff, hammering her farther into the latticework.

Catching her breath, Diane feared that her suit would rip at any moment. The warning lights on her EMU's chest mounted display told her that Sergei had already damaged something, but with her body lodged in the framework at such unnatural angle she needed time to free herself.

Struggling to remain focused, Diane pulled on the woven line, but before her fingers could grab the power saw, Sergei descended on her once more. Tightening her stomach muscles, Diane took the blow better than her suit, which emitted a high-pitched noise that told her she was losing pressurization.

Sergei floated himself up once more. Diane began to feel dizzy and lightheaded as her suit began to lose life-supporting pressure. Fortunately, her prebreathing had removed all nitrogen from her bloodstream, preventing the bends caused by a sudden drop in external body pressure. Quickly, she turned the emergency oxygen knob fully open to maintain an endurable level of pressure.

With the image of the Russian's boots coming down on her again, Diane Williams switched on the power saw and firmly held it with both hands against the approaching boots. Every ounce of strength left flowed into her arms, locked at the elbow. She could not afford another blow. Her EMU would not take it. She had to stop him.

The Russian landed over her. Diane drove the spinning blade into the base of his left boot, letting the serrated edge sink deep into the aluminum, creating a cloud of sparkling white debris.

Twenty-nine

Sergei noticed that the American held out her arms to prevent him from crashing against the EMU. He sensed the resisting motion and got ready to propel himself back up when he felt something strange. For a moment he wasn't sure what it was. It sounded like a malfunctioning fan, or a grinding noise of some sort.

Suddenly, his suit's pressure began to drop, and a burning pain from his heel reached his brain, telling Sergei that the American had pierced the AX-5. Instantly commanding the thrusters to push him back up, he noticed the white cloud surrounding Diane Williams, and he also noticed the object in her hands.

A power saw!

His suit's pressure dropping rapidly below two PSI, Sergei bent in pain from the millions of nitrogen bubbles expanding in his bloodstream. His joints ached to a climax and the cramps in his stomach and intestines scourged him. He could no longer control his body. He was paralyzed, unable to make the smallest movement, except for his eyes, which he focused on the chest-mounted display that told him that he should already be dead. A moment later he passed away.

Thirty

As the limp body of the Russian floated away from her, Diane Williams used her hands to free her right leg, caught in between two crossbeams. That gave her the leeway to position her body so that it became easy to release her other leg from a pair of tubes running along the length of the latticework.

Feeling dizzy, Diane used the HHMU strapped to the side of her backpack unit to move toward the airlock's open hatch. Finding it harder to breathe, she pushed herself through the opening, forcing her mind to remain focused. Her fingers groped around the control panel on the opposite wall, managing to engage the servomotor to close the hatch before pressurizing the compartment.

She fumbled with the visor assembly latch for a few seconds, finally removing it, letting it float overhead while releasing the helmet joining ring. The locking mechanism snapped, and she pushed the clear hemisphere up.

A breath of air. She exhaled and breathed deeply again, coughing, inhaling once more.

A distant rumble brought her gaze toward the airlock's porthole. The missile's thruster fired to commence Earth reentry. Regretting having disabled the laser, Diane removed her EMU suit, leaving on only the cooling garment as she unlocked and opened the hatch leading to Unity and the cupola beyond it, where she engaged the K-band antenna.

Thirty-one

Jake Cohen sat upright when Diane William's voice crackled through the overhead speakers in the Flight Control Room at Johnson Space Center.

"Houston, come in, over."

"Houston here. What in the world is going on up there?"

"Houston, the station is under control, but we have a serious problem. The terrorist managed to fire one warhead. It just started its deorbit burn."

"Stand by," Jake said over the radio, before calling NORAD to advise them of the situation. He then contacted Andrews Air Force Base to call back the F-22s. The terrorist aboard the International Space Station had been neutralized. The Air Force would try to halt the attack, but Jake was warned that it might be too late already.

The veteran CapCom slowly hung up the phone

before reaching for the mike in front of him. He had to warn Diane of the possibility of ANSAT missiles heading her way.

"Houston here."

"I'm still here, Houston, go ahead."

Jake struggled to remain as professional as he could, particularly when all eyes in the Flight Control Room were on him. "Situation report?"

"Just accessed the station through Unity. Currently performing a visual check, looking for the rest of the crew. So far I haven't found anyone else."

"I'm afraid we might have bad news for you. A squadron of F-22s is currently trying to shoot you down with ANSAT missiles. We're trying to call them back, but we might be too late."

"Did you say ANSAT?"

"Affirmative. You're might have to use the laser."

"That's a negative, Houston. I disabled the laser before coming inside the station. It's out of commission until we can get a crew to come up here and repair it. I'm afraid if any of those ANSATs are fired, this place is going be in real trouble."

Jake closed his eyes. "Okay, listen. In that case you need to be ready to get into the Soyuz escape vehicle and leave the station immediately. You've stopped the terrorist from launching any more warheads. We'll deal later with the damage those missiles might do to the station."

"That's a negative, Houston. There has to be another way."

Dammit, Diane! Jake thought, before saying as calmly as he could, "ISS, Houston. There is nothing you can do. Repeat, there is nothing you can do without the laser. If the ANSATs are fired, they will destroy the station."

"Houston, I have an idea."

Thirty-two

Colonel Keith Myers kept the rearward pressure on his sidestick as the F-22 soared above 80,000 feet. Brief side glances out of his canopy, and the forty-eight-year-old colonel verified the tight inverted-V formation of his five-jet squadron.

The F-22 was a beautiful plane, and Myers loved to fly it. The advanced tactical fighter-bomber, brought into full production only last year, was a worthy replacement of the venerable F-15 Eagle, which had carried the Air Force through the latter portion of the twentieth century. Myers had been one of five test pilots of the two prototypes built by McDonnell Douglas, and at the end of the evaluation period he had been assigned to lead the first wing out of Andrews.

A medium-built, muscular man with fair skin and short brown hair, Myers looked and acted the role of the typical Air Force squadron commander. He was cocky and sometimes borderline-arrogant, but he knew how to carry out orders and get his men motivated to follow them as well. On the ground he was a bastard, who pushed everyone to do and act their best, but once airborne, he was the ideal flight leader, wise and courageous, fully capable of making lifesaving, split-second decisions.

Myers definitely knew how to follow orders, even when those orders meant the destruction of one of the world's greatest technological achievements: the International Space Station.

"Leader to Ghosts, Leader to Ghosts," Myers said over the squadron frequency. "Prepare to release."

"Roger," came the response from his other four jets, each carrying a single ANSAT missile attached to the underfuselage pallet.

Myers activated the ordnance-release system. Firing the ANSAT was quite simple because of the nature of the missile, which was already preprogrammed to home in on the station flying 105 miles overhead. There was no radar control from the parent craft or from an overhead satellite to guide it to its target. The ANSATs were shoot-and-forget. According to the briefing, Myers would fire his missile first. Each of his men would follow serially until all five missiles had been fired.

Shoving the sidestick back while pushing full throttle, Myers pointed the nose to the upper layers of the stratosphere before pressing a button on the sidestick.

A silver missile glided upward in a parabolic flight as he rolled the jet and pulled away. The missile continued skyward solely on the momentum it had gained from the F-22, until right before reaching its apex, when the single solid-propellant booster kicked in and projected it up at great speed.

"Leader's out," commented Myers as he watched his wingman get into position for his release.

"Ghost Leader, Ghost Leader, Eagle's Nest, over."

"Nest, Leader, over."

"Abort, Leader. Repeat, abort mission. Authorization code Three-Niner-Alpha-Zulu-Seven-Six-Lima-Charlie."

Myers glanced at the small notepad strapped right below the Heads-Up Display. *Abort Code 39AZ76LC. That's a match.*

"Leader to Ghosts, Leader to Ghosts. Abort, abort. RTB, RTB."

"Roger," responded the other four jets, acknowledging not just the abort, but also the Return-To-Base order.

Colonel Myers watched his wingman rolling his jet out of the climb and returning to formation with the ANSAT still strapped to his F-22's belly.

Myers said, "Nest, Ghost Leader. One demon got away. Repeat. One demon got away. Other four demons secured. RTB."

"Roger, Lead. Will pass it on."

The runaway ANSAT's thruster still burning in the distance, Myers cut back throttles and dropped his F-22's nose. His squadron followed him.

Thirty-three

As she floated inside the Habitation Module, Diane Williams only had two more minutes before the AN-SAT missile reached her orbit. She inserted the keys she had removed from the GPATS' launching station into the key slots on the top of the keyboard of the Multipurpose Application Console, connected to the central electronic brain of the station.

The screen came up with a list of menus, each containing its own list of submenus and commands. She chose a menu that controlled the station's rotational verniers. A three-dimensional drawing on the screen showed the ISS's current attitude with respect to Earth, and also indicated that the station was operating under automatic computer control. She switched to manual, transferring control of the verniers to a joystick controller next to the station.

She then programmed the station to split the large

screen in two. The bottom section still displayed the station's attitude, but the top section now showed a color radar map of the ISS and its surroundings. The resolution was set to 250 miles out, and it showed no sign of the ANSAT yet.

"Houston, ISS. I'm all set, over."

"All right, ISS," Jake Cohen responded from Mission Control. *"ANSAT is three hundred miles high two hundred ninety miles downrange with a closing velocity of seven hundred miles per hour. It should show on your screen any moment now."*

Diane's eyes never left the display as she said, "I see you." The blue dot entered Diane's range from the east and approached the station at great speed. She estimated another minute to impact.

The fingers of her right hand caressed the plastic surface of the joystick. Her eyes followed the blue dot, blinking its way across the screen.

She waited, knowing she would only have one chance at this. Her military background told her that the radar-controlled ANSAT would home in on the area with the largest mass, namely the core of the station. A direct hit there would certainly destroy the ISS.

The ANSAT got within fifty miles. That was the mark. She moved the joystick to the right, and the station's rotational verniers responded by firing counterclockwise. She watched the screen as the station's 3-D drawing began to rotate. *Twenty seconds to impact.*

The ANSAT was too close to make any large corrections as its electronic brain detected a shift in the relative location of its target's center of mass. The microprocessor stored inside the missile's cone ordered the firing of the small attitude control verniers to make a slight adjustment in the flight path, and in another few seconds the missile struck the south section of the boom, near the only functional set of solar panels, over two hundred feet away from any module. The ensuing explosion severed the solar panels in a brief display of orange flames.

Diane was thrown against the food galley, bounced and landed feetfirst against the large panoramic window next to the crew's recreational station. Her shoulders and back burned. Through the largest and thickest piece of tempered glass ever put in orbit Diane Williams saw the damage as the station rotated clockwise, out of control, but at least in one piece. She had spared the core of the station from a direct hit. However, the blast had sent a powerful electromagnetic pulse through the cables connecting the solar panels to the station's batteries, shorting them out.

Alarms blared inside the Habitation Module. Red lights, indicating a major power malfunction, flashed at each entrance to the module. Just as suddenly, sparks and smoke spewed from underneath the floor tiles near the Multipurpose Application Console. The bright overheads suddenly went off, replaced by green emergency lights. The computers, sensing that they had lost power from the main batteries, automatically switched to the emergency shutdown program, which began to power down all systems according to a priority sequence.

Stunned but fully conscious, the forty-five-year-old ex–Marine aviator thrust herself through the smoke and sparks and back to the Multipurpose Applications Console, where she snagged the joystick and tried unsuccessfully to stabilize the station. She tried to switch to automatic control, but the system did not respond.

Another alarm began to blare inside the station.

Diane recognized its high pulsating pitch: The station was losing pressurization and oxygen. The air pressurization and revitalization system had shut down. At least the station had survived, but it would take a couple of shuttle flights to get it back in shape to support life.

Time to go.

Finding it harder to breathe, her ears beginning to ring from the air-pressure drop, Diane kicked her legs against the MPAC and floated out of the Habitation Module and into Unity. The Soyuz capsule was coupled to the node through a four-foot-long narrow tunnel.

Feeling dizzy, her vision fogging, Diane reached the connecting D-shaped hatch, opened it, and dived through the tunnel into Russian technology.

Her head feeling about to explode, she floated inside the cramped interior of the Soyuz capsule. Closing the access hatch, locking it in place, Diane strapped herself to the center of three seats arranged side by side.

Her vision tunneling, Diane's fingers groped over the control pane searching for the pressurization lever, finding it, throwing it.

Hissing oxygen filled the capsule. The pounding against her eardrums stopped, and after a few deep breaths, her vision cleared, allowing her to inspect the capsule, which lacked an interior wall. Most of the electronic wiring and hydraulic tubing ran fully exposed along steel walls. A porthole directly above provided her only window to the outside, and at that moment it showed Diane the side of Unity.

Placing her hands on a set of levers on the sides of her seat, Diane pulled them up and twisted them ninety degrees.

The capsule jettisoned away from the station,

throwing Diane against her restraining harness. Soon she saw nothing but space through the porthole.

Following a preprogrammed reentry sequence, the capsule fired the attitude-control verniers to position the Soyuz's main thruster in the direction of flight. As she waited for the capsule to reach the point in orbit when the rocket would fire to start the reentry, Diane Williams snagged the radio headset secured with a Velcro strap by her left knee, and put it on. She switched on the communications radio and selected a frequency of 252.0 MHz to make a connection with the TDRS-White Sands-Houston link.

"Houston, SES, over," Diane said from the Soyuz Escape System.

"Diane! What happened. We lost communication!"

"The station lost pressure and oxygen. It lost the south end of the boom and solar panels to the AN-SAT. I'm afraid some systems and subsystems may have been damaged. But the station is in one piece and still in orbit."

"Status of GPATS module?"

"Deactivated. I have both control keys—"

Her words were cut short by a powerful jolt as the single thruster fired. "Houston, SES. Just started de-orbit burn," Diane reported.

"Roger, SES. We're tracking you. Estimated landing site is southern Ukraine."

"Status of the warhead that got away, Houston?"

"Not good, SES. It struck a Russian tank battalion near the border with Chechnya fifteen minutes ago. First estimates are over two thousand dead and many more wounded."

"Damn."

"It could have been a lot worse, SES. The tanks were spread out over a large area. If it would have hit a heavily populated area casualties would have been much higher."

Her eyes watched the star-filled cosmos rush past her porthole as the capsule decelerated from its 24,000-miles-per-hour flight.

The burn ended and was replaced by a strong vibration as the first air molecules began to strike the capsule's underside heat shield, heating it to incandescence.

Soon the vibrations grew, accompanied by a pink glow around the edges of the window. Inside her pocket of life traveling inside a decelerating hell of steel-melting temperatures, Diane Williams sat back and watched the pink glow turn into a bright orange just before the Soyuz craft became engulfed by the flames.

Closing her eyes, the ex-Marine tried to relax. She had made it against staggering odds. The remaining weapons aboard the station would remain safe until NASA could get another crew up there to repair it. But that no longer her concerned her.

The rumble of the capsule rushing through the upper layers of the atmosphere increased to a soul-numbing crescendo. Thin air and insulation compounds collided in a scorching outburst of flames. With the might and beauty of a meteor dropping from the sky, the Soyuz capsule sliced through the air at great speed.

Diane Williams dropped like a rock, the flames slowly fading away as the capsule decelerated to the point when the deorbit program disengaged the heat shield to expose three retrorockets to be used ten feet over ground to cushion the fall. At an altitude of thirty thousand feet, bright red twin parachutes deployed from the top of the capsule, giving Diane the jerk of a lifetime.

The first rays of sunlight shafted through her round windowpane, filling the interior of the Soyuz capsule with wan orange light. Mission Commander Diane Williams watched it in silence.

R. J. Pineiro is the author of several technothrillers, including *Ultimatum, Retribution, Breakthrough, Exposure, Shutdown,* and the millennium thrillers *01-01-00* and *Y2K.* His latest thriller, *Conspiracy.com,* was published in April 2001. He is a seventeen-year veteran of the computer industry and is currently at work on leading-edge microprocessors, the heart of the personal computer. He was born in Havana, Cuba, and grew up in El Salvador before coming to the United States to pursue a higher education. He holds a degree in electrical engineering from Louisiana State University, a second-degree black belt in martial arts, is a licensed private pilot, and a firearms enthusiast. He has traveled extensively through Central America, Europe, and Asia, both for his computer business as well as to research his novels. He lives in Texas with his wife, Lory, and his son, Cameron.

Visit R. J. Pineiro on the World Wide Web at www.rjpineiro.com. R. J. Pineiro also receives e-mails at author@rjpineiro.com.

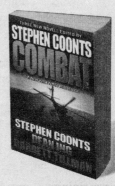